"Vickie McDonough gives readers a special treat as she blends her signature vivid descriptions of the prairie with fascinating details about the land rush. More than simply a tale of love and adventure, *Gabriel's Atonement* is a story of an important but rarely seen period in American history."

—Amanda Cabot, author of *At Bluebonnet Lake*

"Vickie McDonough is at the top of her game with *Gabriel's Atonement*. Historical facts are deftly woven into a plot that sings and characters that seem so real as to want to walk off the page. The exciting story of a young widow and rugged gambler set during an Oklahoma land rush was a delight to read."

—Margaret Brownley, bestselling author of The Brides of Last Chance Ranch and Undercover Ladies series

"Vickie McDonough's brilliant storytelling shines in *Gabriel's Atonement*. Gabriel will capture your heart. The best 'bad guy' I've ever fallen in love with! And the best land run romance since *Far and Away*."

—Amy Lillard, Carol Award–winning author of *Caroline's Secret*

"I've long known about Vickie McDonough's interest in Oklahoma history, especially the Oklahoma land runs. She took the details of history and skillfully worked them into the lives of her characters, who leapt off the page and grabbed my heart. Using several plot lines that could have been ripped from the pages of Oklahoma history, she wove them carefully together to give an interesting and thoroughly satisfying tale. You won't want to miss this wonderful read."

—Lena Nelson Dooley, multi-award-winning author of *Catherine's Pursuit*, book three of the McKenna's Daughters series

"Get out the popcorn. *Gabriel's Atonement* reads like a movie you don't want to end. The suspense of Gabe keeping his 'secret' and what the reaction of the widowed Lara will be is 'just right.' McDonough paints the setting with details that make the story come to life. Looking forward to reading more by her as she keeps getting better and better."

—Diana Lesire Brandmeyer, author of *The Festive Bride*, *A Bride's Dilemma in Friendship, Tennessee*, and *Mind of Her Own*

"This delightful prairie romance brings together a handsome gambler, looking for a reason to change, and a lonely widow with a sweet spirit who just might provide the motivation. Their involvement with the Oklahoma land rush adds to the fun and adventure of the story. Vickie McDonough is known for her well-drawn characters, realistic settings, and heart-stopping romance, and she has done it again with *Gabriel's Atonement*. Readers who enjoyed her previous books will love this new story."

—Carrie Turansky, award-winning author of
The Governess of Highland Hall and *The Daughter of Highland Hall*

"Guilt and regret can destroy a man or lead him into the arms of love. Hold on tight to the reins and prepare for a thrilling ride!"

—DiAnn Mills, bestselling author of the FBI: Houston series

"Once again Vickie McDonough delivers a great novel that comes sweeping down the plains to Oklahoma in the days preceding the land rush. Gabriel is seeking atonement for past sins and a new life in Oklahoma Territory. Lara Talbot desires a new home for her son, sister, and father. When they meet, sparks fly in a story that captures the spirit of the times and will keep the reader turning the pages."

—Martha Rogers, author of the series The Homeward Journey
and Winds Across the Prairie

"*Gabriel's Atonement* is packed with action, romance, and suspense. I loved the characters, loved the setting, loved the historical detail. Thanks for another great read, Vickie McDonough!"

—Susan Page Davis, author of the Prairie Dreams series

"*Gabriel's Atonement* tops my list of Vickie McDonough's historical romances to date. What isn't there to love about a handsome gambler in the Old West who's trying to do the right thing and a lovely widow who's struggling to make ends meet—with a love story that develops amidst action, adventure, intrigue, and a setting that comes to life on the page? Don't miss this one—it's a keeper."

—Miralee Ferrell, bestselling author of *Blowing on Dandelions*

GABRIEL'S ATONEMENT

— Land Rush Dreams 1 —

Vickie McDonough

SHILOH RUN PRESS

An Imprint of Barbour Publishing, Inc.

Print ISBN 978-1-62836-951-9

eBook Editions:
Adobe Digital Edition (.epub) 978-1-63409-154-1
Kindle and MobiPocket Edition (.prc) 978-1-63409-155-8

Cover design: Faceout Studio, www.faceoutstudio.com

Published by Shiloh Run Press, an imprint of Barbour Publishing, Inc., P.O. Box 719, Uhrichsville, Ohio 44683, www.shilohrunpress.com.

Our mission is to publish and distribute inspirational products offering exceptional value and biblical encouragement to the masses.

ecpa Member of the
Evangelical Christian
Publishers Association

Printed in the United States of America.

The rich man's wealth is his strong city, and as an high wall in his own conceit. Before destruction the heart of man is haughty, and before honour is humility.

PROVERBS 18:11–12

Chapter 1

Kansas City, Kansas
March 16, 1889

The cool metal of the Morgan silver dollar warmed as it rolled over Gabe's knuckles and between his fingers. One thing he'd learned in the last nine years was how to read people, and the cocky cowpoke at the bar looked ripe for the picking.

Like an early morning fog, hazy smoke floated in the saloon's tepid air. The cowpoke swigged back his drink and slammed his shot glass onto the counter, patted his pocket, and looked in the direction of the gaming tables. Gabe caught his gaze and nodded.

With a leering grin, the cowboy brushed past Trudy, one of the buxom saloon girls, and strode across the room toward Gabe. "I'm of a mind to double my money."

"Are you now?" He leaned back in his seat, one arm over the back of the chair, and waved a hand. "Have a seat," he hollered to be heard over the din of the crowd. He recognized the man from a month ago when he lost his paycheck at Tricky Dan's table. If he remembered right, the cowboy worked for Walt Whiteman, owner of the largest cattle ranch in the area—and the best paying one.

"The name's Tom Talbot." He nodded and pulled a pouch of coins from his pants pocket.

"Gabe Coulter. What's your game?"

"Five Card Stud."

Slim Trenton and Will McDaniels, two other regulars, pulled out chairs and joined them. The tinny music of the piano mixed with masculine laughter and chatter as men at each table talked loud enough to be heard over the racket. With his thumb and forefinger, Gabe slowly pulled his pistol out of his jacket holster as usual and laid it on the table—a sign that he brokered no funny business.

Two hours later, the cockiness had gone out of Talbot's blue eyes, replaced by disbelief at the first hand he lost, and then simmering anger as he tossed the last of his coins into the pot. Gabe had seen that look many times in his years as a gambler, even felt it himself often in the beginning of his career. But he couldn't tell whether Talbot was angry at himself or Gabe.

Talbot ran a shaky hand through his disheveled, curly blond hair and shoved away from the table. "That's it. I'm broke."

Slim pushed up from the table. "Guess that pretty wife of yours ain't gettin' no money again this month."

Talbot grabbed the man by the collar. Gabe rested his hand on his pistol and watched. With a loud growl, Talbot heaved Slim backward into the wall. Then he turned and sidestepped, bumping into a barmaid, and wove his way to the exit. The double saloon doors banged and remained swinging as Talbot lurched outside.

"Come on, Will. Time to head back to the ranch." Slim rubbed the back of his head where it had smacked the wall then bent and picked up his hat from the floor.

Will, the last cowpoke still seated, pushed upward, wobbled, and then grinned as he got to his feet. "I just need one more drink afore I hit the trail."

Slim grabbed his arm. "You've had enough for tonight. Let's go."

Gabe watched them leave. He glanced around, knowing nobody was paying him any attention now that the action was over. He slid the glass of whiskey that had been sitting on the table most of the evening toward him, then dumped it down the knothole in the floor near the leg of the table. He couldn't stand the taste of liquor and didn't like what it did to a man, but in order to keep his table, he had to buy a few drinks now and then, as well as fork over a percentage of his earnings.

He pocketed the coins along with a scratched but decent pocket watch he'd just won. Then he stood and stretched. Long ago, he'd eased his mind over taking hard-earned money from businessmen and poor cowboys. He never forced anyone to gamble. Men played games of chance for fun and relaxation after a hard week's work, and if they wanted to risk their wages, who was he to deny them the opportunity? Occasionally he lost, but he read people so well now that he generally came out on the winning end. Stretching, he decided to call it an early night.

Selma, a pretty brunette saloon girl, sashayed over and nuzzled up to him. "How about some company tonight, Gabriel?"

He didn't miss the sensual way she purred out his full name, or her pouty lips and the pleading in her dull brown eyes. But he never indulged in women of the night. The memory of his mother—a kind and godly woman, a lady who smelled of flowers and fresh bread, not whiskey, cheap perfume, and smoke—kept him from compromising himself. That, and the promise he'd made his ma.

Gabe shook his head. "Not tonight, Selma."

She stuck out her lower lip as he set her aside. "It's never *tonight* with you." She turned and brushed up against one of the town's bankers, who leered at her then tugged her to him.

Gabe pushed through the doors, glad to be out of the smelly

building. He glanced up at the stars and breathed deeply, relishing the fresh air. Being outside at night reminded him of the days back on the farm when he rose before the sun to do the milking—before life had turned inside out.

He rolled his head, popping his neck, and headed toward his suite at the hotel. A smile crept to his lips at the thought of his ma scolding him for going to bed in the middle of the night and sleeping till noon. A day wasted, she'd have said.

Up ahead, a group of cowboys stood by their horses, preparing to return to the ranches where they worked. Gabe hesitated then ducked down the alley—a place he generally avoided. But right now, it provided a better alternative than being caught alone with a pocket of coins by a rowdy group who'd mostly lost their hard-earned money and had far too many drinks.

A full moon illuminated the path behind a doctor's dark office and one of Kansas City's many stores. Gabe's boots thumped out a soft thud in the dirt as he listened to the peaceful noises of the night. Crickets sang in the tall grass just past the edge of town, and the piano music and the saloon ruckus dimmed. A cool breeze swept past his sweaty neck, sending a chill down his back.

The crickets suddenly quieted, and a man stepped out of the shadows, his pistol pointed straight at Gabe.

Halting midstep, Gabe assessed the situation, his hand aching to draw his weapon. He'd known walking back here was risky, and now he wished he hadn't. Though he was a quick draw, he had no chance against a man whose gun was already drawn.

"You cheated me out of my money."

Gabe recognized Tom Talbot's voice and lithe form. The hairs on his nape rose. Was the man alone? Were his cohorts hiding in the shadows as Talbot had?

"I never cheat." Gabe growled out each word slowly as he attempted to gauge Talbot's soberness. Having concentrated on the card game, he hadn't noticed how much Talbot was drinking. A mistake he wouldn't make in the future.

If the man was inebriated and his reactions slowed, Gabe just might have a chance, even though the man's gun was already drawn. First, he needed to distract him. "I didn't force you to play. You knew the risk when you sat down at my table."

"My wife and boy need that money."

Gabe shrugged, tucking his jacket out of the way in case he needed to draw his weapon. He felt sorry for the man's family, but Talbot should have thought of them sooner. Gabe forced away the unwanted memory of a hungry, crying boy.

"Toss me my money, and I'll be on my way." Talbot stepped closer, moonlight illuminating his body.

"Can't do that. I won it fair and square. I wouldn't be in business long if I returned every sad cowboy's money."

"Talbot!" a voice in the distance called. "We're leavin'."

In the split second that Tom Talbot cocked his head toward the voice, Gabe whipped out his gun. Talbot turned and fired. Gabe's hand jolted as his Colt 45 blasted.

His opponent jerked and stared at him with disbelief. The weapon fell from Talbot's hand. He grabbed his chest with one hand and sank to his knees.

Instant regret flooded Gabe as he lowered his gun. What had he done? Holstering his weapon, he rushed to Talbot's side, wishing he'd handed over the money.

"S—sorry, Lara. . ." Talbot tugged at something in his shirt pocket then wheezed his last breath.

Gabe hung his head, remorse weighing him down. Things had

happened so fast. Too fast.

Moonlight reflected off the paper in Talbot's pocket. Gabe pulled it out. A photo. He cocked it toward the moonlight, and the picture of a pretty woman with sad eyes took shape. In her arms rested a baby. Lara—Talbot said her name was—and somehow it fit. Had Talbot loved his wife? The man sure hadn't been much of a provider from what Gabe had seen.

He squatted next to Talbot's body, once again gutted with guilt. He'd just made this woman a widow—and the baby, fatherless. Something he knew all about.

He flipped the photograph over and held it up to the moonlight. *Caldwell, Kansas. 1886.*

Guilt ate at him like a bad case of food poisoning. He shoved to his feet as people ran his way. The sheriff pushed through the crowd and studied the scene. Gabe could only hope the man would believe his story.

⌒

Caldwell, Kansas
April 2, 1889

Michael tugged on Lara Talbot's skirt. "Mama, somebody's follo-win' us."

Lara glanced over her shoulder and her heart jolted. Sure enough, a man she'd seen in town was riding through the prairie grass toward them.

"Is it Pa?" A mixture of hope and yearning flashed across her four-year-old son's face.

"No, sweetie, it's not him." They hadn't seen Tom in over a year. His creditors, however, frequently knocked on her door.

Michael stared at the rider again, her son's golden curls dancing on the light spring breeze. "Maybe he's comin' to see Grandpa."

"Maybe." Lara's stomach swirled as she searched for a hiding place among the waist-high grass. But surely the rider had already spotted them. She couldn't tell Michael that she'd noticed this same man watching her in town. She hadn't thought much about it then, since men tended to stare at women, but if he had business with her, why hadn't he approached her in Caldwell?

She tightened her grip on her son's hand and quickened her steps, wishing she weren't a whole mile from town and another half mile till home. The large bundle of mending she'd picked up from Mrs. Henry's house weighed her down. If she dropped her burden, she could whisk Michael up and maybe hide in a gully by the creek, but she'd never be able to replace the expensive clothing should something happen to it.

"Slow down, Mama."

Michael's short legs pumped hard to keep up with hers. She slackened her pace and glanced back. The man was gaining ground.

Tom's debts were like a trail of bread crumbs leading to her door. Would this man be kind and compassionate or rude and demanding like most of the others?

Not that it mattered. She had nothing to give any of them.

The man must have realized she'd seen him, because he kicked his horse into a trot. Lara's heart stampeded. Most folks in the area were friendly, but there were always those unsavory scoundrels who yearned to catch a woman alone.

She shoved Michael behind one of the cottonwood trees that hugged the creek bank, dropped the load of mending, and grabbed the largest limb she could find on the ground.

"Stay there until I call."

Her son looked up with wide blue-green eyes and nodded. His curly blond locks sprang up and down in spirals across his forehead.

Lara sucked in a breath, tightened her two-fisted grasp on the branch, and stepped to the middle of the trail. As the horse neared, the animal's eyes widened and its nostrils flared. The rider soothed his mount then hoisted his stout leg over the horse's rump and dropped to the trail with a huff. On the ground, the short, portly man wasn't nearly as intimidating. From the cut of his clothing she could tell he was a city fellow.

He offered a stiff smile, lifted his derby, and swiped the sweat from his wide forehead. The horse lowered its big head and plucked the top off some nearby buffalo grass.

Trembling, Lara glanced up and down the dirt path, hoping someone would arrive to help her, but this lone trail led only to her home—and unless someone was purposely going to visit them, there was little chance for rescue. She peeked at Michael, relieved to see him obeying and hiding behind the tree.

Determined to protect her son, she tightened her grip on the branch and faced the stranger. "Why are you following me?"

He raised his palm in the air. "Now don't be fearful, Mizz Talbot. I don't mean you no harm."

Lara stiffened, and her heart galloped like a runaway horse. She lowered the branch and wiped each sweaty palm on her skirt. How was it this stranger knew her name?

"What do you want? If you're looking for Tom, I haven't seen him in over a year."

The man dropped the reins, removed his dusty derby, and twisted the thin brim with his pudgy hands. "Truth is, I *have* come 'bout your man."

Lara heaved a sigh and shook her head. This stranger would have to get in line to collect his debt. *Oh, Tom, what have you done now?*

The stranger reached into his pants pocket. Lara tightened her grasp on the branch again, knowing how little help it would be if the man pulled out a gun. She swallowed the lump in her throat. If he did, she'd have to react fast.

Something crinkled in his fist, making Lara go weak in the knees with relief. Paper, not a pistol.

The stranger cleared his throat. "I have a letter for you from my employer and. . .uh, something else."

Keeping hold of the club with one fist, she held out a shaky hand, retrieved the damp, wrinkled missives and shook them open. As she stepped back, her gaze darted from the man to the letter. She scanned the brief, hard-to-read note asking her to come to a Kansas City hotel to collect some cash Tom left behind. She couldn't make out the scrawled signature. It made no sense. If Tom had money, he'd never leave it anywhere—except at the gaming tables. Her heart clenched as if squeezed through a wringer, and then she glanced at the second paper—a death certificate.

Tom was dead. *Oh my. . . How. . . ?*

He was only twenty-six years old.

Shot, the certificate stated.

What was he doing to get himself shot? And who pulled the trigger?

She waited for grief to overwhelm her. That's what happened when a woman lost her husband, wasn't it? She remembered how inconsolable Grandpa had been when Gram died. Of course, he had *loved* her.

Numb and dry-eyed, Lara stared at the stranger. She carefully worded her question because of Michael. "Where is he now?"

The sun glinted off the man's shiny bald head as he studied the trail, fidgeting and wringing his hat half to death. "You'd have to talk to my boss 'bout all that, ma'am. My orders were to find you and fetch you back to Kansas City."

"Kansas City! Why would I want to go there?" Lara blinked. Stunned at the news of her husband's death, she had dropped her guard. She raised the club up between her and the stranger again, the papers crumpling in one fist around the limb. "I'm not going anywhere with you, mister."

Would he force her?

The man scratched his head. "But the boss said I was to bring ya."

Swallowing back her fear, Lara stood her ground. "How did you know where to find me?"

Shuffling his feet, the man avoided her eyes. "There was a picture—of you and the boy."

"Mama?" Michael sniffed and rubbed one eye as he peered around the tree.

"It's all right, sweetheart. Stay right there and guard the laundry for me."

Michael nodded, looked around, and snatched up a little stick. She wanted to smile but returned her focus on the stranger.

"You don't understand, Mizz Talbot. Your husband left some cash behind, and my employer insists you come to Kansas City and collect it yerself."

"Why didn't he send it with you?"

The man shrugged one beefy shoulder and grinned wryly. "Maybe he don't trust me."

"Then why should I?"

He opened his mouth and slammed it shut, looking perplexed. His gaze took in her ragged dress and bare feet. She tucked her toes back under her skirt. It was none of his business if she wanted to save her only pair of shoes for cold weather.

"Looks to me like you and yours could use the money. Won't take long to ride the train to KC."

Lara sighed. "I knew my husband well, Mister. . .uh. . ." She lifted her brows and peered at him.

"Jones. Homer Jones."

"I am *not* going anywhere with you, Mr. Jones. My family needs me. Besides, Tom never had a pocket full of coins—ever. Much less enough to make it worth journeying to Kansas City."

"The boss ain't gonna be happy about this." The man slapped on his hat and snagged his horse's reins. The animal jerked its head and snorted. Mr. Jones muttered under his breath, "Nope, he won't like it one bit."

"That isn't my problem. Good day, Mr. Jones." As much as she wanted to hope Tom had left behind some money, she knew the truth. Her husband was a wastrel.

Lara tossed the heavy branch into a patch of the thick buffalo grass and wildflowers that battled the trees lining the creek for the precious liquid. "You can come out now." She held her hand out to her son. The boy jumped up and ran to her, burying his face in her skirt. Had he understood that his father was dead? Or had he been frightened by the situation?

She smoothed Michael's white-blond curls, so much like Tom's, then gave him a hug. A boy shouldn't have to grow up without a father, but then Tom had been home so few times since his son's birth that she wasn't even sure if Michael would have recognized him.

She hoisted the mending bundle over her shoulder and then reclaimed her son's hand. Together they tramped down the trail, leaving Mr. Jones alone to figure out how to remount his horse.

It was a strong statement about her marriage that all she felt was relief now that she knew Tom was gone. And guilt, because she wasn't grieving.

Tom had been so charming when she'd first met him when she was fifteen. He was so unlike the solemn, hardworking men she'd known before him. He'd made her laugh, and spending time with him helped her get through her tough days that held far too much burden and responsibility. Lara's papa and mama had died four years before she met Tom, and her grandma died just ten months after her parents, leaving Lara as cook and housekeeper on her grandpa's small horse ranch at only eleven years old. Maintaining the home while watching her troublesome sister was more than a little difficult. Her older brother Jack's anger and talk of leaving tore out her heart, and then he left, too. On top of everything, she'd had to cheer up Grandpa and help him see he still had a reason to live—she and Jo needed him desperately.

She clenched the mending bag tighter. Life seemed unbearable for a time. And then she met Tom at a town festival. And he gave her a reason to smile. At least for a short while.

"You've got to be the prettiest gal in all of Kansas," he'd said the first time they met.

She'd worn a faded calico and had just walked two miles in the scorching August heat. Lara knew she had all the appeal of a split tomato, but Tom still seemed enamored with her.

Once he turned the full power of his charm on her, she'd fallen fast for him. And look where it got her.

At least Tom would no longer be incurring debts that she was obligated to pay, nor would he show up out of the blue, expecting her to act like a loving wife who'd been pining for her husband.

A shiver charged through her. As hard as she'd tried, in their five years of marriage, she'd never been able to get Tom to give his heart to God. Just like her younger sister, Joline, Tom craved adventure. He was always running off, searching for the next way to get rich fast. The remorse she felt was for a lost soul—for the man she had once loved so much that she'd gone against her grandfather's counsel to marry him. And most of the time since then, she'd regretted her decision.

She glanced up at the bright blue sky, hoping in Tom's final moments he'd cried out to the Savior. Birds chirped in the few trees along the trail. Prairie grass swished on the morning breeze, and the poppy mallows and prairie violets turned their colorful faces to the sun. God's world still looked the same, but hers had changed. At just twenty-one years of age, she was now a widow.

But then, hadn't she been living as a widow for a very long time?

Chapter 2

Gabe slammed his fist down on his desk, rattling his coffee cup. "What do you mean she wouldn't come?"

Homer shrugged one shoulder in his typical noncommittal way. "Said she don't b'lieve that no-account man of hers left behind enough money to make it worth travelin' all the way here."

The chair squealed as Gabe pushed back from his desk and stood. He padded across the thick Persian carpet to the window and stared down on the streets of Kansas City. People ambled about their business, and a tired horse tethered to a rail across the street drooped its head and swished flies with its tail. A wagon pulled by a team of mules moseyed down the road as its driver waved to a man on the boardwalk.

Gabe rolled his head from side to side, trying to relieve the tension knotting his neck. Why hadn't the woman been reasonable? Surely she needed the money.

He'd tried to do something good for someone else for once. . . . Now what?

Leaning his palms against the windowsill, Gabe rested his forehead on the cool glass. "Did she ask about the circumstances surrounding his death?"

"No, and I didn't say nuthin'. She didn't seem too overly upset about it, neither." Homer wheezed a raspy chuckle. "You shoulda seen her swinging that branch at me like it was a club. Don't know that I coulda overpowered her if'n I had to."

Gabe turned and lounged against the windowsill, wondering what kind of woman wouldn't be upset over her husband's death. There were few respectable jobs for women, especially one with a child, so life was surely going to be more difficult for Mrs. Talbot. Any woman who would turn down a hundred dollars in gold coin intrigued him, especially a spunky one. But then she didn't know how much he planned to give her. Talbot only lost his twenty-dollar monthly pay, but adding Gabe's own funds to the kitty would help the widow more and ease his guilt over killing her husband. He still woke up most nights in a cold sweat when he dreamed of the shoot-out.

"She's a purty little thang." Homer ran his hand over his thick stubble, making a scratching sound. "Got the most unusual pale green eyes I ever did see."

Green. The sad eyes that had haunted his dreams since the ambush in the alley were light green. An unusual color for sure. "Her hair?"

"Golden brown, like a glass of fine whiskey held up to the light—and curly, just like that boy of hers."

"Boy?" So the babe in the photo was Talbot's son.

"Cute little feller." Homer yawned then smacked his lips. "Sure looked like they coulda used that money. Neither of 'em had on shoes, and their clothes was ragged. Found out Mizz Talbot's been doin' mending for some of the townfolk."

Gabe sighed. He couldn't stand the thought of a child going without basic needs. It was only April, and the ground still held a chill. Neither mother nor son should be going without shoes so early in the year.

"You got somethin' else you want me to do, Mr. Coulter?" Homer Jones wiped his nose with his sleeve.

Gabe could barely abide the uncouth man, but Homer was loyal and did as he was told for the meager pay doled out to him.

"That's all for now." Gabe pulled two dollars from his pocket, tossed it to Jones, then turned to face the window.

"You gonna be playing poker at the saloon tonight?"

"Where else would I be?"

"Now that I've got some money, maybe I'll get in on the game myself." The door latch clicked as Homer left the room.

Gabe shook his head and chuckled. Likely, those two bucks would be back in his pocket before long. Homer ought to know better than to gamble with a professional.

Gabe flopped down in his chair and stared at the bottom right-hand drawer of his desk. Next month he'd be twenty-five. The deathbed promises he'd made to his mother plagued him like a bad bout of influenza. He hadn't been able to keep his first promise. "Read the Bible every day, Gabriel," she'd said. "And become an honorable man like your father was."

Too late for that. His dear mother would be so disappointed with how he'd turned out. But perhaps it wasn't too late to keep the second promise. Was there any hope a gambler could become an honorable man? He snorted and shook his head. Not likely.

He glanced across the room to the framed picture of his mother and real father on their wedding day. They'd been younger than he was now.

It was odd that he could love his ma and her memory but still resent her for making him promise those things. Knowing he'd committed to both read his Bible and become an honorable man had kept him from growing truly comfortable in his choice of career. And the closer he got to turning twenty-five, the edgier he grew.

Ma had no idea how badly his stepfather had mistreated him. He'd hidden all but the worst of the beatings he'd taken from the man he hated, and had explained the injuries away as falling off a horse or some other accident. But they'd taken their toll and had left him as crushed both emotionally and physically as a man who'd been run down by a herd of stampeding cattle.

He pulled the drawer open and stared at his mother's aged Bible. He touched the decorative leather cover then slammed the drawer closed with his boot, hoping to shut out the haunting memories.

Now what? His plans to soothe his befuddled soul by doing something noble had included seeing that the Widow Talbot received the money her husband left behind. Money Tom Talbot lost fair and square.

Gabe leaned his head back and closed his eyes, exhausted from the lack of sleep. Every time he tried to rest, he saw Tom Talbot's stunned expression as life quickly ebbed from the man's body. Talbot couldn't have been much older than he was.

And now the man was dead.

And a little boy was fatherless.

Sighing, he stared up at the decorative tin ceiling. Maybe the boy's mother would remarry—but having a stepfather could be far worse than having no father at all.

He looked around the classy hotel suite he lived in, with its stylish wallpaper and top-of-the-line furnishings he'd purchased. He had all a man could desire as far as fancy things and good food. So why did he feel so unsettled lately?

Was it because of the promises he'd made to his ma?

Or the blank look in Talbot's lifeless eyes?

He shook his head, trying to replace the image of Talbot with that of the man's wife. He pulled the photo out of his jacket pocket. A lean, pretty face stared back, albeit melancholy. Homer hadn't mentioned if she was tall or short. Those eyes haunted Gabe's dreams. And now they had color.

Lara Talbot sounded like a good woman, not swayed by money and ready to fight if need be to protect her son. His mother was the only truly good woman he'd ever known. If Mrs. Talbot was anything like his ma, he owed it to himself to make her acquaintance and to make restitution—if it was possible to make reparation for the life of Mrs. Talbot's husband.

This was a good time to get away. Other than to exercise the fine horse he'd won a few months back, he hadn't left Kansas City since he'd arrived ten years ago as a determined boy.

The town of Caldwell, on the southern Kansas border, wasn't all that far away. He could take the train, deliver the pouch of coins to Talbot's wife and son, and for once, be proud of something he'd done. He'd won Talbot's twenty dollars honestly, but it was blood money, and he needed to be rid of it.

Maybe after he made things right with the man's widow, he could journey down to Texas for his birthday. He'd always had a hankering to see the great state and to visit the Alamo.

He rose and walked to the window, his gut swirling with uneasiness. He couldn't forever put off the promise he'd made to his ma. His God-fearing mother was the only woman he'd ever loved, and he aimed to keep his word—just not yet. She wouldn't be happy knowing he made his living as a gambler in a fancy saloon. He could see her finger wagging in his face as she lectured him on the woes of gambling.

He blew out a loud breath.

Ma was long dead. She'd never know if he didn't keep his word. But he would.

First he'd find this green-eyed widow and hand over the money. Then he'd see about reforming his life.

For the first time in years, excitement surged through him.

⌒

As Lara approached the sod shack that sat on the acre of rented land where her family lived, she slowed her steps. Her trio of nanny goats bleated to her and stuck their heads over the short fence, hoping for a handout. Michael plucked a dandelion and stuck it out, giggling when the billy goat snatched it with his big teeth.

She had kept the information she'd learned yesterday a secret while she examined her feelings and tried to comprehend that she'd never see her husband again.

How would the news affect her grandfather? Would he share her relief, mixed with the sadness of a life snuffed out at such a young age—a mostly wasted life?

Five years ago, she'd been so eager to get help for her grandfather that she had gone against his wishes and married Tom with the hope that having another man around would ease her grandpa's workload. But they'd lost the ranch after Tom went off searching for riches and adventure. Many times over, she'd regretted marrying him. Lara remembered something a woman at church once muttered when a local farm girl ran off with a traveling peddler. *"Marry in haste, repent at leisure."*

Lara sighed. That sure was the truth.

The sun glistened off the top of Joline's head as her sister ducked down and stepped through the low doorway of the soddy. Jo looked up, and her blue eyes sparked when she saw Lara.

"Where were you?" Jo glared at her.

"Out pickin' greens."

"Well, it's about time you got back. Grandpa's had another of his swamp fever attacks."

Lara closed her eyes and allowed the news to wash over her. "How bad is it?"

"Better than some, worse than others." Jo stooped down to hug Michael and gave him a kiss on the cheek. "Eww! You're all sticky."

He giggled and tried to touch her with his dirty hands.

Jo jumped up and stepped back. "Oh, no you don't."

Michael laughed out loud and chased her around the yard, Jo playfully shrieking as if a bear were after her. Lara smiled, glad her worries hadn't affected her son. He needed to play and laugh.

She set down the bucket of greens, blowing out a sigh as Jo walked toward her.

"How much of Grandpa's medicine is left?" Lara asked, even though she knew exactly how few pills were still in the bottle. She had desperately hoped she could finish this month's mending and collect payment before Grandpa ran out of his quinine tablets.

"Six. He's been trying to not take them."

Lara wanted to sit down and cry but knew it wouldn't accomplish anything and would only upset her son. She glanced up at the sky and silently beseeched her heavenly Father for help.

"Does he have a fever yet?"

Jo shook her head. "No, but he's tired and achy, and his head hurts. I hope for his sake this is a short episode."

"Me, too. Did you finish weeding the garden?" Lara held her hand over her eyes to block the sun and studied her sister, hoping she had done her chores. Jo usually seemed willing to help until it came time to do the actual work. She'd rather be dreaming of fancy clothes, a house with wood floors and pretty furniture, or a handsome beau.

Joline waved a hand in the air, dramatic as ever. "I've been taking care of Grandpa. When would I have time to work in the garden?"

Michael ran up beside Lara, his face and hands dripping wet. "I can pull weeds."

His childish exuberance warmed her heart, but if she let him hoe alone, he'd cut down the vegetables along with the weeds. Lara stooped down and gave him a hug. "Thank you, sweetie. Maybe we'll go do it together and let Aunt Jo watch over Grandpa, since he's not feeling well."

Michael glanced at Joline and smiled then tugged Lara toward the small vegetable plot.

The southern breeze cooled her damp back but blew her hair into her face. For early April, the weather had been quite warm, and she hoped it wasn't a sign of an extra-hot summer. A clump of hair tickled her cheeks and clung to her lips. The rebellious curls refused to stay in the confines of her braid, so she pulled a triangle of fabric from her pocket and tied back the wayward tresses. She'd often envied women with straight, manageable hair. Hers would be a mess to brush out later.

"I'll get the shubbel."

Lara shook her head. "No, son. We don't need the shovel to pull weeds. We'll use our hands or a hoe."

"I'll get it." He ran to the lean-to attached to the grass house they lived in and disappeared inside. Just as quickly, he came back out, dragging the hoe with both hands.

"Lara?" Jo closed the distance between them.

At sixteen, Joline turned many heads with her curly blond hair and dark blue eyes. She had been fortunate to get their mother's beautiful eye color and not the unremarkable pale green of some unknown ancestor like Lara had gotten. In spite of her faded dress, Jo was a beauty. Lara couldn't help wondering how long it would be before some handsome young man stole her sister's heart and took her away.

"Have you thought any more about the land run?" Jo fidgeted, toeing circles in the dirt.

Lara peeked at Michael and saw him reach for the green stems of a carrot. "Son, why don't you take the bucket and get some water for the plants?" Since they were only about fifty feet from the creek, she could keep an eye on him, and distracting him with fetching the water would keep him from pulling any of the precious vegetables.

He smiled and nodded his head, his ringlets bouncing up and down. She really needed to give him another haircut but hated to clip away his adorable curls.

"I'll get water," he sang as he skipped over to an empty bucket sitting near the soddy and dragged it toward the creek.

Jo shoved her hands to her hips. "So, have you thought about it? Everyone's talking about the free land. And it's good land that'll grow wonderful crops, and there's fresh game running all over the place. Grandpa told me, and Samuel Carter has seen it. He said parts of the Unassigned Lands look a lot like the area around here, although other parts are much drier. That's why it's so important to get a good spot and be in front when the race starts." Jo's eyes danced with excitement. "I wish I was old enough to ride."

Lara huffed out a disgusted breath. She was sick of hearing about Harrison's Hoss Race, as the land rush into the Oklahoma Territory was being called. President Benjamin Harrison sure did open a can of worms when he signed legislation opening the Indians' lands to settlement. Joline yearned for adventure like a parched man craved water, and with everyone talking about the last chance to get free land in the United States, hope and excitement were as plentiful as grass on the prairie. Reality was something else. Dreams didn't put food on the table or clothes on a body. Lara shook her head, tired of fighting her sister on this subject.

"How could we compete?" Lara held out her callused hands, watching Michael dip the bucket in the two-inch deep water at the edge of the creek. "We have no horse, only a tired, old mule and a rickety wagon. Grandpa's sick. How could he possibly race and have any hope of getting property when he has to compete with young men on fast mounts?"

Jo's eyes sparkled with excitement. "You could run on foot. Other women are racing. I'm willing, but I'm too young. You have to be twenty-one to race."

Lara closed her eyes, pushing away her frustration. Why couldn't she have a quiet, helpful sister who liked cooking and cleaning? "Think about that. Me on foot, fighting my skirts, trying to beat out men on horseback and in wagons to get one of the few sections of good land?" Lara pursed her lips and shook her head. "Be realistic, Joline."

Her sister crossed her arms and scowled. "You're becoming a boring old fuddy-duddy." She leaned in closer. "It's a chance for us to get land of our own—for Grandpa to have his own property again. Losing his ranch to the creditors was almost the end for him." Jo tossed her braid over her shoulder. "Just think. No more waiting for Tom to get lucky or for Providence to rain down gold coins from heaven."

Lara straightened. "Joline Marie Jensen, do not blaspheme God."

Jo had the sense to look chagrined. "I'm so sick of eating squirrel, mush, and turnips. If we had more land, we could grow all kinds of things."

Behind her sister, Lara watched her son slowly lug the bucket toward the garden. If she could just keep Jo distracted until after the land run, then she wouldn't have to listen to this particular harebrained idea anymore. Of course, Jo would just come up with something else to occupy her imagination.

"The Lord blessed us with a rabbit today. Please remove it from the snare, then you can skin it while you sit with Grandpa—but do sit outside while you tend to that task."

"I'm not stupid, you know." Jo sighed, the fight gone out of her for the moment. She dragged her feet in the dirt as she trudged up the hill toward the rabbit trap. "Why do I get all the nasty jobs?"

"Jo, wait." Lara had a sudden urge to see her grandfather. With his quiet faith in God and his gentle demeanor, he had a way of helping her keep things in perspective. "Watch Michael for a minute and let me check on Grandpa."

"Skin the rabbit. Milk the goats. Watch Michael." Jo flung her arms up. "Make up your mind, will you?"

Lara stifled an ugly response and ducked into the sod house. Her eyes took a moment to adjust to the dimness, then she saw the lump on the floor pallet where they all slept. She tiptoed over, hoping not to awaken her grandpa. Gently, she reached out and touched his forehead with the back of her hand, wincing at his ashy coloring and the heat emanating from his brow. So, the fever *had* set in.

She bowed her head and prayed under her breath. "Lord, please let this be a quick and easy episode. I ask that You help Grandpa through this time. Heal his body, and help him not to feel useless and a burden to me."

He must have heard her movements, because he opened his eyes. "H'lo, punkin."

"How are you feeling?" She smiled.

He shrugged one shoulder. "Aw. . .you know how it goes. Aches. Fever. Chills. I'm sorry to add to your worries."

"*Shh*. . .none of that now." Lara patted his thin chest then reached out and tugged her quilt over to add to the one covering him. "What can I do to make you feel better?"

"A drink of water would be nice."

"I'll let Michael get it. He just fetched water from the creek for the garden. The last time he got water for me, the bucket only had an inch of liquid in it. At that rate, the beans will be ripe before the whole plot is watered."

Grandpa grinned. "He's a good boy and tries hard to please you."

"I know. I wish you had seen how proud he was of that tiny bit of water." Lara nodded as her chest warmed with love for her son. Michael was the only good thing Tom had ever given her. She wanted to tell Grandpa her shocking news, but it would have to wait until he was over his bout of swamp fever. Otherwise he'd lie here and stew about everything, when he needed to concentrate on getting better. Sharing the news would take some of the burden off her shoulders. Tom's death had also removed any futile hopes that he might somehow strike it rich and come home with enough money to buy land and build a real house so they could quit renting the acre from Herman Hancock.

The reality of it all suddenly struck her. There would be no money from Tom. No hope of any money, either. She couldn't understand why that portly stranger had tried to persuade her otherwise, especially since she knew in her heart that traveling to Kansas City would be a waste of time.

"I've been th–thinking."

Her grandpa's teeth rattled so loudly, it pulled Lara from her thoughts. She grabbed Jo's worn patchwork quilt, shook it open, and laid it over him. Dust she'd stirred in the air from the earthen walls danced in the sunlight shining through the open doorway. "Just rest now, and don't worry about things."

Lara pushed upward to stand, but he grabbed her wrist, tugging her back.

He cleared his throat. "Lara, c—consider the land rush. I know Jo has some crazy ideas, b—but this one just might be the Lord's will."

Masking her surprise, she patted his hand, like she would Michael's. It was the fever talking. Her levelheaded grandfather would never consider such a risky endeavor. "Just rest. We can talk later."

"There's not time! L—less than three weeks. Gotta get r—registered. Get a h—horse." His brows dipped and his eyes narrowed.

Lara's heart stumbled. Rarely had she seen her mild-mannered grandpa so serious and determined. "All right, I'll look into it."

As if he'd spent all his energy in that one plea, he immediately relaxed and dropped his hand. Lara took the bottle of quinine pills from her apron pocket, removed one, and handed it to him, and he swallowed it.

She lifted the layer of bed covers and slid his arm underneath, feeling the heat of the fever. His swamp fever attacks, a remnant of his soldiering in the War Between the States, occurred almost as frequently as the new moon, but thankfully, with the help of the quinine, he could get over them fairly quickly.

She stepped outside. Jo's and Michael's giggles shattered the quiet of nature as her eyes adjusted to the sun's brightness. Michael snagged a dirt clod and lobbed it over the young cabbage plants, narrowly missing Jo. She squealed and tossed a clump of dried weeds at the boy.

Lara wanted to join in their lighthearted fun, but her heart was too heavy with the burden of keeping things running and making sure they had food.

"Jo!"

Her sister jumped and turned, hiding her dirty hands behind her skirt. "What? Is something wrong with Grandpa?" Jo's dingy apron, grayed from use and so many washings, had a clump of mud sticking to it. The girl needed a mother, not a nagging big sister with so many worries.

"Grandpa needs a drink. I told him Michael could fetch the water."

"I'll get it!" Michael dumped out the last of the garden water and dragged the wooden bucket outside the fence, leaving a trail in the dirt behind him.

"If you'll show him how to wash off and then get fresh water upstream, I'll take over in the garden."

Jo nodded then jogged to catch up with him. The rickety gate squeaked as Lara tugged it open. They'd erected the fence made of branches to keep their goats and other animals out of the small garden. She walked over to where Michael had been playing with Jo and noted a foot of carrot tops lay half smashed. She sighed then molded dirt around the base of the plants to help support the stems.

Glancing up at the beautiful sky, she watched a fat cloud drift by. A red-tailed hawk screeched then dove down, rising again with a squirming critter in its talons. The wind had shifted, coming from the northwest, and would most likely bring a cooler breeze.

"Lord, please watch over our garden. Keep the critters out, and send a refreshing rain. Be with Grandpa, and let this malaria attack be a short one. And please help me to know what to do about this land run. We can't compete without a horse, so I guess if You want us to ride in the race, You're going to have to provide a mount."

"Mama!"

Heart pounding at Michael's scream, Lara jumped up and searched for her son, hoping—praying—he wasn't injured.

"Bad Billy got loose." The boy ran her direction but pointed past her.

Lara pivoted and gasped. Their ornery billy goat charged straight for the open garden gate.

Chapter 3

The train shuddered to a stop at the Caldwell Depot with a squeal of brakes and a loud hiss. Gabe looked out at the cluster of buildings that made up Caldwell. Several rows of one- and two-story brick and wooden structures rose up from the prairie. Not much of a town compared to Kansas City. He knew Caldwell was a big cow town years earlier, but with more and more fences going up and crops being planted, the big cattle drives had all but ceased, and from the looks of it, the town had suffered.

Gabe grabbed his satchel and hurried down the aisle, anxious to see how his horse had fared on the train. He'd won the black gelding in a poker game a few months ago and had quickly become attached to the fine creature. Animals made good friends. They never argued with you, although Tempest could be temperamental when riled. They wouldn't desert you in favor of someone better looking or with a deeper pocket, and they generally vied for your attention. If only people were the same.

Gabe handed his claim ticket to the freight conductor and waited on the ramp for the man to bring out Tempest. He recognized the gelding's loud whinny and figured the conductor had his hands full with the feisty animal. The clunk of hooves sounded as his horse kicked the side wall of the train. A loud curse echoed in the freight car, and Tempest bolted past Gabe, almost knocking him off the ramp. Gabe's heart ricocheted in his chest as he made a flailing grab onto the handle of the boxcar door and regained his balance.

He searched for the ornery beast and saw him corralled by a circle of men. A woman with curly hair slipping from her loose bun eased up to the frightened creature, her hands held apart. Gabe jogged toward the group, concerned for the woman's safety and determined not to lose his horse.

As he drew near, he could hear the woman's soft muttering. Tempest's ears flicked in her direction, but his eyes no longer held that wild, frightened look. He snorted and thrust his big head toward the woman, and she quickly grabbed the loose lead rope then patted Tempest on the neck.

"What a good boy you are. And pretty, too."

As Gabe stepped behind her, he realized how small she was—probably no more than five-three, and the top of her head reached no higher than his chin, yet she'd bravely faced down his spooked horse. He opened his mouth to thank her, but then she turned, taking away his breath. The pale green of her eyes made his heart jolt. Could this possibly be Tom Talbot's widow? How many women in Caldwell could have eyes with that unusual color?

He struggled to match the face in the faded photo he'd memorized with the real-life woman in front of him. Homer had said she was pretty, and that was true in a tomboyish way. A faint sprinkle of freckles not visible in the photo dotted the bridge of her nose and splattered onto her cheeks. Her skin held the sun's gentle kiss, and except for being on the skinny side and wearing worn clothing, she was easy on the eyes.

When she noticed him staring, she stepped toward him. "Is this your horse, mister?"

He nodded, accepting the lead rope from her. Tempest nickered, and Gabe scratched the rascal between the ears.

"He's a fine animal."

Gabe pressed his lips together. He didn't like surprises. Didn't like losing control and hated that his mind swirled with haphazard thoughts. But those eyes. . .

"Guess he doesn't like the train all that much. It can be rather loud and jarring." The woman's lips tilted up in a shy smile. "Better keep a close eye on him, what with horses being in such high demand right now." She stepped around him, squeezed past two men, and disappeared into the crowd.

Tempest nudged his arm, wanting attention. Gabe watched the woman go, a hundred questions racing through his mind. He'd never seen a woman with eyes the color of—what? They didn't resemble anything he could think of. Maybe the light green satin of one of the saloon gals' dresses back in Kansas City, but this woman, clothed in a dowdy, faded dress, was much lovelier than a saloon dancer in her finest. Something about her tugged at his heart.

"Hey, mister. Ya wanna sell that horse?" Gabe blinked and focused on a tall man dressed in a three-piece suit coming his way. He waved a handful of dollars in the air. Tempest snorted and jerked his head, but Gabe kept him under control.

"I asked if you want to sell that horse."

From behind him he heard someone yell, "Hey, John, this feller's got a horse for sale."

Before he could respond, Gabe was quickly surrounded as men elbowed one another to get closer. Tempest pranced sideways and snorted. Gabe tightened his grip on the leather lead and patted the horse's jaw. "*Shh*. . .you're all right, boy."

"I'll give you twenty-five dollars for that horse," a man said above the din of the crowd.

Men pushed closer, and Gabe had to return to the ramp leading to the freight car. Tempest eyed it, snorted, and stood his ground on the depot platform.

"I'll give you forty dollars," a bald man with a bushy beard cried.

"Forty-five." A tall stranger shoved the bald man, who back-stepped several paces. "I claimed the horse first."

Gabe raised his free hand in the air, palm forward. "Gentlemen, please." When they quieted, he continued: "Sorry to disappoint you, but this horse isn't for sale. He's my personal mount. I apologize for the confusion."

The crowd moaned as one but quickly dispersed amid grumbling murmurs. Relieved, Gabe looked around and found his satchel partially hidden under the ramp. He glanced past the depot, wondering what to do with Tempest now. Would the horse be safe in a livery, or would he need to hire a man to guard him?

A dark-haired adolescent boy jogged toward him, obviously hoping for a coin or two. "Need some help, mister?"

"Know a good hotel and a reliable livery where I can board my horse for a few days?"

"Yes, sir." The boy bobbed his head and smiled. "Can I lead your horse?"

Gabe held out his satchel. "You carry this, but better leave ole Tempest to me. He's a bit spooked by the train and crowd."

The boy accepted the satchel and shrugged one shoulder. "Sure. Hopkins Livery can board him, and the Blue Bonnet's got clean beds and fair food, but the Leland Hotel is the best in town."

"It is, huh?" Gabe grinned. "So, what's your name?"

"Jasper."

"Since you seem to know a lot about this town, can you tell me why that mob wanted to buy my horse so bad?"

"It's the land grab. Folks are buying up every horse and wagon they can find. Some even got them fancy bicycle things, but I cain't see how they're gonna ride them over rocks and through gullies. Give me a horse over one of them crazy contraptions any day."

An idea sparked in Gabe's mind. Bill Swanson had some saddle-broke horses for sale back in KC. If he could buy them cheap and have them shipped here, he stood to make a nice profit. He'd assumed that men riding in the land run would already own a mount, but after the way those men had dickered for Tempest, he felt confident he could quickly sell a half-dozen good horses.

All he had to do was get them to Caldwell before the land run.

Silas Stone tossed a final shovelful of dirt onto the fresh grave. Using a branch broken off a nearby cottonwood tree, he swiped the red soil around the grave and tossed several handfuls of leaves on it until the area blended in with the undisturbed ground. He threw the branch aside and studied his handiwork. Nobody would find the cowboy's final resting place for a long, long time—if ever.

Tired from the strenuous physical labor, he wiped his forehead with his sleeve and rolled his shoulders to work the kinks out. With shovel in hand, he followed the faint path and made his way down the hill to where the cowboy's dugout sat, nestled in the side of the knoll. The man had the misfortune of settling on the only piece of land that Silas had determined long ago would be his one day. And this was that day.

The other man had done the exhausting work of chiseling the earthen house out of the hard dirt and rock on the side of the hill, but Silas and his brother would reap the benefit, staying warm in the winter and cool on hot summer nights—as long as the soldiers hunting for Sooners didn't discover them in the Unassigned Lands before April 22.

He slid on the loose rock and jogged his way down to the nearby Cottonwood Creek then knelt at the bank and splashed the cool water on his face. Though only April, the warm afternoon sun glaring on him, combined with hard physical labor, made Silas long for a drink of whiskey. Water would have to do, though, since the nearest saloon was miles away, across the state line in Kansas. He slurped his fill then looked back at the dugout.

The door would be easy to miss. With the opening hidden among a copse of trees, wild shrubs, and tall prairie grass, nobody would know the dugout was there unless they were looking for it. He would have missed it himself, if he hadn't seen the smoke from the cowboy's campfire.

Now all he had to do was steal a small herd of cattle, and he'd be in the ranching business—right in the heart of Indian lands.

He stood and let his gaze wander across the area that had been allotted to the Creek and Seminoles. For some reason, no Indian had ever settled here. It was their loss.

Warm satisfaction seeped through him as he surveyed the valley he'd first laid eyes on during a trail drive years ago. He'd passed through several other times, and each time, his desire to settle here grew stronger.

The crickets and other insects suddenly went quiet, setting his senses on alert. A snap cracked behind him, and Silas swiveled, reaching for his gun. His frantic heartbeat slowed, and he lowered his hand as his younger brother, Arlan, approached.

"Thought you was diggin' that cowboy's grave, not lollygaggin' by the creek." Arlan glared at him, his rifle resting in crook of his arm.

"Thought you was on guard duty." Silas lifted his chin and glowered back.

"A man's gotta eat, don't he?" After a moment, Arlan cracked a smile. "Besides, I been sittin' up on that there hill standing guard all day, and there ain't been nary a soul in sight. We's too far out for them soldiers t'find us."

Silas grabbed the shovel and started for the buckboard that held their food supplies. After dinner, they could move everything into the dugout, hide the buckboard, and no longer have to worry about critters getting into their supplies during the night. He'd miss bedding down under the stars but not sleeping in the rain.

"I've got a hankering for some fish tonight." Silas tossed the shovel on top of a crate and pulled a cane pole off the wagon's tailgate.

Arlan reached for it. "I'll catch 'em while you fix the biscuits."

Silas raised the pole out of his brother's reach. At seventeen, Arlan was still nearly a foot shorter than Silas. Arlan jumped up, but Silas stretched high, until his overalls pinched his shoulder.

"Give it to me."

He shoved his brother back. "Hold yer horses. I figured we could both fish to celebrate our new home. We'll eat sooner that way."

"You reckon it's safe to live inside a hill? Don't seem right to me." Arlan's worried glance shifted toward the hidden dugout. The boy hated small, dark places ever since their pa had locked him in the root cellar when he was young. It wasn't like Arlan could help being simple-minded, but their pa had been embarrassed to take the boy into town and had locked him up to keep him safe while the family was gone. Then as if the dugout were never a concern, Arlan shrugged. "Guess we *could* eat faster with us both fishin'." He crossed to the wagon and rummaged around until he found their second pole.

Silas mixed together a cup of flour, a bit of sugar, and a spoon of grease from the pan where they'd fried the rabbit they ate for lunch, then rolled out some dough balls for bait. His brother reached around Silas's arm and snatched one, ran his hook through it, and squeezed it tight as he headed for the creek. Arlan glanced over his shoulder, grinning, as if he'd stolen a cookie from a bakery. Silas shook his head. His brother was just a big kid. Sometimes he wondered if Arlan would ever grow up.

Two hours later, after they'd gorged themselves on fried bass, Silas leaned against a tree while Arlan stretched out next to the glowing embers of the fading campfire. They really ought to throw some dirt on it so the smoke and scent wouldn't alert soldiers to their whereabouts, but he didn't have the strength to move. All that grave digging had plumb worn him out.

The sun would be setting soon, and they needed to get the food supplies transferred from the buckboard to the dugout, but he couldn't seem to make his lackluster body move. Riding herd on three thousand longhorns was a heap easier than digging through hard red dirt and rock. Muscles ached, and blisters burned his hands. He felt a lot older than his twenty-six years.

"I heard tell folks call people like us Sooners." Arlan scratched his belly. "You don't reckon the soldiers will find us afore the race, do ya?"

"Doubt it." Silas yawned. "Startin' tomorrow, we'll lay low and hide out in the dugout until the twenty-second."

Arlan bolted upright. "But that's more'n two weeks away. I cain't stay indoors all that time."

Silas heaved a sigh. He didn't much like the idea either, but it had to be done to avoid the soldiers hunting for Sooners. The closer it got to race day, the more the soldiers would be searching for people illegally entering the area reserved for the land rush. He and Arlan weren't the only ones who'd entered the Unassigned Lands early and staked a claim. The gently rolling hills were full of squatters. Once the race started, the legitimate racers would be hard pressed to find a piece of land that a Sooner hadn't already taken. Silas chuckled. Play by the rules and you lose.

"What about the horses?" Arlan sat up and stared at him, hair hanging over his eyes, looking like a kid.

"What about 'em?"

"We gonna take 'em into the dugout, too? It'll be mighty smelly if'n we do."

Silas shrugged his stiff shoulder. "Haven't quite worked that out yet."

Arlan flopped back down, sending a puff of red dirt into the air. "What about the buckboard?"

Silas grunted. That was something else he hadn't worked out. Somehow, he needed to hide or dispose of the wagon. They could use it as firewood, but then they wouldn't have a way to haul things.

Silas glanced past Arlan to where his brother had leaned the rifle against the wagon wheel when he'd searched for the fishing pole. He held affection for Arlan, but the boy wasn't too responsible. He'd been watching out for his younger sibling most of Arlan's life, even seeing that he got a job herding cattle whenever Silas signed on.

Silas's eyelids drooped. He really needed to get moving and put the food away before the sun set. Maybe if he rested a few minutes he could find the strength to do the job. Arlan's soft snores lulled him into a relaxed state. Only a few minutes' rest. . .

A horse's loud whinny jolted Silas out of his dream of dancing saloon girls. *Dumb animals.* He rubbed his eyes and sat up.

"Soldiers!" Arlan squawked as he jerked upright.

In the dimness of twilight, Silas's heart jolted as soldiers on horseback charged into their camp, rifles aimed straight at him and his brother. Arlan scrambled on hands and knees toward the rifle, still leaning against the wagon wheel.

"No!" Silas yelled and raised his hands. A soldier lifted his weapon and fired as Arlan grabbed the rifle. His brother's body jerked and flew sideways in the air. He landed with a dull thud four feet from where Silas stood.

Numb with shock, Silas stared at his brother's unmoving body. The rank smell of gunpowder filled the air as a cloud of smoke began to settle. Rage seeped through him. He growled a deep guttural roar and charged the closest soldier, pulling him off his horse. The frightened animal squealed and trotted off as the soldier fell to the ground. The loud blast of rifle fire splintered the twilight again. A sharp, burning pain stabbed Silas's shoulder, and he reached for it, feeling a warm stickiness.

"You shot me." He swirled around to face a young soldier, still aiming his rifle at him.

"Take another step and I'll shoot you again, you stinkin' Sooner." The private sneered in the waning light.

Suddenly, Silas remembered his brother. He pivoted, looking to see if Arlan had moved. With one arm stuck under his body and the other just a foot away from the rifle, Arlan lay still—dead—with a bullet wound in his chest, eyes wide open in stunned shock. A pain unlike anything Silas had ever known spiraled through him.

"Tie him up and tend his wound," the captain said.

A soldier grabbed Silas's good arm and shoved him toward the campfire. He gritted his teeth as pain burned from his elbow to his shoulder, but it was nothing compared to the ache lancing his heart. A lump swelled in his throat, choking off his breathing. The soldier shoved him to the ground near the campfire, but he barely felt the contact. His brother was dead.

Another young private who looked no older than Arlan added several branches to the fire then tossed on a handful of dry prairie grass. It flickered and flamed to life, popping and snapping.

A man sat down beside Silas, cut away his shirt, and doctored his wound. "Good thing the bullet went clear through. Should heal quickly, as long as infection don't set in."

Ignoring the man, Silas ground his teeth together, trying to understand how his life could change so quickly. Why had he been so stupid and let down his guard?

"You two, dig a grave for that man." The captain pointed to two soldiers then at Arlan.

Silas shivered at the thought of his brother buried in a cold, dark hole. Arlan would hate being cooped up in so small a place forever.

Trying to ignore the pain in his shoulder, he looked around the camp. The fire illuminated a flickering circle of light, but shadows of night threatened to sneak in and steal its brightness. Thanks to the lateness of the hour when the soldiers had arrived, they hadn't noticed the dugout yet. Maybe it would remain safely hidden in the brush.

Silas had never wanted anything so badly in his whole life as this little piece of earth. He'd planned to give Arlan the home he'd never had—and now never would.

He covered his ears to block out the *swish-thunk* of the shovels of dirt where the soldiers were digging Arlan's grave. His brother would always remain on this piece of land, and some way, somehow, Silas would come back to reclaim what was his.

Chapter 4

Lara leaned on the hoe, staring at the damage Bad Billy had done to the garden, and her vision blurred. It had taken both her and Joline a good fifteen minutes to wrestle the determined goat out of the garden and back into his pen. Tiny baby carrots lay exposed to the sun, and tender lettuce and chard leaves shredded by Bad Billy's hooves lay sprinkled all over the front third of the garden, looking as if a cyclone had struck.

Swatting at a tear with the back of her hand, Lara knelt down and carefully patted the carrots back into the ground, hoping they would continue to grow in spite of their early uprooting. She inhaled a deep breath and lifted her chin, taking a moment to compose herself. She would not cry. Not here. Not now. If she got started, she might never stop. Someone had to be the cornerstone of the family, and that someone was her, whether she wanted the job or not.

Moving down the row of carrots, she continued pressing them into the ground and setting aside the ones that had been damaged. Why did this have to happen? Couldn't God have kept that ornery goat out of the garden? They had precious little food to eat without this destruction.

"How bad is it?" Jo's long shadow darkened the row Lara worked on.

"Could be worse. Lost some carrots, but I hope most will survive. The lettuce is another matter." Lara glanced over her shoulder. "Maybe you and Michael could start picking up the bigger leaves. Some may be salvageable."

"Bad Billy's a bad boy." Michael leaned against Lara's back, and she turned to envelop him in a one-arm hug, needing the comfort of his little arms around her neck.

After a moment, Jo tugged him away. "Come on, Shorty, let's gather the lettuce."

Michael planted a warm, sloppy kiss on Lara's cheek, and then he knelt in the dirt to bury a carrot. Her heart warmed by her son's affection, Lara pressed in the last carrot, fetched the bucket, and headed down to the creek.

She stood by the water's edge, listening to the quiet ripples bubbling over the rocks. This place was so peaceful, so free of problems. It soothed her troubled spirit. Glancing up, she peered at the bright blue sky. Not a single cloud marred the view. She knew God could see her—knew that He was aware of their situation and struggles, but why didn't He help them?

She scooped up a bucketful of water and returned to the garden. As she poured a ladle of water on each carrot, she tried to shake off her melancholy. Most likely, some of it was due to Tom's death. It must have affected her more than she realized. Plus, not having a body to bury made it hard to comprehend he was actually dead and never coming back.

The thought both relieved and troubled her. In the dark of night, she had cried a few tears over the man she'd once loved, but it was time to look to the future. Grandpa wanted her to find out more information about the land rush. Now was as good a time as any.

An hour later, after she'd cleaned up and put Michael down for a nap, Lara headed to Caldwell. Even before she entered the town, she was shocked by the swells of people everywhere. Tents lined the road and onto the prairie as far as she could see. Only three days had passed since she'd last been in town to return Mrs. Henry's mending, and yet Caldwell's population had grown surprisingly in that time.

As she walked past the Leland Hotel doorway, a man stepped outside and nearly collided with her.

"Pardon me, ma'am."

She quickly sidestepped then looked up, surprised to see the same man whose horse she'd rescued at the depot.

He stared at her for a moment, then recognition sparked in his dark eyes. Tipping his hat, he smiled, sending trickles of unexpected awareness shooting through her.

All right, she would admit the man was handsome, but he was clearly a dandy. His stylish three-piece suit probably cost more than she could make mending clothes for a year, not to mention the shiny gold watch peeking out from his vest pocket. His skin was light, like a man who stayed inside a lot, and he could stand to lose a few pounds. Probably a banker who'd never worked hard physical labor a day in his life.

"Ma'am, I didn't get to thank you for calming my horse the day I arrived in town. He's fast, and if he'd gotten away, I'd have been sore pressed to capture him on foot." He smiled with teeth so white Lara couldn't help staring. "Do allow me to escort you to dinner to express my appreciation."

Her heart jolted. No man had ever asked her to dinner. She stared down at her faded dress and tucked her bare feet under her skirt. As much as she'd like to eat a meal cooked in a restaurant—a meal of meat other than squirrel, turtle, or rabbit—she couldn't accept. Why, she didn't even know the man's name.

"Just exactly who are you?" She tried to ignore how clean he smelled and how his engaging eyes seemed riveted to hers.

"Ah, so sorry. I'm Gabriel Coulter from Kansas City, but my friends call me Gabe." He tipped his hat again and bowed. "A pleasure to make your acquaintance Miss. . . ?" His dark brows rose as he straightened.

Friend indeed. Lara scowled, knowing she had no business standing on the boardwalk talking to this stranger, even if he was quite mannerly and smelled better than anything she could think of. "It's *Mrs.* Talbot, sir. And thank you for your generous offer of dinner, but I'm afraid I must decline." With a swish of her skirt, she swirled past him, trying to ignore her quickly pounding heart. Oh, he was charming all right, but she wasn't about to succumb to his wiles.

Putting thoughts of the handsome man behind her, she scoured the town for a poster or something that would tell her about the land run. Finally, she resorted to eavesdropping. Lingering outside the door of the mercantile, she fanned herself and hoped she looked as if she were waiting on somebody. A trio of old men sat in front of the barbershop next door discussing the land run.

"All y'all have to do is register," an elderly gent with bushy gray eyebrows said.

"You don't got to pay no fee?" A skinny bald man tipped his chair back against the wall. "You mean to say it's free?"

The man with bushy eyebrows nodded. "That's what I heared. Over two million acres of free land, just for the taking. All you have to do is be the first to stake a claim on the twenty-second of April."

Lara's heart pounded. Two million acres of land! That much? Surely Grandpa would be recovered by the twenty-second, and if he rode in the race, maybe he could get a claim. But how much land would that be?

"You reckon anyone can ride in the race?" the third man asked as he scratched his bristly chin.

"If'n you kin read, the rules are posted outside the newspaper office."

Lara quickly pushed away from the wall and crossed the street, dodging a slow-moving wagon pulled by an old mule. She stumbled on a rut in the dirt road, grabbed her skirt up, and took a few quick steps to right herself, carefully avoiding the piles of fresh manure.

A crowd had gathered outside the *Caldwell Tribune*, but she worked her way close enough to see the announcement tacked to the wall. Holding one hand to her nose to avoid the ripe aroma of so many people clustered together, she scanned the announcement: HARRISON'S HOSS RACE. APRIL 22, 1889, AT NOON. The purpose of the run was to populate the Unassigned Indian Lands.

"What's it say?" someone behind her asked.

"Free land! One-hundred-and-sixty-acre plots will go to the first person to stake a claim," Hurbert Galloway said.

Lara tightened her fist around the edge of her apron as excitement took wing. A whole quarter section of land free for the taking!

"Who can ride?" a voice in the back called out.

"Says here anyone over twenty-one," Mr. Galloway hollered over his shoulder.

A big Negro man to Lara's left leaned in closer as if he were reading the bulletin. "Dat mean colored folks, too?"

Mr. Galloway scanned the announcement then nodded his head. "Sure does. White men. Black men. Even women. As long as they're twenty-one."

The Negro man's yellowed teeth gleamed against his dark skin. "Well, glory be." He turned and hurried down the road.

Lara pushed her way to the outer edge of the crowd where the air was fresher, and stood there listening to everyone's comments. Hope and excitement were more abundant in Caldwell than dust—and the feeling was contagious. A spark of hope flickered in her chest for the first time in a long while. Maybe Grandpa and Jo were right. Maybe the land run was the answer to their prayers.

⁓

Gabe stood off to the side, watching Lara Talbot. Homer had been right in saying she was quite a beauty. The first time he encountered those pale green eyes at the train depot, he was stunned speechless. Now he realized they reminded him of some light green crystals that a man had tried to gamble away one night. At least today he'd been able to gather his composure when he nearly collided with her at the hotel.

She'd seemed taken off guard by his sudden dinner invitation. He was unaccustomed to women turning him down. There was a sadness in her eyes, probably from so recently losing her husband. He watched her as she stood on the edge of the crowd, as if waiting for someone. She intrigued him, but he couldn't say why. Maybe it was the way her rebellious curls framed her face. Or her tattered dignity. He regretted her refusal to dine with him and would have enjoyed spending time getting to know the lovely *Mrs.* Talbot.

She didn't know he was the one responsible for making her a widow. What would she say if she knew the truth? Or if he walked up and handed her the money he'd won from her husband?

He ought to do just that, but he'd learned in town that she was a proud woman—a hard worker who wouldn't accept charity. No, giving her the money wasn't the answer. But somehow, he'd find a way to help Mrs. Talbot and her son—and atone for Tom Talbot's death. He had to, for his own peace of mind.

Gabe watched her tuck several wayward strands of golden-brown hair behind her ear as she stared at the bulletin posted on the newspaper facade. Deciding to risk talking to her again, he crossed the dusty street. He couldn't explain it, but as if a rope were tied from his waist to hers, he felt pulled to her. For some reason, he wanted to protect her. Both times he'd been close to her, an awareness unlike anything he'd ever experienced before had surged through him. Maybe it was because she needed him.

He squeezed his way through the growing crowd and sidled up beside her. "So, are you thinking about riding in the big race?"

"What?" She turned her confused gaze upon him, but when she recognized him, her full lips tilted down in a frown.

Wounded pride needled him for a moment, but he shoved it away and pointed to the sign. "Are you going to ride in the land run?"

She pressed her lips together, and her brows dipped down. "I haven't decided yet."

"Sounds like a great opportunity. I might even take a gamble and ride myself."

A sad smile tugged at her intriguing mouth. "You'll most likely do well ridin' that fine horse of yours."

"Yes, Tempest sure does like to run." He lifted his hat, smoothed his hair, then set his derby back on his head. "You ought to go ahead and register if you're serious about it."

She shrugged her too-thin shoulders. "It's not that simple."

"Tell me about it."

"If'n you two's gonna yammer all day, could you do it somewhere else?" A thin man scowled at them then stood on his tiptoes, trying to see around Gabe to read the announcement.

A blush tinged her cheeks. "Sorry, sir." Mrs. Talbot sidled past the man and hurried away.

Gabe pushed through the large crowd, not quite ready to let her go yet. He caught up and settled into step with her. "So, why isn't it simple?"

She glanced sideways, looking both cautious and curious. "Why do you want to know?"

"Why not?" He flashed her the smile that made other women swoon.

She scowled. "I don't know you, so why would you be interested in my business?"

"What's not to know? I'm charming, handsome, interesting. . ."

"You sound like a snake oil salesman hawking his wares."

Gabe slowed his steps, slightly insulted by her comment. He'd never known a woman immune to his charms—and it intrigued him even more.

"I still think you ought to register if you're serious about riding. It doesn't cost anything. And besides"—he waved his hand in the air—"people are surging into town. The line will only get longer if you wait until closer to the race."

She seemed to be considering his comment and stepped back to allow an elderly couple to pass between them. "I'll think about it."

A sudden thought pummeled Gabe. Was she even old enough to ride? Now that he considered it, she barely looked eighteen, much less the twenty-one-year minimum required to race.

"We don't have a horse." She bit her lip as if she'd just confessed a deep family secret. "Just an old mule that only has one speed—sluggish." Then as if she'd revealed too much, she waved her hand in the air. "I really should go. Good day, Mr. Coulter."

Gabe watched her scurry away in her faded dress. He had the ability to make her life so much easier, but if he offered her the money, then he'd have to explain his part in her husband's death. He couldn't stand the thought of seeing censure in her lovely eyes. Still, there had to be something he could do to help. His mind swirled with ideas, until suddenly—Gabe snapped his fingers in the air.

Yes sirree, he'd act on the idea that just popped into his mind—and just maybe he'd find some peace in helping the Widow Talbot and her son.

Maybe then he'd sleep at night.

Chapter 5

Feeling only slightly guilty for having sneaked off again, Jo hid behind Caldwell's livery until Lara disappeared from view on the trail toward home. Lara was always giving her chores to do or telling her to keep an eye on Michael. Her work-minded sister had forgotten that a young woman needed time to visit her friends and to just have fun.

As Jo stepped out from behind the building and walked toward Main Street, she studied the striking dandy who stood on the corner staring off in the direction her sister had gone. He looked to be deep in thought.

She'd seen him talking to Lara as the two had strolled along the boardwalk. Who was he? And what did he want with a poor, married woman like her sister?

Suddenly, he snapped his fingers and turned. Jo ducked back, lest she be caught staring, but she couldn't help admiring his handsome, citified appearance. His stylish three-piece suit looked as if it had been made to fit him by a trained tailor rather than homemade, like her two faded dresses. She ran her hand down her patched calico, wondering what it would feel like to wear clothes tailor-made just for her. Jo peered around the side of the building, watching the dandy again as he strode with long-legged confidence along the boardwalk and into the telegraph office.

She walked down the street, amazed at how many people had swarmed into Caldwell since the last time she'd been in town. Must be land seekers, all hoping for a chance to get a claim. Excitement swirled in her stomach. She knew Grandpa could get land if only Lara would register him. By the time he recovered enough from his swamp fever bout to come to town, it could be too late.

She slowed her steps and peered at her reflection in the mercantile window, twisting her head sideways as she tried to see her profile out the corner of her eye. Could she pass for twenty-one?

Standing straighter, she wrapped her long braid into a knot at her nape and held it there with one hand as she examined her reflection. She heaved a sigh, knowing she still couldn't pass for the required minimum age. Riding in such a grand race would be so exhilarating.

She moseyed down to the telegraph office and slowed her steps. The dandy stood in the doorway, studying the sheet of paper in his hand with a big smile on his face. He looked even more dashing up close, but he was too old to interest her. Why, he had to be at least in his midtwenties, like Tom. The man rolled up the paper and smacked it against his palm with pleasing satisfaction.

The dandy looked up and noticed her. He smiled then tipped his hat to her and walked across the street. Jo caught a faint whiff of some kind of musky fragrance and closed her eyes. She ought to be insulted that he'd barely glanced at her, well. . .she would have been if she hadn't already deemed him nearly a codger. Someone bumped her shoulder as they passed by and jolted her back to her senses. She moved to the edge of the boardwalk, looped her arm around a post, and watched the fine-smelling dandy disappear into the hotel.

Leaning her head against the post, she studied the activity of Caldwell. Riders on horses and long-eared mules pulling wagons headed down the dirt road—one of the main streets of Caldwell. Fragrant aromas of café food blended with the familiar smells of dust, animals, and leather.

Across the street, a woman in a lovely lavender gown exited the hotel on the arm of an older man in a fancy suit. Jo sighed as she dreamed of what she might look like in that dress, dining on a five-course meal in the hotel. What would it be like to live in a town and wear nice clothes and shoes every day? Or to even stay in a clean room in a boardinghouse with beds that had frames and feather pillows and a café that served hot, belly-tingling meals? Where other folks did the chores and waited on you as if you were a queen or someone grand?

Her stomach gurgled in response, and Jo laid her hand across it. She was sick of eating squirrel meat and other things most people would turn up their noses at.

Security was what she longed for. A nice house to live in with wooden floors, glass in the windows, and a roof that didn't let in rain or critters while she slept.

Was that too much to ask for?

Oh, why had she been born into a poor family?

If only she had some money. What she needed was a job. She pushed away from the post and looked at the various stores and places of business. Caldwell wasn't a huge town, but there was a variety of different shops. Maybe one of them could use some help. She was a good worker, even if Lara didn't think so.

Jo tossed her braid over her shoulder, smoothed the hair around her face, and proceeded down the boardwalk. The buzz of unfamiliar voices filled her ears—voices all talking about the land rush. On the other side of the street a crowd had gathered in front of the newspaper office, and they were staring at something on the wall.

Lifting her skirt a little, she jogged across the street and leaped over a pile of fresh manure.

She squeezed her way to the front of the crowd and read the information about the land run. One hundred and sixty acres. This was the answer to all her problems, she just knew it. Somehow, she had to get Lara to register. Maybe they could get a claim in one of the new towns being plotted out by the land-run officials, find work, and build a clapboard house. Or maybe they could start their own business.

Even though she knew the age requirements, she checked them again to make sure she hadn't misread them, and blew out a frustrated sigh. Horse feathers! She missed being old enough to ride in the race by five years.

Why was she was always too old or too young? Never just the right age—whatever that was.

Making her way out of the crowd, she spied her best friend coming out of the dressmaker's shop. "Alma Lou!"

Her friend glanced around the crowded streets then peered over her shoulder. When she caught sight of Jo, she waved and turned in her direction.

"What brings you to town?" Alma Lou carried a thick package wrapped in paper and tied with twine. "Did your sister finally give you a day off?"

Jo snorted. "Not likely. Lara put Michael down for a nap, and Grandpa was resting, so I snuck into town after Lara headed here."

Alma Lou looped her free arm through Jo's. "I miss seeing you. It seems I hardly ever get to visit with you now that we're no longer attending school. So, you want a Hires Root Beer?"

Jo glanced sideways at Alma Lou. "Are you serious? You know I don't have any money."

Her friend shrugged a shoulder. "Daddy gave me enough money to buy a bottle of root beer and some candy, but I'm getting too old for childish things like candy. C'mon." She tugged Jo back into the dirt street toward the general store.

"Then I'd love one. I've never had root beer before." Though Jo eagerly anticipated her first soft drink, she didn't think she'd ever get too old to enjoy the sweet taste of candy.

Alma Lou had grown up since the last time Jo had seen her about a month ago. Her trademark braids were now rolled into a tight bun at her nape, and the dress she wore looked more matronly than Jo would have expected to see on someone her age. Alma Lou even wore the new style of lace-up shoes, but then she always did have the prettiest clothing of anyone in their school.

Over the years Jo had fought hard not to be jealous of Alma Lou and her wealthy father, who owned the hotel. Her friend always had nicer clothes and better food to eat at lunchtime, but because of Alma Lou's generous nature, Jo never felt inferior—until now. With her free hand, she tried to hold her skirt out so that it hid her bare feet.

Ten minutes later, they sat in two rockers in front of the mercantile, drinking their soft drinks.

Alma Lou took a ladylike sip, wiped her mouth with a lace handkerchief, and looked at Jo. "I have some thrilling news." Her brown eyes danced with excitement.

Jo took a long swig, savoring the sweet-tasting drink, thinking she'd never had anything so delicious. A man and woman passed in front of them, casting their shadow on Alma Lou and then Jo. Their shoes tapped softly against the dry wood of the boardwalk. The woman leaned over to the man and whispered something in his ear then giggled. Jo sighed. Would she ever have a beau to cuddle with and whisper sweet words of love to?

Oh, there were plenty of silly boys back in school who had eyed her golden hair and wanted to claim her as their own, but there'd never been a man in her life. Her thoughts flew back to the handsome dandy.

Alma Lou shoved her, jostling her soda bottle so that Jo had to tighten her grasp to keep from dropping it. "I'm telling you the most important thing in my life, and you're not even listening."

"Sorry. I was thinking about something." Jo pulled her gaze back to her friend. "So. . .what's the news?"

"Oh, it's so exciting I can hardly stand it." She squeezed her soda bottle with both hands, her face beaming. "Jeremiah Watson has been courting me and has asked me to marry him."

Stunned, Jo blinked her eyes and tried to understand what her friend had said. "Jerry Watson? Jokin' Jerry?"

Alma Lou hiked up her chin. "Don't call him names. He's not like that anymore."

"Well. . ." Jo searched her mind for something to appease Alma. "I haven't seen him much since we finished school, so I suppose he could have matured." The picture of Jokin' Jerry that came to mind was of him dipping her braids in the inkwell and stealing her lunch while she ran screaming mad after him.

"You're invited to the wedding." Alma Lou sniffed. "I wanted to have you stand up with me, but Mother thinks I should ask Jeremiah's sister."

The root beer turned sour in Jo's stomach. All their growing-up years, she and Alma Lou had talked arm in arm about being each other's maid of honor when they got married. They even talked about having a double wedding. But that would never happen now. She could hardly get married without a groom.

Jo stood, searching for something to say. "Congratulations. I'm happy for you."

"You won't be upset if I have Sally Watson stand up with me, will you?"

Biting back her overwhelming disappointment, Jo shook her head. "Lara will be mad if I don't get back home soon. Thank you for the soda pop. It was mighty tasty."

Jo stepped into the store and set the half-empty bottle on the counter then slipped out the back door, lest Alma Lou see her tears. Jo hated crybabies, and it made her mad that she couldn't stop her own tears.

Nothing would be the same between her and Alma Lou again. Why, by this time next year, her friend might even be a mother. The thought of losing her best friend brought fresh tears. Jo swiped at them and plodded down the road.

Why did things always have to change? She didn't mind it so much when she was the one causing the changes, but she didn't like it one bit when that change was beyond her control.

⌒

When she returned home, Lara searched the valley and along the creek for Jo but didn't see her sister. Maybe she was off hunting something for dinner or fishing. A mess of trout fried in cornmeal would taste delicious.

She slipped inside the soddy and allowed her eyes to adjust to the dimness. She could hear Michael's soft breathing as she spied him curled up on his quilt in the corner.

"What d'you find out in town?" Grandpa whispered as he turned on his side to face her.

Lara felt his forehead, relieved that it was cooler than last time she'd checked. "It's pretty much what you said. A quarter section of land—if you get a claim. Plus, there will be town lots available. There sure are a lot of people in Caldwell, though. I would guess the population has doubled—several times over. Do you think there will be enough land for everyone who wants it?"

"Prob'ly not. Elsewise there'd be no need for a race."

"I suppose you're right. I have to admit there's land rush fever in town—and it's contagious. If only we *could* get a claim. . ."

"We need to pray." Grandpa glanced up at the sod roof, where roots of prairie grass hung down like cheap chandeliers.

"We'd need a horse. Our poor old mule wouldn't stand a chance winning that race. Why, Grandpa, there's folks in town with racehorses and even those two-wheeled bicycle contraptions."

He chuckled and shook his head. "I cain't see how one of those fancy conveyances would have a chance against a fast horse."

"I can't even imagine how someone could stay on one of those things on a smooth trail, much less through tall prairie grass and over rocky ground."

"So. . .did you register?"

Lara shook her head. How could she explain that if they won a claim they'd have to pay fourteen dollars to file it? Even after she did all the mending and collected her wages it wouldn't be enough.

"What's goin' on in that pretty head of yours?"

With a sigh, she explained her thoughts.

"Well. . .we don't need that money now, so God hasn't provided it." Grandpa patted her hand, so sure that the Lord would supply. "He gives us what we require when we need it. Right now, we should pray for a horse."

Lara nodded, thinking her grandpa needed quinine and they needed food supplies, but those things hadn't been provided. She wasn't sure if her faith was strong enough to believe God would give them a horse. Oh, she had no doubt He could do it if He wanted to, but it was the *wanting to* part she wasn't sure of. She'd once been a young bride filled with hopes and dreams, but then her dreams died one by one, until her life became a lonely struggle to stay alive and put food on the table.

"Don't look so long in the face, punkin. Things will work out."

She managed to give him a wobbly smile, not wanting him to worry about her. She hated that she didn't trust God more. In her heart, she knew that He could do anything, but it was her practical mind that was doing the arguing. It grew harder and harder to believe, when she had watched her family go hungry and live with so little for months on end.

After covering up both Michael and Grandpa, she sat there trying to decide what to fix for supper. All of her staples were getting low, and she needed to finish up the mending in order to replenish them.

Guilt washed over her knowing how disappointed her mother would be with her lack of faith. Oh, if only her parents hadn't died, surely things would be different. Life had changed so much after the fire that killed her folks and burned their home to the ground. The move from their Topeka farm to their grandparents' ranch in southern Kansas had been a blessing to Lara after all that had happened, and she was terribly relieved her siblings were able to stay together. But Jo had cried for her mama for ages, and Jack was angry. Grandpa tried to comfort and guide him, but Jack saw it as Grandpa wanting to control him.

Crying over what-ifs didn't change things. She mustered up a weak prayer for God to send them a horse and a stronger plea for Grandpa to have a quick recovery. He was down to his last two quinine pills. She wrung her hands together. *Please, God, help me find a way to make some money so I can purchase Grandpa's medicine.*

A horse nickered, and a shadow filled the open doorway. People rarely meandered out to their little acre of land, and curiosity pulled her to the door like a magnet.

Their landlord, Herman Hancock, dismounted his horse and turned to face her. He pulled his hat from his head and held it tightly in front of him. "Good day, Mrs. Talbot."

"Same to you, Mr. Hancock." Lara motioned him away from the soddy and toward the creek, dreading the conversation to come. She still didn't have the money to pay their rent. "Could I offer you a drink of water?"

He squirmed and looked toward the creek then followed her. "No thanks." He glanced at the soddy. "Is Daniel here? I need to talk to him."

"He's here, but he's having one of his episodes."

Mr. Hancock pursed his lips. "Right sorry to hear that, ma'am." He glanced up at the sky for a moment then looked at her. "I—uh—have some news that I'm sure you won't be too happy to hear."

Her heart dropped. Not more bad news.

He shuffled his feet in the dirt then glanced at her. "Guess you may have heard my son Gavin got married last month while he was up in Nebraska visiting my oldest son. Right fine weddin' they had, too." He smiled, his eyes holding a faraway stare.

"Gavin had thought to stay up there and learn blacksmithing, but he's changed his mind. His wife don't like the cold weather and has a hankerin' to come down here to live. I'm sorry to drop this on you all so sudden like, but I just got a telegram saying they'll be back on the fourteenth, and I'll need this place for them."

"Why that's only a few days away!" Lara felt the skin on her face tighten as the blood drained from it. Her mind swirled. What in the world would they do? She wanted to rant and rave. Scream and cry "unfair!" but the concerned expression in Mr. Hancock's kind eyes held her silent.

"I'm real sorry, ma'am. I was hoping you folks might have plans to ride in that big horse race for free land. I do hate putting you out so suddenly."

Lara straightened her back and held up her head. "It's all right, Mr. Hancock. The good Lord will provide." The words tasted bitter on her tongue, and guilt instantly assaulted her at the doubts coursing through her.

"Thank you for being so understanding, ma'am." He set his hat back on his head. "I know you've had hard times with Daniel being ill, and you probably don't have the rent money you still owe for last month or this month so far."

Lara's poor heart was getting a workout, and she slipped her hand over her chest. If he required payment, there'd be no money for food—or medicine.

His gaze traveled from the goats to her garden. "What say we swap a goat and the future pickings from your garden in exchange for the rent you owe, and call it even?"

Her throat tightened and eyes stung. His offer was kind and generous, but how could she part with one of her beloved goats? She was very tempted to leave behind Bad Billy, but they needed his services so that the nannies would continue to have kids and give the milk that Michael needed. But maybe she could part with one. She really had no choice.

"All right, sir, it's a deal." She held out her hand, and he shook it.

She swallowed the lump in her throat. "We'll be out by the end of the week. Would you like to go ahead and take the goat rather than me leaving her here unprotected?"

He eyed the fence holding the smelly animals and nodded.

"Which one do you want?" *Please don't pick Mildred.* Lara's grandmother had given her Mildred when the goat was a kid, just a month before Grandma died. Lara couldn't bear to part with her.

"I reckon any of them will do as long as it's healthy. Gavin's married a widow with a couple of little girls, and they'll need the milk." Mr. Hancock uncurled a rope that had been tied to his saddle and handed it to her.

With heavy feet, she shuffled over to the goat fence and enticed Lolly out with a handful of grass. She patted her brown and white hide then slipped the rope over the goat's head. As Mr. Hancock rode off, Lolly's frantic tugging at the rope and confused bleats brought tears to Lara's eyes.

The other goats joined in, making a ruckus that was sure to awaken Michael. "Hush, you all."

Lara looked heavenward, tears filling her eyes. They were just starting to gather a few peas and some other things from the garden, and she'd even decided the carrots were going to pull through, but now they'd have to leave it all for others to enjoy. With all the people crowding into the area, how was she supposed to find a place for them to live? If they moved to another city, she'd lose her mending customers. How would they survive?

"Why this now, Lord?" Lara tightened her fist. "Have You forgotten about us? Grandpa has such faith in You. Please don't let him down. When will You answer our prayers?"

Chapter 6

As Gabe looked around the crowded train depot, a sense of pride filled him—and pride was something he hadn't felt in a long time. The horses he'd ordered Homer to buy from Mr. Swanson and have shipped on the train from Kansas City had sold in minutes. Only one was left.

"Forty-five dollars." A red-faced man Gabe recognized as John Hawkins waved his beefy hand.

"Fifty."

"Sixty!" Arthur Drexel shouted.

Gabe stood back, leaning against the depot wall, amazed at how much these people were willing to pay for an average horse with no saddle or bridle. With only two weeks to go to the land rush, desperation was growing faster than stacks of coins at a poker table.

"Sold! To the man in the gray hat." The skinny auctioneer Gabe had hired pounded his gavel on a fence post. "Gentlemen, you all who won bids can pay Mr. Coulter and then collect your horses. We're much obliged that you came out today."

One by one, the men paid Gabe then gathered their horses. He counted the money, gave the auctioneer his pay, and stuffed the rest into his pocket. He stood straighter, enjoying the guilt-free sensation of having completed a legitimate business deal.

"You plannin' on having any more horses for sale before the run?" a tall man with a pencil-thin mustache asked.

Gabe rubbed his thumb and index finger on his chin and glanced at Homer, who nodded, indicating Mr. Swanson had more horses he was willing to part with. Gabe focused on the tall man again. "Same time next week."

The man smiled and nearly shook Gabe's arm off. "Great! Wonderful! Save one for me, will you?"

"I'd like to do that, but they'll be auctioned off just like the ones today were."

The man's brows dipped. "All right then, I'll just have to get my hands on some more money by then."

As he ambled away, Homer waddled toward Gabe. "Swanson said he had five more mares he could sell and two geldings. His wife has been naggin' him for a bigger house, so he was more willin' to part with them than usual."

"Perfect timing for us." Gabe reached into his pocket, pulled out several bills, and handed them to Homer. "This is for you. Good job." He counted out another hundred dollars. "Give this to Mr. Swanson, and tell him I'll give him the balance of what I owe as soon as I sell the other mounts next week."

Homer nodded and shoved the bills in the pocket on the bib of his overalls. "You gonna play poker tonight?"

"Nah, don't think so."

Homer gave him an odd look. "I am, though I've gotta call it an early night. Gotta ticket for a noon train back to Kansas City tomorrow."

"Good. Timing is critical, so be sure you make that train—and see that you don't gamble with any of my money." Gabe stared at Homer until he nodded. So far Homer had proven trustworthy, but one hundred dollars would tempt many men. "You know anyone else up there with horses for sale?"

Homer grinned, and his three chins melded into one. "Maybe. I could check with the liveries and ask Travis Martin and Jake Farley."

Gabe nodded. "Do that, and find me a fast saddle horse that's gentle."

Homer cast a sideways glance at him. "How come you need another horse?"

"That's my business." Gabe pinned Homer with a stern stare.

Homer nodded and lumbered out of the depot.

Patting his pocket, Gabe headed toward his hotel room. He tipped his hat to a pair of women he passed on the boardwalk, and then his feet slowed as a man shoved open the doors to the Lucky Chance saloon and nearly collided with him. As the stranger scowled and sidled around Gabe without even an apology, the familiar scents of smoke and booze left in his wake taunted Gabe's senses. He never was a drinker, but that old pull to find a game of chance and double his money lured him just inside the saloon. He surveyed the smoke-filled building, listening to the masculine chatter and laughter. Since coming to Caldwell he hadn't once played cards or gambled. There was something wholesome and exciting about earning money in a legitimate, honest manner—and he liked it.

Yes sir, he enjoyed that good feeling warming his chest. He released the swinging door and continued down the boardwalk, ignoring the lure of the tinny-sounding piano and familiar scents.

The aromas emanating from Myrtle's Café, however, were too much to resist. Gabe entered the small restaurant, his stomach rumbling, and found a table looking out over the street. Every day, more and more people surged into town, hoping to participate in the land rush. As he'd been exercising Tempest, he'd discovered that just outside of Caldwell, for nearly as far as one could see, were tents, wagons, and families filled with hope and glimmering eyes.

All except for Lara Talbot. He watched her cross the street, coming almost straight toward him. Her head hung down, and when she glanced up, her eyes looked sad—desperate—like a man who'd gambled away his whole paycheck and had to go home and tell his wife.

Gabe wanted to call her in and have her eat until she filled out her skin. She was far too thin and seemed to be carrying a burden too heavy for her slight shoulders.

She'd made it clear, though, that she didn't welcome his advances. He watched her until she disappeared down the boardwalk. Why did she tug at his heartstrings so much?

A girl who looked to be fourteen or fifteen set a plate heaping with beef stew and corn bread in front of him. She batted her long lashes, and a coy smile tugged at the corners of her mouth. Gabe knew that look. He nodded his thanks and turned his gaze away. Not interested.

The only woman to snag his attention lately was a grieving widow who couldn't care less about him.

As he scooped up a spoonful of steaming stew, he thought about the promise he'd made to his mother on her deathbed. At the time, he'd agreed to find a God-fearing woman to marry, simply to calm his mother. He'd never been a man to give his word lightly, but he couldn't help wondering how a professional gambler was supposed to find a Christian woman willing to marry him. Most churchgoing folks he recognized in KC shunned anybody who made a living in a saloon.

He buttered a thick square of corn bread and took a bite. His thoughts continued to travel back to Lara Talbot.

Why did he think of her when he thought of his promise? Gabe shook his head. What a crazy idea!

～

The tantalizing aromas of cooking food made Lara's mouth water as she trudged down the steps of Pearl's Boardinghouse to the street. She hadn't placed much hope in getting rooms but figured it was worth a visit to check, in case Pearl might swap two rooms in exchange for her and Jo cooking and cleaning. But the boardinghouse was so full that extra people were sleeping on pallets in some rooms.

Lara was at her wit's end. Nobody had rooms for rent, no houses were available, and no one had land to lease, either. Their only option was to leave town and try to find something somewhere else. Grandpa should be resting, not worrying about packing up their meager belongs, and Jo would be devastated because all of her friends lived here. Lara had lost touch with her old school buddies because she was always working and didn't have time to attend quilting bees and other social functions. Nobody in Caldwell would miss her, except her mending clients, and even they would find someone to replace her easily enough.

She entered the mercantile and gave her eyes a moment to adjust to the dimmer lighting inside the building. The familiar scents of leather, coffee, spices, and the nearby pickle barrel gave the place a homey feel. Passing the counter, she went to the corner where the potbellied stove sat. On cold days, some of the older men in town gathered here to play checkers and gab, but on warm days they tended to congregate outside where the ever-present breeze could cool them. A section of the southern wall of the store was covered in cork, but the cork was concealed by a passel of notices and advertisements.

She quickly scanned the mostly hand-printed and few typeset ads, hoping to find one that offered them the possibility of a place to stay. Nothing. Her hope sagged, like the soddy roof after a heavy rain, but she must keep trying. She wanted to believe, wanted to hope, but with so many bad things coming, one after another, she found it difficult. Grandpa's stalwart faith and her family were the only things keeping her going these days.

"Thanks for bringing in that bucket of milk earlier. I already sold it." Mary McMann, the store clerk, smiled. "You want cash for it, or do you plan to make purchases today?"

Lara returned the cheery woman's smile. "I'll use the credit now. I need a small bag of cornmeal, a half pound of coffee, and two pounds of flour." As Mrs. McMann measured out the items, Lara counted the coins she'd made doing mending. She eyed the jars of penny candy on the shelves behind the counter, wishing she could purchase some for Michael and Jo.

"Just let me wash out your bucket, and you'll be all set." Mary hurried into the back room, and Lara heard the door slam that led outside.

A few minutes later, she gathered the packages, put them in the bucket, and exited the store. For a fleeting moment, she wished she'd brought the wagon. Carrying a bucket of supplies wasn't as awkward as a pail of milk, but it was heavier, and she had to carry them over a mile. At least Jo had helped her lug the milk to town. With them both holding the end of an old broom handle, the bucket had swung gently between them. But Jo and the broom handle were no longer in sight. Her sister needed time with her friends on occasion, and Lara supposed Jo had gone visiting. Unlike Lara, Jo needed to be with other people to feel complete and content.

Lara smiled at the old men sitting in front of the store, not surprised to hear them still jawing on about the land run, then she glanced at the long line at the land office, wondering if all those people were registering. She passed by the chatty crowd and continued down Main Street. It was time to tell Grandpa the news about having to move. She couldn't do it yesterday, but today he was better, thanks to the quinine tablets. When she left for town he'd said that he and Michael were going fishing in hopes of catching something for their lunch.

As she neared the end of town, the sound of music from the church's pump organ drew her. She stopped beside an old oak tree and leaned against it, her eyes closed. The music ministered to her aching spirit as the words ran through her mind. *My hope is built on nothing less than Jesus' blood and righteousness.*

A sharp pang of guilt stabbed her as if her chest had been pierced by an Indian's arrow. When had she shifted to relying on herself and on Grandpa's faith instead of trusting in the Lord?

The song's refrain wove itself through her mind like the cool spring breeze fingering its way through her hair. *On Christ the solid Rock I stand, all other ground is sinking sand.*

No wonder things had been so bad lately. She'd been trying to claw her way through the sinking sand, with each new problem pulling her down, deeper and deeper. Grandpa was right, but she'd been too stubborn, too set on making everything work out, that she'd stopped clinging to God. Her foundation had shifted from the solid Rock to quicksand.

Lara lifted her gaze heavenward, her eyes stinging with unshed tears. She cleared her throat. "Forgive me, Father. It's my nature to try to solve everyone's problems, but I can't do it all on my own. I'm so tired, Lord. I need Your help. We desperately need a place to live."

She closed her eyes again and listened to the music, mixed with the chirps of birds singing and chattering in the branches above her and the distant murmur of countless people. For the first time in a long while she felt peaceful. She didn't have to carry her burden alone.

As the music transitioned into another song, Lara thought of all the work waiting for her at home. Behind her, she heard the thud of feet running on the hard ground.

"Come back here, boy!" a masculine voice shouted. "Stop!"

Her curiosity got the best of her, and she pushed away from the rough tree trunk and turned to her right, holding the heavy bucket in front of her with both hands.

"Look out!"

A lithe body slammed into the bucket, sending it flying out of Lara's hands. Shoved hard, she fell backward, grappling at the trunk as she tried to keep from falling. Her fingernails clawed the uneven bark, but she couldn't gain hold and fell to the ground. Pain radiated from her fingertips to her hip, which had landed hard on a gnarly root. The boy who'd knocked her down raced away without even a glance over his shoulder.

Footsteps hurried toward her, and then a shadow darkened the ground, just before Gabe Coulter stepped into view and knelt beside her. "Are you all right?"

Lara sucked in several deep breaths, trying to push the sharp burning sensation away. Lifting her hand, she stared at her bleeding fingertips. One nail was ripped almost in half, and she dreaded having to pull it off the rest of the way. Numb, she stared at the man who always seemed to appear at her side whenever she came to town.

"Mrs. Talbot, are you hurt? Do you need a doctor?"

"No, please. No doctor." She couldn't afford the doctor, even if she may need his services. She had no way to pay for them.

"Here, let me help you up, if you're ready to rise."

He reached his hand toward hers, and Lara grimaced. She didn't want to stick her dirty, callused palm in his neatly manicured hand, but with one hand injured, she had no other choice. She raised her arm, but he slipped around behind her, placed his hands on her waist, and gently lifted her. Lara held her breath against the pain swirling through her as she stood. She tested her limbs, relieved that other than her hand, she would probably only be bruised, thanks to the bulkiness of her skirt and petticoats, which had padded her fall. Mr. Coulter took her wounded hand by the wrist, and his mouth quirked.

"You need a doctor."

"I need to get home." Lara carefully extracted her hand from his, trying not to wince. She glanced on the ground for her bucket. "No—" Closing her mouth, she held back her angst at seeing her packages broken open and spilling onto the ground. Tears burned her eyes, but she blinked them away. She wouldn't cry in front of this man.

"This is all my fault." He grabbed the bucket and sifted through her food supplies. With a semi-victorious smile, he held up the still-intact package of coffee. "Be happy for small victories."

Lara nodded. She could have done without the coffee but not the flour and cornmeal. What would she feed her family all week? She held her injured fingers in front of her, cradling them in her other hand. At least the bucket wouldn't be so heavy now.

Mr. Coulter sorted through the flour and cornmeal then shook his head, his lips pursed. "Sorry, but these are ruined. I'll replace them for you after the doctor tends your hand."

She shook her head. "That isn't necessary."

He lifted his palm as if to halt her objections. "I insist. It's partially my fault that you were injured." He looped the bucket over one arm then gently took hold of her elbow and steered her away from the church. "I was paying the clerk at the store for a purchase. The boy who knocked you down had been standing by the counter, looking as if he wanted to buy something. But the second I laid my money down, the kid grabbed it and tore out of the store at a dead run. So, you see this *is* my fault. If I hadn't chased him, he wouldn't have run into you and knocked you down."

Lara allowed him to guide her back into town simply because she didn't have the strength to resist him. She glanced down at her dirty, faded skirt then over at his clean, stylish suit. Suddenly he stopped and met her gaze. A boyish gleam twinkled in his eyes and a smile tugged at his mouth, making Lara's insides tingle. In spite of his citified dress and fair complexion, he wasn't a bad-looking man.

"I just realized that I don't know where the doctor's office is."

The irony of the situation tickled her, and she smiled in spite of her aches. Here she was, allowing him to lead her, and he had no idea where he was going.

The blind leading the blind.

She swallowed at the unwarranted thought and waggled one finger westward. "It's the second door past the sheriff's office. But really, it's not necessary."

He gave her a mock glare then propelled her forward. "Guess that's handy at times."

Confused, she glanced up as he guided her down the street. "What do you mean?"

He flashed her a wicked grin. "Oh, you know, having the doctor's office so close to the jail. I imagine the sheriff has need of the doctor on occasion."

She supposed so, though Caldwell was normally a sleepy little town except when the cowboys from the area ranches came into town after riding herd on cattle for a month.

A short while later, they exited the doctor's office. Lara's hand still stung from his removing the torn nail and putting some smelly, burning medicine on her fingers. How would she get any work done with her hand bandaged?

She must be getting used to Mr. Coulter's assistance because she looked up to discover herself being escorted into the mercantile. She didn't like the man's bossiness but couldn't help enjoying the feel of someone caring for her for a change.

"We need ten pounds of flour, five pounds of cornmeal, and three pounds of sugar."

"What? No, that's too much." Her gaze darted to his. "I didn't have any sugar."

"I insist." He held up his palm to halt her objections. "I realize it's more than you originally purchased, but I hope the difference will make up for the pain and trouble I've caused."

Mrs. McMann glanced curiously at them but turned aside and starting filling bags, obviously happy for the sale.

Embarrassed to be caught in Mr. Coulter's intense gaze, Lara slid hers to the window and studied a frenzied fly struggling futilely to get outside. Mr. Gabe Coulter was just as insistent as that fly. "It wasn't your fault that boy ran into me."

He pressed his lips together and looked patronizingly at her, his dark brown eyes serious. "As I said earlier, he wouldn't have done so if I hadn't been chasing him."

Lara had no argument for that. She peeked around the store, thankful that no one else would witness her humiliation at having someone buy supplies for her. The townsfolk still considered her a married woman, and having this man so new to town doing things for her was sure to raise questions. She needed to get away from him as soon as she could, even though she was more than grateful to him for helping her and replacing the supplies.

"So did you catch that little thief?" Mrs. McMann thunked the heavy bags onto the counter, sending up a puff of flour.

"No. The rascal got away."

"It's a crying shame." Mrs. McMann shook her head as she wiped her hands on her apron. "We never had this problem until all them Boomers swarmed into town, bent on getting free land. Probably less than half of them will get a claim. I hate to think what will happen to all of the others. Anything else you folks need?"

He looked around, stroking his chin with his thumb and forefinger. "Give me two pounds of coffee and a dime's worth of those peppermint sticks."

Lara wondered what he needed with coffee and a whole ten-cent bag of candy. Surely if he was only in town on business he'd be staying at one of the hotels in town and wouldn't need a stock of food.

"What happened to your hand?" Mary McMann laid the package of coffee next to the other bags. "You only just left here a short while ago."

"I had a run-in with a tree."

Mrs. McMann quirked one eyebrow then selected ten peppermint sticks and dropped them into a small bag. Thankfully, she didn't question Lara further, though she cut a quick, curious glance at Mr. Coulter. Peeking up at him, Lara caught him staring at her, a twinkle dancing in his eyes. He lifted both brows, as if to say, "A tree?" She shifted her gaze away from his intriguing eyes and studied the worn gray planks of the mercantile floor.

"How are you going to carry all this home?" Mrs. McMann set the small bag next to the others.

Lara shrugged. Even with both hands healthy, she wouldn't have been able to carry so much all the way home.

"I'll see that she gets there." Gabe reached into his pocket and pulled out a stack of folded dollars.

Heat rising to her face, Lara peeked up at the store clerk. "Mr. Coulter arrived right after that boy knocked me down and has been very kind to help me."

Mrs. McMann bent to tally their purchase. "It's none of my business if he wants to be a Good Samaritan."

Shifting from foot to foot, Lara ached for escape. Mrs. McMann was generally kind, but the woman made it her business to know everyone else's business. She could only hope that the clerk didn't tell others about Mr. Coulter assisting her. It was highly improper for an unmarried man to aid a married woman—even if she wasn't officially still married.

Not nearly soon enough for Lara's taste, Gabe touched the small of her back and guided her out of the store, under the probing stare of Mary McMann. Lara couldn't begin to imagine what the woman thought, and prayed she wouldn't begin any idle gossip.

Mr. Coulter carried the bucket overflowing with all their purchases in one arm, as well as the sack of flour under his other. He barely touched her elbow. People she knew nodded their heads or cast inquisitive glances her way. Oh, why hadn't she stayed home today?

He stopped in front of the livery and set the bucket down. "If you'll wait right here, I'll get a buggy and drive you home."

Lara straightened and hiked her chin, hoping to maintain a minuscule shred of dignity. The pain from her fall must have dulled her senses for a short while. How else could she explain allowing a stranger to take such control over her life? "That isn't necessary, Mr. Coulter. You've done more than enough already."

His wide, ornery smile made her stomach flip-flop. "I insist." He strode past her before she could object further, sending a whiff of fragrant cologne in her direction.

What a rascal!

With her good hand, she tried to lift the heavy wooden bucket laden with supplies. As much as she hated to admit it, she was right in thinking she couldn't carry it all the way home one-handed. Facing the town, she lifted the brim of her bonnet and searched the busy streets for her sister. Most likely Jo had gone to visit Alma Lou. She thought about asking Mr. Coulter to run by there, but she didn't want to be beholden to him for anything else. And she didn't particularly care to answer Jo's questions about Mr. Coulter. She hadn't even told her sister about Tom's death yet.

A horse whickered behind her, and Lara jumped at its nearness. The buggy creaked as Mr. Coulter stepped down right in front of her and gave a bow. "Your carriage awaits, madam."

Had she been a young schoolgirl, she would have been giddy at the charming man's attention, but she was a widow—one who should be in mourning and wearing widow's weeds—not gallivanting all over town and the countryside with an alluring bachelor.

Pushing aside her reservations because she had no other options, she allowed him to help her into the buggy. He retrieved the heavy bucket as if it weighed nothing and set it on the floorboard near her feet. The buggy creaked and tilted to her left as he climbed in and sat beside her. Ignoring his manly scent, she scooted as far to her right as she could, hoping the ride would be over with quickly.

Chapter 7

Payton Reeves flicked his cheroot to the ground and stamped the life out of it as he watched his nemesis escort Tom Talbot's wife into the mercantile. A white swath of gauze covered her hand, and she cradled it as if in pain.

He narrowed his gaze and pressed his palm on the handle of his pistol. What was going on?

How did a gambler from Kansas City even know Lara Talbot? And what was his business with her?

Besides that, what was Coulter doing in Caldwell? Payton rubbed his trigger finger against his thumb, thinking how he'd like nothing more than to pull out his 45 and blow that thieving snake away.

The swell of people crowding the streets of Caldwell faded as he remembered that fateful day in Kansas City. Gabe Coulter had been playing cards at his usual table in the back of the Lucky Chance saloon when Payton and his younger brother, Judah, had come into town for some fun. They'd been herding cattle at the Double S Ranch all week, and Payton was thirsty and hankering to win a bundle of money. He'd talked Judah into coming with him, even though his brother had preferred to stay on the ranch. Judah was saving his money and planning to return home to his young wife at the end of the month, but Payton wanted his brother's company.

He knew Gabe was a professional gambler, but he'd never seen a luckier man. Coulter won all but five hands that night, including the last three games, and had taken every last dollar he and Judah had.

Payton ground his back teeth together as he remembered his brother's desperation. At the end of the month, Judah went home to his pregnant wife, but when he turned up nearly empty-handed, she left him and went back to her parents' home. No amount of pleading and begging on Judah's part could change her mind. Finally, Judah sold his little house, sent the money to his wife in Topeka, and rode off. Payton had tried to stop him, begged him to stay, but Judah was determined to leave.

His gaze focused, and he looked toward the livery where Coulter was settling Mrs. Talbot into a rented buggy. He snorted a laugh. *I wonder if Tom Talbot knows his wife is two-timing him.* Not that Talbot had a right to say anything after the time he spent with the trollops above the saloon. Still, it didn't sit well with a man to know his wife was spending time with another man. It was different somehow. Wrong.

If Payton had time, he'd ride back to that ranch up near Kansas City where he'd worked with Talbot for close to a year and see if the man was still there. See if he would partner up with him in taking down Gabriel Coulter, but he didn't want to lose Coulter's trail now that he'd found him. He needed his revenge, although he wasn't exactly sure the best way to get it. Merely shooting Coulter was too simple—unless maybe he did the deed when they were far from town. He could take that pretty horse of Gabe's and leave the man gut-shot and dying. It would be a long, painful death—unless a wolf or some other critter found him first.

He pushed away from the wall outside of the saloon and jumped off the boardwalk into the street, feeling vengeance within his grasp.

A cloud of dust covered his already dirty boots. A fire burned in his gut, aching to be quenched. He climbed on his horse, wondering if he'd ever see his brother again.

Judah had never even laid eyes on his own son, born five months after he left town.

Somebody had to pay for all the pain his family had endured.

⌒

Gabe jiggled the reins and made a kissing sound at the horses. Lara Talbot's surprised crystal-green gaze zipped his way, as if he'd tried to sneak a smooch. A reddish tinge stained her cheeks, and she quickly looked away.

He smiled and held back a chuckle. The young widow was as edgy as a newly captured mustang. She made it quite obvious that she didn't want his help, but the problem was. . .she *needed* his help. Evidently that didn't sit well with her.

He couldn't help wondering if her aloof attitude had to do with him being nearly a stranger to her or if she was merely highly independent.

Either way, she intrigued him more than any woman he'd ever met. He was surprised to learn he enjoyed doing things for Lara Talbot and making her life easier. He would have bought half the store if he thought she would have accepted his gift.

His attraction to her didn't make sense. He cut a glance Lara's way, remembering the roughness of her hands when he'd helped her into the buggy. Glancing at his palm, he rubbed his thumb over his smooth fingertips. A shaft of guilt choked its way down his throat and lodged in his gut at the imbalance of it all. He was a man. He should be the one with callused hands and clothes dirty from hard work. There was a time when they had been.

The continual *clip-clop* of the horse's hooves lulled him into a relaxed state. The swishing of the tall prairie grass against the sides of the buggy reminded him of when his little brother, Stephen, and he had sat in the back of the family buckboard and dangled their feet in the grass, hoping to catch some grasshoppers to use for fishing bait. The years he'd lived on the farm with his mother and stepfather came into focus in his mind. They were the best—and the worst—years of his life.

Six years younger, Stephen always wanted to do whatever Gabe was doing. He'd enjoyed his brother's admiration but also found Stephen a pest at times. Then they both came down with the measles. A week later, Stephen died but Gabe lived, and the guilt of it had nearly been too much for him. He could still feel his mother's arm around him as they both cried and comforted each other.

Gabe realized he was clenching his teeth, and he forced himself to relax. He glanced at Mrs. Talbot, but she seemed deep in her own thoughts. With nothing but the boring prairie or the horse's rump to stare at, he allowed his mind to drift back again.

Stephen had been Gabe's stepfather's only blood heir. And Elliott Jarvis had grieved hard, taking out his enormous pain on his stepson. Gabe cringed. He'd lost count of how many times Elliott had questioned why Stephen had died instead of Gabe.

His life changed after Stephen's death. Elliott had never been overly warm to Gabe, but he'd never hit him before, either. The whippings began the day his brother was buried—the same day Gabe turned eleven.

He tightened his hold on the reins. Every little thing he'd done wrong had incurred his stepfather's wrath. Elliott had worked him like a slave, making him care for all the animals, labor in the fields, and tend the barn, while Elliott softened his pain with liquor—

precisely why Gabe never indulged in drinking whiskey.

Around Gabe's ma, Elliott never touched him. He remembered his stepfather's warning that if he ever tattled to his mother, the beatings would get worse. So while his mother tried to work through the grief of losing her youngest son, she was oblivious that her remaining family was being torn apart.

How could a quiet, hardworking man crack so suddenly and become such a harsh taskmaster? Gabe shook his head, still not understanding it even after so many years.

His mother had died when he was fourteen, ripping out his heart. The next day, she was buried beside Stephen, and that night, Gabe slipped away in the dark to begin life on his own. He determined then that he'd never endure a lickin' again.

A horse's whinny pulled Gabe away from his troubling past. He looked around, realizing that he had no idea where he was going. He'd followed the road out of town that Mrs. Talbot had pointed out to him and figured she would have told him if they were going the wrong way. He peeked at her, noticing she held her injured hand carefully in her lap. He'd not heard her holler out when the doctor was in the other room tending her injuries, but when he went to the back room to retrieve the widow, her eyes glistened with unshed tears. She might look soft, cuddly, and needy, but Lara Talbot had a backbone to her.

The cool spring breeze lifted a wavy strand of wheat-colored hair that had come loose from her bun. It flittered around her cheek like a hummingbird exploring a flower. His fingers twitched. He wanted to reach over and tuck that wayward strand behind her ear—or better yet, rub it between his fingers to see if it was as soft as he imagined.

Sighing, he turned his attention back to the road. He could look but not touch. What he'd really like was a taste of those slightly full lips of hers, too often pursed together as Lara was deep in thought. And he wanted to see her smile—see those lovely eyes sparkle with delight.

Gabe shook his head, wishing there was a creek nearby where he could douse his head. What in the world was wrong with him?

He glanced sideways and caught Lara staring at him with those pale green eyes. Had he unconsciously muttered something out loud?

She cleared her throat. "You'll need to take the trail that veers to the right, the other side of the next hill."

Turn right. Good. That gave him something to concentrate on besides his intriguing companion.

He couldn't deny that she attracted him in ways the saloon gals never had. In time she might be interested in pursuing a relationship with him, but women needed to mourn after losing a spouse. He'd noticed she wasn't wearing black, and for some reason that made him happy. He didn't want to see her in such a gloomy-colored dress. She needed bright colors. . .a flowery yellow or green to match her eyes. How could he get her to accept some new clothes?

And where was her son? Gabe thought about asking after the boy, but he didn't want to tip his hand that he knew so much about her.

He gritted his teeth, suddenly angry with Tom Talbot. Why had the crazy fool been gambling when his family so obviously needed the money he earned?

Like most men who gambled, Talbot had probably hoped to double his purse and return home with a pouch full of coins to please his wife.

That rarely ever happened, though, when a weekend cowboy gambler took on a professional.

For the first time, Gabe got a glimpse of how his occupation as a gambler hurt the innocent. A shiver ran through him as the buggy hit a rut and dipped down. Lara bumped his shoulder, but she quickly grabbed the side of the buggy and pulled herself back to her half of the seat.

Shame charged through Gabe at the trouble he'd caused her, but just as suddenly, anger followed on its trail. He never forced anyone to gamble with him, and if Tom Talbot hadn't gambled at *his* table, the man would have sat down at someone else's. And he was certain his fellow gamblers wouldn't have bothered to help Talbot's widow in the least. So, why was *he*? To mollify his guilt over killing the man?

Gabe worked his jaw, irritated with Talbot for challenging him in that dark alley. If only the man had gone back to the ranch where he worked, he'd be broke but still alive. He stared at the monotonous landscape. Why was he getting so melancholy? Caring for Lara Talbot wasn't his job.

Still, deep down, Gabe knew aiding the needy woman helped to soothe his guilty conscience. Like an angry hornet that continued to pester him, Tom Talbot's lifeless body, lying in that dirty alley, invaded his mind. Gabe hadn't meant to kill the man. He was merely defending himself.

He'd like to just hand the money he'd won from Talbot over to his wife. Then he could be on the first train back to Kansas City— or Texas—before he had a change of heart and needed to find a new career—one that his ma would be proud of. But Lara Talbot would never accept the money, no matter how badly she needed it.

He stared out at the prairie grass dancing in the light breeze. If he was clever enough, he could find other ways to pay it back, like he had today with buying the extra supplies. His ma had always said not to let the left hand know what the right hand was doing where giving was concerned. He'd never understood that phrase as a child, but now it made perfect sense.

Mrs. Talbot waved her hand to the right as a faint trail appeared. He tugged on the reins, and after a moment of resistance, the horse turned down the grassy path. Waist-high prairie grass whispered along the sides of the buggy, sending up debris from the snapped off tops of the tall stalks. A small grasshopper landed on Mrs. Talbot's dingy skirt. She jumped but then casually flicked it away. A scissortail flycatcher and a pair of purple martins hovered nearby, swooping down every so often to snatch a flying insect. A small smile tugged at his passenger's lips as she watched the circus act of birds snagging their prey. Her son would have enjoyed seeing this. Where was the boy? Had Mrs. Talbot left him with a neighbor? The long walk would be tiring for a young child.

Thinking of the fatherless child, he shook his head. Buying a few provisions didn't begin to atone for killing this woman's husband, but it *was* a step in the right direction. If he had his way, Lara Talbot and her son would be living in a fine house with all the food she could eat and everything she ever needed.

Maybe then his guilt would be assuaged.

"You can let me off here." Her soft, sweet voice broke the peaceful quiet of the prairie.

Gabe glanced around, but when he didn't see a cabin or house, he turned her direction in the seat and lifted one eyebrow.

She blushed, making her cheeks look sun-kissed. Gabe-kissed—that's what he wanted. Clenching his jaw, he faced forward again. He was acting like a schoolboy with his first crush.

"Where's your home?"

She cleared her throat and pointed ahead. "Just over that hill. Really, it's not far."

"I'll take you. That bucket is too heavy for you to carry with your injured hand."

"I'm sure I could manage, if you'd just remove your items."

He cut her a quick peek, wondering what she was talking about. Clucking to the horse, he jiggled the reins, moving the animal forward.

"Please, just let me out here."

Curiosity got the best of him, and he ignored her. She fidgeted in her seat. What was she trying to hide? The buggy crested the hill, and Gabe noticed a small, well-tended garden, but as his gaze traveled past that, it landed on a disheveled grass soddy leaning to one side. A pungent odor assaulted his nose, and a trio of goats, raising a ruckus, drew his attention to a pen on the far side of a tilting soddy. His gaze jerked back to the pitiful hovel where Mrs. Talbot and her son lived, and it took great effort not to shake his head. The awful place needed to be torn down before it fell down.

As he helped her out of the buggy, he thought of his fine hotel suite in Kansas City and of all the luxuries that he indulged in at the expense of women like Lara Talbot. His mouth dried, and an iron blanket of guilt pressed down on him. He set the bucket of supplies on the ground, tipped his hat to her, then hopped up in the buggy. Making a smooching sound at the horse, he guided the animal in a half circle and then headed away from the source of his guilt. If only he could shake her from his mind. But her circumstances were far worse than he could have imagined.

Behind him he heard Mrs. Talbot's thank-you then her cry, "You forgot your groceries."

He pretended not to hear her and snapped the reins against the horse's back, urging him to go faster. He'd bought those supplies for Mrs. Talbot and her son. They'd both enjoy the candy sticks, he hoped.

He was certain it would be a long while before he enjoyed anything again.

Chapter 8

Lara stared at the bucket overflowing with supplies. Had Mr. Coulter forgotten the items he bought, or had he meant them as a gift for what he'd called her "pain and trouble"? He'd said that in the store, but she was so numb at the time, she didn't believe him.

Since he'd unloaded the bucket from the buggy for her, she felt safe in assuming he meant for her to have them. Using her good hand, she wrangled the bag of flour off the top of the bucket, carried it into the soddy, then returned for the coffee and sugar. Oh what a blessing! Months had passed since she'd been able to purchase sugar. Excitement trickled through her as she thought of all the treats she could make for her family.

She stepped out of the stuffy grass house and shaded her eyes with her hand, looking toward the creek. Grandpa and Michael were probably still fishing. Glancing back up the trail, she wondered how many hours would pass before Jo would wander home. She couldn't help feeling a bit anxious for her little sister. With all the people coming into town, there were bound to be some unsavory types.

Would she be safe walking alone?

Worrying over Jo's well-being and knowing that she'd need her assistance in preparing dinner, Lara couldn't help wishing now that she'd asked Mr. Coulter to go by Alma Lou's house so she could get

Jo and bring her home.

But it was too late for that.

She closed her eyes and tilted her head up to the warm sun. What she needed to do was to talk to Grandpa while Jo wasn't around. Her sister would be terribly upset to learn they would be moving. And Lara could no longer prolong talking to Grandpa about Tom. He would hug her and take it in stride, just as he always did, but she hated to burden him more. Although, now that she thought about it, Grandpa would most likely be relieved that Tom was out of her life for good.

When she reached the creek, she looked both ways but didn't see her grandfather or her son. Michael would be intrigued and curious about the bandage on her hand. Grandpa would be concerned.

She knew Grandpa didn't like being a burden on her, but they were family, and family cared for one another. Besides, how could she ever make it through the day without his gentle encouragement, which always turned her to God?

Frogs croaked and birds chirped as they flitted from branch to branch. The soothing sounds of water bubbling over rocks made Lara want to sit down in the warm sun and take a nap, forgetting all about her troubles for a time. But naps were for sick folks and children, and she was certain her feisty little boy needed one by now.

She heard a squeal and jerked her head toward the sound as her heart jolted. Grandpa and Michael were standing side by side at their favorite fishing hole, leaning over a fish one of them had caught. Michael glanced up, saw her, and waved. He smiled and ran in her direction.

"Mama! I caughted three fishes." His fervent smile warmed her insides, turning them to mush.

Cautious of her wounded hand, she knelt down and engulfed

him in a hug, relishing the feel of his skinny arms around her neck and his sweaty boy scent.

He pushed away, all too soon, his eyes dancing. "Can we have shushpuppies wif the fishes?"

Lara smiled. "If we can get the chickens to cooperate and lay us an egg or two, I can make some hush puppies tonight. I got flour and cornmeal in town today."

Michael bounced up and down then yawned as he looked at his great-grandpa. Lara captured his hand.

"I'm taking Michael back home for his nap."

Grandpa nodded. "We got enough fish already, so I'll clean them and then mosey back." When his gaze landed on her bandaged hand, his fuzzy gray brows dipped into a V. He gave her a glance that said they'd talk later.

"But I don't want no nap." Michael tugged and jerked, trying to get loose. "I gots to help Grandpa."

Lara tightened her grip, gritting her teeth at the pain Michael's flopping caused her injured hand. "Michael, stop. You're hurting me."

He halted his movements and stared at her bandage, his blue-green eyes widening. "How come you gots your hand wrapped up?"

She took advantage of his distraction to tug him toward the soddy as she explained what happened. His darling little brows dipped with concern for her, making her want to cuddle him and keep him small forever.

She answered Michael's many questions about her injury while he ate a leftover biscuit, then she put him down for a nap. When she stepped outside, Grandpa was there with a mess of cleaned fish, lying in a big wooden bowl. Her mouth watered at the thought of fried fish coated in thick cornmeal batter. With the big sack of cornmeal Mr. Coulter had given her, she wouldn't need to scrimp on the batter. He was kind to replace her groceries. Perhaps she had misjudged him.

Grandpa headed toward the lean-to to put away the fishing poles. Though almost as thin as one of the cane rods he carried, he'd rebounded well from his latest bout of swamp fever. She hated to see him suffering so often but knew she should be grateful to God that he had lived to see his sixties. Many men who'd contracted malaria during the War Between the States, twenty-four years ago, were long gone. God had known how badly she needed her grandfather.

He ambled around the side of the soddy, brushing his hands together in a gesture that Lara knew meant he'd finished a task. He smiled at her then glanced at her bandage, his lips pursed. "What happened?"

"Long story." She offered him a weak smile. "Let's sit down outside so we don't disturb Michael."

He followed her over to the rickety buckboard that rested in the shade of a persimmon tree and helped her up onto the open wagon bed. With a litheness that belied his recent illness, he hopped up beside her. She arranged her skirts and dangled her bare feet off the edge like a carefree young girl, though her heart felt anything but cheery. She glanced at her grandpa, and he returned her gaze, lifting his brows.

"So? Out with it." He crossed his arms and leaned against the side of the wagon.

Lara studied the dark circles under his eyes, knowing what she had to share would tax him further. She told him about what happened in town and how Gabe Coulter had helped her; however, she omitted the fact that she'd met the man before.

"Right nice of that stranger to help you out like he did. Wish I'd been around when he brought you home so I could have thanked him."

Now that Mr. Coulter was gone and could no longer boss her around, her attitude toward him softened. She realized she hadn't been very nice to the kind man who was only trying to help. Shame coursed through her.

"Was there something else you wanted to talk about? I have chores piled up after being down on my back for three days." He scratched his chest and stared off in the distance. "Where's Jo?"

"In town. She helped me carry the milk to the mercantile then disappeared. I figure she's gone to visit Alma Lou."

Grandpa shook his head. "That gal needs to help you more. I haven't done right in raising her. She's got more grandiose ideas than I don't know who. Jo needs a mother."

Lara winced and turned her head away so he wouldn't see how his comment pierced her heart. She'd done the best she could to raise her sister, but she was only ten years old when her parents died. Jo was only five. Shoving aside her pain and apprehension, she looked at him again.

"I got some news. Tom is dead."

His blue eyes widened, and his mouth dropped open for a moment. "When? How?"

Lara shrugged. "I don't know."

"Then how do you know he's dead?"

"A man stopped me a few days ago as I was leaving town. He said Tom died in Kansas City and gave me the death certificate. He said Tom left a bag of money there, and he wanted me to go back with him to claim it."

Snorting a laugh, Grandpa shook his head. "Not likely. That Tom Talbot never had a dollar to his name, much less a whole bag of coins." Suddenly he got quiet. "What do you mean that man tried to get you to go with him?"

Concern crimped her heart at his worried expression, and she laid her hand on his arm. "I don't mean he tried to force me. Actually, the man was quite polite. He said his boss needed me to come in person to collect the money. Of course, I told him no and said the same thing you did."

"That sure is odd." He wrapped his arm around her shoulder. "I'm sorry, punkin. You know I never cared much for Tom, but he was your husband and Michael's father, such as he was."

She leaned into his embrace as tears clouded her eyes. "I realize now that I never should have married him. I just wanted so badly to get you some help."

"Me?" He gently pulled away to look her in the eye. "You married him to help me?" he said, his tone incredulous.

Her cheeks heated with embarrassment. She'd never planned to tell him that, but it simply slipped out. She fiddled with her skirt, noticing several small rips, probably from her fall, that needed patching.

"I always wondered what you saw in that man. I'm so sorry you felt you had to do such a thing." He shook his head and stared at the ground. "I should have done better by you gals."

"You did fine, Grandpa. If not for you, who knows where Jo and I'd be now." Lara's feet swung faster. The last thing she wanted to do was to make him feel incompetent. "It's all in the past. Tom's gone, and hopefully we no longer have to worry about his debt collectors coming around, begging money."

"So, you're not upset about him. . .being gone?"

How could she explain what she truly felt? "I did shed a few tears for Tom, mostly because I doubt that he came to know Jesus as his Savior before he died."

Grandpa picked up her good hand and wrapped his around it.

"You don't know that for sure. Many a man will cry out to God when he knows the end is at hand. I saw it over and over again on the battlefield."

His soft words comforted her, and she leaned her head on his shoulder, absorbing his strength. "Thank you. I sincerely hope he did make things right with God before dying."

In the distance, she heard the screech of a hawk and the bleat of a goat. The leaves of the trees fluttered in the breeze casting dappled shadows on the ground. Lara sucked in a strengthening breath and sat up, knowing there was more to tell.

"Herman Hancock came by yesterday when you were resting."

Her grandpa smiled. "Sorry I missed seeing him. Did you give him the rent money?"

She shook her head. "No, I didn't have it to pay, but it doesn't matter now. He told me his youngest son is married and returning home with his wife. They need the soddy to live in, and w—we have to move."

He sucked in a sharp breath. When he didn't say anything, she darted a glance his way. What was he thinking?

His mouth was puckered as if he'd eaten an unripe persimmon, and he looked deep in thought. Suddenly, peacefulness washed over him, and his features relaxed. "God will provide."

A nearby rustling noise made Lara jump. Jo burst out of the tall grass, her pretty features crinkled in a scowl. "We have to move? How can you say that God will provide?" She stomped toward them. "When did He ever provide for us?"

She swerved her glare toward Lara. "Tom is dead?" she said in a loud whisper then glanced around, probably looking for Michael. "How come I'm always the last to find out these things?" Jo waved her arms in the air like a hen with clipped wings trying to take flight.

"What are we going to do? Where will we live?"

Grandpa sighed and stood. "The Lord will take care of us, just like He always has. Though you can't see it now, He's arranging our steps."

"Ahhh!" Jo pressed her hands over her ears. "I'm so sick of hearing how God will provide, when He never does. How come Alma Lou can have so much, and we have so little?" She turned suddenly and stomped off toward the creek, murmuring to herself.

They both watched her march away, then Grandpa chuckled. "Feels like a cyclone just blew through, don't it?"

Lara stared at him and couldn't help feeling a tad bit of irritation herself. How could he not be even a little concerned?

He turned to face her, sober again. "Like I said, God ordains our steps. I feel His hand in this. When the good Lord closes one door, He opens another. Do you trust me, punkin?"

She nodded, sincerely wishing she had the faith he did. How could he be so physically weak and yet so spiritually strong?

He looked at her, all serious now. "Tomorrow, first chance you get, I want you to go back to town and get us registered for the land run."

⌒

Holding his leather satchel, Mark Hillborne stepped off the train from St. Louis and walked straight to the Caldwell ticket counter. As he stood in the short line, he studied the people coming and going. There were all sorts to behold—rich men in fancy suits like his father wore, poor men in ragged overalls, and even an Indian dressed in buckskins. Boy oh boy, he'd finally broken free from his father's iron thumb.

Soon he'd be participating in the race of the century, but he wouldn't be riding a horse or driving a wagon in a dusty race to claim farmland. No sirree. He wanted a plot in Guthrie, and the best way to achieve that was to take the train there. Excitement raced through him. The man in front of him stepped aside, and Mark moved forward.

"I'll take one ticket on the first train out of town on April 22nd."

The depot clerk pressed his lips together. "Well, now, I can sell you a ticket, but you'll have to get yerself over to Arkansas City if you want to ride that first train. Ain't none headed out of Caldwell into Oklahoma that day. And then it's up to you to beat all them others out to get a seat on that first one."

"Arkansas City?" He'd arrived in the wrong town for his venture? This could be disastrous. "How far is that?"

The man scratched his beard. "I reckon it's around thirty miles or so."

Mark blew out a loud sigh. "Let me have a ticket leaving from Arkansas City on the twenty-second and one that will take me there in three days." Next he needed to find a telegraph station and make sure his cargo went to Arkansas City instead of Caldwell.

He shook his head at his faux pas, still not sure how he got his research wrong. While the clerk prepared his tickets, he thought about having to race a bunch of yahoos to the train. Mark hadn't counted on that, but he supposed it made sense. He had read in the newspaper how hundreds, if not thousands, of people had already filed into the Kansas border towns in preparation for the land opening. Were there as many in Arkansas City as there were here? With the run still over a week away, many more would surely come. He'd be fighting a lot of people for a seat on that first train. He clenched his jaw as he saw his dreams of opening the first store at the Guthrie Station blowing away like chaff. He'd never hear the end of it from his father if he failed.

His grip tightened on his satchel. He never should have wasted so much time arguing with his father. Mark paid the fee then pocketed his coveted ticket.

The Podunk clerk handed him his change. "You reckon to set up house in the Oklahoma Territory?"

"Something like that." Mark exited the depot and scanned the rugged town so different from St. Louis.

A couple of boys ran up to him. "Need some help with that, mister?" the tallest of them asked as he tugged on Mark's bag.

"No, but you can point me to the telegraph office and a general store." Gripping his satchel tighter, Mark followed the boys' directions. He made short work of wiring one of his father's employees who'd been tasked with helping him to let the man know to send his two carloads of supplies to Arkansas City instead of Caldwell. A few minutes later, he walked into McMann's Mercantile.

A plump older woman nodded at him. "Can I help you with something, mister?"

"No, just looking." Mark quickly scanned the store's canned goods selection and smiled. He'd ordered a far wider variety than this woman carried. Suddenly, he sobered. What if he'd ordered items that people in Oklahoma couldn't use?

He'd listened to his grandfather, who'd built up his trading post off the Mississippi River into the largest general store in all of St. Louis. Mark ran a finger along a variety of cans then past containers of liniment and all manner of medicines. He stopped at the small clothing section and studied the wares. He hadn't thought to include overalls, and judging by the large number here, he needed to do that. Tugging out a piece of paper from his coat pocket, he licked the end of the pencil that accompanied it and wrote down *overalls*.

As he circled the store, he listed several more items.

The clerk watched him eagerly, as though she thought he was making a shopping list. He'd need to purchase more farming tools and seed, what with all the people who'd be planting crops after getting their land. And other tools and nails for building.

He finished his list then looked at the woman. Her hopeful smile made him want to laugh in her face. "Can you direct me to the best hotel in town?"

Her eyes blinked in confusion, then she cleared her throat and glanced longingly at the list. He stuck it in his pocket.

"Um. . .of course. Take a right out the door and walk past the next two alleys. You'll see the Leland Hotel across the street on your left. Would you like me to fill your order and have it ready to be picked up later?" She glanced at his pocket again.

"That won't be necessary." He stepped outside, ignoring her confused stare, and made his way down the boardwalk. After a bath to remove the coal dust from his hair and a warm meal, he'd see if there was any high-quality female companionship to be had.

He walked into the hotel lobby, excitement about the future racing through him. He gave the bell on the counter a sharp tap with his index finger and signed his name to the registration book. Yes sirree, it felt great to be out from under his father's harsh control. Mark Hillborne was his own man and not a puppet to paternal power. Not anymore. The Oklahoma Territory was the last place his wealthy, refined father would care to visit.

Gabe paced in the street outside the newspaper office, kicking up a cloud of dust over his newly polished boots. *Should I or shouldn't I?*

He'd read and reread the notice advertising the land rush, and the idea wouldn't go away. It was crazy for him to be contemplating such a thing. He'd never participated in a horse race before, but the very thought of it made his gut swirl with excitement.

He could do it. He certainly had a horse that was fit enough to compete. And the danger of racing thousands of people would be invigorating. Not to mention the thrill of winning a claim.

But what was the point? Did he want to be a sodbuster again? In the Oklahoma Territory, no less? Could he even adjust to country life after living high on the hog in the city for so long?

Pivoting again, Gabe nearly smacked into the head of a horse. The buckskin jerked its head and danced sideways. "Hey, watch out!" the rider yelled.

Gabe jumped back, yanking out his pistol. He aimed it at the man and returned the rider's glare. Sweat trickled down Gabe's back as he realized he'd probably overreacted, but instinct had kicked in. There were times a gambler had to react quickly, and Gabe had honed his skills. The cowboy rested his hand on his pistol for a moment then broke eye contact and nudged his horse forward. Gabe watched the man until he was sure the rider meant no harm then dropped his gun into his holster. Shaking out his tense fingers, he turned back toward the newspaper office.

As usual, a ragtag group stood in front of the land rush poster, and Gabe worked his way forward. One hundred and sixty acres of land. Free to whomever claimed it first.

Ideas churned in his head. If he won land, he could keep it awhile and then sell it. Or maybe he'd try farming again. His real father had been a farmer, and at one time Gabe had dreamed of following in his footsteps. He'd actually never disliked the hard work, just his bitter life after Stephen's death.

But dreams change, and farming held little lure. Now ranching—

that was something else. He'd always loved horses. And if he raised a small herd of cattle, he'd have plenty of beef to eat. The more he thought about it, the better the idea sounded.

He pushed out of the crowd. "It's just plain crazy to even consider it."

A man with a bushy mustache and round spectacles passed by, glancing at Gabe as if he were an oddity.

He thought of his comfortable suite back in Kansas City, the plush carpeting and soft bed. Anything he wanted to eat could be cooked downstairs by Moe, a former slave, then delivered to his door by a dainty gal with flirting eyes. He even had his own table at the Lucky Chance and a reputation for winning fairly. Could he really give all that up to become a rancher?

His steps slowed in front of the land office. For the first time since he'd been in Caldwell, there wasn't a long line of people registering for the run. Was this providence?

In actuality, he could race and still keep his hotel suite. As long as he continued to pay the rent, Hattie wouldn't lease it to anyone else. He might lose his table, though, because there were always other gamblers willing to take his place.

Do it. A voice in his head urged him on.

His fingertips began to tingle, and a shiver of excitement charged through his body. The land run was the biggest gamble of all for most. He'd heard that many people had left their former homes and families for a chance at the free land. For them, failure left them with nothing. For him, it could be an exciting adventure.

What did he have to lose? It cost nothing to ride in the race, and if he won, he'd have land. If he got a claim, he could try ranching for a time, and if he didn't, well. . .he could always go home and return to gambling again—or continue on to Texas, a land he'd always wanted to see. As far as he could tell, it was a win-win situation.

Gabe entered the dingy office that smelled of dirt and sweat.

"Come to sign up, did'ja?" A stooped man standing near the window walked behind the counter and picked up a pen. He held it out to Gabe. "Just put your John Henry on that there line and you're all set. These here are mighty exciting times, m'boy."

Unable to hold back a wide grin, Gabe took the pen and signed his name.

"Yep, I tell you, it's history in the making." The old-timer reclaimed his pen and laid it under the counter. "You sure did come at a good time. First time in a week that there ain't been a line."

Gabe nodded. "I know. I've been watching."

"You'll be needin' to get a sturdy stick and tie some cloth on it to stake your claim, if'n you're one of the lucky ones. There's markers—usually stacks of rocks—indicating the corners of each property, but I imagine they'll be hard to find on the run. Good luck to you, son."

Gabe walked into the sunshine, feeling as if his life was about to change. Funny, how simply signing his name to a piece of paper could make him feel that way.

As he returned to his hotel, he thought of the land he'd like to claim. A pretty little valley somewhere with a creek running through it with enough trees for some cooling shade but not so many that he'd have to clear the land. Maybe then he could find a wife and settle down, thus keeping the promise he made to his ma.

The idea didn't sound nearly as distasteful as it had in the past.

Lara Talbot's face came to mind, and he wondered if the young widow would ever marry again.

Chapter 9

Lara's shoulder ached from the heavy pole pressing against the base of her neck. A few feet ahead of her, Jo walked with the other end on her shoulder, a bucket of goat's milk swaying gently in between them. Cheesecloth covered the pail to keep out flies and dirt. Lara hoped the sale of the milk added to the few coins in her pocket would be enough to buy Grandpa some more quinine. She needed to stock up since they'd be leaving town, and she didn't know when she'd have another chance to purchase any more.

"You know, if you had agreed to register for the land rush like Grandpa and I wanted, we might not have gotten kicked out of the soddy."

Lara's mind swirled as she tried to comprehend how the two events were related. She scrunched her brow together, trying to make sense of Jo's cryptic statement.

"But no-ooo, you refused to obey, just like Balaam's donkey in the scriptures."

Lara pursed her lips together at Jo's scolding tone. To her way of thinking, the donkey had saved Balaam's life by diverting from its path to avoid the avenging angel bent on killing Balaam because he'd angered the Lord. She failed to see how her situation resembled his—unless she'd somehow disobeyed God by not following her grandpa's wishes. But he'd only *suggested* she register—at least until yesterday. "You heard what I said yesterday. We have to leave the soddy because Mr. Hancock's son is returning, and he needs it for his family. It has nothing to do with what I did or didn't do."

"Sometimes God has to give people a shove to get them moving." Jo lifted the pole, rubbed her shoulder, then lowered the thick wooden rod again, causing the bucket to slide dangerously toward Lara for a moment. "I guess He shoved us by making us lose the soddy."

Hearing Jo talk of God—albeit skewed—gave Lara hope that her troublesome sister was at least paying some attention during Sunday services. "I doubt the two situations are related." As soon as the words left her mouth, she wondered if maybe there wasn't a bit of truth to Jo's convoluted thinking. Had God forced them from their home so she'd be willing to register for the land rush because they had no other hope of getting land? With no money to buy land or even to rent an acre if one were available, the run was their best hope of obtaining a place to live.

Lara sighed. "There may be some truth in what you say."

Jo snorted. "Never thought I'd hear you say that I'm right about something." She stepped to the side of the road to allow a covered wagon pulled by an oxen team to pass by, and Lara followed her. The couple on the seat nodded in their direction. She smiled at them.

The road south of Caldwell had always been a fairly isolated one, traveled mostly by folks who lived outside of town or were journeying to the Twin Territories. Now it seemed busier than the streets of Caldwell with so many people going to the Kansas border to prepare for the land rush.

Just outside of town, a buckboard piled high with furniture, bedding, and crates approached, surrounded by a passel of children of all sizes, laughing, squealing, and dodging in and out of the tall prairie grass alongside the road. By the end of the day, she was sure, they'd all be dragging their feet.

A thin woman, who sat next to a man on the wagon seat, nudged him in the side. She whispered something in his ear. He glanced at Jo and Lara then handed the reins to his wife and jumped off the slow-moving wagon as his wife reined the horses to a stop.

He walked toward them and seemed to be studying the dirt road. Finally, he looked up and removed his hat. His gaze darted everywhere except at them. "My missus wants to know if perchance y'all might have some milk or eggs in yer bucket."

Jo nodded before Lara could respond. "We've got goat's milk."

His hands wrung his hat half to death. "I don't reckon you'd care to part with it, would you?"

Lara's heart jolted. She had no doubt the large family needed the milk, but it was her only chance for getting Grandpa's medicine. "We plan to sell it in town," she blurted before Jo could offer to give it away.

"I'd be willing to pay you for it. Say, half a dollar. Our cow died several days back, and our young'uns are in terrible need of some fresh milk."

Jo glanced over her shoulder and lifted her brows. Lara didn't need to consider the offer, because it was more than twice what she'd get in town. "Sold." She offered a smile, and the man looked her full in the face for the first time and grinned.

He took the bucket and poured the milk into one of his own. The six stair-step children chattered loudly and gathered around the back of the wagon. They looked well fed and nicely clothed, making Lara wonder why the family didn't buy another cow. But it was no concern of hers. She gladly accepted the half dollar and carried the bucket while Jo walked with the pole as if it were a shepherd's staff.

"I want to go say good-bye to Alma Lou and visit with her a little while."

Lara wanted to tell Jo that they had lots to do, but the truth was, there wasn't all that much to pack. "I'll need your help later. I want to put new grass in the ticks before we leave. I've heard that some of the land in Oklahoma is quite barren."

Jo glanced sideways at her. "I sure hope it isn't all like that."

"Me, too."

A sparkle lit Jo's blue eyes. "Can I go with you to register?"

She shrugged one shoulder. "If you want, but your time would be better spent with Alma Lou than standing in that long line."

Jo seemed to be thinking that over as they entered Caldwell. When they came to Main Street, she waved and trotted off toward her friend's house. People swarmed the boardwalks, and the loud murmuring of voices reminded Lara of a mass of bees surrounding a hive. Caldwell had certainly become a hive of humanity with all the people passing through.

She walked toward the land office, thankful that the line was short today. She was the only woman waiting to register, and she listened to the men talk of the run. Turning her head to avoid the rank smell of the old man in front of her, she watched the people coming and going, suddenly surprised to realize she was looking for one particular dandy. She owed Gabe Coulter an apology. That must be the reason she was searching him out.

As the line shrank, Lara's angst grew. What if they didn't get land? They'd be stuck in the Oklahoma Territory with no money and no means of support in a place with few towns. Grandpa had insisted they stick together. He didn't want to leave the family behind so that he could travel to the border for the run. Of course, the rest of them would have to wait near the starting line, hoping and praying Grandpa got a claim. She worried about him competing when he wasn't in top condition. And that old mule of theirs was likely to collapse if he pushed it very hard.

The man behind her coughed, and the ghastly odor of his stale breath and rotting teeth made her want to retch. She covered her nose and mouth with her bandaged hand and stepped forward. Swallowing back the bile in her throat, she kept her feet still, knowing if she ran outside, she'd lose her place in line—and she was so close now. The stuffiness of the dim room mixed with the pungent odor of dirty men almost became too much.

She set her bucket down, pulled her handkerchief from under her cuff and fanned herself with it. Oh, what she wouldn't give for her hand fan, even if it did have an advertisement for a burial service on it. Just when she was certain she'd swoon, the man in front of her stepped away, revealing an aged clerk. His pale blue eyes twinkled with mirth. "I know it ain't right to ask a woman's age, but it's my job. Have ya reached twenty-one yet, missy?"

Lara nodded. "Yes, sir. I have."

"Then just sign your John Henry, ma'am, right on that line." He pointed at the ledger book then rattled off the same spiel he'd given every other person before her.

Lara signed her grandpa's name, Daniel Jensen, and started to leave. She glanced at the list, and when the old man turned his back, she added her own name. Picking up the bucket, she spun and hurried outside. She pushed her way through the line of waiting men, darted into the alley, and bent over, trying to catch her breath. What she needed was a cool glass of water. Maybe she could beg one off the doctor when she went there to buy Grandpa's quinine.

She gasped in several deep breaths then straightened, willing her blurred vision to clear. That had been a close call. Maybe skipping breakfast so that she could slip Michael and Grandpa her share of the johnnycakes hadn't been a good idea. Holding on to the side of the wall, she slowly made her way back to the boardwalk. Several men gave her curious stares, but no one offered their assistance, much to her relief.

Embarrassed by her display of womanly weakness, she stepped back into the shade of the boardwalk and wove her way through the crowd toward the doctor's office. The kind man gave her a drink of tepid water and a wet cloth for her face, then with two dozen quinine pills in a small bottle in her pocket, she stepped outside the doctor's office and ran smack into a solid body. The empty bucket went clanging to the ground. The man's hands quickly came out to steady her, and she anchored onto his arms as another wave of weakness washed over her.

"Are you all right, Mrs. Talbot?"

The doctor's door jingled shut behind her as Gabe Coulter guided her to sit down in the chair outside of the office. She took a moment to collect herself, knowing she was going to have to eat more to be able to function. If not for the abnormally hot April day and the foul odors in the land office, she probably would have been fine.

"I'm getting the doctor." Gabe rose from his squat, but she grabbed the edge of his jacket in a very improper manner for a lady.

"No, please. I'm fine." She had no money to pay the doctor and wasn't about to get into Mr. Coulter's debt further. "I just got overheated."

He retrieved her bucket then eased down in the chair next to her, looking less than convinced. "Are you sure? Do you need some water?"

Lara shook her head. "Truly, I'm fine. I just need to sit for a few moments."

The scent of fresh-baked bread wafted by on the warm breeze, making her empty stomach gurgle a protest. She covered her middle with her hand but feared Mr. Coulter had heard. With warm cheeks, she glanced up to see him smiling like a rogue.

He cocked an eyebrow. "Hungry, are we?"

Mortified, she looked away. Why was she always at her worst when he was around? Looking down, she noticed her dirty toes sticking out from under her dress and slid them beneath her frayed skirt. Could things get any worse?

"What were you doing in the doctor's office? Are you sicker than you're willing to admit?" His warm smile wilted, as if he was truly concerned about her welfare.

"I am not sick."

"I suppose you came back so he could check your hand. How's it doing?"

She waved her freshly bandaged hand in the air. "Fine, but the doctor wants me to keep it covered for another day or two."

"I'm glad you didn't break it." His mouth pulled into a tight-lipped smile, which made Lara wonder if he still felt responsible. He tugged a shiny gold watch from the pocket of his vest and cleared his throat. "I was just heading over to the café for lunch. I'd be delighted if you'd accompany me." He held out his hand as if the decision had already been made.

She shook her head. "Thank you, but I can't." She may be a widow, but nobody in Caldwell knew that yet. How would it look if she were to dine with a man other than her husband?

Her stomach growled again, and she sank lower in the chair.

With her bucket looped over one arm, Mr. Coulter took her

hand and tugged her up. "I insist." He stood so close that she caught a whiff of his spicy bay rum scent. She never knew a man could smell so refreshing. After the reeking, hairy hoard of grubby men in the land office, he smelled delightful. And she'd yet to see him dirty or unshaven. She admired a man who cared enough to tend to his daily ablutions. Suddenly feeling crowded by his closeness, she tried to step back, but the bench pressed against her calves.

He quirked a rascally grin, as if he knew her thoughts, then took her uninjured hand, looped it around his arm, and gently pulled her with him down the boardwalk. When she tried to tug her hand away, he applied enough pressure to hold her securely in place.

"Please, Mr. Coulter, it isn't proper for you to accompany me around town. I'm a widow, but most of the townsfolk don't know that. Besides, I'm in mourning."

His gaze traveled the length of her faded dress, making her want to turn and run. "You don't appear to be in mourning. And call me Gabe."

She wanted to slap that smug expression off his face but had no free hand to do so. She tried yanking away again, but he placed his left hand on her arm to hold her there. "I'll set you free after you've eaten a three-course meal. You are far too thin, Mrs. Talbot."

"I can't. Please let me go. I've got to get back home."

He stopped in front of the café door and looked at her. "You need to eat a decent meal. You're so weak you can hardly stand up straight. After we dine, I'll rent a buggy and drive you home, if your duties in town are completed."

"You have no right to order me to eat." Lara stopped suddenly, refusing to go another step as his prisoner. "Turn loose of me, you cad."

She glared at him, but he just grinned back at her like she'd given him the world's nicest compliment. The bell on the café door jingled as two cowboys stepped out. They glanced at her and Gabe but kept on walking. She considered asking for their help, but the fragrant odors of food that followed them out the door made her waver.

When Mr. Coulter ushered her inside, her rebellious feet followed. He seated her then took the chair across from her and smiled. "See, that wasn't so difficult, was it?"

Lara crossed her bandaged hand over her other arm and glared at him. She had no idea how she'd ended up in this chair. What she ought to do was storm outside and run home, but she doubted she could get that far. All she'd had to eat since lunch yesterday had been two hush puppies and a sliver of fish. The tantalizing odors of roast beef and fried chicken melted her last resistance.

"Fine. I'll eat with you, Mr. Coulter, but no buggy ride. I'm perfectly capable of walking such a short distance." She hiked up her chin.

His dark eyes twinkled. "We'll see. And call me Gabe. I insist."

She narrowed her brow. "You're quite insistent at ordering me about when you hardly know me." She refused to call him by his first name. What point was there arguing about that since today was probably her last day in Caldwell?

Something deep inside her winced at the thought of having to bid him good-bye for the last time. He was the only man ever to truly treat her like a lady, even though she'd been as skittish as a wet cat trapped in a rain barrel. Not even when she and Tom were courting had Tom ever treated her so nicely. Lara sighed.

Humbled, she cleared her throat. "I want to thank you for your assistance yesterday. I really don't know how I would have managed otherwise."

He waved his neatly manicured hand in the air. "It was the very least I could do after causing you so much pain and trouble."

She wanted to argue that the boy had caused her problems, but she kept silent. If it made him feel good to help her, she wasn't going to steal his joy.

The waitress came, and Gabe ordered roast beef while she requested the fried chicken. Her mouth watered, and she hoped there'd be enough food that she could take some home for Michael. The growing boy needed to eat more meat.

"Are you in town on business, Mr. Coulter? I don't recall seeing you until recently." She toyed with a fraying corner of her cloth napkin.

"It's Gabe, remember?" He grinned and leaned back in his chair, crossing his arms over his chest. "I'd just arrived the day I met you at the depot when you calmed my horse. Thank you again for that, by the way."

She could feel a blush rising to her cheeks. She'd just happened to be cutting through the depot on her way home from delivering the Henrys' mending, when she saw the spooked horse. While working on Grandpa's ranch, she'd learned young that she had a knack for handling the beautiful animals. "My pleasure."

"I live in Kansas City but came down here to look for someone. I've discovered since then that selling horses here can be very lucrative."

Lara hoped he wasn't cheating desperate people by selling them overpriced mounts. Her stomach growled on cue as the waitress approached with two plates filled with steaming food. Her eyes widened and her mouth watered at the sight of a half chicken coated with crispy fried batter, mashed potatoes and gravy, green beans, and a plate of hot rolls.

Gabe nodded his thanks to the waitress and picked up his fork. He glanced at her, brows tucked. "Something wrong?"

Shaking her head, Lara cleared her throat. "It's just that we always say grace over our meals."

"Sorry, it's been awhile since I've done that. Go ahead." He laid his fork down, looking contrite.

She asked God's blessing for the food then cut off a plump thigh and looked around the café. Since it was only a quarter past eleven, a crowd hadn't gathered yet. She took the remaining pieces of chicken, dropped them discreetly into her bucket, then laid the cheesecloth over them. She avoided Gabe's searing gaze and concentrated on eating everything else on her plate. Soon, she was as stuffed as she could ever remember being.

When she looked up, he glanced at the bucket then quirked one brow. Heat rushed to her cheeks. "I couldn't possibly eat all this, and now I'll have some for later."

"Sounds like a wise plan." He pushed the plate of rolls toward her. "I need some coffee after that delicious meal."

When he looked around the café as if he was searching for the waitress, she dropped her thigh bone into the bucket, imagining the soup she would make from the leftover bones, and placed the remaining rolls on top.

Gabe's dark eyes glistened with amusement. "I hope the waitress doesn't think you were so hungry that you ate the bones."

Lara darted a glance at the plump woman who was waiting on another table. Gabe tossed some money down beside his plate. "Shall we go?"

"What about your coffee?"

He stood and waved his hand. "I can always get some later, unless of course, you'd care for some pie."

"No, but thank you for offering." She allowed him to escort her outside, grateful that he didn't embarrass her for taking the chicken.

Now she was eager to make her getaway, lest he offer her a ride. She didn't want to like Gabe Coulter, but he'd done nothing so far to make her dislike him, other than being overly insistent about things.

"I'll go fetch the buggy. Would you like to wait here or walk to the livery with me?"

She looked up in his handsome face. If only he would spend some time outside, doing some physical labor to help him lose a little weight and allow the sun to darken his skin, he'd be close to perfect. Her eyes widened at that thought. She had no business thinking such things about him.

She ducked her head to avoid his questioning gaze. "I allowed you to buy me dinner, but I insist on walking home."

"You insist?" He chuckled, making her look up. "That's my line."

Lara couldn't help returning his smile. "Be that as it may, I'll be walking home. Thank you for the lovely dinner. It was delicious." She turned and started moving away, but he quickly caught up.

"It's just plain crazy for you to walk. I'm bored half to death here. You'd be doing me a favor."

She shook her head and looked around, hoping to see Jo. When her gaze landed on the heavyset man who'd told her about Tom's death walking toward her, she took a step backward. What was he doing here again?

The man's gaze darted apprehensively to Gabe and back to her. This time he had a different horse—a fine-looking buckskin with a black mane and tail. "Good day, Mrs. Talbot." His gaze shifted toward Gabe. "Mr. . . .uh. . ."

"Coulter. Gabe Coulter." He held out his hand, and the man shook it.

Lara wasn't certain, but she thought she'd seen a spark of amusement in Gabe's eyes for a moment, but she failed to understand why.

"I'm lucky to run into you here in town, Mrs. Talbot." He tipped his hat. "Sorry to bother you again, ma'am, but my boss was mighty displeased that you refused to come to Kansas City to meet him."

Of all the nerve! She stiffened her back and glared at him. "I don't owe your employer anything, Mr. Jones, especially my valuable time. It's quite rude of him to expect me to travel so far to visit a stranger. If he wants to see me so badly, why doesn't he come here?"

He looked at Gabe, almost as if he feared the man. Was it possible the business Mr. Jones had with her was of a private nature?

He cleared his throat. "Well, anyway. He weren't too happy. But we found out that your husband had this here horse stabled at the livery. My boss figured you'd want it."

An explosion of hope burst in Lara's heart before she doused it with a bucket of common sense. This wasn't the old nag Tom had ridden away from home on over a year ago. This fine animal was young and strong. The horse danced sideways as a dog barked nearby. Lara's gaze landed on the worn saddle. Her heart jolted again as she stepped forward. There, engraved on the back corner of the leather skirt, were two overlapping T's—Tom's brand. She rubbed her fingers over it.

"Looks like your husband left you a fine horse, Lara." Gabe stroked the animal's neck. "You'll have a good chance in the race with him—if you decide to ride."

Could it really be true? Dare she hope?

Grandpa had said that the Lord would provide. She spun around to face Mr. Jones. "You're certain this was my husband's horse?"

"Yes, ma'am. The livery man talked with him when he first arrived, and they swapped names." He coughed then cleared his throat. "Took him awhile to realize that the horse's owner was the man who got hisself shot in the alley."

"So this really was Tom's horse?" Lara patted the horse's golden neck, a bit stunned at the realization that God had answered her prayers for the first time in a long while.

The man nodded. "Yes, ma'am." His thick lips lifted in a tentative smile.

She accepted the reins and looked at Gabe. "What a surprise!"

His wide smile warmed her heart. "Yes, it is. Do you ride?"

"Yes! I rode a lot when I was young."

"Can you manage the reins with one hand?"

She nodded. Gabe took the bucket from her and hooked the handle over the saddle horn. Then he stepped behind her and took hold of her waist, surprising Lara to the core, and lifted her onto the horse. She quickly arranged her skirts for modesty and found herself unable to stop smiling. "I can't believe this. It's such an unexpected surprise."

Delight brightened Gabe's expression.

"I sure don't need that buggy ride now. Thank you for dinner, Mr. Coulter, and thank you so much, Mr. Jones, for bringing Tom's horse all this way. I sincerely appreciate that." She waved and turned the horse for home, excited to tell Grandpa their prayers had been answered.

Chapter 10

Jo sat on the well-cushioned sofa in Alma Lou's parlor, elbows on her knees, and stared at the colorful Persian carpet. Saying good-bye to her best friend was harder than she'd expected.

Alma Lou bolted upright on the sofa. "I know! You can stay here with me."

Jo's heart jolted. "You'd let me do that?"

"Of course, but it would only be for a few months. Once I'm married you would need to find your own place." Alma Lou clutched her hands to her bosom. "Oh, it would be such fun. You could help me prepare for the wedding."

Could she do that? How would she support herself? The only work she'd done other than gardening was trap and skin rabbits, hunt, fish, cook over a campfire, and help Lara with the laundry. She'd worked with the horses before Grandpa lost his land, but no one would hire a woman for such work. And could she leave her family?

Yes, she actually could. She longed to be free of Lara's bossy dominance, but leaving Grandpa and little Michael would be much harder. What if she never saw them again?

"What are you thinking? I thought you'd be more excited by my offer."

She shrugged. "Just wondering if I could find work and if I could actually leave my family."

"You'll leave them once you find a man to marry, and with your pretty looks, I doubt it will be too much longer."

Jo wrinkled her nose. "I'm not sure I want to marry—at least not yet. I want to do something fun, go on an adventure, to experience life before I settle down to being a wife and mother."

Alma Lou's eyes grew bigger with each word Jo said. She shook her head. "I'll never understand you. Why, there is no greater adventure than meeting the man who is the only one for you, getting to know him, and planning your future together. Courting is an adventure all its own."

Jo rose and walked to the large picture window. Her friend was right. She would never understand. Alma Lou's parents had been married over thirty years, and as far as she knew, had a happy marriage. Jo's parents died when she was only five, and she barely remembered them, much less had their marriage as an example to follow. Tom and Lara's marriage had been a joke. She'd never told her sister about the times Tom had tried to get her to take a walk with him or when he'd captured her alone and stole a kiss or two. How was a woman to find a good man when she didn't know what to look for? If only she could find someone like her grandpa—not old, but loving and kindhearted.

A knock at the door drew Alma Lou from the parlor. She squealed, and Jo walked to the foyer to see what was happening.

"Mama!" Alma Lou hurried to the bottom of the winding staircase and shouted up, "Miss Moss is here for my dress fitting."

Alma Lou spun toward Jo, her brown eyes dancing. "You get to see my wedding dress."

Forcing a smile, Jo nodded. Seeing the dress would only reinforce that she wouldn't be here for the wedding—unless she could figure out a way to stay. She'd leave right now if it wouldn't hurt her friend's feelings.

An hour later, Jo was kicking herself for not leaving sooner. She'd sat in the corner, watching Miss Moss and Alma Lou's mother fuss over her, pinning and rearranging and gushing about how lovely she was. When Miss Moss packed up, Jo gave Alma Lou a hug, with a promise to let her know soon if she planned on staying with her, then she slipped out the door.

When she cleared the house, she glanced at the sun. It was setting a bit later these days, so she could piddle around town another half hour before she needed to head home. She'd never been a fearful person, but with all the strangers in and around Caldwell lately, she didn't want to be caught alone on the road after dark.

She turned onto one of the streets in the business district and moseyed past the shops. Even on a good day, it would be hard for a woman her age to find work in Caldwell, but with so many people in town, she doubted anyone had an opening for help. Still, it wouldn't hurt to take a look at the corkboards in the general stores. Maybe one of the wealthier families needed a nanny or housekeeper. Caring for children wasn't her favorite thing to do, Michael not included, but if it meant she could stay in Caldwell, it might be worth the trouble.

Jo paused in front of a dress shop to admire a beautiful burgundy gown with ivory accents. Wide ivory-colored buttons ran down the front with matching cuffs trimmed in lace. The front of the skirt opened, revealing a frilly underskirt with more lace and ribbons. She sighed. What would she look like in such a creation?

"A brighter shade of red is more suitable to your coloring."

She spun at the masculine voice and was stunned to silence at the decidedly handsome man whose attention was solely focused on her. His fancy camel-colored sack coat and vest rested on a wide set of shoulders. Sandy brown hair and deep blue eyes accentuated his comely features.

"Ah, now that I see you full on, I've changed my mind. Blue is definitely your color, to match your lovely eyes. A royal blue or perhaps cornflower would go best."

Jo's cheeks felt warm, more than likely because her bonnet rested on her back instead of her head. "And who are you?"

"My apologies. I'm Mark Hillborne, of the Hillbornes of St. Louis."

He stated his name as if it should hold some meaning to her, but she'd never been to St. Louis. "I'm Jo—Joline Jensen."

"A lovely name for a beautiful woman."

She'd received many compliments on her beauty, so she knew a charmer when she saw one, but few rogues had intrigued her like this man. She'd guess he was a few years older than Lara, maybe twenty-three or -four. "I haven't seen you around town before. Are you here for the land rush?"

"That I am. I assume you live here?"

"For now," she mumbled as she turned back toward the dress. Suddenly she swirled around again. "How do you know what colors would look good on me? That seems an odd thing for a gentleman of your age to know. Or is that your usual opening comment when you meet a woman you don't know?"

He smiled and looked even more appealing. "My family is in the general store business, so I've worked there my whole life. My mother insisted I learn which colors look nice with the various complexions in order to help women with their fabric selections."

"I've never known a man who was interested in fabrics."

He leaned casually against the building, crossing one leg over the other. "Maybe *interested* isn't the proper word." He ran his thumb and forefinger down his lapel. "I do appreciate fine clothing, and I learned what I had to about fabric in order to assist our customers. Wouldn't you prefer to purchase a dress that enhances your beauty rather than diminishes it?"

Jo blew a puff of air from her nose. As if she'd ever own a store-bought dress.

"What is that look I see in your expression?"

She turned away from the window and started walking. She might just as well leave this dandy with a fair memory than let him know the state of her financial poverty, not that he probably couldn't tell by her patched dress and bare feet.

"Wait! What did I say?"

She shook her head. "Nothin'. I just need to be getting home." Lara would need help with dinner since her hand was still bandaged.

"Miss Jensen, please wait." He tugged on her arm, not really giving her a choice but to stop or make a scene. And with hundreds of people on the street, it would be a big scene.

"What?"

He smiled. "Would you allow me to escort you home?"

Jo shook her head. "It's too far. By the time you walked back to town, it would be dark and you'd probably get lost."

He blinked, as if not used to being turned down—or maybe her comment about him getting lost challenged his masculinity. "I can hire a buggy and get back in plenty of time before dark, unless, of course, your home is an extraordinary distance from here."

Jo kept walking, hoping he'd take the hint. When she saw a ragged land rush announcement, posted on a wall, she paused and read over the information once more. Just imagine, one hundred and sixty acres—all for one family. . .

Mr. Hillborne stopped beside Jo. "I'm participating in the land rush. Are you planning to?"

She shook her head. "I wish I could, but I'm not old enough."

He frowned. "You're not? That surprises me."

She stood a bit straighter. Most people recognized she was still somewhat young, even though she was old enough to marry—if she wanted to. Alma Lou was only sixteen, and a few months older than Jo.

"I'm hoping my grandpa can ride, but he's been sick lately."

"I'm sorry to hear that."

"Thank you." Jo turned toward her charming admirer. The man truly was handsome. She stole a long peek at him while he was scanning the announcement. "So, do you have a fast horse?"

"No horse at all."

Jo blinked. "But how will you get land if you don't have a horse to ride? You don't have one of those odd-looking contraptions with the big wheel, do you?"

"You mean a bicycle?" He laughed. "No, I wouldn't be caught dead on one of those neck-breaking things. The first big rock you run over, you're likely to end up flat on your face in the dirt."

Jo smiled at the image in her mind. "I suppose they would be difficult to ride."

"Not so much on a smooth city street, but I fail to see how anyone could have success with one on the open prairie."

"I feel the same way. Give me a fast horse any day." She started walking and repeated her earlier question. "How are you going to get land if you don't have a horse?"

"I'm riding the train and plan to get a plot in town at the Guthrie Station and open the first general store there. No horse is needed since the town plots are near the depot."

Jo had to admit his plan sounded like a good one. "I'm sure you'll do well."

His eyes glowed as he basked in her praise. "I'll need employees. Why don't you come and work for me?"

Her heart took flight for a moment before landing back at its roost. "That's kind of you to offer, but I'm hoping to find something here in Caldwell. All of my friends are here, and I don't want to leave."

"I see. Well, I wish you good luck in your search, and if you ever get down to Guthrie, be sure to look me up."

"I will." Jo smiled and glanced down the street. The sun had sunk lower than she'd expected. "I'd better go. It was nice meeting you, Mr. Hillborne."

"It's Mark." He took her hand, bent, and kissed it. "I have a feeling we'll meet again, Joline."

⌒

Lara worked hard to stifle her grin as she rode into the yard in front of the soddy. The female goats rushed to the side of the fence and bleated a greeting, hoping for a handout, but Bad Billy only lifted his head, stared at her for a moment, then returned to eating.

She dismounted and patted the gelding's neck. "You're a good horse, aren't you, boy?" She combed the tangles from his black mane with the fingers of her left hand, wishing she had some grooming tools. She'd have to be satisfied with rubbing him down with a burlap sack.

Lara stared at the trail to town. Jo would be jealous that she'd had to walk home when she learned about the horse, but Lara had no idea how long her sister would be visiting. She couldn't wait until Jo was finished, because she had many things to do to prepare for their move. She shook her head, still amazed that the ride from Caldwell had taken only ten minutes instead of the normal thirty-minute walk, and she hadn't even galloped the horse. If she needed to get to town in a hurry, she now had the means.

She walked around the horse, checking his legs and hooves. At first, she'd thought there had to be something wrong with the animal for Mr. Jones to hand him over to her without expecting payment of some sort, but his tale about the horse belonging to Tom must be true. The initials on the saddle proved it.

Grandpa could ride in the land run now, and she knew just what he would say when he heard her story about how she'd inherited the horse: "Praise the Lord!" And then he would tell her he knew God would provide for them. And God had provided. Guilt nibbled at her like a mouse at a loaf of bread because her faith hadn't been stronger.

A shuffling noise pulled her gaze back to the open doorway of the soddy as Michael stepped out. He yawned, rubbed one eye with his fist, and looked around. "We got comp'ny? Whose horse is that?"

Unwilling to ground tie the gelding until she knew his personality better, Lara held on to the reins and motioned for her son to come to her. "We don't have company, sweetie."

"Then how come there's a horse here? Is it lost?"

"No." She smiled. "Not lost, but it has a new home. He's our horse."

Michael's eyes widened. "Ours? Can I ride 'im?"

"What's this?" Grandpa shuffled out of the soddy, lifting the arm of his spectacles over one ear. He eyed the buckskin then approached the horse and ran his hand down one leg. "Nice-looking animal. Who does it belong to?"

"He's ours," Lara and Michael said in unison. She chuckled and brushed her hand across her son's curly hair.

Grandpa grinned and pushed his hat back on his head, revealing his pale forehead. "Well, glory be! God provided, just like I said He would."

"He certainly did."

"So, can I ride 'im?" Michael clapped his hands and bounced on his toes.

Grandpa looked at her and lifted a brow.

"I rode him all the way home from town, and he's a good, calm horse. If you're going to ride, I think it's fine for him to go with you."

Grandpa nodded. "I would like to give him a try. Been awhile since I've been on a horse as nice as this one. Where did he come from?"

Lara's joy wilted. "Take a ride, and then I'll explain it."

He eyed her again but nodded. God had given them the horse they needed. If only He'd let them get land where they could finally settle down and build a house with wood floors and a roof that didn't leak, and windows where she could look out upon the prairie. God could do anything—she knew that and believed it—but it was hard to keep believing when only bad things happened, month after month.

"Lift me up, Mama. Lift me!" Michael's tugging on her skirt yanked her from her thoughts. She picked him up, groaning at his weight, and hoisted him in front of her grandpa. "My, you're getting heavy."

He grinned like a possum and held on to the saddle horn. Grandpa looped one arm around the wiggly boy and held the reins with his other. He nodded at Lara. "Back in a bit."

She watched them go, pride welling up in her at how straight a seat her grandfather sat in spite of his sixty-three years, spending weeks at a time in bed because of his malaria, and the years he fought in the War Between the States. He was a strong man, and she loved him so much. How would she get by without him when the Lord took him home?

She shoved that thought away, but another took its place. Too bad she couldn't find such a man to marry. Not that she particularly wanted to marry again. Gabriel Coulter's image blossomed in her mind. She snorted, drawing a *maa-aa* from Mildred. Lara shook her head, freeing it from the picture of the sweet-talking dandy, and plucked a handful of grass and carried it to the fence. Her goats crowded one another as they attacked the treat—the same grass that fell over the fence into their pen. She smiled and shook her head. "You silly critters." Mildred lapped at Lara's skirt, and she pulled it away before the goat sank her teeth into the fabric.

In the soddy, she found an empty can and a large spoon and set them on the table next to a skinned rabbit. She swatted away a pair of flies. As she looked around the small house, she realized how little they had to move. She and Jo had three dresses each: two for working in and one for Sunday services and special events, although they rarely were able to attend either lately. Grandpa and Michael both had one extra pair of clothing. She wished she'd been better at providing for her family, but food came first.

Behind the soddy, she rummaged through a stack of crates, selected one, and dusted it out with the hem of her apron. Back inside, she filled it with her meager supply of canned goods, reserving a can of peaches to serve with dinner. She eyed the rabbit and decided to put it on to simmer. After starting a fire, she filled her pot half full with water and the rabbit, and set it on the fire. She washed her hands then went to pack some more, all the while praying God would bless them with a claim as He had a horse.

"Mama, we're home."

Grabbing an empty can and a spoon, she spun toward the door and met her guys outside.

"Grandpa letted me steer the horse, and I made him stay on the trail."

"Good job, son. I'm proud of you. Hop on down because I have a job for you."

"Aww. . .do I haf'ta?"

"Do as your ma says." Grandpa lifted Michael halfway down and let go.

The boy dropped the rest of the way and fell partly under the horse.

Holding her breath, Lara rushed forward and pulled him back by his suspenders. The horse looked their way but never moved.

Grandpa dismounted, albeit a bit stiffly, and patted the horse's neck. "He's well trained and has a comfortable gait."

"We runned him." Michael grinned up at her.

Lara looked at Grandpa, lifting an eyebrow.

He smiled and shrugged. "The boy wanted to go fast, and so did I. What can I say?"

She shook her head. "Sometimes I think I'm raising three children."

"Nuh-uh. You only gots one. Me!"

"That's right, buddy." She scooped her son into her arms and gave him a loud smooch on the cheek.

He giggled, his eyes sparkling with delight.

"Now, how would you like to dig some worms so you and Grandpa can go fishin'?"

"Yippee! That's not work. That's fun."

She handed him the can and pointed to a shady spot with little grass. "Why don't you try over there? Grandpa and I need to talk."

Her son jogged over and plopped down. She hoped he'd stay happy with his task long enough for her to say all she needed to.

She walked over to where Grandpa was unsaddling the horse. "Where will we put him since we have no barn or paddock?"

"I'll hobble him in a nice patch of grass."

"I hate to tie him up like that—and do you think he'll be safe? Will we need to post a guard?"

"I don't think the good Lord would send us a horse and then allow him to get stolen by some miscreants. And besides, if anyone came near here at night, those goats of yours would sound the alarm."

"I suppose you're right."

He looked over the back of the horse at her. "What's on your mind?"

He could always tell when something bothered her. "It'll wait until you're done with the horse."

She checked on the stewing rabbit then walked over and sat on the end of the buckboard, keeping watch on Michael. After a few minutes, Grandpa joined her.

"What's turning that smile I love upside down?"

She shrugged one shoulder. "I don't know. But today, I saw that man again in Caldwell—Mr. Jones, the one who tried to get me to go to Kansas City with him—and he gave me the horse. He said it was Tom's, but I didn't believe it until I recognized the saddle."

Grandpa's head jerked her way. "It was Tom's?"

She nodded.

"No wonder I thought that saddle looked familiar. I didn't see the initials though. So, how did you come by it?"

"It came with the horse. Mr. Jones came up to me while I was talking to someone today and gave me the horse. He said it had been in the livery ever since Tom's death, and Mr. Jones wanted to be sure I got it."

"Seems like an awful nice fellow, this Mr. Jones."

"I don't know. He's not very tidy, and there's something about him that puts me on edge. I think he works for someone. Well, I know he does since he mentioned his boss wanting to meet me."

Grandpa chuckled. "Most folks do work for someone."

She bumped his arm. "You know what I mean. He said his boss had the money Tom left and wanted me to come and get it. Doesn't that seem odd? Why didn't he bring the money when he brought the horse if that was true?"

"I don't know, dear. Some folks do odd things. But I'm sure glad he brought the horse. It's a much finer one than Tom owned in the past."

"I thought the same thing."

"God works in mysterious ways."

"Yes, He does." Lara studied the small farm that had been their home for the last few years. "What are we going to do?"

"We'll load up and move out. And pray that God allows us to get a parcel of land. He knows our needs before we have them."

She wanted to ask if God saw their well-patched clothing and small stock of food, but that would be irreverent. Mildred stuck her head over the fence and bleated at Michael. "What are we going to do about the goats when we leave?"

"I don't reckon I could talk you into selling them."

She gasped and glared at him.

"I didn't think so. Sure would make traveling easier."

"That's true, but I'm not selling them. I already gave Lolly to Mr.

Hancock since we couldn't pay the rent we owed him."

"I'm sorry you had to do that. I wish I was able to work somewhere and better provide for you three."

"Please don't feel bad about that. Like you said, traveling will be easier with one less goat."

He nodded and slid off the end of the buckboard. "I need to see if that old halter I have will fit the gelding."

"Where should we go when we leave here? I couldn't find a place for us to rent, not with so many people surging into the area."

"I'll ride into town tomorrow and see what I can find out. There'll be talk about the run and the best places to go."

"I thought you rode through the area on your cattle drive days."

"I did, but the government is opening up millions of acres. That's a lot of land, and some places will be better for farmin' than others. Guess I'd better see to that horse."

"Supper should be ready in an hour. I need to cut up some carrots and potatoes and get them cooked."

He glanced down the trail. "When's Jo gonna be home?"

"I don't know. She stayed behind to say good-bye to her friends."

"She ought to be here helpin' you."

"That would be nice."

Michael jumped up and ran toward her, spoon waving in the air. "Ma! I named the horse."

"You did? What name did you choose?"

"Sunshine, 'cause he's kind of lellowy."

"He looks yellow to you?"

He nodded, curls bouncing.

"Sunshine is kind of a girly name for a male horse," Grandpa said.

Michael frowned, as if deep in thought.

She hated seeing him disappointed, but Sunshine did not fit

their big gelding very well. "What if we shorten the name to Sunny?"

Michael's lips lifted in a big smile. "Yeah. That's a good name."

She slid off the buckboard, glad that issue was settled so easily. If only the race for a homestead would be as simple.

Chapter 11

Lara, with Jo's help, shook out the last of their quilts and then folded it. She handed the bulky bedding to her sister. "Go ahead and put that with the others, and I'll do a final check of the soddy to make sure we didn't leave anything behind."

Jo nodded. "I still don't think it's fair that we have to move, especially on such short notice and with so many people crowding into town."

"We'd have to leave soon anyway to participate in the land rush." Grandpa backed the old mule up to the wagon and started harnessing it.

Michael leaned over the front of the wagon. "Can I drive?"

Grandpa chuckled. "I thought you wanted to ride on Sunny with Jo."

Lara walked toward the wagon, curious about his comment. "Why would we have to leave?"

"We need to move down to the border of Kansas and the Oklahoma Territory soon so that we can get a good spot to race from."

"How far is it from the border to the Unassigned Lands?" Jo leaned over the side of the wagon and set the quilt on the stack of other ones.

The harness jingled as Grandpa strapped it on the mule. "It's a fair piece. Nearly halfway across the state. I'm guessing somewheres between seventy-five and a hunnerd miles."

Jo let out a slow whistle. "Do you reckon Sunny has it in him to run that far?"

Grandpa paused, resting one arm on the mule's back. "I don't think he'll have to gallop all that way. Folks are fussing with the government, trying to talk the powers that be into allowing us racers from the north to cross the Cherokee Strip before the race begins."

"How wide is that?" Lara asked.

"Fifty or sixty miles, from what I've heard."

Lara joined Jo and leaned against the wagon. "Crossing that before the race could make all the difference in getting land or not getting it."

Grandpa nodded. "That's true. We all need to pray that they allow us to traverse it early."

Jo crossed her arms. "Why do we all need to go?"

"It's too far to come back, if I get land," Grandpa said. "We all need to be close to defend it from claim jumpers who might try to take it away, especially before we get the land registered."

Lara hated to voice the question running circles in her brain, but knew she had to. "And what if you don't get land? What will we do then? Surely there can't be enough for all the thousands of people surging into Caldwell."

Grandpa straightened and patted the mule. "Then we'll pray and ask God what we should do."

Lara returned to the soddy and searched the small home a final time to make sure they'd packed all of the belongings. They simply had to get land. If they did, they could build a wood home where snakes and critters didn't drop from the ceiling and they didn't get wet and muddy when thunderstorms raced through dropping buckets of rain in a short while. They could make some real beds and not have to sleep on the cold floor anymore. She walked to the door and glanced over to the tree where Sunny was tied. Jo struggled to lift Tom's heavy saddle onto the buckskin's back and finally succeeded. Why else would God have given them the horse, if not to ride in the race and win a claim? Having their own property—one hundred and sixty acres that no one could evict them from—was a dream come true. It would give Grandpa a place where he could raise horses again, and she could have as big a garden as she wanted. "Please, heavenly Father. Grant us favor."

Michael ran toward her. "Mama, Grandpa's wantin' to know if you're ready to go."

"Almost. I still need to see what I can harvest from the garden." She bent and picked up the bucket she'd left near the door for that purpose.

"Can I help?"

"You'd better make a trip to the privy first."

"Aww, I don't need to."

She lifted her brows and gave him a stern look.

He ducked his head and turned. "Yes, ma'am."

Smiling, she opened the gate and made her way through the garden. If only they could have stayed a few more months, they would have been able to harvest more than a few small carrots, beets, and onions, which barely covered the bottom of the bucket. At least they would help flavor tonight's soup. With the money she'd made from her final load of mending, she'd bought several potatoes, a one-pound bag of rice, and a small hunk of ham. Her mouth watered.

She closed the gate behind her for the final time. Mr. Hancock's son's family would be the one to enjoy the fruit of her labor.

With her bucket safely tucked into the rear of the wagon that held all of their belongings, she climbed onto the seat, next to her son. Grandpa released the brake and slapped the reins against the mule's back, and they were off—at a tedious pace. A fly whizzed past her ear, and she swatted her hand in the air. "Where are we going?"

"I scouted out a place south of here near where the Beaumont family used to live. There are some trees near a creek, and there weren't many people camped there yet. I figured if we traveled about four miles today and about the same the day after, we'll make it to the state border."

"What about food? Are there any places to purchase supplies?" Not that she had much money.

"I doubt it. But we've got a good supply of flour and cornmeal. Could be we can barter for whatever else we need."

As they reached the main trail, Grandpa turned right instead of going on the trail that led to Caldwell. He was the one member of her family to have ever traveled south of the town. "Can you tell me what it's like in the Oklahoma Territory? Will we encounter—" Lara glanced at her son then mouthed the word *Indians*?

Jo rode up closer to Lara's side, as if she, too, wanted to hear his response.

"Much of Oklahoma is grasslands situated on rolling hills. Some places have lots of trees and others are bald of them. It's a lot dryer in the southwestern part than the central and northern areas. As long as we get a place with a good water supply, we should do fine."

"Does it snow as much there as it does in Kansas?" Jo asked.

Grandpa shook his head. "I don't believe so, but I was never there during wintertime. Still, it's farther south, so my guess would be that we won't see as much."

"That would certainly be a blessing." Lara thought of how hard it was getting to town in cold weather. Snow made it impossible to venture very far. If they hadn't had the good fortune of smoking a deer and catching quite a few fish last year, they might not have made it through the bitter weather. The Oklahoma Territory certainly sounded like the Garden of Eden, but she'd learned the hard way to not get her hopes up. People had a way of exaggerating and making things sound better than they really were. She'd pray for land, but at the same time, she wouldn't allow her hopes to build. She couldn't afford another big disappointment.

Gabe rode past the last of the tents in the makeshift village on the outskirts of Caldwell and gave Tempest his head. The eager horse leaped forward, charging down the lane. Gabe enjoyed the feel of the cool morning air whipping at his face and clothing. There was little sign of last night's rainfall as the thirsty land had sucked up every last drop. The hard-packed dirt of the trail wasn't even muddy.

After a few minutes, he reined Tempest back to a walk. The turnoff to Lara Talbot's land was close, and he didn't want to miss it. The day he drove her home, he'd noted an odd redbud tree that had most likely been hit by lightning. The small tree had split, and though one part of it rested on the ground, it was still covered in fresh buds. It was a tribute to the determination needed to survive on the harsh but lovely prairie.

Gabe spied the tree, although instead of buds, tiny pink flowers now covered it. He reined Tempest down the narrow trail. The grass was crushed, revealing the tracks of a wagon that had recently passed this way.

As he came to the final bend before reaching Lara Talbot's soddy, he pulled Tempest to a stop and took a deep breath. He patted his coat pocket, knowing the stash of cash was still there. He wished he'd planned out what to say to her—how to explain the sack of gold coins he was giving her, but he'd never been able to come up with anything that he thought she'd believe—and he didn't want to lie to her. If he told her the coins belonged to her husband, she'd want to know how he ended up with them. And then he'd have to tell her that he killed her husband—and he didn't think he could do that. He didn't want to see hate in her eyes as she glared at him.

Perhaps this was a bad idea. Could he somehow leave the money without her knowing he'd come?

He shook his head and started to turn Tempest around when the chatter of voices stopped him. Had someone come in the wagon to visit Mrs. Talbot?

Curiosity compelled him to nudge his horse forward. As he rounded the bend, Gabe spied an older couple. The man was working on the front door while the woman watered the garden. Both straightened and turned his way as he rode toward the house. The man pushed his hat back on his forehead, eyeing Gabe, then walked toward him. Gabe guessed the overall-clad stranger was probably in his early fifties, and he seemed friendly. But where were Mrs. Talbot and her son?

"Howdy, mister. What can I do for you?"

Gabe smiled and dismounted, hoping to show he wasn't a threat. "I'm Gabe Coulter, and I'm looking for Mrs. Talbot. Is she home, by chance?"

The man pursed his lips and shook his head. "Herman Hancock." He held out his hand, and Gabe shook it. "They're gone." Mr. Hancock hung his head. "I sure hated turning them out, but our son and his family are arriving tomorrow, and they needed a place to live. Didn't seem right for our own young'uns to live in a tent when we had this nice soddy. Wish I had more than one, but I don't, and so I had no choice but to tell Mrs. Talbot they needed to leave."

Gabe gritted his teeth. As if her situation weren't bad enough, living in a dirt house. Where were Lara and her son now? It wasn't likely she'd find a better place to live, not with thousands of newcomers swarming the town. "Do you know where they went?"

Mr. Hancock took off his hat and scratched his head. "I heard tell that Mrs. Talbot registered for the land rush. I imagine they headed for the state border. It only makes sense with the date gettin' closer."

The woman ambled over and joined her husband. She shook her head. "What's this world comin' to when a woman rides in a race to get land? It just ain't right, I tell you."

"Desperation drives people to do things they wouldn't normally do, Maudie. It makes perfect sense to me that she'd want to own land that no one could evict her off of."

The woman harrumphed and turned to her husband. "I need you to fetch more water, Herman. Can't let those vegetables wither. Not with Gavin and the kids comin'."

In spite of his anger that Mr. Hancock had evicted Mrs. Talbot and her son, he nodded at the couple and mounted Tempest. He rode back the way he had come, trying to figure out what to do next. When he got to the turnoff to head back toward town, he studied the wagon tracks, leading away from Caldwell. Were they Lara's tracks? He didn't want her driving out of his life. He wasn't done helping her.

The thought of her and her young son heading for the border alone made his gut swirl. Tonight, they'd most likely be sleeping outside, possibly in a tent. With all the rain they'd had lately, her boy could take sick. And she was a pretty woman. What if some unsavory cad found her alone? There'd be no one to protect her.

He reined Tempest toward Caldwell and kicked the gelding's sides. He lunged forward like an eager racehorse and galloped toward town. Gabe had a lot to do. He needed to buy a tent and supplies. Tomorrow, another load of horses was scheduled to arrive. If he hired a cowboy to help, they could move the horses toward the border, where he could get top dollar for the coveted animals.

Plan decided, he enjoyed the rest of his ride. The only problem he could see in locating Lara and her son was if there were as many people at the border as there were in Caldwell. He had to find her. He wasn't ready to say good-bye to the pretty green-eyed widow.

Late in the afternoon, Jo finally found a reason to grin. As the wagon rolled into the creek, the goats, tied with ten-foot ropes to the back, pitched a conniption fit about getting wet. Goats may like a lot of things, but one thing they hated was water. They bleated louder than she'd ever heard and jerked at their tethers, but as the wagon rolled on, the furry trio was pulled into the water, and they had no choice.

Jo nudged Sunny into the creek, following the wagon Grandpa drove that had almost finished fording the creek. Water traveled up the rotating wheels, creating an interesting paddle-wheel effect— the most interesting thing on this trip so far. Well, except for the numerous young men who'd winked and smiled at her as they passed by.

She yawned, wishing she could curl up in the back of the wagon like Michael and take a nap. At first, her charming nephew had waved and hollered at her, but he'd soon grown bored and finally laid down at Lara's insistence.

Traveling wasn't as much fun as she'd expected, and they still had a ways to go to reach the Unassigned Lands. When she first heard about the land rush, it sounded like a big adventure, but each step the horse took, she ventured farther into untamed land. They had passed the last of the farmhouses an hour ago and were probably halfway to the border of Indian Territory.

Jo flipped her braid over her shoulder. Would they encounter any of the red-skinned natives? Did they still collect scalps? She shivered at the thought. Obviously, she hadn't fully considered what participating in the land rush meant. She had to leave Caldwell, the town where she'd mostly grown up and attended school. Leave Alma Lou and her other friends, and the stores she enjoyed walking through and dreaming of what she'd buy if she were rich. At least she had the hope of seeing charming Mark Hillborne again. She sighed. What a handsome man he was. And wealthy, from the look of his clothing.

If Grandpa was fortunate enough to get land and it wasn't too far from the Guthrie Station, perhaps she could get a job working in Mark's store. Wouldn't that be a delight! Rubbing elbows and spending all day in the presence of the comely man would be a dream come true. And to think, even though he was older than Lara, he thought she was pretty. She still found it hard to imagine that he knew what color best suited her—blue. It had always been her favorite, next to purple, but her sister rarely bought new fabric, and on the rare occasion she did, Lara purchased bland colors—to help hide soiled spots.

Jo tightened her knees and held on to the saddle horn as Sunny slogged out of the water and up the hill. Grandpa drove the wagon several yards ahead and stopped under a tall oak tree. Stomach grumbling, she nudged Sunny to a trot and hurried to join her family, glad it was finally time to set up camp and start supper.

As she hobbled the horse in a patch of fresh grass, she gazed back across the wide creek they'd just crossed. She'd never been this far south before. Part of her wanted to jump back on Sunny and ride for Caldwell, but another part was still excited about the race and the prospect of winning land. If they did, they could build a proper house, with wooden floors and a roof that didn't allow critters and mud to fall on them. And she could have a real bed to sleep in, possibly even a room of her own. Oh, how heavenly that would be.

"Hurry up, Jo. I'll need your help preparing supper."

"I have to unsaddle Sunny and groom him," she shouted back at her sister.

She loosened the cinch. "Jo, do this," she mumbled. "Jo, do that." Why did Lara have to hurt her hand? It just made more work for *her*.

Footsteps sounded behind her, and she spun, her heart pounding. She relaxed when she realized it was Grandpa, leading the mule, and not Lara. He had trouble hearing somewhat, so it was unlikely he'd heard her murmuring.

"Go on and help your sister. I'll tend to the animals."

"But I like working with them."

Grandpa lifted his hat and looked at her. Wrinkles creased his face, and his expression revealed a tired man. "Lara wouldn't ask you if she didn't need your help. It's not her fault that she hurt her hand. She bears a heavy burden for this family, and you should respect her more."

Jo's eyes widened. Grandpa rarely scolded her. She wanted to offer a rebuttal, but she knew he must be exhausted, and the last thing she wanted was for him to have another swamp fever attack and not be able to ride in the race. "Yes, sir."

As she moseyed toward their campsite, she dragged her feet. She loved her sister, but why did Lara have to be so bossy? If she'd been born first, she would have treated her younger sister more kindly.

Jo blew out a sigh. In all fairness, Lara was never unkind. She just worked all the time and didn't know how to relax. Even in the evenings when all the chores were done, dinner was over and the dishes washed, her sister would mend clothes until she ran out of daylight.

Jo hopped over a rut in the grass as she plotted how she would marry a wealthy man. Then she could hire a maid and no longer have to be an indentured servant with no deadline to her servitude.

Chapter 12

By the time Lara had Michael in bed for the night and put away all the supplies, several dozen tents had gone up around theirs. Campfires dotted the darkness. The soft buzz of conversation blended with the trill of tree frogs and the distant hum of a fiddle. With so many people crowding into the area, Grandpa had moved the animals closer to the wagon and plopped his mat alongside them to be nearby in case anyone decided to steal one of them. She'd argued that he should sleep in the tent and not outside in the cool night, but he said if anything happened to any of their animals, they'd be in trouble. And she couldn't argue with that.

Lara relaxed against a tree trunk. Her hands felt empty without the mending she normally tended to. She looked across to the camp next to them and saw Jo sitting beside Melinda, the daughter of Bill and Emma Jean Parker, whom they'd met earlier. Leave it to Jo to make friends so quickly. Lara envied her sister's easygoing manner. But then Jo didn't have the weight of the family on her shoulders. Grandpa being healthy again certainly helped soften her load, but his malaria could flare up at any time, putting him flat on his back again. She hoped he didn't have another attack until after they staked a claim.

She yawned and checked on Jo again, wishing she'd take her leave and come back so Lara could go to sleep. Morning would come far too quickly. Grandpa wanted them up by sunrise and rolling shortly after, in hopes that they could get a spot right on the border. The better their position at the start of the race, the more likely he was to get a claim.

She closed her eyes and imagined the perfect place for a home. A small bluff near a creek. A place with a view but also with fertile flatland for farming. Though the promoters of the land run promised millions of acres of good farmland, she'd heard cowboys in town saying that some places were too sandy for growing crops and other sections had no water source. They needed water to survive, for their animals and garden. They *had* to find a place with a creek or large pond. In the beginning, they'd probably have to build a soddy to live in, but she hoped that one day they could have a two-story clapboard house with lots of windows. But that dream was years away.

She'd never pictured Tom in the house of her dreams. That seemed odd now that she thought about it. Had she had a premonition that he would die—or was it simply because he so rarely came home? Jo, although too young, would have been a better match for her adventure-loving husband. Lara wasn't the best wife. Maybe if she'd tried harder to please him. . .

No, she couldn't travel down that path. She'd tried her best, but Tom had itchy feet.

Her brother had been the same. Jack was almost seventeen when their parents died. He'd taken their deaths hard, like Jo. Grandma and Grandpa had tried to help him through his pain, but when Grandma died suddenly after a cut became severely infected, less than a year after their parents' deaths, Jack left. He'd said he couldn't stand to watch someone else he loved die. Lara knew he'd always wanted to be a cowboy on a big ranch, and imagined that's where he was. They received a few sporadic letters from him the first few years but none in a very long while. He'd be twenty-eight by now. Was he even still alive?

She blew out a sigh. Was Gabe Coulter the same type of man? Did he also crave adventure? She couldn't remember him ever stating what kind of work he did, although it really was none of her business. Her stomach swirled at thoughts of the kindhearted dandy with the dark, twinkling eyes. It made no sense why he wanted to help her so much. Did he simply see her as needy? She glanced down at her worn dress—a castoff Mrs. Henry had given her several years ago. The brown striped fabric had faded to the color of dirty dishwater, and the cuffs and hem were ragged, but if she raised the hem any more, the length would be indecent. No wonder he found her lacking. She exhaled a loud breath. It hardly mattered. She would never see Gabriel Coulter again.

⁂

Late afternoon on their second day of travel, Lara guided the mule behind Grandpa, who rode Sunny, weaving the wagon through the tents that had already been pitched. As far as she could see in both directions, campsites, buckboards, covered wagons, and buggies littered the plains with horses, oxen, and mules grazing alongside. She wanted to camp on the outskirts of the massive tent city, but he insisted they needed to try to get as close to the border as possible.

An elderly woman smiled and waved, while a man she passed frowned at them. Finally, Grandpa motioned for her to stop in a tiny clearing.

She set the brake then stood and looked around as she rubbed the aching spot in the small of her back. If she hazarded a guess, she'd say there were more people here than still in and around Caldwell. How could the nearby creeks supply enough water for so many people?

Michael tugged on her skirt. "Can I get down, Mama?"

"Yes, but stay close." If he wandered off, finding him would be nearly impossible in such a mass of humanity.

Jo hopped off the end of the wagon and walked around to the side, reaching up for Michael. "C'mon, Shorty."

Grandpa tied Sunny to a sapling and looked around. "I hadn't counted on so many folks bein' here already." He scratched his head behind his ear. "The goats may be a problem. No place to pen them up, and they don't like bein' tied for long."

"What if they chew through the ropes?" Jo leaned against the wagon wheel.

"They didn't last night, so maybe we'll be okay for another night. They're most likely worn out from all the walkin'." He untied Bad Billy, led the goat to another small tree near the mule and tied him to it. "Good thing there's shrubs and grass here similar to what they're used to eatin'," he said as he untied the female goats. "We won't have to worry about them bloating."

Lara nodded. "That's good. One less thing to be concerned about." The makeshift fence they used for the goat pen back at the soddy had been packed into the wagon, serving as the sides that kept the crates from falling out. Once they settled somewhere for more than a night, they'd have to rebuild the pen. The goats certainly could be a noisy nuisance when traveling, but their milk was a blessing—if they gave any after their long trek.

Lara slowly climbed down, stiff after sitting on the hard bench seat for so long. With the land rush still a week away, at least they'd have time to work out their stiffness before moving on. At the rear of the wagon, she pulled the crate with her cooking utensils toward her then looked for her sister. "Jo, come and help me unload this, please. It's rather heavy."

Jo did as requested, but Lara could see the stiffness in her shoulders. Why did her sister resent helping so much? One day she'd have her own place and need to know how to cook and sew. And Lara did say please.

Together, they lifted the crate. "Let's put it over in that clearing. I'll start a fire with the wood I collected today," Lara said.

"I told Grandpa I'd groom Sunny."

Lara searched for Michael and found him lying across Mildred's back. She turned back to her sister. "I wondered if you might want to go find some water. I know we filled the barrel this morning, but with so many people around drawing from the same water source, I'd like to keep it full if we can."

Jo perked up. "I can do that after I groom Sunny."

Lara nodded. Her sister jumped at any opportunity to get away from home—or camp—and be around other people. Lara was happy at home and had never understood her sister's need to wander and visit. At least Jo could meander around while doing something useful.

"Howdy, neighbor."

She spun around to see a portly red-faced woman waddling toward her. Lara smiled and nodded. "Good day."

"It is at that. I'm thankful the weather isn't too cold for this time of year, because it can be."

"That's true. I'm Lara Talbot."

"A pleasure to meet ya. M'name's Betty Robinson. My brother Lester Biggs and his boy, Sam, are around here somewheres. Probably off jaw-jacking with some other fellows about the land rush.

Isn't it all so exciting?"

Lara smiled at the friendly woman with kind blue eyes. She figured the woman was probably in her fifties, judging by her partially grayed hair. "Yes, it is, although I wonder what will happen to those who don't get land. Surely there can't be enough for everyone."

"There's millions of acres. More than I can imagine. I reckon if some folks don't get land, they'll go back where they came from. We came from Nebraska, but before that we lived in Arkansas. How 'bout y'all?"

"We just traveled from Caldwell. Not anywhere near as far as you."

"We been here for a week now. There was some other folks camped where you are, but they gave up and went back where they came from. Said what you said—too many people to compete against. Course, they had family they could live with."

Lara peeked at Michael, who was sitting on the ground next to Grandpa, then refocused on her neighbor. "Seems a shame to come so far and not even try to get land."

"I know. I told Lester the same thing. Say, why don't y'all take supper with us tonight? I made a huge pot of duck stew."

Lara's stomach rumbled at the thought of fresh duck. It had been a long while since she had eaten any, but she didn't want to impose. "There's four of us, and that's too many for you to feed."

Betty swatted her hand in the air. "Oh, pshaw. I had planned to feed the Norman family, but since they left a few hours ago, I have far too much for just us and no way to preserve it out here. I've never been able to cut back after my Edward died and Lester's two daughters moved out. It would be a delight for me to have the comp'ny of another woman."

"If you're sure you don't mind, I'd enjoy your company, too.

Would you allow me to bring some corn bread?"

"No need to start a fire when I already have one. Y'all just come. Don't worry about bringin' nuthin'."

Lara nodded, thinking how nice it would be to eat a meal she didn't have to prepare, but she couldn't show up empty-handed. She mentally ran through her supply of canned goods. There were several cans of applesauce she could contribute. "Will you holler when you're ready for us to come over? We need to get our tent set up so that I can put my son to bed right after we eat."

"Will do. It was nice meetin' you."

Lara waved. "You, too."

Two hours later, Betty called for them to come to supper. With the tent pitched, bedding laid out, and the animals fed, Lara led the way to their neighbors' camp. The aroma of Betty's stew had been tormenting her for the past hour.

Betty looked up from her huge stew pot and smiled. "Howdy, neighbors. I'm mighty glad to have you join us for supper."

"Not as glad as we are to come," Grandpa said.

Betty's gaze roamed toward him, and her brows lifted. She straightened and patted her hair. "Now who's this handsome gent?"

Grandpa stood taller and smiled. "The name's Daniel Jensen. I'm Lara and Jo's grandpa and this little guy's great-grandfather." He patted Michael's head.

"I'm Michael." He pointed to Lara. "She's my ma."

Betty bent down and tousled Michael's hair. "Aren't you a fine young man? I sure wish I had curly hair like yours."

Lara tugged Jo forward. "This is my sister, Joline."

"Just call me Jo." She frowned at Lara.

"My men oughta be back anytime now. I sent them for water so's I could clean the dishes after we're done."

Lara held out the two cans of applesauce. "I brought these. I hope you can use them."

Betty's eyes lit up. "That's mighty kind of y'all. I haven't had applesauce since we finished off the last of the jars I canned this past fall."

"We're grateful to you for the invitation to supper." Grandpa smiled at Betty.

A shuffling sound drew Lara's attention to her left, where two men lumbered in, carrying buckets of water. Both men's gazes paused on Grandpa then flicked to her and then Jo. The younger man's mouth curved up on one side, at least she thought it did. With his thick beard, she wasn't sure. She guessed him to be in his mid-to-late twenties.

Betty hurried toward them. "Our guests are here. Put the water on the tailgate and wash up."

"We can see they's here." The older man ambled past Betty and set the buckets down.

Lara glanced at Jo, who rolled her eyes. If not for the offer of food, she was certain her sister wouldn't have come.

Sam dunked his hands in one of the buckets then splashed water on his face. He swiped his sleeve across his beard to dry it then turned toward them, his eyes staying focused on Lara.

Betty introduced them, and Mr. Biggs shook Grandpa's hand then nodded at her and Jo.

Michael bumped against her skirt and glanced up. "When're we eatin', Ma? I'm hungry."

Betty clapped her hands. "Supper's ready now, son. Lester, would you bless the food?"

Lester yanked off his hat and mumbled a quick prayer. Sam remained where he was, hat still on, and Lara could feel his gaze. If he stared at her the whole meal, it would surely be a long one.

Bowls of stew and biscuits were passed around, and everyone took a seat on the ground. Grandpa and Lester started talking about the land run. Sam took a seat near Lara, with Michael in between. Her son dunked his biscuit into the broth then took a bite.

Sam stared at her over his head. "Where's your man?"

"Sam! Don't be so rude." Betty waved her plump hand in front of her face.

Lara thought him ill-mannered, too, but she hoped it didn't show in her expression. She hadn't yet told Michael about his father, so she had to voice her response carefully and hoped he'd drop the subject. "I'm a widow."

Sam lifted one woolly eyebrow, giving her the impression the news pleased him.

"What part of Nebraska are you from?" she asked Betty.

The friendly woman launched into a long tale about their home in a small town south of Omaha and her deceased husband and how his two daughters had married and moved away. Betty talked so much that Sam didn't have a chance to ask Lara any more questions. His focus eventually turned to the men.

After dinner, Jo took Michael back to camp and put him to bed while Lara helped Betty with the dishes. She liked the woman, but her menfolk were sorely lacking in manners.

She thanked Betty for the fine meal and her company, while Grandpa said good night to Lester and Sam. As she turned to leave, Sam hurried over to her, and Lara's heart dropped to her stomach.

"Might'n I have a word with you, ma'am?"

She tried not to look annoyed, but she was tired after the long day. She nodded. "A brief word. I need to check on my son."

Grandpa looked over his shoulder but continued on. She wished he would have waited, but she knew he was giving Sam time alone with her. Time she didn't want.

Sam scratched his beard. "I aim to get me a section of land, so I can settle down on my own place. You don't got no man, and I'm huntin' a wife, so I think you and me oughta get hitched."

Chapter 13

Gabe listened covertly to two mounted soldiers while he watered a pair of horses he planned to sell.

"How many Boomers did they catch?" the dark-haired soldier asked.

"There was over thirty of 'em encamped along Turkey Creek near the Kingfisher Station with a dozen wagons and a passel of horses and cattle. They'd already made several dugouts, put up a paddock, and started on a cabin."

"They must have been there awhile."

"Yep. Looked that way. Some soldiers in Troop K happened across their wagon tracks and followed 'em." The blond soldier shook his head. "I don't know why folks can't follow the rules."

"So what happened to them all?"

"We escorted 'em back across the lines, took their names and photographs, and wrote down the sections they was in."

The dark-haired soldier allowed his horse to drink from the creek. "Will they get to ride in the run?"

The other man shrugged. "Don't know. If'n it was up to me they wouldn't."

Gabe shook his head and tugged on the reins, leading the horses back to his camp. Even though he'd made his living as a gambler, he had never cheated. He was good at reading people, and that's where he gained an advantage. It would be a simple thing for him to sneak through the wide area between soldiers and ride into the Unassigned Lands like those settlers had, but the fun—the challenge—of getting the land was competing in the race for it, especially against such a large number of people.

As he walked back, he scoured the crowd of Boomers, as the land rushers had been called by some newspapers. He'd searched for Lara Talbot since he arrived two days ago, but he hadn't yet located her. He couldn't explain the craving need to find her and make sure she was safe. Most of the folks in the crowd seemed nice, although many remained aloof, as if they expected you to steal the particular piece of land they wanted. His gaze landed on a trio of wagons whose owners had printed *Oklahoma or bust* on the canvas covers. He smiled at the sight, but the sign was true. Many people wouldn't get land, and it would be a bust for them. Where would Lara go if she failed? That hovel she called home already had others living there by now. Did she have someplace else to go if she didn't get land?

He gritted his teeth. Why couldn't he shake her from his mind? Her light green eyes haunted his dreams. She walked with a lantern in the dark, calling his name, and try as he might, he could never get to her. He'd even awakened one night in a sweat from his effort.

The tantalizing aroma of cooking bacon made him quicken his pace as he approached his campsite. Luke McNeil, the cowboy he'd hired to help with the horses, had proven to be an excellent cook. Too bad Luke had aspirations of his own to get land. Gabe would have liked to keep him on to work for him once he got land— and he had a gut feeling he would. Most times that gut feeling had proven true.

He secured the two horses to the picket line then walked over to Tempest and patted him. The gelding tended to get jealous when other horses were around if he didn't get enough attention. Gabe scratched the white diamond on Tempest's forehead then straightened his black forelock. "Too bad you can't eat bacon, boy. Sure smells great."

The horse nudged him in the chest, and Gabe chuckled. Tempest was the closest thing to a good friend that he'd had in as long as he could remember. The townsfolk didn't trust gamblers, and the people he was around in the saloon weren't exactly the types he'd care to spend his free time with or confide in. Yeah, he'd joke with some of the regulars, but he wouldn't turn his back on any of them.

He sighed. After ten years of working in a noisy, crowded saloon, he found it odd to discover he was lonely. Gabe patted Tempest's neck. "How about we go for a ride after breakfast?"

The horse nodded his head as if agreeing, and Gabe turned back to the campfire, where Luke was dishing up their breakfast.

"My belly's gnawing on my backbone. I'm sure glad you can cook like you do." Gabe eagerly accepted the plate Luke held out.

Luke set the cast-iron skillet on a stone beside the fire and stood, holding his own plate. "My ma was sickly a lot when I was younger. If I hadn't cooked, we wouldn't have eaten."

"How is she now?" Gabe bit off half a piece of bacon, enjoying the salty flavor.

Luke shook his head. "She died when I was seventeen."

"Sorry. What about your pa?"

His cook frowned. "Never knew him, and Ma didn't talk about him much, other than to say he got a cravin' to strike it rich and went off to Alaska. I've always imagined he probably died there."

Gabe knew it was easier for Luke to believe that than to think his father had abandoned his family. Gabe's real father was thrown from a mustang and broke his neck when Gabe was five. Maybe his pa hadn't willingly abandoned them, but it had the same effect and opened the door for Elliott Jarvis to marry his ma, eight months later. Elliott had never been kind and loving like his real pa, but life hadn't been too bad until the day Gabe's younger brother died.

Life changed for him that day. Ma never recovered from Stephen's death, and Elliott never stopped blaming Gabe.

Wincing, he stroked one shoulder. If only he could rub away the memory of the leather strap crashing down on it. For a time, he felt he deserved the beatings for contracting the measles at school and bringing them home, where Stephen caught them. But Elliott had rattled off a litany of Gabe's misdeeds, from forgetting to milk the cow, to not chopping enough firewood, to neglecting to shut the privy door. The smallest oversight could bring a whipping.

Gabe stared at his half-empty plate, having lost his appetite. After a few moments, he forced himself to finish. Food was too precious to waste when traveling.

While Luke cleaned up the breakfast dishes, Gabe, needing a distraction from his morose thoughts, pulled out the *Homesteader's Handbook* and studied it. All of the land available for settlement had been divided into townships, with each of those divided into thirty-six sections, which were each one square mile. Those sections were divided into four quarter sections, each one numbered, so that every claim would have its own number. When a man registered his land, he had to give the agent the location number. Gabe had to admit the whole system of mapping out the land as it had been was rather ingenious.

"Are you aiming for a certain piece of land, Luke?"

The young cowboy's eyes lit up. "I've heard talk that Guthrie may be the capital if Oklahoma ever gains statehood, so I'm of a mind to ride southeast toward there. Kingfisher and the Oklahoma Station are both planned town sites, but most of the talk seems to be focusing on the Guthrie Station."

"Yeah, that's what I've heard, too. Makes me wonder if it might be better to head for one of the other town sites."

Luke shook his head. "The Oklahoma Station is too far south. All them folks on the southern border of the Unassigned Lands will have more of an advantage. If you want land there, you'd better ride farther south before the race starts."

He wouldn't, of course, because Lara Talbot was here somewhere. He also needed to talk to some of the soldiers and find out what they knew about the town sites. For certain, he wanted to be fairly close to one of them. It would make getting supplies easier and save time traveling back and forth.

"You the man with the horses for sale?"

Gabe looked up from the handbook. Two tall cowboys stood just outside his camp area. He stood. "Yep. Got a string of four fine geldings and three mares. All saddle broke."

"How much you want for 'em?" The older of the two asked.

"Depends on the horse." Gabe motioned his hand, indicating for the men to go ahead of him. Something about them didn't sit right with him, so he didn't plan to turn his back on them.

The men split apart, the older man headed toward Tempest, while the other aimed for the middle of his picket line. Gabe glanced back to get Luke's attention, but the youth had his back to him. "That black gelding isn't for sale. He's my horse."

"Too bad. He's a fine animal."

"Yep. The others are sound horses, too. Most of them are around four years old."

The younger man had proceeded down the line to the far end,

bent, and lifted the hoof of the dun mare. Gabe stood back watching, hoping his gut was wrong about the scruffy duo.

The tall man walked around behind Tempest, keeping his hand on the gelding's rump. Then he turned to face the next horse in line, a gray gelding.

"How much for this mare?" the guy on the end asked. "She looks sound."

"They're all sound." Gabe walked toward him. "That horse is one hundred dollars."

"A hunnerd dollars?"

Gabe shrugged. "Horses are in high demand right now. In fact, I've heard some people are renting them for fifty dollars a day, so I figure you're getting a good deal."

Tempest snorted. Gabe turned to see what the problem was and saw the tall man jump up and slide his leg over the gelding's back. "Hey! I told you he's not for sale."

The man lashed Tempest with the lead rope that had been unhooked from the picket line. The horse pranced sideways, reared, and then trotted away as the man kept kicking him.

Luke jumped up. "What's wrong, boss?"

Gabe broke into a run then suddenly halted and turned back. The shorter man had mounted the mare and was riding off in the other direction. Gabe stuck two fingers in his mouth and whistled. Tempest halted suddenly, sending his rider flying over his head.

"Get that man and take him to the soldiers while I go after the mare."

Luke broke into a run, dodging campers and their wagons as he raced toward the thief. Gabe snatched Tempest's bridle off the tree where Luke had hung it, while the horse trotted back to him. In half a minute, he had the bridle on and was mounted, following the other thief. He hated to leave the other horses unprotected, but he couldn't allow that man to get away with the mare.

He trotted Tempest, weaving around wagons, people, and all their goods, while keeping his eye on the man riding the mare. The dun stopped suddenly as it reached a line of wagons, and the man reined it sharply to the left, giving Gabe a few seconds to close the gap. The man spied him and kicked the mare. She reared then trotted forward. No tame horse would run with so many obstacles in its way.

Gabe narrowed the distance as the man turned again. The river wasn't far away, and if he got across, Gabe might lose him. He reined Tempest to the south and nudged his horse to a fast walk. Suddenly, a small boy ran out in front of him.

A woman screamed. "Michael!"

Gabe pulled hard on the reins.

Heedless of the danger, the woman charged forward and grabbed the child. She turned away from him and hunched over the boy, as if expecting to be run down. But Tempest had stopped in time.

After a long few seconds, while Gabe's heart pounded, she looked over her shoulders. A pair of wide green eyes made his heart jolt.

"Lara!"

Lara stared up at Gabriel Coulter—at least she thought it was him. He was wearing more casual clothes than the other times she'd seen him, and he'd shaved off his mustache.

He smiled and tipped his hat, his intriguingly dark eyes gleaming. "Fancy seeing you here. I'd love to talk, but I'm chasing after a man who stole my horse. I'll return later, and we'll chat then."

And he was gone, weaving his horse through the crowd, toward the state line.

She still hugged her son, and she wasn't sure if her heart was throbbing because of the close call or the fact that she'd seen Gabe again. She watched him ride off, sitting tall in the saddle. This cowboy look was far more becoming on him than the dandy style.

Michael wiggled, and she released him.

"Why did you run off like that?"

"I was following a kitty."

She blew out a breath, hoping for patience. "Sweetie, you can't run away like that. Not with all these people here. What if you had gotten lost? We might never have found you."

"But I wanted to pet the kitty." A pair of innocent, blue-green eyes stared up at her. He clearly had no idea of the danger of wandering off. She'd just have to keep a closer watch on him.

"Let's go back to camp."

"But the kitty. . ."

She stroked his hair as she searched for the cat. "It's gone now, and we have work to do."

She made a mental list of what she needed to accomplish today. Feed and milk the goats. Wash some clothing. Scrape together something for them to eat. Maybe she could barter some goat's milk for a hunk of meat to make soup with.

As they walked into camp, she noticed Grandpa had dug out his wrinkled shirt with the GAR patch on the sleeve and was wearing it. She didn't know much about the Grand Army of the Republic organization, other than it was a group for Union war veterans. She smiled. "You found your old shirt."

He nodded and rubbed his hand down the front of it. "I ran into Jess Filbert, from my old troop, and he had his on. Lots of veterans are here, hoping to get land to leave to their families when they're gone."

She winced, hating to think about life without him. But she was fortunate he was still here, considering the struggles he faced whenever a malaria attack hit him. All she could do was help ease his daily workload and pray that God wouldn't take him home for a long while.

"A group of us are gettin' together after supper to catch up on things."

"That sounds like a nice evening." She glanced around camp. "Where's Jo?"

"She and that friend of hers went for a walk."

Lara pursed her lips. Leave it to Jo to disappear when there was so much to do. "Do you know when she'll be back?"

"Lunchtime, I reckon." He winked at her. "You know how that girl loves to eat."

"And hates to work."

He chuckled. "Speaking of work, I already fed and milked the goats. What do you want to do with the milk?"

At the mention of the goats, Michael tugged a weed loose from its roots and trotted over and held it out to Mildred.

"Let's pour one bucket into the milk can and see if we can trade the other for a piece of meat."

"You want me to check with the Biggses? See if they're interested in barterin'?"

"That would be nice. I need to take some clothes to the river and wash them." Maybe she'd see Gabe there. She hoped he found his horse. "I heard a man had one of his horses stolen this morning."

Grandpa's eyes shot to hers. "Sad thing when folks steal from one another, but I reckon we'd better keep a closer watch on Sunny and them goats."

"The goats? Why?"

He lifted a brow. "There's lots of folks here, and fresh meat is hard to come by."

She gasped. "I can't even think about that."

"All the same, we need to keep a close watch on all that's ours. I don't plan to be gone long tonight. Don't want to leave you girls alone too long."

"We need to get Jo to stick around more. I don't like her wandering off with so many unmarried men around. I know many are trustworthy, but the theft proves there are others who aren't."

He nodded. "Desperate times make folks do things they normally wouldn't."

"I'm glad we're so close to the border and near the soldiers. They may be a deterrent."

"That's true, but we still need to be cautious."

"All right. So will you stay here while I go to the river and do laundry?"

"Yep. I'll head over to the Biggses' camp now while the milk is fresh."

"Good idea. I'll gather the laundry. While I'm gone, could you please string a line to hang the clothes on? I'll need to do that when I return."

"Soon as I get back, I will."

Lara glanced at Michael, who was making a circle of pebbles, then she walked over to the back of the wagon and tugged the wicker basket of dirty clothes toward her. She dreaded hanging up her and Jo's unmentionables where so many people could see them, but everyone else was doing it, too. Heat warmed her cheeks at the thought of Gabe Coulter seeing them. Maybe she could hang their drawers and chemises under their dresses and petticoats. She smiled. There was a solution to every problem.

Gabe reached the border and reined Tempest to a halt. He'd lost track of the thief when he nearly ran down Lara Talbot. He gritted his teeth, hating the thought of losing his horse to a trickster. He could ford the river and hunt for the man, but then soldiers might think he was a Sooner. He couldn't afford to get arrested and miss the run. Better to just count the one horse as lost. He did get Tempest back, and they'd caught the man who'd tried to take him—at least he hoped Luke had managed that task. He patted the gelding's neck then loosened the reins so he could get a drink.

A commotion to his left, just across the river, snagged his attention. A pair of soldiers was wrestling with a man on the ground. If he wasn't mistaken, that was *his* horse grazing not far from them. He tapped his heels to Tempest's side, walking the horse along the line of the river to a group of soldiers on the near side who were watching the wrestling trio. Gabe dismounted and approached a corporal. "Excuse me, sir."

The man turned and lifted one brow. "Can I help you?"

"That man stole one of my horses." He nudged his chin toward the mare. "That dun grazing over there is the one he took. He crossed the river, trying to get away from me."

"You got a bill of sale?"

Gabe nodded. "Back at my camp."

The men eyed him for a moment, as if taking his measure, then faced the river again. "I don't guess we'll need it. You look like a man whose word is good."

Gabe straightened, savoring the rare compliment. Most folks didn't believe a gambler's word was worth much, but the soldier had no idea what his trade was. Feeling respected made Gabe stand a bit taller. It was something he could easily get used to.

"If you can hang around for a bit, I'll see that you get your horse back."

"Thanks. I appreciate that."

An hour later, Gabe walked into camp with both horses.

Luke looked up from where he was grooming one of the geldings and smiled. "You got her. I didn't know what to think with you gone so long."

He dismounted and patted Tempest's neck. "The soldiers stopped the thief after he crossed the river. Guess they thought he was trying to sneak over to stake a claim."

Luke chuckled. "I bet them soldiers was surprised to find out he was a horse thief."

"That's true. I told a corporal what happened. They questioned the thief, and when they threatened him with hanging, he spewed out a tale about the other man forcing him to help him steal the horses. Did you get that tall fellow to the soldiers?"

"Yep. He was a bit dazed after that fall he took off yer horse. Followed along like a docile ole dog."

Gabe grinned at the image. "Things been all right here while I was gone?"

"Yep, quiet as a saloon at noontime."

He liked the young cowboy with his quirky comments. "I need to tend to some business. Can you groom this mare after you're done with that gelding?"

"Sure thang, boss. Want me to give her a little extra feed?"

"Good idea. Keep a close watch on the horses."

"I will. Got my gun loaded and a rifle leaning against that tree that's nearest the horses."

"Good." Gabe mounted Tempest again and reined him in the

direction where he had last seen Lara. He hadn't thought to ask if her camp was near there, but a boy so small couldn't have run too far without her catching him. His stomach swirled at the thought of seeing her again. He didn't even know what he would say—only that he wanted to talk with her. Be near her.

He blew out a breath and reined in his thoughts. He needed to be careful. Lara Talbot was a new widow—and he was the man who'd made her one. That was the last thing he wanted her to discover, although keeping the truth from her didn't sit well with him. But if she knew he was the one who shot her husband, she'd want nothing to do with him. She needed to get to know him first—see that he was an honorable man—then he would tell her. Or maybe they'd end up going their separate ways and she'd never need to know.

His gaze roamed the various campsites as he searched for her. Finding anyone in this menagerie was nigh on impossible, but he was determined. He wove in and out of the campsites for nearly an hour, and then his heart thudded. A woman with golden hair bent over and kissed a small boy with lighter hair. When she straightened, he knew he'd succeeded in his mission. As if she sensed him, she turned his direction, and when she spotted him, she waved. A gentle smile lifted her pink lips.

He dismounted and strode forward, his heart pounding as if he'd run a long race. He couldn't remember the last time he'd ever been so excited to visit a woman—if he ever had.

"Good afternoon, Mr. Coulter." Lara walked toward him, holding the boy's hand.

"It's Gabe, remember?" He sent her a smile that matched the giddiness he felt on the inside. His gaze lowered to her son. "And who is this handsome young man?"

"This is my son."

"I'm Michael." The boy eyed Gabe seriously.

Wanting to make friends with the child, he squatted and held out his hand. "Mighty happy to meet you, Michael."

After staring at Gabe's hand and taking a quick peek up at his mother, the boy laid his small hand inside Gabe's. His closed around it, and he gave it a gentle shake, as an overwhelming desire to protect the youngster and his mother washed over him like a flash flood. He stood, a bit stunned at the sensation.

"Are you all right?" Lara took a step closer, lifted one hand but then dropped it to her side.

Gabe smiled, hoping to set her at ease. "Most certainly, I am. How could I not be in your lovely presence?"

A bright red tinged her cheeks, and she brushed her hand across the stained apron covering her worn dress. He'd encountered few people whose clothing was so shabby. Too bad he hadn't thought to give her some fabric with his last gift to her.

"So, did you find your horse?"

"I did. I feared I'd lost her at first, but the soldiers had captured the thief as he tried to cross the river."

"I'm glad you got her back."

"Thanks." He felt a tug on his pants and looked down. A pair of blue-green eyes stared up at him.

"Can I sit on your horse?"

"Michael. It's not polite to ask that of people you don't know."

"But you know 'im, don'tcha?"

Gabe's gaze locked on Lara's, and he lifted a brow, sending her a cocky smirk that dared her to deny her son's comment.

"Well, yes, but you don't."

"I don't mind. And you don't have to be concerned. Tempest is a well-trained horse, and I'll keep hold of the reins. So, can he?"

She lifted a skeptical brow. Her lips twitched as if she tried to keep from smiling. "He didn't seem well trained that day at the depot."

"He'd just come off a long train ride, which he didn't particularly like, and he got spooked. Normally, he's a calm horse."

Michael's hopeful gaze swiveled to his mother.

"I suppose it won't hurt to let him sit on the horse. He does love them."

She turned for her son, but Gabe latched onto him first and hoisted the featherlight youngster into the saddle. The urchin was as thin as some on the streets of Kansas City that he had frequently helped. If only there was some way he could help Lara more.

His heart ached as he surveyed her camp. The rickety buckboard wasn't likely to hold together if she used it for the race, but then why would she when she had her husband's horse? A frayed tent sagged against one side of the wagon. He glanced back at the boy, smiling wide as he bounced in the saddle. What would she do with him while she rode in the land run?

"Was there a reason you needed to see me, Mr.—"

"Who?" He captured her gaze and sent a knowing stare that made her squirm. Why was she uncomfortable voicing his name?

"Oh, all right—Gabe." She waggled her brows as if asking if he was happy. "Why did you want to see me?"

He scrambled for a legitimate reason to be in her company and yanked the *Homesteader's Handbook* from his back pocket, holding it out to her. *Because I missed you? Missed looking on your lovely face and seeing that brave set to your shoulders?* "I. . .uh. . . I wondered if you'd seen this."

She took it and shook her head. "No, I haven't. What is it?"

"A guide to homesteading, among other things."

"Oh?" Her interest was obvious. "What does it say?"

"Shall we have a seat, and I'll show you?"

She cast an apprehensive glance around her campsite then to his trousers. "I'm afraid there is little to sit on but the ground."

"I've never been afraid of a little dirt. I wouldn't be in the horse business if I were."

"If you're certain."

"I am." He turned back to Tempest. "Time to get off, son."

"Aw. . .do I hav'ta?"

"Michael, Mr. Coulter has been nice to allow you to sit on his horse. Please get down now, and don't whine."

Gabe passionately felt the child's disappointment. It was a familiar feeling when he'd been growing up. "Don't worry, Michael. Next time I see you, you can sit on Tempest again."

The boy's eyes brightened as he reached for Gabe. "Promise?"

"Yep." Gabe reached into his pocket and pulled out a slightly cracked peppermint stick. He'd been fond of them ever since he'd eaten his first one the day his ma was buried. Mr. Oldham, owner of the general store had given it to him—the only high point in a very low day.

"Oh boy! Can I have it, Ma?"

Gabe hadn't even considered asking her first. He'd been handing them out to the street children for so long that he didn't give it a second thought. He glanced at her, and she nodded.

Michael took his treat and scooted under the wagon, where he twisted off the paper wrapper and stuck the candy in his mouth.

"That was nice of you."

He shrugged. "I like to make children happy."

She glanced at him, as if she'd made an interesting discovery. "And why is that?"

"Maybe because my own childhood wasn't that grand," he blurted out before he stopped to think how revealing his statement was.

"I'm sorry. I wish all children could live happily, but we both know that doesn't always happen."

"Not half as often as it should," he mumbled.

Chapter 14

Lara tried not to stare at Gabe. Her heart ached to learn his childhood hadn't been a good one, but he'd turned out to be a kind, honorable man. That was something he could be proud of.

He opened the *Homesteader's Handbook*, evidently ready to put aside talk of his past. She watched as he quickly thumbed through the pages and told her what they meant. When he turned to the pages of land plots, her eyes widened. "You mean the whole area has been divided into sections and numbered? All of them?"

He nodded. "Pretty amazing, isn't it?"

She couldn't fathom the time and effort it must have taken to map out two million acres.

"I'm hoping to get land somewhere near the Guthrie Station. I've heard tell it will be the capital when Oklahoma becomes a state."

Hadn't Grandpa said the same thing? "Do you think it will? What about the Indian Territory? Seems like there'd be a lot of folks who wouldn't want it to be part of the country."

"I don't think the objectors have a choice. Oklahoma and Indian Territory are smack-dab in the middle of the United States. How could it not eventually gain statehood?"

He scooted over to show her something in tiny writing, and her heart thudded as his shoulder pressed against hers. He was a bigger

GABRIEL'S ATONEMENT

man than Tom, probably well over six feet tall, and his shoulders were wide enough to bear all of her troubles, not that she would let them. She slid a bit to her left, and he followed as he continued babbling on about the land run.

A part of her wished she'd never heard of Harrison's Hoss Race. That she were still back on their one-acre piece of land, living in the sagging soddy.

He nudged her shoulder. "Hey there, what's wrong? You've gone quiet on me."

She turned, looking into eyes so dark they could belong to an Indian or Mexican, but the color of his lightly sun-touched skin held no hint of either culture. "I guess I was thinking."

"About the land run?"

She nodded. "I don't like the uncertainty of it. So many of these good people will be disappointed. There can't possibly be enough land for all of them."

"Probably not."

"I don't know what will happen to us if we don't get a claim."

He stared at her, as if he wanted to say something, but then looked at the booklet again. "We'll just have to make sure you do."

She warmed at the way he said *we'll*, as if they were together in this quest. She couldn't let her hopes rise that something could grow between them. After all, she was a new widow and shouldn't even be talking to a man she barely knew, much less allowing him into her dreams. And he *had* ridden into them, bold as can be, much to her angst.

"These lots here, sections sixteen and thirty-four of each township, have been reserved for schools that will be built later, so we need to know where they are and make sure we don't claim one of those sections."

"But how? Will they be labeled or have a flag or something to indicate they're school lands?"

He gazed at her and blinked his long lashes. "This book shows where they are."

"Looking at a map is not the same as open country." She sighed and glanced at Michael, who'd fallen asleep, the partially eaten candy still in his hand.

"Stay close to me when the race starts, and I'll see that you get land."

He didn't know she wouldn't be the one to ride, but then she'd never told him about her family. For some reason, she wasn't ready to share that information with him. Maybe if he knew about them, he'd no longer want to help her—not that she wanted his help—but she enjoyed his company. No man had made her feel cared for other than Grandpa in a long time, and she rather enjoyed that element of their relationship. She frowned. Was she taking advantage of him to want even that much, when she was supposedly a widow in mourning?

"Would you like me to leave this here so you can read over it tonight? I could come by and pick it up on the morrow."

"That would be nice. I'd like to read through it so I'll know all of the rules." Grandpa would like to see it, too. How come he hadn't known about the handbook?

Gabe rose and held out his hand to her. "I have an appointment to talk with a man about buying one of my horses, so I need to go."

She allowed him to help her up, enjoying the feel of his strong warm palm next to hers. He was always the gentleman, unlike Tom. She stood a few feet from Gabe and realized she didn't want him to leave, but he needed to. Grandpa would be back soon, and who knew when Jo would. . .

He rolled up the handbook and held it out to her. "See you tomorrow?"

She smiled and nodded, knowing she'd be counting the hours.

He mounted his fine horse, tipped his hat, and winked at her. A blush warmed her cheeks, and she waved, enamored like a schoolgirl. She watched him ride away, peeked at Michael, then turned to start supper. Another man strode into her camp—a scowling man she'd never seen before.

"Can I help you?"

He strode a few feet from her and stopped, his gaze shifting from hers to behind her where Gabe had been.

"Let me give you fair warning about that gambler."

"What?" She didn't know any gamblers, other than Tom. But how could this man possibly associate her with him? "Who are you talking about?"

"Gabe Coulter. You'd best stay away from the charming snake."

Lara lifted her hand to her throat. "What did he do to you?"

"Not me, my brother. He stole his hard-earned money when my brother gambled at his table. The loss cost my brother his family— and me, my brother. He's not a man who can be trusted."

Just that fast, the stranger stormed off.

Lara swallowed the egg-sized lump in her throat. Gabe was a gambler? A man who lured unsuspecting cowboys, like Tom, to his table in hopes of stealing their wages?

Could the stranger be mistaken? Who was he? And why should she believe him? She shook her head. His enmity was too real. He must be speaking the truth. Lara fell back against the side of the wagon and stared at the book in her hand—Gabe's book. She remembered the day she first bumped into him as he exited the hotel, dressed in his dark suit, his skin fairer than it was today. She'd thought him a suave businessman, but maybe she was wrong.

How could she have fallen for another untrustworthy man?

⁓

Half an hour after Gabe left, Grandpa rode Sunny into camp. He dismounted, tended to the horse, then hurried toward her, smiling. "I got some news."

Lara stirred the soup then straightened and rubbed a kink in her lower back. "Good news, I hope."

He nodded. "The soldiers are gonna let us move up to the northern border of the Unassigned Lands so that we'll be on the starting line of the race on the twenty-second."

Lara smiled. "That *is* good news." She'd wondered how they would have any chance at getting land when they first had to cross the sixty-seven-mile-wide strip of land that paralleled the Kansas border before they even reached the beginning of the Unassigned Lands. "So when do we cross the Cherokee Outlet?"

"Day after tomorrow."

A loud roll of thunder rattled the sky, as if displeased with the news. Lara looked up, as did Grandpa. Rain would only make things harder for them.

"I hope we don't get much rain tonight. If the river swells, it will make crossing more difficult." Grandpa leaned over the soup pot and sniffed. "Smells good."

Lara smiled, knowing it smelled the same as it did most nights. If only she had a piece of beef or chicken to add to the pot, but no one had any to spare. At least Grandpa had caught a turtle earlier. Although not her favorite meat, it did make the weak soup a bit hardier.

"Grandpa! You're back."

She turned to see Michael crawling out from under the wagon. Quickly, she grabbed a rag and dipped it in the bucket then carried it to her son and relieved him of the stickiness on his fingers, as well as what was left of the peppermint candy.

"I wasn't done with that." Michael's lower lip pooched out.

"You may have some more tomorrow, but you've had enough for now. Supper will be ready soon."

"Me and the boy will walk to the river and get some water for the goats."

"All right. Have you seen Jo?"

He shook his head and grabbed two buckets, and then he and Michael left camp.

Lara looked around. She'd only unpacked the things she needed most, but packing would still take a bit of time. She dreaded moving out of Kansas but was excited over the fact that she was leaving the state for the first time. Would they find a new home in the Oklahoma Territory?

God alone knew.

❪

Jo smiled at the trio of cowboys that surrounded her and her new friend, Melinda. She'd hated leaving Caldwell, but she never expected she would meet so many interesting people while traveling.

"Did you really fight Indians?" Melinda batted her eyes at Pete, the most handsome of the three Texans.

"Yep. Some Apaches snuck across the Red River into Texas and tried to steal some of the boss's cattle. We couldn't let them get away with the beasts, so we shot at the Injuns and they shot back."

"Was anyone hurt? Did you kill any of the savages?"

Jo nearly rolled her eyes at Melinda's fascination with Indians.

Most of the Indians she'd seen were the peaceful type, who only wanted to survive and be left alone. She'd even read about some Indians who were part of the Civilized Tribes who were doctors and lawyers. She and Lara had traded milk with a family who were part Cherokee for small game more than once. "So, why are ya'll in Kansas? Seems like you'd start the run on the southern border."

Rafe, the tallest and thinnest of the group, pushed his hat up on his forehead. "Came up here to deliver several dozen horses and are headed back. Thought we'd give the run a try and see if we could get land of our own. If not, we'll keep on going back to Texas."

"What a brilliant idea." Melinda clapped her hands.

Jo liked the girl, who was the same age as she, but she was learning that Melinda could be annoying and immature.

Buck, the most homely of the three, stepped closer to Jo and smiled, revealing wide front teeth that stuck out too far—probably how he came by his name. "Yer about the prettiest thing I ever did see with all that golden hair and them eyes as blue as the sky."

Jo tried not to show the repulsion she felt. She might talk to cowboys, but she'd never let one get close. She had lofty plans for her life that didn't include a smelly husband who lived in a crumbling shack. She wanted a pretty house with shiny wood floors, all the food she could eat, and a handsome husband with deep pockets, and if she had to use the beauty God had blessed her with to get it, she would.

She turned to Melinda. "It's nearly suppertime. I need to get back to camp."

Buck sidled up to her again, his elbow stuck out like a broken wing. "I'd be happy to escort you, ma'am."

Jo shook her head. "That isn't necessary."

The man's congenial expression darkened. "What's the matter?

Am I not good lookin' enough for yer hoity-toity ways?"

Jo blinked, surprised by his swift change. "No, it's just that I don't want my pa seeing me with men he doesn't know. He's a sure shot and doesn't like fellows following me around."

Rafe nudged Buck in the arm. "C'mon. You don't want to mess with a hair-trigger pa and get shot before you even get a chance to own your own land."

Pete nodded his agreement, but Buck still frowned. Jo tried to soften the tension. "Perhaps I could tell him about you, and maybe tomorrow you could meet him rather than taking him by surprise this evening."

Buck's shoulders lowered as if he'd relaxed. "That sounds like a fine idea." He took her hand, bent, and slobbered a kiss on the back of it.

Jo struggled not to shudder, and forced a smile. She waved, trying to ignore the glistening spot on the back of her hand. "Until tomorrow."

Melinda took her arm and hurried her away from the cowboys. "I thought you said your pa was dead."

Stomach curdling, Jo wiped her hand on her skirt. "He is, but that was all I could think of to get rid of him."

Chuckling, Melinda shook her head. "You're a sharp one, Joline Jensen. I'd have never thought to lie my way out of such a situation. I probably would have fainted if he had'a kissed me."

"Well, that's the only time he will ever kiss me." Her stomach rolled, and she pressed her palm against it.

"What about tomorrow? What will you do then?"

"He'll never find our camp in all this disarray, and I plan to stick close to home tomorrow."

"I hope you're right, because you'll have a hard time explaining that you don't have a father."

"Maybe I could pass off my grandpa as him, but then he'd never go along. And Lara would be livid if I brought a man back with me."

They wove around campsites, tents, wagons, and staked-out horses and cattle. Most people nodded a greeting, but some didn't even look their way. Jo wondered what she was doing in such a place. She was meant for something better, she could feel it in her bones. She was meant for silk not shabby calico. For diamonds not dust. She just knew it.

Suddenly someone stepped into her path, and she bumped into a solid chest.

The man grabbed her arms, steadying her, and she looked up. A pair of intriguing blue eyes stared back at her from a relatively handsome face. His lips turned up to create a cocky smile. "Well, well, what do we have here?"

"We have nothing. Please unhand me, sir." Tired of pushy men, Jo flipped back her head and stared the man in the eye.

"What if I don't want to unhand you?"

"What if I decide to scream?" She lifted an eyebrow. "There are plenty of people around who will rush to my aid."

The man chuckled. "Maybe. Maybe not. They're all busy with their own business."

"C'mon, Jo, we need to go." Melinda's voice trembled, revealing her anxiety.

The man's eyes flicked toward Melinda with a show of disinterest, then back to Jo. "Why don't you stay and spend some time with me? We could have a good time, and I got a big fat steak ready to cook."

Jo couldn't remember the last time she had steak, but she couldn't endure this man's company. More than likely, he would drive away her appetite. "Thank you for the offer, but I need to get back or my five brothers will come searching for me, and you don't want them to find us alone."

For the first time, the confidence left his eyes. He seemed to be mulling over her comment, and then he turned her loose. He reached up as if to trail a finger down her cheek, but she jerked her head back. "Too bad, pretty miss. We could have had a good time."

Melinda tugged on Jo's arm, and she hurried away with her friend. If she didn't know better she'd think there was a run on women, not land. Jo didn't mind the company of a handsome, suave man like Mark Hillborne. In fact, she welcomed it and hoped she could find his store if she ever got to Guthrie. Maybe he'd even give her a job, and then she could get a place of her own.

Melinda sighed. "I sure wish I was pretty and could attract men like you. And you're so brave. Weren't you quiverin' in your petticoats back there?"

"Naw. You have to show a man you're not afraid, or they're more likely to take advantage of you. Just face them square on, and even if you're scared spitless, don't let them know it."

"I could never do that. Even my own brothers make me tremble at times."

"It's hard for a woman to get by on her own. We need men, so you might as well get used to that fact." And she definitely needed a man—a wealthy man—to set her plan of living in a fine home in action. She simply had to find the right one. But maybe she already had. If Mark was as wealthy and as prosperous as he was a braggadocio, he might just be the man for her. He certainly was handsome enough with his sandy brown hair, deep blue eyes, and muscular frame. She sighed.

All she had to do was figure out a way to snag the man and get him to marry her.

Chapter 15

Lara stood up in the stirrups and stared at the long row of soldiers, looking dapper in their uniforms, lined up in front of an ocean of prairie schooners. Everyone was eager to be off and on their way across the Cherokee Outlet and moving closer to the Unassigned Lands. Jo had been especially helpful in packing this morning, and they'd gotten done early, so Grandpa suggested Lara ride to the front of the line to see if she could learn anything while he greased the wagon wheels and got the livestock ready to travel.

An officer rode forward and slowly made his way between the soldiers and the people, shouting instructions. When he drew near her, he said, "I expect everyone to keep in line, and I'll treat each of you the same, so no fighting or rushing to get ahead. We leave at ten when the bugles sound. No one crosses early."

"That's Captain Woodson." A mounted man to her right said as he gestured at the soldier.

Lara nodded. Excitement swirled inside her. Soon they'd be in the Oklahoma Territory. Would the land be the same? Would they see Indians? And if so, would they be hostile toward the people moving across their lands?

A short while later, the captain rode back in their direction. He lifted his arm, and mounted buglers all down the line raised their horns. When he lowered his arm in a swift jerk, the bugles sounded. All around her, the excitement was tangible—something you could feel in each person and animal.

Captain Woodson shouted, "Forward—march!"

The cavalry soldiers turned their horses, and the lead wagons and horsemen started forward into Oklahoma. She reined Sunny around and trotted back to their camp, not far from the front of the line. All was packed when she arrived, and Grandpa, Jo, and Michael were seated on the wagon, ready to go. The goats bleated at her as if scolding Grandpa for tying them behind the wagon again.

"The lead wagons have started moving."

"We heard the horns, Mama." Michael stood up, bouncing on the seat.

"Did anyone give instructions?" Grandpa lifted his hat, brushed down his already sweaty hair, and then replaced it.

"Not much. Just that we should stay in line and each of us would be treated the same."

Jo looked around at the rows of wagons surrounding them. "I don't see how they expect all of these wagons to stay in one line."

Lara shrugged. "We'll have to cross the Bluff Creek Bridge. I'm guessing we can only do that a wagon at a time."

An hour later, as the mob narrowed into a single line in preparation to cross the Bluff Creek Bridge, Lara stared at the mass of humanity. There were wagons that looked brand new being pulled by strong stock, while other folks had rickety ones pulled by a broken-down horse or slow-plodding oxen. There were buggies of all kinds, schooners, buckboards, even a few people pushing handcarts. And there were hundreds of riders on horseback, many who wore the GAR patch on their sleeve, with all they owned tied up behind their saddles.

Lara yawned. The day was sunny and warm, in spite of the rains they'd received the night before. The pace was achingly slow, but they were now close to the bridge. Once on the other side, she'd trade places with Jo and see that everyone had some lunch.

As they rode up the trail leading to the bridge, Lara noticed a big covered wagon pulled by four horses that had the words *The Great War Show* printed on the canvas cover.

"Look at that!" Behind them, a large wagon hauled a single-mast ship. "What do you think they plan to do with that on the prairie?"

Grandpa shook his head. "Gives a whole new meaning to prairie schooner."

Lara chuckled. "Look at that boat, Michael."

Her son oohed and aahed as they watched the big wagon circle around and out of sight. It seemed everyone's spirits were high, and many were singing. Still, most every man she saw was armed. Every now and then, a shot rang out and someone bagged a meadowlark, jackrabbit, or prairie dog.

As she reached the end of the bridge and had the advantage of high ground, she spied an unusually tall, old-fashioned buggy pulled by two shaggy yellow horses. A gangly-legged colt trotted alongside, nuzzling at its mother. A woman drove the wagon, holding the reins in one hand and a baby in the other. A tow-headed boy followed along behind, lobbing clods of dirt at a disgruntled cow. As long as Lara lived, she'd never forget the sights she'd seen this day.

By nightfall, they reached Pond Creek. Lara set about making dinner while Jo and Michael pitched the tent and got out the bedding. Grandpa tended to the animals. In spite of doing nothing but riding all day, Lara was tired and ready for sleep. Tomorrow was the twentieth, and the land run was just two days after that. Soon they would know if they had a home or not.

As she lay down on her pallet in the tent with Michael, her thoughts turned to Gabe Coulter. The man hadn't returned for his booklet as he'd said. Had he gotten tied up selling his horses? Or maybe he never really intended to return. Why should he? She was nothing to him except a needy woman.

She hated such thoughts, but they were the truth. Although she was only twenty-one, she felt worn down, haggard, ugly. What man would look at her twice when all she had to wear were faded, raggedy dresses? And what did she care if one did? She wasn't looking for a man. Gabe had sneaked over her defensive walls and helped her. She knew not to trust a man. But how could one as kind and generous as he be a wily gambler? The picture she had of him in her mind didn't fit with the gambler image. Could the stranger have been wrong?

She blew out a sigh. What did it matter? More than likely she would never cross paths with Gabe Coulter again, not with thousands of people crowding into the same area.

Gabe stretched out on his cot in the large Rock Island Hotel tent. It was his first time to stay in a makeshift hotel. All around him, men's deep chatter blended with the loud snores from those already asleep. Rain splatted on the top of the tent. He hoped Luke would be able to stay dry and get some sleep where he'd camped near the horses. Even though the hotel clerk had assured them they'd hired armed guards to watch over the animals, Luke wanted to stay close. Gabe admired the man. Even more so, he actually liked him. Luke had become the closest thing he'd had to a friend in as long as he could remember.

He turned on his side, thinking over the day. His only regret was that he hadn't gotten back to see Lara. So many people haggled over his horses that he'd organized an auction and ended up selling all except for Tempest, Luke's palomino, and their packhorse. His pockets were full of cash—enough money to purchase the supplies he would need to establish a home and ranch. He could even afford to hire some men to build a solid wood house. In his rented suite in Kansas City, he owned enough furniture already to furnish his bedroom, study, and parlor. The only problem was that whenever he closed his eyes and dreamed of the new place, Lara Talbot invaded those dreams as she walked through the rooms of the new house and decorated them. She was the one he wanted to share it with.

But she never would.

He couldn't—wouldn't—marry her, even if she was willing, without telling her that he'd killed her husband, albeit not intentionally. Once she heard that news, she wouldn't want anything to do with him.

He saw no answer to his dilemma.

He yawned and flipped onto his back. Hopefully, tomorrow's crossing of the Salt Fork would go as easily as today's trek did. Although if the rain continued, it would make fording the river much harder. People like Lara who had wagons would face the worst of it. Would her pitiful mule even be able to make it across a swollen river pulling their rig?

Gabe's body relaxed and felt heavy as sleep drew near. The sudden pop of gunfire erupted, and he jerked awake. He bolted up, yanked on his boots, and rushed outside. The gunfire came from the direction of the horse corral. Men yelled. The high-pitched squeals of the frightened animals rent the air that was already filled with the acrid stench of gunpowder.

Several men rode past Gabe, with several riderless horses in tow. Gabe stepped into the path of Luke's riderless horse, his hands held out to his side. "Whoa, boy."

The gelding slid to a halt and reared, his slashing hooves narrowly missing Gabe's face. When the animal set all four hooves on the ground, Gabe grabbed his halter and then smoothed his hand across the gelding's neck, cooing soft, soothing sounds. The well-trained horse quickly settled under his gentle touch. Gabe led the animal back and found Luke bending over one of the guards, who'd been shot. When he glanced up and saw Gabe with his horse, relief softened his expression.

"I can't tell you how glad I am that you caught Golden Boy. I've had that horse three years, and I'd sure hate to lose 'im."

Gabe nodded, his gaze searching the corral for Tempest. He didn't see the horse, but it was night and there were few lights about. He whistled, and the tension fled when he got an answering neigh. Tempest pushed through the other horses and stuck his head over the fence, obviously happy to see his owner after the mayhem. Gabe held on to Golden Boy while scratching Tempest's face and between his ears. "You're all right, buddy."

Other people rushed to the corral, and soon the breach had been repaired and the injured man carried off to the doctor's tent.

With Golden Boy back in the corral and standing next to Tempest, Gabe finally relaxed. Rain dampened his clothing, but he wouldn't be sleeping in his dry cot tonight. Not when there could well be others who'd like to steal their horses. He hadn't yet seen their packhorse, but dawn would reveal if it was still there.

As he leaned against the railing beside Luke, he blew out a frustrated breath. "I'll sure be glad when this land rush is over so we can get a full night's sleep."

"Yeah. Somewhere dry with hot food."

Gabe nodded. "Why don't you take my place in the hotel tent, and I'll stay here for a while, keeping watch. We can trade off later."

Luke eyed him. "You really wouldn't mind? I am drenched to the bones and would love to get out of these clothes."

"No. Go on. I couldn't sleep now anyway, and I'm used to staying up late. Four a.m. has been my normal bedtime for years."

"If you're sure."

"Go!" Gabe swatted his hand in the air. "Get some rest."

Luke nodded then trotted away. Gabe crossed his arms over his chest, wishing he had his duster. No sooner had he wished it than Luke came jogging toward him, holding the coat.

"Thanks!" Gabe took it and settled into the dry jacket, relishing its warmth. He leaned back against the corral railings, hooking one boot over the lowest one. Tempest leaned his head over and nudged Gabe's shoulder, and he reached up and patted the horse's muzzle. Gabe yawned. He'd been looking forward to a good night's sleep in a dry bed, but that wasn't going to happen now. At least they'd managed to save their saddle horses.

He nodded at one of the guards who walked past him. To keep his mind off the rain and how miserable the night was, he mentally ran through the course of travel he planned to take on the land run. He wanted to get property along the Cimarron River, near Guthrie. And he hoped that Lara Talbot got a section of land that bordered up next to his, but the odds were against that happening. Still, a man could dream.

He smiled as he thought of all the ways he could help the pretty widow. Maybe if he bided his time until she finished mourning her husband—well, maybe something could develop between them. The image of those beautiful green eyes rarely left his thoughts. He blew out a loud sigh. When he first started on this venture, he'd never have guessed he would meet a woman who intrigued him so much.

～

The blazing campfire cast a brave circle of light into the misty night. Two of the riders Payton Reeves had hired rode in fast and yanked their mounts to a quick stop, the horses trailing behind bumping into the rumps of the leaders. Payton searched the half-dozen nags for one particular horse and cursed. He kicked the water bucket, sending it flying into the shadows. One of the horses squealed and sidestepped when the bucket landed nearby.

"That was stupid." Albert Swan scratched his chest and yawned. Keeping hold of the ropes tied to the horses trailing his mount, he stepped to the ground.

Payton glared at the man he'd hired to help him steal Gabe Coulter's horses. "You're the stupid one, Swan. You couldn't even swipe the right horses."

"It was dark, and the one you wanted is black. How'd you 'spect me to find the right one at night and with no lantern?"

"That was your problem. I paid you to get two particular horses—the palomino and the black with the diamond on its forehead."

"That palomino was following us until some yahoo cut 'im off."

Payton spat. "Coulter, most likely."

"At least we got some good mounts you can sell," Raul, the second rider, said. "Prices are running high for horses."

"That may be true, but that wasn't the point of this venture. I wanted to keep one particular man from riding in the run."

"If you don't want the horses, we'll take them. I nearly lost my head stealing them." Albert poked a finger through a hole in his hat.

"There was extra guards posted. If two of 'em hadn't fallen asleep, we pro'bly wouldn't have gotten any."

Payton shook his head. "Get them on a picket line." He suddenly swung about and stared into the darkness, listening. His camp was a ways north of the mayhem at the border, so no one should come this way unless his men had been followed. The crickets resumed their ruckus, and he relaxed.

This scheme hadn't gone as planned. He'd just have to come up with some other way to get back at Gabe Coulter for ruining his brother's life.

And he would.

He had to.

Chapter 16

The day before the land rush, Lara sat with her family in a crowd surrounding a minister, and celebrated Easter Sunday. The man's loud voice carried well, but right behind them another group was playing baseball.

The minister turned slowly, and Lara was able to catch most of his comments. "Have you ever considered how the disciples felt after Jesus died? They thought He was the Messiah, but now He was dead."

Crack! The smack of a bat hitting a ball reverberated in the few seconds the minister paused to allow his thought to seep into the minds of his listeners.

"Run! Run!" Cheers rang out.

"Slide!"

Jo rose onto her knees and turned toward the ball players. Lara tugged her down and frowned, shaking her head. Jo scowled and flounced back onto the blanket, her arms crossed.

"They'd lost someone who was so precious to them," the man continued as the crowd behind them quieted, "and their expectations had to have been crushed. Woe is we." He shook his head. "What about you? Tomorrow is a monumental day. A historical day. But what if you fail to obtain land tomorrow? Will your faith in God be crushed, like the disciples'?"

He turned a slow circle again. "Remember folks, Jesus rose from the grave! Hallelujah!"

Many in the crowd repeated his praise to God, as the baseball players' chants rose in volume again.

"When the disciples were at their lowest, Jesus appeared to them in the room, with the doors still locked. And what did He say to them?"

"Peace!" several men yelled out.

"That's right!" The minister smiled. "Peace be with you. And tomorrow, whether you win land or not, remember this—peace be with you. God has not forgotten you, nor will He forsake you."

The crowd murmured their agreement, and Lara felt a deep peace within her for the first time in weeks. God saw them. He was aware of their need for a place to live, and He wouldn't forsake them.

"Rise and let us sing, 'O for a Thousand Tongues to Sing,' for we do indeed have a thousand tongues today." He raised his hands in the air and swung them inward then out, and the crowd joined him in song.

Behind them the baseball rooters yelled again as the bat cracked. It was a strange communion of churchgoers and game players.

When the song finished, the minister started singing "Beulah Land." Those gathered round joined him singing the words:

"I've reached the land of corn and wine,
And all its riches freely mine;
Here shines undimmed one blissful day,
For all my night has passed away."

The ball players quieted, and slowly more voices, those outside of their circle of worshippers, rose up together in song:

"O Beulah Land, sweet Beulah Land,
As on thy highest mount I stand,
I look away across the sea,
Where mansions are prepared for me,
And view the shining glory shore,
My Heav'n, my home forever more!

"My Savior comes and walks with me,
And sweet communion here have we;
He gently leads me by His hand,
For this is Heaven's border land."

And when the song finished, a quiet hush fell over the crowd. Taking advantage of the moment, the preacher hollered, "Let us pray." He led all those listening in a prayer of thanks to God and for safety on the morrow. Then he prayed for those who wouldn't get land—that God would grant them peace and provision. When he said "Amen!" the ballplayers cheered and resumed their game.

Jo hopped to her feet. "I'm going to watch the game now."

"What about dinner? Those who attended the service are pooling food. There's liable to be some fresh meat and sweets to eat."

Jo wavered. She glanced at the game then at Lara and shrugged. "I guess I'll eat first and then go to the game."

Lara glanced at Grandpa and smiled. He winked at her. Food always was a good motivator for her sister.

Benches had been moved to a central spot and boards laid across to fashion a makeshift table. Then the women moved in, filling the tables with all manner of delicious food items. Lara's mouth watered as she set down two jars of peaches. Grandpa followed with a pot of fish stew. She hoped to be able to sample some of the other women's cooking.

Lara distributed a plate to each member of her family, making sure to keep Michael close. The women and children proceeded through the line first. Lara had her eye on a plate of sliced ham, but before she reached it, the last piece was taken. She sighed in disappointment and focused on a big crock of green beans with ham pieces and tiny new potatoes. Just as she was ready to step forward and claim the spoon, a woman slid in front of her.

"Excuse me, please. I just need to grab this empty plate." She did, and passed it off to another woman, who then handed her a platter of fried chicken.

Lara felt her eyes widen, and she stared at the delicacy. The moment the woman stepped away, she snagged a chicken leg and thigh then glanced over her shoulder. "Jo, look. Fried chicken."

Jo had the same reaction, and she grabbed another thigh and speared a fat breast, which she passed to Grandpa. Lara spooned green beans and potatoes on her plate and Michael's, thanking God for the magnificent feast. She added a slice of fresh bread and several desserts then moved away so others could fill their plates.

Betty Robinson waved them over, and although she'd just as soon avoid the Biggs men, she couldn't refuse Betty. Thankfully, the men didn't join them. Sam had avoided her ever since she turned down his proposal. The meal was a quiet one, with even talkative Betty engrossed with her dinner. Soon the feast was over, and Jo rose, eager to be off.

"Don't wander too far," Grandpa said. "I'd hate for you to get so lost you can't find your way back to us."

"I won't." Jo swatted her hand behind her as she hurried away.

"Can I go?" Michael yawned.

"I think you need a rest, little man."

"But I don't want'a."

"*Shh*. . .no arguing. After your nap, we'll go see if there's a ball game we can watch."

Her son's eyes lit up for a moment, then he shoved the crust of a peach pie slice in his mouth. Lara's gaze drifted to her grandfather, and she frowned. He sure hadn't eaten much. She lifted her eyes, noticing how tired he looked. The days of travel had been harder on him than she'd realized. She needed to do more to help him. He had a long, hard race to ride tomorrow and needed to be in good shape.

He set his plate down. "I think I'll join that great-grandson of mine for a nap. You can go sightseein' if you want, Lara."

"Are you sure?" She would love to walk around for a bit but hated to leave them.

"We'll just be sleepin'. It would help me relax more to not have you watchin' us."

"I can keep an eye on them, if you'd like," Betty offered.

"That's very generous of you." Lara rose and took the plates to scrape and wash them. "Let me walk Michael back and get him settled, then I'll return for our dishes."

"I don't have anything to do. You go on, and I'll tend to them."

"Why don't we do them together, then you can come walking with me?"

Betty shook her head. "I may not need a nap, but I've had enough movin' around to last me a month. I'll sit and work on my mendin' pile."

"Are you sure?"

Betty waved her hand in the air. "Shoo! Go on and have a nice walk. And don't worry none about them two or your belongin's. I'll keep watch."

Lara smiled at the woman's kindness. "Thank you very much."

Once Michael had a drink and was settled in the tent next to Grandpa, Lara strode out of camp. She made note of the nearest tree and planned to keep it in sight so she wouldn't get lost. She moseyed up next to Jo, who stood with Melinda, and watched the baseball game for a few minutes, but it made no sense to her. What fun was it to hit a ball with a wooden stick and then run in circles? She shook her head. "I'm going for a walk. You want to join me?"

Jo shook her head. "I'm enjoying the game."

Lara moved away from the crowd watching the ball players and wandered through the hodgepodge of wagons and buggies. She smiled and nodded at many people, stopped to admire the handiwork of several women sewing on a lovely quilt, then she ended up at a haphazard array of store supplies on a buckboard.

"Pots, canned goods, and paraphernalia of all kinds. If you want it, I've got it!" the skinny panhandler cried out. He caught Lara's eye and gestured to her. "C'mon and have a look. Don't cost nuthin' to look."

He was right. Looking didn't cost her anything. She eyed the colorful bolts of calico then forced her gaze away. Lusting wasn't good and wouldn't accomplish anything. She paused to finger a blue ribbon that matched Jo's eyes, when she heard a familiar voice.

Surely not.

She turned, and there, standing in a group of men, was Gabe. He leaned back his head and laughed at something another man said.

Her heart galloped. She swiveled to face the wagon and moved down to look at a pair of brushes at the end then thanked the peddler and hurried away. Gabe was the last person she'd wanted to run into today.

Gabe chuckled at the stranger's joke. He looked past the group of men he'd been talking to and saw a woman walking away from a panhandler's wagon. Lara! He'd recognize her slim form and that ugly faded dress anywhere.

"Thank you, gents, for a nice conversation, but I see someone I need to talk to." The men nodded their good-byes, as did Gabe, and he rushed off, determined not to lose Lara in the crowd.

He jogged past the peddler's wagon, ignoring the man as he tried to hawk a silver cigar case. That was the last thing he needed. He searched for Lara among the other wagoners selling wares but didn't see her. His pulse pumped faster. How could he have lost her so quickly?

He stopped. Narrowing his eyes, he scanned the campsites, looking for someone moving away from him. There! She darted around a gold-fringed surrey and rushed on. What was her hurry?

Gabe broke into a lope, quickly closing the gap with his long legs. "Lara!"

She stopped suddenly, stood there, then slowly turned with her arms crossed over her chest, as if talking to him was the last thing she wanted to do. He slowed his pace and walked the final steps, sending her a smile that he hoped would charm her.

But it didn't.

What had happened? And where was her son?

"Is everything all right?" He swooped off his hat and held it in front of him, rolling the brim. He knew the answer to that already, but he had no idea what the problem was.

"Everything is fine. Thank you."

"So where's your son today?"

"He's taking a nap."

Gabe blinked. "You didn't go off and leave him alone, did you?"

Her nostrils flared. "Of course not. A woman in a neighboring campsite is watching him, but I've been gone long enough. I really should go." She spun around, but Gabe stopped her with a hand on her shoulder.

"Lara, what's the matter? Please, tell me."

She turned, arms again crossed across her middle, as if she needed a shield. "All right. Since you insist. Is it true that you're a gambler?"

Gabe's eyes widened, and he sucked in a quick breath. How in the world had she discovered that? "Yes, it's true that I've made a living as a gambler, but I'm hoping to change professions."

She lifted a skeptical brow. "To a farmer? I find that hard to believe."

"Why? Is a man not allowed to make a radical change in his life if he wants to?"

She wilted a bit. "Of course. It's just been my experience that gamblers rarely change."

Her husband. That's who she referred to, but he couldn't let on that he knew. "I'm guessing someone in your life lived off the cuff?"

She relaxed a smidgen more. "My husband, Tom. He was fond of visiting the saloons and trying to multiply his monthly pay at the gaming tables, but he never did."

And she was the one who paid the price. "I was a good gambler. Won much more than I lost."

Lara lifted her head, her expression pained. "Did you ever once stop to think about how you were hurting the families of those men whose money you won? Women and children went hungry so that you could line your pockets or buy another fancy suit. Did you ever think about that as you walked home at night, gloating over your winnings?"

"To be honest, I didn't. But my eyes have recently been opened, and that's one reason I'd like to change professions."

"It would be good if you could, but have you ever farmed before?"

"Actually, I was raised on one, but I don't intend to farm. I want to raise horses."

Her tense posture softened. "I love horses. My grandfather raised them before—" She cleared her throat. "Riding was often the highlight of my day."

So she might actually have a chance then, when she rode in the race. He enjoyed the fact that they had some common ground. "I've always liked them, too. We had stock horses on the farm, and my stepfather had a riding horse, but I never had my own until I left home."

"Might I ask, if you were raised on a farm, how did you become a gambler?"

His jaw tightened as he thought of his stepfather's cruel treatment. "It's not something I like to talk about."

"I see. Well, I probably should get back and check if Michael is awake."

"Mind if I walk with you?"

She shot him a look that said she did, but he fell into step with her.

"So, are you ready for tomorrow?"

She lifted one shoulder in a noncommittal shrug.

He paused and turned her toward him. He gazed into her pretty green eyes, which today looked almost lifeless. Because of him? Or was something else bothering her? "Tomorrow is one of the most exciting days in the history of this nation. How can you not be excited?"

She inhaled a long breath and then blew it out. "Because I worry about the thousands of people who will be brokenhearted in thirty hours because they didn't get land." She turned and stared off in the distance. "I worry about my family."

He didn't like the thought of her losing. He hadn't even thought that much about the horde of people who would be devastated tomorrow evening because they failed. "I guess they'll go back to wherever they were before they came here. I imagine most folks have family they can live with."

"Most, maybe, but not all."

She was talking about herself again. He thought back to that tiny soddy she'd been living in. That was no decent place to raise a boy. Even in his worst days, he always had a solid roof over his head. He'd thought life was so hard then, but he'd never lived in poverty. Well, maybe his first year or two after he left the farm and before he became a gambler, but even then, he stayed in the supply room of the saloon, sleeping on a cot. What had she endured?

He wanted to help her. See that she got the house she deserved, but her stubborn pride wouldn't allow her to accept a home even if he gave her one. He'd been more than a little lucky that Homer had discovered her husband's horse at the Kansas City livery and brought it to her. Gabe was willing to buy her one, but she wouldn't have as easily accepted it as she had her husband's buckskin.

Behind her, a man tuned his fiddle. A small crowd sat around a cold campfire. The man tuned up his fiddle then started a jaunty song. Toes tapped and people clapped. A couple stood, and the gent bowed to the woman and she curtsied. They began sashaying to the lively music.

Lara turned to watch. Gabe noticed her index finger tapping against her arm in time with the music. He grinned and stepped in front of her. "Madam, may I have the honor of this dance?"

She shot him a glance that said he was loco and shook her head.

He leaned in closer. "Please."

"It's Sunday. Easter Sunday, at that."

"True, but it's not an ordinary Sunday. You need to catch the spirit, Lara. The excitement that comes with tomorrow's sunrise. Dance with me."

She shook her head. "I can't."

Ignoring her objection, he grabbed her hand and placed his other hand on her tiny waist. "I beg to differ."

"Let me go, Gabe."

He grinned. "Nope. Not until you dance with me."

She dropped her gaze, her cheeks blazing red. "I don't know how to dance."

Gabe blinked, not a little bit stunned. Had she never attended a social when she was young? How had a pretty gal like her grown up not knowing how to dance? Not to be swayed, he smiled. "No time like the present to learn. Just follow me."

"Gabe—"

He tugged her close and moved his feet in time with the music, all but dragging her along. Though he rarely danced, he wasn't used to unwilling partners, but Lara was smart, and he knew she'd catch on. And she did.

She joined him in a makeshift polka, keeping time to the fast music. He enjoyed holding her hand and waist and being close to her. He had no idea how it had happened, but the independent woman had stolen a chunk of his heart. He didn't want to let her go, but he knew that he would have to. When the dance ended, far too soon for his pleasure, he smiled down at Lara. "See, that wasn't so bad, was it?"

Her cheeks were flushed, and the sparkle had returned to her lovely eyes. "I suppose not, but I really must go."

"All right, but I'd like to ask you to ride with me tomorrow."

Her brows dipped. "Why?"

"For protection, of course. Things will be chaotic tomorrow. Once the race starts, it will be every man—or woman—for himself." He waved his hand in the air. "All this camaraderie, this festive spirit, will be a thing of the past, and it will be dog-eat-dog."

Her throat moved as she swallowed, but she lifted her chin. "I can take care of myself. But I do thank you for the warning." She turned but then paused. "I still have your *Homesteader's Handbook*."

"Keep it. I got the information from it that I needed."

She nodded as her gaze roamed across his face, then she held out her hand—uncharacteristically for a woman. "Thank you for all the kindnesses you've shown me, but this is good-bye, Gabe."

A numbness settled in his brain. Her good-bye sounded so final. "What do you mean?"

She lowered her hand. "It means that I don't expect I'll see you after the race. You'll go your way, and I'll go mine. Things will be crazy tomorrow, as you said. And if I don't get land. . ." She shrugged, nibbling her lip in a way that made him want to pull her into his arms and kiss away all her fears.

He didn't want her to go. "Lara, give me a chance. Please. I can help you. I *want* to help."

She pinned him with a glare. "Why?"

Because I killed your husband and made you a widow. Because I've come to admire your spunk. Because I care. . . .

He couldn't tell her that. So he did the only thing he knew to show her how he felt—he tugged her into his arms and kissed her.

Lara stood stiff in his arms, but as he plied his lips to hers, a bit harsh at first but then softer, she relaxed. Not as much as he'd like, but she didn't fight him.

The fiddle music faded, and in its place hoots and cheers. Lara jerked away—fast. Her cheeks flamed. Her lips still damp from his kisses. The look in her eyes shifted from pleasingly sated to angry, and she reached up and slapped him. Loud. Hard.

Chuckles sounded all around as Lara marched away.

Used to being in the limelight somewhat, Gabe turned, yanked off his hat, and offered the crowd a gentlemanly bow. Then he took a final look at Lara's retreating backside and strode away, smiling. The woman might have slapped him to regain her honor in the face of the crowd, but she'd kissed him back, whether she'd admit it or not, and that small detail gave him hope.

Later that night, as he walked through the crowds, pondering how to get Lara to ride beside him, he overheard something that chilled his bones. He paused on the far side of a wagon and looked around. All was dark, and most folks were already sleeping.

"It's true," a deep voice stated. "There are women riding alone in the race."

Someone else chuckled. "Wouldn't be hard at all to follow one and steal her claim if'n she gets one."

"Yep. Although what if she didn't?" a third, alto voice said. "Then you'd'a wasted your chance to get land. I say ride for yourself. You're better off doin' that than chasing after a skirt and hopin' *she* gets a claim."

"No, I think I'm'a gonna follow a skirt. That way I'll get land *and* a woman."

Gabe froze at the tone of the man's voice.

"You're a fool, Leo."

A ruckus ensued as Gabe imagined the deep-voiced man pummeling the other fellow, and Gabe made his getaway. There was no doubt now that he had to ride with Lara. Maybe not with her exactly, but at least right on her tail. He smiled as he wove his way back to his camp. Yes sir, that's just what he'd do.

It was the only way he knew to protect the stubborn woman who was quickly stealing his heart.

Lara lay in the tent beside Jo and Michael, listening to their soft breaths of sleep. The ground vibrated from the wheels of Boomers just arriving. A cow mooed, and someone in the distance laughed.

She wished she'd told Gabe the truth—that she wasn't riding tomorrow, Grandpa was. But as far as she could remember, she'd never told him about Grandpa or Jo. She wasn't sure why she'd held back that information, but then she really didn't know the man very well.

And yet, she'd kissed him.

Well, truth be told, he'd kissed her, but instead of insisting he release her immediately, she'd allowed herself to enjoy the moment of being held and feeling special to someone. And she'd kissed him back.

Oh dear.

She'd never kissed anyone other than Tom before.

What had she done? More was the question, why had she enjoyed it so much? Yes, she was attracted to Gabe, and yes, he'd sneaked in and claimed a portion of her heart before she'd even known it was happening, but she would never—never!—get in a relationship with another wastrel, much less a cardsharp. She prayed Gabe would get land and could change his ways, but she wouldn't be around to watch. Grandpa would ride tomorrow, and God willing, he'd stake a claim, and they'd finally have a place to call home—

far away from Gabe's claim. She couldn't bear to think what would happen if Grandpa wasn't successful. *God, please. We need land. We need a home.*

She felt God saying He would provide. But she thought of how they'd struggled the past few years since Grandpa lost his homestead. Was that dirty soddy God's provision? Yes, it was better than sleeping in a tent as she was now, but still. . . Couldn't God provide a real house for her family? He owned the cattle on a thousand hills, but how could she reconcile the simplistic way they'd lived in the past with God's favor? Maybe she'd done something that caused Him to remove His favor from their lives. Was that even possible?

Gabriel's help had been a true blessing. Had God sent him to her to help her family?

She rolled onto her side, contemplating that possibility. She knew a person often never recognized when God had come to their aid, and that aid often came through others.

Why did life have to be so complicated?

Why couldn't it be simple for once?

Please, Lord, help us.

Outside her tent, she heard a cough. Grandpa?

She sat up, listening. He'd seemed overly tired today, but she thought it was because of their three days of travel. He tried to do so much to ease her burden. Had he overtaxed himself? She'd have to watch him more closely.

"Lara. . ."

His weak call pushed her into motion, and she hiked up her gown then crawled out of the tent, taking care not to knock it down in the process. She hurried to the wagon, which he was sleeping under, and kneeled beside it. "Grandpa, are you all right?"

"S—sick. Need m—my quinine. B—blanket. C—cold."

No! What about tomorrow? What about the race? "I'll get it. Hang on."

At the front of the tent, she rustled through the crate that held his medicine. Jo tossed for a moment and then sat up. "Is something wrong?"

Lara swallowed the lump building in her throat. "It's Grandpa. He's having an episode."

Jo gasped. "What about the race?"

Lara shook her head. "I can't think about that right now. I have to care for Grandpa." Her hand folded around the precious bottle, and she extracted one pill. She tugged on her quilt and started to back away, but Jo grabbed her arm.

"Lara, you *have* to ride. You're the only one who can now."

She stared at her sister, not wanting to accept the truth. Grandpa's episodes lasted for days. The timing couldn't be any worse. There was no chance that he'd be well enough to ride tomorrow. The burden of getting land had fallen on her shoulders.

Chapter 17

Lara awoke to the sound of talking, goats bleating, and the stomach-tingling aroma of bacon. She stretched then bolted upright. Today was the day! And Grandpa. How had he fared the rest of the night?

Jo had awakened Lara sometime in the middle of the night and told her to go back to bed and she would attend their grandfather. Lara hadn't wanted to leave his side, but since she had a long, hard ride today, she acquiesced. What time was it now?

She quickly dressed and then crawled out of the tent. Michael spied her and came running.

"Mama, Grandpa's sick again. Aunt Jo made breakfuss'." He frowned. "I like your food better."

"I heard that," Jo hollered.

Michael's eyes widened, but then he grinned and fell forward, wrapping his arms around her neck. "You sleeped late."

"I was up part of the night caring for your great-grandpa." Lara gave him another squeeze then stood and gazed up at the sun. Midmorning had already passed. She needed to hustle if she was going to be ready to ride at noon.

The two nanny goats bleated and wailed, calling to be milked. She walked to her sister's side where Jo was washing the bowls she and

Michael had used for breakfast. "Why haven't they been milked?"

Her sister just shrugged. "I've been busy. I woke a bit late—fell asleep watching Grandpa. Then I had to prepare breakfast. Your boy was starving."

Lara smiled. "Don't I know. I'm sure both of his legs are hollow the way he's always hungry." She glanced toward the buckboard. "How's Grandpa?"

"Last time I checked, his fever was down. He probably should have another pill this morning."

"Did he eat anything?"

"He's been sleeping, so I didn't want to wake him."

Lara nodded. "I'll go check on him."

As she started to walk away, Jo cleared her throat. "Are you gonna ride?"

"Do I have a choice?" She swung back to face her sister. "Could you please fix me a couple of sandwiches and make sure the canteen is filled? I probably should get to the starting line as soon as possible to get a good spot."

Jo nodded.

Lara started to walk away then stopped again. "Are you going to be able to take care of Grandpa and keep watch on Michael and the goats?"

Jo straightened. "It's not the first time I've done it."

"No, but before, the goats were penned and Michael knew his boundaries. It's far different here. And I don't even know if anyone will be left here once the race starts."

Jo swatted her hand in the air. "Of course there will. Not all of these wagons will be racing. Half of them wouldn't make it two miles at a fast pace, and many folks have a passel of little kids. They can't race with them."

"All right. I'm counting on you to stay here in camp and protect our belongings and Grandpa and Michael—and yourself. No wandering off today."

"Stop worryin' so much. We'll be fine. Just see that you get a claim."

"I aim to try hard." Lara peeked under the wagon at Grandpa and pulled the quilt up to cover his chest. Though barely past midmorning, the sun had already warmed the day so that she didn't need a cloak, but with his fever, he was probably chilled.

She started to back away, but Grandpa grasped her hand, heat radiating from his.

"Lara, you have to ride."

"I know."

"Take a gun. Be careful. And ride toward Guthrie." He took a labored breath. "My gut says that's the best area."

She nodded. "Can you eat something?"

He turned up his nose. "Jo cooked."

Lara smiled. "I'm sorry about that, but she allowed me to sleep in so I'd be well rested."

"That was nice of her." He scratched his chest. "I might could drink some coffee and maybe get down a slice of bread if we have any left."

She smiled. "Good. I'll get it."

"No, tell Jo. You need to prepare for the ride and get to the starting line."

She listened closely as he explained that she was to ride due south and whenever she had to adjust her direction, to take a small tack to the east. The Guthrie Station was almost due south of Caldwell. If she went too far east, she'd ride out of the Unassigned Lands. He explained how she needed to find a place with water. That was the most important. Also a somewhat flat section of land to make farming easier.

Lara's mind swirled. How was she supposed to do that while trying to beat thousands of other racers to the land? The burden of it all weighed her down. What if she failed?

"Lara. Look at me."

She did as he asked. "You can do this. You're the strongest, most capable woman I know. You will succeed."

His pride in her lifted her spirits. "I'll do my best."

"That's all I can ask for. Be careful, punkin. I don't want anything to happen to you. You're far more precious to me than any piece of land."

Tears stung her eyes. "I feel the same way. Love you, Grandpa."

He nodded and closed his eyes, obviously spent. Lara pushed into action. She had so much to do. She should have thought to check Sunny's hooves yesterday, but after Gabe's kiss, she'd been able to think of little else. "Jo, Grandpa would like some coffee and bread."

She nodded. "The coffee's ready. You want some?"

"Yes, but let me milk the goats first." She checked to see where Michael was and saw that he'd crawled under the wagon and now sat beside Grandpa, playing with some rocks and sticks. She grabbed a clean bucket and hurried to Mildred, who greeted her with a long, complaining, where-have-you-been bleat.

"I know I'm late, but there were extenuating circumstances." Thirty minutes later, both female goats were in a much better mood. Lara set the buckets of milk on the tailgate then hurried to see to Sunny. Thank goodness, Jo had fed the horse earlier. She quickly verified his hooves were in good condition then saddled him and tied a bedroll behind as well as her bag of food. She stuck the flag she'd use to claim their land down firmly into the bag. She didn't dare lose it.

Excitement bubbled up within her now that the time had come, and it suddenly struck her that she was actually happy she was the one to participate in this great historical event. All around her, others were packing and moving forward toward the starting line. She was relieved to see that some campers looked settled in for the duration, most of those with small children. With Sunny ready, Lara strode over to Betty's camp. The woman had become a friend, and she wanted to say farewell.

She wasn't surprised to see Betty's campsite packed up. She waved when the woman turned her way. "So you're leaving?"

Betty nodded. "Lester wants me to drive to Guthrie, and he'll come find me there."

"By yourself? Are you sure that's safe?"

Betty shrugged. "I had hoped Sam would stay with me, but he's bent on riding in the race and getting his own land."

"I don't like the idea of you traveling alone."

"I'll be fine. There are too many folks around for something to happen."

She was probably right, but it angered her that Lester and Sam would leave her. "Thank you so much for all you did to help us."

"Happy to do it." Her gaze shifted past Lara, and her brow pinched. "Is Daniel all right? It's not like him to stay in his bed so late in the morning."

Lara knew the kindhearted woman had taken a shine to Grandpa. "He's had one of his malaria spells. He'll be better in a few days. What he needs now is rest."

Surprise engulfed Betty's chubby face. "But what about the land rush? Are you folks giving up on it?"

"No. I'm riding."

Betty gasped. "They let women do that?"

Lara smiled. "Yes, ma'am, they do."

"Well, I wish you luck, and I certainly hope to see you again." She glanced wistfully toward Lara's camp. "If I hadn't promised Lester I'd be in Guthrie by nightfall, I'd stay and tend Daniel."

"That's mighty kind of you. I'm sure he'd favor your cooking over Jo's."

They shared a chuckle and another hug.

Lara backed up a step, knowing she needed to go. "If you find a bulletin board in Guthrie, leave me a note as to whether or not you got land and where you'll be going. I'd like to stay in touch."

"Bless you, dear." Betty placed her palm on Lara's cheek. "You be careful out there. And good luck to you."

"Thank you. You be careful, too."

As she walked the short distance to her camp, she felt she knew what having a mother at this age might feel like. Betty sure was talkative, but she was as kindhearted as any woman Lara knew.

She checked on Grandpa a final time then squatted next to Michael. "You be good for Aunt Jo, and say a prayer that I get a claim today."

"I will. How long you gonna be gone?"

"I don't know, sweetie. Probably a day or two. Give me a hug and kiss." He crawled out from under the wagon, smelling of dirt and boy, and wrapped his arms around her neck. "I love you."

"Me, too." He scrambled back to his spot under the wagon, and Lara stood.

Jo approached. "I wish I were the one riding. I know I could get land."

And there it was—the challenge she'd half expected. "I'll do my best, but you and I both know there isn't enough property for everyone. Not by far."

"Just don't let any rowdy men push you out of the competition. Ride like I know you can. Like you did when we were girls racing Grandpa's horses back at the ranch."

Lara smiled. "That's what I'll do. I'll pretend I need to outrun you. That should give me the motivation I need."

Jo grinned. "I'm sure it would."

Lara enjoyed the rare close moment with her sister. "I'm trusting you to take care of everything here—and take care of yourself. No wandering off."

"And I'm trusting you to get some land. No getting lost."

"I'll do my best." She gave her sister a quick hug and then checked Sunny over one last time to make sure she had all she needed. She strode to the wagon, tugged Grandpa's extra pair of trousers out of his crate of clothing and hurried to the tent. Inside, she donned the britches under her petticoats. Having such stiff fabric hugging her legs felt odd, but she didn't want to have to worry about her skirts flying up and revealing something she preferred to keep hidden. Next, she strapped on Grandpa's holster and made sure the pistol was fully loaded. He'd taught her and Jo how to shoot it, although she hadn't done so in years—and she hoped she wouldn't need it today. But if God blessed her and allowed her to get land, then she might find herself in the position of having to defend her claim from others who'd like to take it from her.

Outside the tent, Jo looked her over, raising one brow as she did. "Going huntin'?"

"I hope not, but I plan to be prepared just in case."

She mounted Sunny then waved good-bye to her family and rode toward the very crowded starting line. Being on horseback, she was able to look around and see where there were places she could squeeze the horse through and move forward. Excitement filled the air as if lightning had struck the area. Like the air on a humid day, the buzz of expectancy was so thick, it seemed it could almost be cut with a knife.

A man sitting on a horse beside her glanced over then eyed her pistol. She smiled, and he nodded.

Her stomach swirled, and her limbs felt weak from anticipation. Sidestepping, Sunny obviously sensed her excitement as he bumped the rider on her right. "My apologies, mister."

"Don't worry about it, ma'am. All these horses are anxious." The man, who looked to be about her grandfather's age, grinned and tipped his hat at her.

She glanced up at the sun nearing its zenith. It wouldn't be long now.

⌒

The morning of April 22, Gabe slowly reined Tempest through the massive crowd, gaining scowls from many folks. Trying to weave through the tight throng of horses, wagons, and buggies, all squeezed in as close to the starting line of the race as they could get, was like trying to walk through a massive buffalo herd without making it stampede.

"Just park yerself somewhere and wait for the bugle call, mister."

Gabe nodded and offered the man a smile as he barely squeezed in front of the stranger's horse. "I would, except I was supposed to meet someone, and I can't seem to find her."

Hoots sounded around him from the high-spirited crowd.

"The biggest race of all time is about to start, and he's looking for a woman," someone to his right shouted.

Cackles filled the air, much to Gabe's chagrin. He shouldn't have spent so much time over breakfast and making sure Luke knew where to look for him after the race. If they failed to meet up later, he instructed Luke to wait for him in Guthrie near the depot.

An army captain rode along the river's edge, where soldier after soldier had sat for hours to keep the Boomers from crossing the river early. Three soldiers left their posts and rode up to the officer. The minute they stopped their horses, several riders on horseback let out a *yeehaw* and shot through the gap their leaving created and plunged into the river. Angry roars filled the air from the Boomers, and two soldiers charged after the men.

The disruption and the space their absence created left room for Gabe to ride down the line to where Lara should be. He was making the assumption she'd ride straight south from her campsite, and he sure hoped he was right. He glanced at the sun, which had nearly reached high noon. He only had minutes left to find her. His gut twisted. He couldn't stand the thought of Lara out there all alone with unscrupulous men willing to steal her claim. Was she armed? Did she even know how to shoot?

Maybe if he helped her get land he could atone for accidentally killing her husband. At least he'd sleep better knowing she had a place to call her own. He might even hang around long enough to help her build a house.

Standing in his stirrups, he searched the infinite line of racers, all wearing eager expressions with eyes filled with hope. When he didn't see her, he changed plans and looked for Sunny's buckskin coloring. He'd seen few of the light-colored horses in the past few days, and that should make it easier to find—his pulse stumbled. There! He spotted her, but she was still a good twenty yards away.

A soldier rode down the river's edge, shouting, "No one crosses the river until the bugles sound and rifles fire. If you do, you will be tracked down and removed from the race. Follow the rules, folks, and this will be a good day for all of us. Two more minutes."

Cheers filled the air, so loud they made Tempest prance sideways. Gabe searched for a way to get to Lara, but it was impossible. With the two-minute warning, everyone had eased forward. He was so close to the riders on either side of him, if he had a razor, he could have given them a shave. He smiled at the thought and focused forward. Those on horseback would have the early advantage. They could cross the river far easier than the heavy buggies and wagons. As soon as he got across, he'd angle his way toward Lara. She didn't need to know he was there to watch over her. He just hoped she rode as well as she claimed she did, because if he dawdled, he'd have no chance at getting land himself.

Maybe he should worry about himself and forget about the feisty widow who despised his choice of careers. As soon as the thought breached his mind, he knew he couldn't let her ride alone. Even if she hated him, too much of his heart was invested in her well-being. He could at least see that she got a spot of land. She needed it far more than he.

All around him, the tension rose as each racer focused on the soldiers, waiting for the lift of the bugles and rifles that would signal the start. He'd never participated in something so exciting, and his limbs actually trembled. Tempest snorted and pawed the earth, as if he, too, sensed the importance of the day. Gabe glanced again at Lara, memorizing her dark blue dress and straw hat. He blinked. Was that a gun belt around her tiny waist? He grinned. Maybe he'd underestimated her abilities.

A tense hush fell over the crowd, with horses blowing and the jangle of harnesses the only sounds to be heard. The captain stared at his watch. He lifted a hand, and Gabe hunkered down across Tempest's neck. There were only a few horses ahead of him, so he should be able to break free fairly quickly. He held his breath.

On both sides of him for as far as he could see, anxious Boomers lined the river, resembling a massive writhing serpent, waiting to strike.

Gabe's heart pounded. A trickle of sweat ran down his temple in spite of the cool temperature.

Horses pranced and snorted, sensing the tension of their riders.

The captain's arm swiftly dropped.

The blare of bugles rang out, and the blast of rifles filled the air.

With a roar, the riders lunged forward in an east–west line that ran for miles. Gabe shot into the river, crossed it with no problem in spite of the high water, and made it up the other side. The rider next to him slipped on the muddy banks, allowing Gabe to slide over and fill his spot. The faster horses pulled away, quickly leaving the struggling horde of wagons behind. His hat flew off, and he was glad he'd taken the time to affix the cord around his neck earlier. An exhilaration he hadn't experienced since he was a young boy flooded him.

He searched for Lara. Had she made it across the river, swollen from the recent rains? Glancing back and forth between the land in front of him and the riders to his right, he continued his search. Where was she?

A group of riders fanned to the far right while others surged forward. There! She was slightly in front of him—something he hadn't expected. He spotted her buckskin horse and her straw hat. He angled Tempest to the right and realized that Lara had reined her horse to the left. She must be taking his advice and heading to the Guthrie area. The distance between them narrowed.

The wind whipped at his face as Tempest's hooves pounded the ground. Fortunately, even though they received rain almost nightly this week, the ground was still hard. The sun warmed his head, and his heart pounded with possibilities. He couldn't help grinning. What happened today might well change his whole life.

After an hour of riding, all but a handful of riders had veered off or stopped to stake a claim. When Lara slowed her horse to a trot to rest him, so did Gabe, keeping a ways behind her. At some point, he needed to catch up to her, but for now, he was content to follow and make sure she was safe.

In just a few hours, they might both be landowners. Neighbors.

Chapter 18

Jo kicked at the buckboard's wheel, stubbing her toe. Wagon after wagon drove past, leaving behind only a smidgen of the people who had been camped there this morning and a huge cloud of dust, which coated her face and clothing. Grit settled on her teeth and in her hair. She scratched at her chest, sure that dust had made its way into nearly every part of her clothing. If only she could have ridden instead of Lara.

Maybe she should have taken Sunny last night and sneaked off. She might have if Grandpa hadn't taken sick and Lara hadn't sat up half the night with him. She'd seriously thought about it, but in the end, she didn't want to jeopardize her family getting land. If she staked a claim and someone else contested that she was too young and that she'd been there before the start of the race, they would lose everything. She sighed. She may not want to live on a farm, but she would like to know her family had a home.

Bad Billy cried out and yanked at his tether. The crazy ole goat didn't like all the ruckus made by the Boomers. She checked to make sure Michael was still playing inside the wagon and walked over to the trees where the goats had been tied. They'd eaten all the leaves off the nearby bushes. As soon as things settled down and the last of the wagons crossed the river, she needed to find something for Lara's beasts to eat.

Wagons had been fording the river for hours, and there were still many more.

"Jo."

She patted Billy and handed him a wad of grass she'd plucked then rushed back to the wagon and stooped down. "How are you, Grandpa?"

He shivered, and Jo tugged the quilt over his chest.

"Do you need another quilt?"

He shook his head. "Need pill."

Jo counted the hours in her head since his last pill. Lara had said to try to spread them out since she didn't know when she'd be able to purchase more of them. She hated seeing him suffer. Since their parents died, he'd been the only one who gave a hoot whether they lived or not. Even Jack, their own brother, had up and left them.

She hurried around to the dust-coated tent and crawled inside. Her hand shook as she opened the bottle. The precious pills popped out. She quickly gathered them up, making sure not to lose even one. Then she carried a single pill and a ladle of water around and helped him drink. "Do you think you could eat some lunch? Although I don't know if I can find anything that isn't covered in dust."

"Not yet. I just need to rest." He yawned and then coughed several times. "Did Lara get off?"

"As far as I know. She rode up to get as close to the start as she could, but I didn't follow her."

"She's a fine horsewoman."

Jo looked away. Just once, she wished he'd compliment her. The question hovering in the back of her mind for days spilled out. "What happens if she doesn't get a claim?"

"I believe that she will. But God will provide if she doesn't."

Jo rolled her eyes and blew out a sigh. That was always his pat answer. Had that miserable soddy been God's provision? And if God was so good at providing stuff, why couldn't he give them a steer so they could eat some beef instead of squirrels, turtles, and pigeons? Why did her parents have to die if God cared so much?

"Aunt Jo, I gotta go. And I'm hungry."

"Go see to the boy. I'm just gonna rest some more."

Jo stood and dusted off her skirt, which was an effort in futility, then helped Michael out of the wagon.

She thought of the pretty house she would have one day and knew it would only happen by hard work on her part. God didn't even know she existed, much less want to provide for her. No, the best thing she could do was to get away from this wretched land— this filthy dirt—and find someplace where she could live the life she'd dreamed about.

The train chugged closer to Guthrie, making Mark's gut swirl. Each mile brought him closer to his dream of owning his own chain of stores—the first one in Guthrie. He had to get land. Failing wasn't an option, not with the two carloads of supplies he had coming in later today. People would need all manner of supplies that they hadn't been able to carry with them on the run—lumber, cookstoves, food, and building materials. Mark stood taller. He was the one with the foresight to plan ahead and realize those needs, and he'd be the one to reap the financial benefit.

The wind whipped his face and threatened to steal his hat away, while coal dust powdered everything like a layer of sooty snow. He held on to the railing surrounding the outside of the platform at the back of the third car with sweaty hands that he had to keep wiping on his pants. At first, he'd planned on getting a seat inside but then decided against it. The train was packed with men sitting on the laps of other men, the aisles were full, and there were even men riding on top of the rail cars. Getting out of the cars would be difficult, especially with the platforms full. Six men even shared his small landing. He glanced up at the top of the car behind the one he was riding, and watched the men clinging to the top.

He shook his head. Fools, all of them. He wouldn't risk his neck like that. At least he'd had the foresight to climb aboard the platform early, claim his spot and hold it, even though he'd been bumped and scowled at by others trying to get on. No matter. What was done was done.

He watched the rolling hills of Indian Territory sail by. He had no plans to ever ride on the platform of a train again, but this one time was quite exhilarating. His father, the great Wilfred Hillborne, and his father's protégé, Mark's older brother, Baron, would be appalled at his behavior. Of course, neither of them would be caught dead participating in such an uncouth event as a land rush. Both were fuddy-duddies with no sense of adventure.

Still, he had to give his father credit for funding this venture even if he didn't agree with it. Just another reason he *had* to get land and make a good profit. The sooner he paid back his father, the happier he'd be. He didn't like being beholden to him.

The train jerked, and Mark tightened his grasp. It wouldn't do to fall off before he got to the Guthrie Station. If he got a fast start at the beginning of the race, he might be fortunate to get a town plot close to the railroad station. It would make transporting wares from the depot to his store much easier.

His thoughts turned to Abigail and how she'd pleaded with him not to go to a dirty town on the prairie. She was scared to death of

Indians and being so far away from a big city. He was sick of hearing her whine about that and about leaving her behind. Part of the reason he chose the Oklahoma Territory was because he knew she wouldn't follow him out there. She was beautiful, but too spoiled for his liking. Too bad he didn't find that out sooner.

"What kind of business do you intend on startin'?" the impeccably dressed man on his left asked.

"A mercantile."

The man nodded. "I'm a tailor. Perhaps I can purchase supplies from you if'n you get a plot."

"I have a good supply of fabrics arriving later today actually, including some plain, striped, and diagonal worsteds, mostly in shades of navy and black. There are also some fine finished tweeds in checks and plaids. Mind you, my stock in the finer fabrics isn't large, but I can order more if you need me to."

The man had started nodding when Mark first mentioned the fabric he had in stock and still continued. "Fine! Fine. That's far more than I would've hoped for."

"I also have a good supply of needles in various sizes, scissors, thread, and the like. My name's Mark Hillborne."

"Everett Daggert. Most folks call me Ev." He held out his hand, and Mark shook it. Ev eyed Mark's sack suit in appreciation. "I'm glad to meet another man who knows how to dress well."

Mark nodded as he checked the time on his pocket watch. He frowned. It was well past one, and the race had already started. What would he do if no land was left when he arrived? Surely the train would beat the riders to Guthrie, even with the late start. He certainly hoped so.

He sighed and studied his platform mates. While he didn't particularly care about making friends, establishing relationships with other men who owned businesses was crucial. The other trio of men on the platform, who looked enough alike to be father and sons, kept to themselves, even facing the opposite direction. They talked so low that the noise of the train drowned out anything they said. No sweat off his brow if they wanted to keep to themselves. One of the men pointed at something on the far side of the train, but Mark couldn't distinguish what it was. He started to turn and face the outside of the train when it suddenly jerked, hissed, and slowed. He spun about and spied a small wooden structure. Was that the Guthrie Station or just another water stop?

Whoops and cheers rang out from the first car, and men jumped off the top of the train. Mark lurched into motion, grabbing his satchel off the floor. He eyed his stake, making sure it was still there, and then, even though the train was still moving, he studied the ground for a flat spot and jumped. He hit hard, rolled, then found his feet and took off running. As he angled his body toward the land behind the depot, he saw a crowd already gathered there, much to his dismay. He pushed his confusion away and aimed for the land past them. His feet pounded hard, and he ran for all he was worth, as a herd of men stampeded behind him.

The train's whistle blasted, announcing its arrival. Even though this was supposed to be the first train to reach Guthrie, there had to already be several hundred men there. Sooners, no doubt. Sneaked in and claimed their spots already. Or maybe the trains from the south had beat them. He gritted his teeth but didn't slow his pace.

Signs marked the streets, so rather than head straight for the most crowed area, he aimed for the street north of the depot and hurried up the slight incline. He passed people with their shingles already hanging from two sticks in the ground, stating their name and sometimes the type of their business. Oftentimes, someone was standing at the front of the lot, waving people on. As far as he could see, men were working. Some already had supplies out and were hawking their wares.

Mark couldn't believe his rotten luck. Breathing hard, he slowed his pace.

A man waved him on. "Don't give up. Just find the last piece of land and claim it. Go on. Others are right behind you."

He nodded his thanks and hurried on. Three blocks from the train station his steps slowed as his eyes landed on the prettiest thing he'd seen since meeting Joline Jensen—an unclaimed lot. The lot on the far side already had a tent on it as did others farther down. How had this one been missed? He stepped across the invisible threshold and drove his stake into the ground. Then he straightened, looping his thumbs in his suspenders and watching the other frantic Boomers pass him.

His neighbor to his left nodded and grinned. "I wondered when someone was going to notice that plot hadn't been claimed. If'n I'd had a son old enough, he'd have gotten it."

Mark smiled, very glad the man didn't have a son. He wasn't as close to the depot as he'd hoped, but the way he figured, with this huge crowd, there would be plenty of men who didn't get a claim who might be interested in hauling freight. Stretching, he surveyed his plot. It wasn't the one he'd hoped for, but with all the wares he had coming, by tomorrow, he would be doing a stiff business. He needed to hire several workers to get his large tent erected and stocked. His thoughts rushed to Jo Jensen again. Where was the pretty girl now?

He shook her from his mind and got back to work. From his satchel, he withdrew a ball of string and a supply of sticks and began staking out his mercantile. He wished he'd thought to bring a fabric sign with him, but by tomorrow, he'd have the one he'd had made just for this event.

Besides the tent, the first things he needed to have brought to his booth were the half-dozen barrels of water he'd sent by train. Gilbert, his father's employee, had thought him crazy to ship barrels of water, but Mark knew that with so many people competing for the land, there was bound to be a shortage of the precious liquid. Just how much he could get for a cup was the question. He grinned.

Yes sir, by tomorrow night, his pockets would be lined with coin.

⁓

Though Sunny wanted to gallop constantly and Lara preferred it, she reined him to a brisk trot, hoping to conserve his energy. He was too valuable to lose. She glanced at the sun, estimating that she'd been riding for close to two hours. Looking around and behind her, she only saw three riders, and one of those veered to the right as she watched. He must be heading for Kingfisher.

Lara angled Sunny to the left slightly, trying to remember all that Grandpa had told her about the lay of the land—but it all ran together with no map to refer to. Should she stop here and claim this section? And how was she to know if someone else already had when she couldn't see the whole one hundred and sixty acres at once?

She crested a hill and allowed Sunny to pick up his speed as he descended it. A man stood in a copse of trees, waving his flagged stake as a signal to ride on. This land was claimed. "Please, Lord, help me find an available claim."

Everything depended on it.

She kept Sunny to a trot across the hilly land as much as possible, knowing the horse could last much longer at that speed. She crossed several more rolling hills and realized there was no one around. She searched right and left. Only a single rider followed her. Was this the spot she should claim?

One more hill—to see if there was a water source—and she would stop. She held her breath as she crested the hill and pulled Sunny to a stop. His sides expanded and shrank with his labored breathing.

A wide creek, surrounded by trees on both sides ran through the beautiful span of land. She looked to her left, and her stomach clenched at the sight of a stack of stones that indicated the corner point where four sections of land met. Her heart picked up speed. She could claim this land. It was perfect. And not a soul was in sight.

But hoofbeats pounded behind her—close behind.

"Hi'yah, Sunny!" She slapped the reins against his neck.

The surprised horse bolted forward and down the hill. Rocks scattered beneath his hooves. Lara held her breath, wishing she hadn't pushed him so hard on the slope, but her family's existence rested on her getting this land.

Suddenly, Sunny stumbled. Lara grasped at the saddle horn, but her hand slipped. Strings of Sunny's mane slid through her fingers as she scrambled for a hold. And then she was flying over the horse, through the air. Darkness claimed her.

⌒

Gabe's heart nearly flew from his chest as he watched Lara sail over the head of her falling horse. He should have called out to her. Let her know it was he who was following her, then maybe she wouldn't have felt the need to hurry so badly. He should have slowed down and not pressed her. This was his fault.

At the bottom of the hill, he jumped off Tempest before the horse stopped and ran to Lara. Blood seeped from a cut above her eyebrow, as well as multiple scrapes on her face and hands.

He jumped up and grabbed the reins of the buckskin, at the same time checking to see if the horse was injured. At least the gelding was standing. Blood ran down his front legs, but all four hooves were securely on the ground. The horse panted and blew, still winded from his long ride. Gabe needed to cool down the animals, but first he had to tend to Lara. He led her gelding to a shady spot and checked to see where Tempest was. The horse had found water and was helping himself to a drink. Gabe jogged over to him, grabbed the reins and tied them to a hackberry bush. Then he unfastened his bedroll and bag of supplies, making sure to keep his claim stake close at hand. Picking a wide-open spot, he shoved the blue-flagged stake into the ground, becoming an instant landowner. Pride swelled through him, but it was short-lived.

Under the shade of an oak tree, he shook out his bedroll then hurried to Lara's side, scooped her up, and carried her to his blanket, where he laid her. She moaned but didn't awaken. He knew little about doctoring, except that he needed to tend her wounds and cover the worst of them. Tugging off his bandana, he jogged back to the creek, dipped a corner of it in water, and returned to Lara's side. Kneeling beside her, he gently pressed the damp cloth against the biggest cut. It probably needed stitching up, but he had no needle or thread.

But maybe she did. He glanced at the buckskin and realized there was no gear attached to the saddle. Looking back at the hill, he saw that Lara's satchel and bedding had come loose in the fall. He quickly fetched the items, along with her battered straw hat, and brought them back. He felt odd rummaging through her unmentionables, but it had to be done. The first thing he noticed was the sad state of her grayed garments. Oh, they were clean, but faded and frayed. He tugged out a petticoat, easily ripping the thin fabric into strips. At the bottom of the bag, he discovered a rolled-up piece of fabric and untied and unrolled it, thanking God for the supplies inside.

The only thing missing was a bottle of whiskey to cleanse the wound and ease her pain, not that he thought she would imbibe. Ten minutes later, he sat back on his heels and studied his handiwork. Lara would have a jagged scar, but it would heal, and maybe her hair would hide it.

She'd be horrified to know that he'd run his hands down each of her limbs, making sure there were no breaks—and thanked God there weren't. Those pants, which surprised the dickens out of him, had protected her legs. She would be sore and in pain for a few days, but she would live. He hoped.

He heard a scuffling and saw a rider sliding down the rocky hillside. Gabe strode out to let the man know the land had been claimed. He started to motion to the man to ride on, but a thought streaked across his mind.

"Hey, mister, you got any whiskey?"

The man grinned and reined to a halt, his horse prancing and blowing hard. "You aim to celebrate gettin' a claim?"

Gabe shook his head. "My woman got hurt. Her horse didn't take that hill as well as yours and mine. I need some whiskey to cleanse her wounds."

"Sorry to hear that." He reached behind him, unfastened his saddlebags, and pulled out a half-empty bottle of scotch. He gave it a lingering look then tossed it to Gabe. "I guess your lady needs it more than I do. Mind if I water my horse a speck from your creek?"

"Go right ahead, and thanks a heap. And no one has passed us in a long while, so the next section may be unclaimed."

"Thanks!" The cowboy grinned and tipped his hat and trotted

his horse toward the creek. Gabe rushed back to Lara's side, mulling over the fact that he had a creek on his own land.

When he poured a small portion of the scotch on Lara's forehead, she groaned and twisted away from him. She raised a hand toward the cut, but Gabe grabbed her hand and pulled it away.

"W—what happened? W—where am I?"

He plugged the bottle and scooted closer to her. "Your horse took a fall, and you fell off. Injured your head, mostly."

Her eyes blinked, and she squinted up at him. "Gabe?"

He took her nearest hand. "Yeah, it's me. You liked to have scared me half to death."

"The land!" Suddenly she bolted up, moaning and grabbing her head.

He clutched her shoulders, halting her progress, and pushed her back down. "Easy there, you had a bad fall. You just need to rest."

She looked toward the hill. "My horse. Is he—"

"Fine. He's shook up and scratched his knees, but he seems fine." Gabe glanced at the buckskin and smiled. "He's even grazing, so that's a great sign."

She stared at him. "Let me go. I've got to get land."

He shook his head. "You're not going anywhere. You don't realize it yet, but you're going to be in a world of hurt come morning."

She pushed an elbow behind her, again attempting to rise.

Once more Gabe gently halted her progress. "You need to rest, Lara."

She glared at him. "Get off me."

"No."

"My family is depending on me."

"You're more important to your family than a piece of land."

She grimaced and looked past him, her eyes latching onto

something. Gabe glanced over his shoulder as a trio of riders crested the hill. He rose and walked toward them, waving them on with one hand while keeping the other resting atop his gun. "This land's been claimed. Move on."

They nodded and kept riding. Gabe relaxed and walked back to Lara. Now that she was doing fairly well, the horses needed his attention.

When he turned, Lara was sitting, albeit a bit shakily, glaring at him. "You? You claimed my land for yourself?"

Chapter 19

Silas Stone clutched the bars of the tiny window of the Wichita jail and gave them a shake, like he'd done a hundred other times. Even if they broke free, it wouldn't help him because the opening was too small for him to climb through. He blew out a frustrated sigh and stared out at the quiet alley.

For weeks, people traveling in wagons of all kinds had passed down his alley, but now it was just—quiet. The land hunters had left town, and some unlucky soul had claimed his land—the land his brother was buried on.

Today was April 22. He glanced up, barely able to see the angle of the sun from his cell. The land rush was over and done with by now. The marshal's fat old deputy had taken pleasure in counting down the days until the run and shoving it in his face that someone else would be rightfully settling on the land he'd already claimed as his own. He gritted his teeth and shoved away from the wall, pacing to the front bars and back. He had to get out of here. Had to get back to his land and throw off the yahoo who thought it was rightfully his. Someone would soon be sorry for intruding on his dreams and stealing what was his. Someone needed to live on that land who would put wildflowers on his brother's grave.

He kicked his empty food plate, sending it skittering across the floor. The tin dish gave a satisfying clink as it hit the bars. If he hadn't been thrown off the land, he'd have put up a corral by now, planted a garden, and maybe even stolen a half-dozen head of cattle to call his own.

He grabbed one corner of the pitiful tick mattress, yanked it off the bed, and tossed it in one corner. Being cooped up in this tiny cell for three weeks was driving him crazy—as was the ear-splitting snores of the drunk in the next cell.

Silas stomped across his tiny cage and reached through the bars, poking the smelly ole man in the side. He sputtered, rubbed his whiskery jaw, then resumed the irritating noise. Silas groaned and reached through the bars again and pushed the man. The drunk rolled away from him, lurched suddenly, and fell to the floor. Silas chuckled. That should fix the ole coot.

He started for the window again, but the door to the marshal's office rattled, and the tall man ambled in. He stood bow-legged, a toothpick hanging from one corner of his mouth, eyeing Silas. After a long moment, he let out a loud sigh. "The judge says I have to set you free. My gut says not to."

Silas's heart lurched at the good news, but he tried not to show it.

"If I let you go, you have to give me your word that you'll stay out of the Oklahoma Territory. You can go north, east, west, I don't care. But you're not to ride south. You understand?"

"Course I do." He understood that he had to agree if he wanted to get out of jail. "What about my horse?"

"He's at the livery. If you agree to stay clear of Oklahoma, I'll release you and authorize his release to you."

Silas held up one hand as if pledging on a Bible and fought to hold back a smile. "I swear."

"This goes against my better judgment, but. . ." He stuck the key in the lock and turned it. The loud click was the sweetest thing Silas had heard in ages. He grabbed his hat off the floor where it had fallen when he tossed the mattress and slapped it on his head.

The door whined open as if it, too, didn't want to let him go. The sheriff stepped back, and Silas walked through the doors, a free man.

A few minutes later, with his holster on his hips, he walked out of the marshal's office and headed to the livery. In a few short days, he'd be back home—to his land—in the Oklahoma Territory.

And God help the man who'd stolen that land.

Lara leaned against the oak tree that had sheltered her from the warm sun most of the afternoon, every muscle in her body aching. All afternoon, she'd dozed in and out. Only sleep half softened her misery.

She shouldn't have taken that last hill so fast, but she was afraid the rider behind her—Gabe, she now knew—would get her claim. All her efforts had been wasted. Even this pain was a waste, because Gabriel Coulter had claimed the very land she'd meant to win.

She glanced over at the handsome scoundrel as he built a fire. They'd be sharing the campsite tonight. Alone. Would she be safe in only his presence?

She allowed some of her tension to flow out. For some reason, she felt sure she would be. Gabe had never done anything—other than steal a kiss that she half wanted—to prove himself less than a gentleman. Except for stealing her land. But to be fair, if he hadn't, someone else surely would have. And where would she be now without his help? Rather than being afraid of him, his presence encouraged her, but that didn't mean she wasn't still upset.

She watched the glorious sunset. The beautiful pink clouds and orange-tinted sky looked as if they were celebrating the people who'd been fortunate to get a claim today. But so many felt as she did—despondent. Why did God allow her to fall? Why didn't He let her get the claim instead of Gabe?

"Are you hungry?" He gazed across the fire at her. "I caught a couple of fish while you were resting."

She was starving, but she didn't want him to know it. She had some food supplies in her bag. Her gaze jerked to her saddle then back to where she fell. Where was her satchel?

Twisting toward the creek, she gasped. Gabe had opened her bag and strewn her unmentionables out on the grass for anyone to see. She cast him an angry glare and rotated onto her knees then gently pushed up to her feet. She closed her eyes to the stabbing pain coursing through her and fought not to fall. Gabe rushed to her side and steadied her with a firm, but gentle hand.

"What are you doing? Tell me what you need, and I'll get it."

She turned toward him and narrowed her eyes.

He blinked, looking confused by her anger.

"You went through my belongings?"

"Oh, that's what's upset you." He grinned and shrugged. "The cut on your head needed stitching, and I didn't have a needle or thread. Good thing you did."

He sewed up her head wound? She reached for the bandage but stopped. She must have been hurt more than she realized. "Did you have to string out my unmentionables for all to see?"

He shrugged again. "I was more worried about you bleeding to death. My apologies for not putting them back, but I've been busy tending the horses, finding us some supper, and shooing off anyone who thought to steal this claim away from us."

His use of *us* wasn't lost on her. "This claim doesn't belong to *us*, Mr. Coulter. It belongs to *you*. First thing in the morning, I'll be on my way back to my family."

His brow wrinkled at her comment. "No need to rush off. I don't think you're in any shape to travel that far. And your horse needs at least a day's rest, too."

She hiked her chin. "I can't stay here alone with you."

"You're doing so tonight. Why would tomorrow night make any difference?"

Did the man have to be so confounded sensible? She looked around. At the moment, she needed some privacy. "Please, let me go."

"Like I said, just have a seat, and I'll fetch whatever you need."

She stared at him. "This isn't something you can tend to."

His ears actually reddened, and if she hadn't been so heartbroken over her loss, she might have smiled.

"Oh. Uh. . .well, let me at least help you to wherever you aim to go."

"I can walk on my own, but thank you."

"Are you sure? That's a nasty gash you have, and you were unconscious for quite a while. You might have a concussion."

"At least give me the dignity of trying."

He eyed her for a moment then nodded and let go, but he didn't leave her side.

Lara took a step, wincing at the pain in her knees. She took another one, wobbled when her gaze blurred, and Gabe was there to steady her again.

"Don't be so stubborn, Lara. Let me help. It's partly my fault this happened." He took a deep breath and then murmured, "Everything is my fault."

She frowned at his odd comment. "My horse stumbled because

I pushed him too hard."

"And you probably did that because I was right on your tail and you were afraid I'd beat you to a claim."

"Which you did." She turned to look him in the eye. "Why were you behind me? I never saw you before the race. How was it you were following me?"

He looked away, and a muscle in his jaw twitched. "I overheard some men talking about how there'd be women riding alone. They'd planned to follow one and steal her land."

He looked at her, and something in his fierce gaze took her breath away.

"I couldn't let that happen to you."

She wanted to admire him for protecting her, but the end result had been the same. "And yet you now own the very piece of land I wanted."

"It's not what I wanted, Lara, but I couldn't leave you, not with you unconscious and bleeding. Would you have preferred I let someone else have this section?"

She had to be truthful even if it hurt. "No. I suppose not. If I can't have it, I'm glad that you at least got your land."

He relaxed a bit and rubbed the back of his neck. "I've been thinking, I want to give the land to you. It hasn't been registered yet, so there's no big deal if you are the one who shows up at the land office and claims it."

Her heart soared for a moment before plummeting. She hiked up her chin. "Thank you for your kind offer, but I can't accept such a generous gift."

"Why not?"

"Surely you know why."

"No one would know but us."

"I won't be beholding to a man I barely know."

Gabe frowned. "That's just silliness."

"Maybe so, but it's how I feel. Now, could you please help me to a private spot?"

He ushered her a short distance away to a copse of trees. Sunny nickered as she drew near, and she ran her gaze over him, more than a little thankful the horse hadn't been badly injured. With her securely holding a tree, Gabe walked away.

"Call me when you're done, and I'll help you back."

Her face was so warm, she was certain it was beet red. She quickly removed the trousers, tended to her business, and walked through the trees, holding on to the trunks as needed. Gabe must have heard her, because he jogged her way. She glanced longingly at the creek.

"Let's get you back to camp."

"I really would like to wash. Could we stop at the creek first?"

He nodded and turned toward it. She handed him the pants then knelt down, ignoring the burning pain, and washed off her hands and face. When she was done, Gabe helped her to a nearby boulder, and she sat, enjoying the serene setting. The water bubbled over the rocks, shallow in spots while pooling deeper in others. The last rays of sunlight cast a warm glow over the shady area. "This really is a peaceful place. You're lucky to have gotten it." In spite of her efforts, she couldn't keep the wistfulness from her voice. It was hard to be happy for him when her heart was breaking and her future was so unsettled.

Gabe stepped around her and lowered himself on the other side of the boulder. "Lara, look at me."

She sighed and turned to face him.

He took her hand and laid his other on top of hers. His thumb moved back and forth across her skin, doing strange things to her stomach. "I want to help you, Lara. And the fact is, I can't tend this land alone. I've been tossing ideas around in my head. What would you think about coming to work for me?"

Gabe stared at Lara as a variety of expressions crossed her pretty face.

"What do you mean? What kind of work could I do?"

His mind raced. He'd really only blurted out the thought as it popped into his brain, but the idea had merit. "If I'm working all day to build a house, plant a garden, put up fences, and the like, it won't leave much time for preparing meals or tending to laundry." He squinted, staring at her. "You can cook. I mean you've got a kid, so surely you know how."

She sat up straighter. "Of course, I can cook." Just as fast, the starch left her, and she crossed her arms, staring at the creek. "But I need a home, not a job."

Ideas rushed through Gabe's mind. How could he keep her here and still give her what she needed? She wanted land. He nearly snapped his fingers at the sudden idea. "Tell you what I'll do. If you'll work for me for a year, I'll give you ten acres of land."

Her mouth dropped open as she blinked, staring at him in wonder. "Ten acres? Why, that would be enough for Sunny and our mule to graze on, and I could maybe even get a cow or two. And think of the large garden I could have. . ." She sat back, her smile dipping. "But you won't actually own the land for five years. What if you decide to sell it before then?"

"I won't. I promise."

She stood, grimaced, and reached up, touching her head.

Gabe vaulted to his feet. "Time for you to lie down. Besides, I need to get that fish cooking before all of the light is gone. You think about things and let me know when you've made up your mind."

She didn't fuss as he helped her back to the blankets. He wished he had a big feather bed for her to rest on. One day, maybe. But not tonight. "Before you lie down, let me move you upwind of the campfire. You don't need to be coughing, not with your head hurting like it is."

When they reached camp, he leaned her against the big oak, dropped the pair of pants Lara had worn under her skirts near her satchel, and hurried to move the blanket. He could tell by the way she sagged against the tree that her energy was spent. He jogged back and hoisted her in his arms. She squealed but didn't object. A true sign that she'd pushed herself too hard. Gabe set her down and wrapped one of his blankets over her. Lara placed her hands together and rested her cheek on them, eyes shut.

He stood there, staring down at her. He couldn't explain why he wanted to help her—to not let her go. He longed to ease her burden. To make her life so much easier, and to see her laugh. He turned and walked toward where he'd left the three fish he'd caught earlier.

Somehow in his effort to make atonement to Lara Talbot for killing her husband, he'd fallen in love with her.

⌒

Lara stretched, instantly regretting the action that reminded her of yesterday's fall. She yawned, blinking her eyes as she attempted to fully awaken. Birds chirped happily in the trees overhead, and the gentle sound of water lapping over rocks belied the tension ratcheting through her.

She glanced across the dying fire and saw that Gabe had respectfully slept on the far side. He was most likely cold, curled up as he was in the early morning chill with no blanket or fire. He was kind to give his covering to her, even though she had her own quilt.

How could she work for him? How could she be close to him day in and day out and not waver in her desire not to marry another man who gambled?

And she was attracted to Gabe. Not only because he was handsome with his dark hair and sparkling eyes and that cocky grin that made her stomach feel as if she had a live fish swimming circles in it. Much more than that, he was kind. Had gone out of his way to help a stranger, with no ulterior motive but to be of assistance. She couldn't reconcile the good man with the gambler. They seemed like two separate people. Maybe Gabe was telling the truth when he'd said he wanted to change his ways.

She sat up, trying to ignore the pain surging through her as every muscle felt bruised. The ache in her head was less than it had been yesterday, but there was still a dull throb. How was she going to manage the long ride back to her family in her condition?

And for some reason she didn't understand, she'd yet to tell Gabe about her family. He knew she had a son but not an ailing grandfather and a rebellious sister who liked to wander. And then there were the goats.

A smile pulled at her lips as she imagined Gabe chasing Bad Billy when the goat next escaped his pen. The image drew a chuckle from her.

Gabe rolled over, his eyes open. When he saw her, he sat, rubbing his hand across his stubbly jaw. With that shadow of a beard and his hair mussed, he was even more attractive. He flashed a sleepy grin and blinked his eyes several times as if trying to force himself awake. "How did you sleep?"

His voice, always a bit on the deep side, sounded husky this morning—and far too intriguing for her liking.

She cleared her throat. "I must have slept fine. This is the first I remember waking." A tendril of hair blew across her face, and she tucked it behind her ear. Her hair must look dreadful, judging by the way Gabe stared at her. Yesterday, she braided it and left it down, not wanting to try to keep it pinned up during the long race. She smoothed the wisps of hair surrounding her face then plucked a leaf from atop her head and searched for her satchel.

"What do you need?" Gabe hopped up, his dark pants covered in dirt and grass.

"My satchel, if you don't mind. I'd like to brush the tangles out of my hair."

While he fetched the bag, she unbraided her hair and ran her fingers through it. Gabe hurried back her way, his steps slowing as he gazed at her with wide eyes. His throat moved as he swallowed and continued to her side. He plopped the bag down then sat on the far side of it and cleared his throat. "We. . .uh. . .need to make plans for the day."

She nodded. "I need to get back. Michael will worry if I'm gone too long."

"First thing, I need to get into Guthrie and register my claim before someone gets it into his mind to steal it out from under me."

Lara gasped. "You mean someone might do that? How would you prove it's yours?"

He flashed that cocky grin, and she dropped her gaze, hating the way her insides reacted to his nearness.

"I have a witness to verify my claim."

Her gaze shot up. "I'm not going with you to Guthrie."

"You don't have to, unless I need you to prove I got this land first, fair and square."

"So, when are you going?"

A muscle flicked in his jaw. "I really ought to go right after breakfast. Will you be all right here alone? Are you sure you don't want to ride along?"

She glanced around the desolate valley, wondering if it was wise to stay there alone, but then the starch flowed down her spine again. "I'll be fine. Go—and when you return, I'll start back."

A worried expression flitted across his face. "What about working for me? I could really use your help, Lara. And I have the funds to pay well."

"*If* I work for you, it will be for that ten acres of land you offered me. My family needs a permanent home, and it would take years of work to save up enough money to buy land." She really had no choice. Since she failed to win a claim, this was her only viable option to get her family the home they needed. "I will work for you on one condition."

Gabe smiled, and one eyebrow cocked up. "And what would that be?"

"I want to pick out my land."

He seemed to mull over her comment for a long moment, then he nodded. "I'll agree to that—on one condition."

"Um. . .what condition?"

"That you pick land along one of the four borders of my claim and not right smack in the middle of it."

Lara nodded. "That's more than fair. Agreed."

"It's a deal." He held out his hand, and she eyed it. Touching him was dangerous, but she had to seal the deal. "I'll shake on it now, but I also want things officially put in writing, so there's no confusion later, especially if you decide to sell the claim at some point." She reached out, allowing his hand to envelop hers. A hot fire sizzled through her as if she'd been hit by lightning as her palm rested against his. Gabe's self-assured expression deepened, and he captured her gaze with his own. Her heart pounded in her ears as she veered into dangerous waters.

He gently tugged her toward him. "Lara. . ."

His voice was far too husky—far too appealing. She yanked her hand back, frightened to realize how attracted she was to him. So inappropriate for a new widow. Living around him daily would be a challenge, but at least she'd have her own home to return to at night.

"We'd better eat some breakfast, so you can be on your way. The sooner you go, the sooner you'll get back. I'd very much prefer not to be here alone after dark."

The sweet moment between them was lost. Gabe nodded, looking disappointed. He stood. "I'll build up the fire and see what there is to eat."

"I have two cheese sandwiches that need to be eaten."

He nodded and walked over to the pile of wood he'd collected.

She watched him go, both relieved and frustrated. Why did she have to be attracted to Gabriel Coulter? Everything would be so much easier if she weren't.

Chapter 20

Near noontime, Gabe rode into Guthrie, more than a bit surprised at the mass of people he encountered. Thousands of tents dotted the land for miles. He imagined the sight resembled a massive army camp. People moved everywhere, carrying wood, hawking food and water, and business after business was open, as if it weren't odd that no one had a building to work from.

His stomach grumbled, but he rode on, anxious to locate the land office and make his claim official. He'd read in the *Homesteader's Handbook* that the land office would be situated near the depot, so he headed there, hoping to find Luke somewhere in the mess of folks. Up ahead, his gaze landed on a small wooden structure, one of the few built so far. He had no doubt that next time he arrived in town there would be many more, because hammering and sawing occurred in almost every direction he looked.

As he dismounted, he thought of all the things he needed to buy: a wagon and team, food supplies, a stove, a bed for Lara and her son, although he could probably make one fairly easily. He'd need rope for supporting the mattress and using around the ranch, and wire for fencing. He blew out a loud sigh as he tied Tempest to a hitching post, and then he walked over and stood behind the last man in line at the land office. Starting from scratch wouldn't be easy, but many besides him would be doing the same thing. And he was in better shape than most because he had money and several rooms of furniture.

An hour later with his claim officially registered and his certificate proving it in his pocket, he went in search of something to eat. A place called Mel's caught his eye, with red-and-white-checkered cloths covering three tall tables. There were no chairs, but a man could stand at the table and eat without having to hold his plate and cup. A large man with muttonchops and bushy eyebrows served him a bowl of ham and beans, the daily special—and the only item on the menu. Lukewarm corn bread and hot coffee finished off the fare. Not the best meal he'd had, but it filled his belly and allowed him to watch the comings and goings of the town.

He needed to finish his business and get back to Lara. He didn't like leaving her alone, especially after the fall she took. She seemed to be all right, but he didn't want to spend any more time in town than necessary.

He rode up and down several of the makeshift streets to see who had the best stock of supplies. It didn't take long to figure out there was one place in particular that had far and above the amount of supplies than the other stores—Hillborne General Store. He tied Tempest to a brand-new hitching post and wandered into the big tent, looking at the stacks of wares as he walked. He hadn't expected to find a store almost as well stocked as one he would see in Kansas City, but someone had been wise and forward-thinking enough to plan ahead. The man had sure taken a risk, because if he hadn't gotten land, he would have been stuck with all of this stock.

As the list in his head grew of things he wanted to take back to camp, Gabe realized he should have first looked into buying a wagon or a packhorse.

A nicely dressed man close to his age smiled. "Can I help you find something, mister?"

Gabe pushed his hat back on his head. "I need more than I can carry. Do you know where I could purchase a wagon and team?"

The blond man rubbed his hand across his jaw. "I've been so busy here that I've hardly left this tent, but I heard some discouraged folks were selling out and hopping the train back to wherever they came from. You might try down near the depot. In the meantime, do you have a list of supplies?"

Gabe shook his head. "I didn't make one because I wasn't sure what all would be available, but I need pretty much everything to start working my land."

The man's blue eyes sparkled, and he held out his hand. "My name's Mark Hillborne, and I'm guessing you're one of the fortunate men who won a claim yesterday."

"Gabe Coulter." He shook hands, smiling. "And yes, I did." His smile faded when he thought of how Lara had planned on claiming that piece of land before her horse stumbled. He'd make it up to her. "I need a good stock of canned goods, flour, sugar, coffee, beans, rice, shovel, axe, saw, fencing wire." He blew out a loud breath. "So much it makes my head swim."

Mr. Hillborne jotted down a list as fast as Gabe spat it out. Then he paused and glanced up. "I hope you're aware that I'm not offering credit, since I don't know anyone here."

Gabe nodded. "I can pay. I sold horses before the land run and did fairly well."

Mr. Hillborne chuckled. "I bet you could buy some of those horses back now for a fraction of what you sold them for."

"I reckon you're right." He tapped his finger on the table that served as the store's counter. "Why don't you gather me a small supply of food stocks while I go see if I can purchase a wagon. No sense in ordering more than I can carry."

Mr. Hillborne looked a little disappointed, but he nodded. "I'll be here when you get done."

Gabe rode Tempest downhill toward the depot. Off to the right, he noticed a half-dozen wagons and a corral of horses and mules and reined his horse toward them. He picked out a decent buckboard and team and dickered with the eager seller until he got the price he wanted, then he returned to Hillborne's. He had a feeling the store's sharp owner wouldn't be as easy to haggle with as the liveryman.

An hour and a half later and a lot poorer, he stood next to his full buckboard. Wouldn't Lara be surprised with all that he'd bought? The cooking and food supplies would make preparing meals much easier for her, as would the big washtub for doing laundry. Tempest nickered at him, probably more than ready to be off.

Gabe wished he could have found Luke, but finding a specific person among thousands was nigh on impossible. He secured Tempest's reins to the tailgate and patted the horse's rump as he walked behind him.

"There's that pocket-pickin' blackleg Gabriel Coulter!"

He spun around, looking for the man who'd slandered his name. The hairs on the back of his neck rose, and an ominous feeling tightened his gut. His gaze landed on a tall man who looked vaguely familiar. How did he know the man?

The cowboy walked toward him, keeping his hand near his holstered gun. "You ruined my brother's life, Coulter, and I aim to ruin yours."

❧

After washing her hair in the creek, Lara strapped Grandpa's holster onto her waist again and wrapped a blanket around her to get warm. The sun would dry her hair, but with it damp, a chill had worked its way into her bones. Walking helped her warm up and seemed to also work some of the tension from her muscles. She followed the creek, meandering in and out of the trees that lined it.

She exhaled a loud sigh. This land Gabe won was beautiful, and the water made it the perfect choice for a farmer or a man who wanted to raise horses on a small scale. It would have been a wonderful place to call home, if only she hadn't lost.

But if she accepted Gabe's generous offer, she could return to her family, partially successful. There really was no choice, even though she didn't want to be near Gabe, because he stirred her senses with his glimmering eyes and gentle touch. Tom had never been so tender. He'd charmed her into falling in love with him when she was only Jo's age, but then he'd taken what he felt was his and often left her crying in his wake. If that was marriage, she didn't want it.

She had to believe that not all men were like that. Her father had been a kind, compassionate man, and she was certain Grandpa never treated Grandma so harshly. Nor would Gabe. But then, she'd have never expected Tom to treat her in such a manner, either.

A creaking noise jerked her gaze to a hill covered in bushes and trees. She paused, searching for whatever made the sound, making sure it was safe to continue on before she ventured farther. Nothing moved except for the leaves rustling in the breeze. A gust tugged at the blanket and her skirts. Her hair fluttered out to the side. The creaking noise emanated through the shadowy area again, raising the hair on her arms. Shedding the blanket, she tugged the pistol from her holster, cocked the hammer, then cautiously crept forward. Stopping behind a wide oak, she swallowed hard and peered around the trunk.

She was surprised to find what looked to be a campsite. There was no sign of anyone there now, but she chose to err on the side of caution and stayed hidden.

The eerie squeal made her jump. Lara took a half step around the tree and gasped. The noise was a door, swinging back and forth in the breeze—a door to an opening in the side of a hill. She'd heard of dugouts before, but she'd never seen one.

"H'lo in the camp. Anyone there?"

Her hand shook as the pistol grew heavy. She lowered her arm to her side but didn't holster the gun. When no one answered, she slowly stepped forward, searching every direction. There was nothing to indicate the camp was fresh, but she couldn't afford to take chances. She made a beeline for the charcoals in the middle of the campsite, kept her gun ready, and poked the ashes with a stick. No sign of smoke or warm embers. No one had used this fire pit in a long while. She relaxed and looked around. A buckboard sat near the dugout, and several faded men's shirts hung from a rope strung between two trees. Someone might have lived here at one time, but they no longer did. A pair of stained socks, with holes in the heels and toes lay on the ground, as well as a couple of fishing poles and dishes. What had happened here? Why would someone ride off and leave their laundry and buckboard?

She turned to the dugout, longing to look inside but also partly afraid to. She swallowed and tiptoed to the door. It was possible someone was hiding in there but not too likely, given the sad state of the camp. She pointed the gun toward the open door. "Anyone there?"

Her heartbeat pounded in her ears. She huffed a breath, embarrassed at her nervousness. Tugging the door open all the way, she stepped forward and peered inside. It took her eyes a moment to adjust to the dimmer lighting, but after a moment, she could see that the inside was actually bigger than their soddy in Caldwell had been.

She sucked in a breath. Gabe had said she could have her choice of his land. Would it be selfish of her to pick land that included the dugout? Her family could have a shelter right away, which was especially important for Grandpa and Michael. Why, the place was plenty big enough for her and Jo to sleep inside, too. Walking farther in, she spotted a table with two chairs. Pocketing her gun, she allowed herself to smile. Grandpa had said God would provide. The good Lord hadn't provided the way she'd hoped or even expected, but He had given them just what they needed. "Thank You, God."

On the table, she found a lantern and a tin mug with some matches. She snagged one and lit the lantern then turned it toward the back wall. The place certainly needed cleaning up, but it was cool now, and she suspected it would be warm in the winter. Maybe by then they could get a stove and put in a vent pipe. On the wall to her right was a double bed. It would be perfect for Grandpa and Michael. The bedding needed boiling and the tick re-stuffed, but the frame was solid. Lara circled the room, unable to believe her good fortune.

There was just one thing she had to make sure of—that the dugout wasn't smack-dab in the middle of Gabe's claim. He'd been clear on that issue.

She returned the lantern to the table and blew it out, sending a plume of smoke into the air. Outside, she walked around the hill and up to the top. The exertion made her head pound, but she wasn't about to stop. She needed to find the stones that marked the edge of Gabe's claim.

After nearly an hour of zigzagging left and right, she found the pile of rocks that marked the southwestern corner of Gabe's property. Lara turned back toward the dugout and smiled. If she asked for the whole southwestern corner, she could have the dugout, a water source since the creek angled along Gabe's southern border, and a somewhat flat valley for planting. There were even plenty of trees for building a pen for the goats and a barn for Sunny, their mule, and the cow she hoped to buy.

Delighted, Lara clapped her hands. The sun shone down, warming her head and drying her hair. She was finally home.

Gabe held out his hands, while his mind raced as he tried to figure out if he'd ever before seen the stranger who now called him out. "Sorry, mister, but I have no idea what you're talking about."

"You're the no-good gambler who cheated my brother and caused him to lose his monthly pay that he was supposed to send to his wife. She up and left him and took their kid with her—and I blame you."

"I never forced anyone to play cards with me. And I never cheated. Besides, those days are past." He glanced at the crowded streets. People all along the dirt road watched, while moving out of the way at the same time. A woman tucked her daughter behind her back, but she didn't make any attempt to leave. If shots were fired, anyone lining the street would be in danger of getting hit.

"I don't even know you. What's your name?" A bead of sweat trickled down the side of Gabe's temple, but he didn't dare make a move to wipe it. More than likely, he could outdraw the stranger, but he didn't want to risk getting shot, especially with Lara waiting for him to return.

"Payton Reeves. My brother's name is Judah. Sound familiar?"

Judah Reeves. Gabe rolled the name over his mind until a picture formed. "Yeah, it does. But like I said, your brother came to me. I never forced him to sit at my table."

"You gamblers are all alike—stealing a man's hard-earned money and grinning all the way to the bank."

Gabe took a step closer when Reeves glanced sideways. "Your argument is with me, Reeves. Let's handle this like men. Take off your gun belt and fight me like a man. That way no one else will get hurt."

Reeves glanced around, probably noticing the women and children in the crowd. Eyes narrowed, he stroked his whiskery chin with his thumb and index finger. Scowling, he turned back to Gabe. "You ruined my family, and I mean to have revenge."

"Look, I'm sorry for the pain I've caused you. I've quit gambling and have a sweet little piece of land I won yesterday where I plan to raise horses." He even had a woman he wanted to call his own, but he couldn't say that. "I only recently realized how my gambling hurt other people, and I'll tell you here and now in front of all these people that I regret the choices I made. If I could do things over, I'd do them differently."

"You ain't sweet-talkin' your way out of a fight like some snake oil salesman, Coulter. You destroyed my brother's life."

Before Gabe could respond, Reeves drew. Unprepared, he fumbled for his gun. A shot rang out, and Gabe jumped, waiting for the fiery pain that accompanied a bullet. But no pain came. Instead, Reeves dropped his gun and stared at the growing red spot on his chest. He glanced up at Gabe with a stunned expression then dropped to his knees and fell on his face.

Still numb from his close call, Gabe looked over his shoulder to see who had shot Reeves. Luke McNeil walked toward him, holstering his gun. The young cowboy grinned. "Good thing I had your back, huh, boss?"

He nodded. "Am I ever glad to see you again! You saved my life. I wasn't expecting him to draw like that."

"I could see it in his eyes. He was just waitin' for you to drop your guard."

Two soldiers jogged up the street and halted beside Payton Reeves's body. One motioned Gabe to him. "What happened here?"

Mark Hillborne strode forward. "I saw the whole thing, Sergeant. This man is a customer of mine, and we had just loaded his wagon when this galoot called him out. He tried to get the man to settle their squabble without guns, but this fellow drew without warning."

The soldier pursed his lips and slid his gaze toward Gabe. "That what happened?"

Gabe nodded. "Yes, sir. I was just about to leave town when that man hollered at me. He blamed me for some rift in his brother's family. I had no clue what he was talking about."

"Did you shoot him?" The man narrowed his eyes at Gabe.

"I did." Luke stepped forward. "That Reeves fella drew without warnin', Sergeant, just like the man said." He nudged his chin toward Mark Hillborne then faced Gabe. "Mr. Coulter here tried to reason with the man, but he just flat wouldn't listen. I saw that Gabe wasn't aware that Mr. Reeves had gone for his gun, and so I shot the man to protect my boss."

The crowd closed in around them, and several men nodded.

"That's just how it happened," a tall bearded man wearing overalls said.

"Yep."

"Uh-huh."

Most of the men in the crowd nodded their agreement.

The sergeant looked at each one, as if hoping to find a dissenter, but nobody disagreed. "All right, then, you're free to go, Mr. Coulter, but I'd better not hear of you gettin' into any more trouble anytime soon."

"Thank you, sir." The relief that washed over Gabe nearly knocked him to his knees, but he turned and grabbed on to Luke's shoulder. "I owe you. I'd be a dead man if you hadn't noticed Reeves drawing."

Luke smiled. "Well, I didn't get land, so I reckon I could use a job. How about you? Did you get a claim?"

Gabe grinned. "Prettiest set of rolling hills you ever did see. With a wide creek cutting across it. I could use your help. I want to get a house and barn built before winter, fences raised, a garden planted." He glanced up at the sun. He thought of Lara waiting for him, and his pulse shot up like a bullet aimed at the sky. "We'd better get a move on if we're going to get back before dark."

"Yes, sir. I just need to get Golden Boy." He spun and took off at a lope.

Gabe turned back for a final look at Payton Reeves and couldn't help feeling the man was dead because of him. The two soldiers picked up the body and carried it down the hill to be buried. Tom Talbot was dead, too, because he'd played cards and lost and then wanted his money back to send to his wife. Gabe clenched his fists. Why hadn't he just turned the money over to Talbot? Then the man would be alive. Although Gabe wasn't sure Lara would be any better off. In fact, he knew she wouldn't. She'd still be living in that dirty soddy, trying to make ends meet and feed her son. He could take much better care of her, if she'd let him.

A woman like Lara deserved to be cherished, not worked to death. Yes, he'd offered to hire her, not to work her day and night, but rather so that he could keep her close in hopes that she would come to care for him like he did her.

He pushed his feet into motion. Luke would wonder why he was standing in the same spot when he returned. Back at the buckboard, he checked to make sure Tempest's reins were securely tied to the tailgate. He patted the horse, thinking about how close he'd come to meeting his Maker.

Mark Hillborne walked back out of his tent. Gabe hadn't noticed the man had left after the shooting. He skirted around Tempest and toward the storekeeper. "I owe you my gratitude for standing up for me."

Mark shrugged. "I was just telling it like I saw it. That man provoked you and deserved what he got."

Gabe wasn't going to disagree. If not for Mark's statement, as well as Luke's, Gabe might be in the soldiers' custody and locked away somewhere right now. "I still thank you. Let me know if I can ever return the favor."

Mark nodded.

As Gabe climbed up and took a seat on the buckboard's bench, he couldn't shake the thought of how close he'd come to dying. And he wasn't nearly ready for that. He swallowed the lump in his throat. He'd thought about changing his ways, and now he knew he had to. He didn't want to be responsible for tearing apart any other families. He'd done enough of that already.

Chapter 21

Lara dumped the load of firewood in the pile she'd been collecting. Finding the wood had helped her feel useful. She'd washed the bedding from the dugout and hung it over some shrubs to dry in the warm afternoon sun. She'd even decided where she wanted to plant her garden and had made a mental list of the vegetables she planned to grow. She glanced in the direction Gabe had ridden this morning, hoping to see him, but she didn't.

The sun would set in a little over an hour, and she had decided if he wasn't back by then, she'd make as big a fire as she could then go lock herself and Sunny in the dugout. She would feel safer than sitting outside alone all night. That was for certain.

She tried fishing in the later afternoon hours but had no luck. With nothing else to do, she walked up the closest hill to watch for Gabe. The grass swished as she passed through it, and grabbed at her skirts. She looked in all directions, and seeing no one, she hiked up her skirt and petticoat and trod up the hill, enjoying the freedom from clawing plants. At the top, she stopped to catch her breath and enjoy the view. The hill she stood on was taller than the others nearby, giving her a clear view for a long way. Everything looked the same—grassy rolling hills, with trees clustered sporadically, mostly near the creek.

A part of her felt sad for the Indians who never got to live there, but she was glad that her family would as well as so many others who needed land. Something moved in the bushes halfway down the hill, and Lara froze. She hadn't thought about the wild creatures that inhabited this land, but there were probably coyote and wolves. Sucking in a breath, she drew her gun and pointed it. Suddenly two rabbits hopped out from behind the shrub. Lara almost laughed out loud, but then she realized she had supper within her sites. Lifting the gun, she aimed and fired. The shot hit a rock close to one rabbit, and it shifted direction and fled. The other one froze, not realizing it made the perfect target. Lara sited the gun and fired. The shot hit its mark, knocking the hare several feet from its original spot. Lara holstered the gun and started down the hill. "Yahoo!"

The rabbit not only gave her a task to tend to, but she would have something for Gabe to eat when he returned, for she refused to believe he wouldn't. He had promised, and unlike Tom who couldn't keep a promise, she believed Gabe would. With supper in her clutches, she climbed the hill again, ready to take one last look around before heading back to camp.

Her heart jolted at the site of a rider on a Palomino coming her way fast. Right behind it was a wagon. Both seemed in a hurry. Her heart pounded. She didn't have time to run to the dugout to hide. And they already knew someone was around because they would have heard her gunfire. She dropped the rabbit and reached to pull out her gun when her gaze landed on the horse behind the wagon. Tempest?

Shading her eyes, she stared at the driver. Gabe? Oh, yes! It was him. Her pulse raced as she waved her hands. She couldn't express her joy that he had returned. He waved back and then slowed the buckboard.

The rider on the yellow horse galloped her way then slowed and stopped. "Are you Lara?"

She nodded. "And who are you?"

The handsome cowboy relaxed and grinned. "I'm Luke. I work for Gabe."

"It's a pleasure to meet you."

He tipped his hat. "Same here. Gabe's been mighty concerned that we wouldn't arrive before sunset. We ran into some trouble in town, but it turned out all right."

She wanted to ask what kind of trouble, but Gabe was topping the hill. He pulled the wagon to a stop and smiled. "I told you I'd be back before dark."

"That you did." She couldn't help smiling in return and didn't bother to hide her delight. "And it looks like you brought a whole store with you."

He shrugged. "We're starting from scratch and have need of many things. And, besides, I only bought half a store. I wish I could have brought more, but this will hold us for a week or two." He glanced at the cowboy. "I see you've met Luke."

She nodded then bent and picked up the rabbit. "I got something for dinner."

Luke's brows lifted to his hairline. "She can shoot?" He chuckled. "You'd better be on your best behavior, boss."

"Didn't I tell you that? Lara is an amazing woman."

Lara's cheeks heated. Gabe had been talking about her? She wished she knew in what capacity. Was he merely telling Luke about his other employee? Or was there more to it?

She glanced at Gabe and caught him staring. He winked, making her stomach flutter. She smiled and ducked her head.

"You want to ride to camp?" Gabe stood and held out his hand as if he knew her answer.

She ought to walk, but she longed to hear about things in town, and she was rather tired after her busy day. She nodded and took hold of his hand, allowing him to haul her up into the wagon. Once seated, she glanced sideways. "I'm sure glad you returned before the sun went down."

"You and me both. We had a bit of trouble finding our way back. Mile after mile of prairie that all looks pretty much the same can be confusing."

She knew what he said was true. They hit a dip in the ground and Lara's shoulder bumped against Gabe's, sending her pulse soaring. She'd tried hard not to like him, but he was so kind and generous. Somewhere along the way, he had staked a claim on her heart. But she wasn't sure he felt the same.

Just because a man was kind to you didn't mean he was in love with you. Maybe Gabe pitied her. Felt sorry for her because her clothes were so shabby? She smoothed a wrinkle in her skirt. She'd wanted to travel light and hadn't packed an apron, which she sorely needed today when she was cleaning the dugout. "I found the piece of land I want," she blurted without thinking.

"You did?" Gabe's gaze zipped toward hers. "Where is this land?"

"In the southwestern corner of your claim, on the border as you stipulated."

He nodded, smiling wide. "Good. That means you're going to stay and work for me."

"Yes, but tomorrow I need to go get Michael. He'll be worried. We've never been separated before."

"I'm sure he misses you," Gabe said. "I still miss my ma."

"Where is she?"

"She died when I was a boy."

Lara leaned against Gabe's arm as they reached the bottom of the last hill. "I'm sorry, Gabe. I know what it's like to lose a parent—both of them, actually."

Luke jogged his horse down the hill ahead of them and out of earshot. He circled the camp and then dismounted. Sunny nickered a greeting to Luke's horse.

"I'm sorry about your parents."

Lara shrugged. "It was a long time ago. My grandpa raised my sister and me—and my brother, but he left before a year was out."

Gabe guided the wagon toward their campsite. "Where are they now?"

Lara scooted away from him, staring toward her small speck of land. She had decided she wouldn't tell him about her whole family until they were already here. Would he change his mind about hiring her if he knew they were coming to live here also?

He slowed the wagon then stopped it and set the break. Gabe turned toward her. "What's wrong, Lara? Did something happen to them, too?"

She swallowed and licked her lips, unsure how to explain. She cupped her fingers together, running her thumb over the back of one hand. If he sent her packing, they were in trouble. She should have told him from the start that she wasn't alone, but the topic had never come up.

His large warm hand rested atop hers, and she stopped fidgeting. "Whatever it is, just tell me. It can't be worse than what I'm imagining."

She thought of how fussy Jo could be at times and the three goats and their antics, and she thought Gabe might be wrong, but she had to tell him. She pivoted to face him and looked into his dark, solemn eyes. "I. . .uh. . .they are watching Michael, except for my brother, Jack. I have no idea where he is."

A crease formed between Gabe's eyes. "Who is watching your son?"

"My grandpa and my sister. They will be coming to live with me. They have nowhere else to go."

He blinked, looking confused. "So, you're not alone? I thought you and your son lived by yourself."

She shook her head. "No, but my grandpa suffers frequent bouts of swamp fever—malaria—and my sister can be. . .trying."

Gabe surprised her by grinning. "She must be like you at times."

"What?" She was trying? She thought of all he'd done for her and imagined that maybe she did seem that way to him.

He nudged her shoulder with his. "I'm teasing, Lara."

She looked into his eyes and saw the truth. When she realized how close she was to him and that if he only leaned a few inches, he could kiss her, she jumped up.

Gabe tugged her back down. "We're not finished with our discussion."

She flopped onto the bench beside him, catching the odor of the fire that Luke had started. "It's getting dark. I need to prepare supper, and don't you need to unpack?"

"It can wait. You're saying that besides your son, your grandpa and sister will be living here?"

She nodded, holding her breath. Praying he wouldn't cast them out.

He blew out a loud breath. "All right. I hadn't counted on feeding so many folks, but we'll make do."

She turned toward him, her heart taking flight. "You mean, you don't mind? I was so afraid you'd tell us to hit the road."

He glanced over his shoulder, and she looked at the camp. Luke squatted near the fire with his back to them. She jumped when

Gabe's hand rested against her cheek. His gaze captured hers and held her prisoner. "Why would I mind? I'm glad you have some family and don't have to live alone with only your son."

She blinked back the tears stinging her eyes. "You're a good man, Gabe Coulter."

A sad looked stole his happy expression. "There are many who would disagree with you."

"Why? You've been more than kind to me."

His gaze hardened, and he dropped his hand, the tender moment lost. "I've done things in my past that I'm not proud of—" His voice caught, and he cleared his throat. "I want you to know that I'm changing my ways. I've quit gambling and intend on raising horses. It will be a slow go of things until I can acquire more land, but we'll make it. I have some savings, so that will hold us over during the thin times."

He said *we* and *us* as if they were a family. As if she mattered to him. And yet she hated the way he had accumulated that savings—by winning money from men like Tom, who should have sent a portion of their earnings to their hungry families. She believed a man could change his ways and hoped Gabe truly had, but what if he couldn't make a go of the ranch? What if his savings ran out? Could Gabe live as miserly as she had back in Caldwell? Could she trust him not to go back to gambling if things here didn't go as planned?

And could she trust her rebellious heart when all she wanted was for Gabe to take her in his arms and kiss her fears away?

❧

Tired from traveling since leaving Wichita, Silas halted at a campsite some previous traveler had used just across the state line. He dismounted and tended to his horse then reclined against a tree. He needed food, but the cheap marshal didn't send him off with any, nor did he return the coins Silas had in his pocket when he was arrested.

A bird flitted in the tree above him, and he glanced up. He'd eaten pigeons and starlings before, but they weren't his favorite. The bird flew up to another branch, and something blue caught Silas's eye. Someone had secured a bundle in the tree. More than a little curious, he rose and managed to climb the tree. He lowered the bunched blanket to the ground, almost praying there'd be food inside, but then he wasn't a prayin' man. He loosened the knot, tossed aside the rope, and flipped back the blanket, revealing a stock of canned goods that made his eyes bulge.

He snatched up something wrapped in brown paper and ripped it open. His mouth watered at the yeasty aroma of bread. He ripped off a corner and shoved it into his mouth, delighting in the still soft texture of the white middle. The only bread he'd eaten in the jail had been rock-hard biscuits or moldy two-day-old leftovers.

When his mouth became too dry to eat any more, he grabbed his canteen and guzzled the lukewarm water. Then he went in search of a knife or something to open the cans with. Half an hour later, with his belly filled with sweetened peaches, beets, and green beans, all he wanted was to curl up and take a nap, but the settler could return anytime. This would be a nice place to live if it weren't part of the Cherokee Outlet and still closed to white settlers. Besides, his heart was set on one specific piece of land. The place where his brother was buried.

He stuffed what cans he could into his saddlebags, along with a supply of jerky and the wool blanket, then mounted and rode away. He yawned and patted his sated belly. Maybe he could ride a mile or two then rest for a while. At this pace, it would take him a week to get back to his land.

But he would get there, and heaven help the man who'd thought to make that land his.

⌒

Excitement sizzled through Lara as she and Gabe crossed the last creek before reaching her family. Three days had passed since she'd last seen them. She prayed Grandpa had recovered from his last bout of malaria, because they wouldn't be able to travel far if not. Her gaze scanned the land that looked almost bare with most of the people gone.

"Is that them over there?" Gabe pointed to her left.

Lara pushed back her hat and narrowed her eyes as she searched in the distance. "Yes! It is." She reined Sunny to the west and nudged him into a trot. She tried to take in everything as she rode up. The camp looked much the same, although it was no longer surrounded by other wagons. Grandpa sat on the tailgate with Michael at his side, working on a fishing pole. Jo was nowhere to be seen, and Betty Robinson's wagon was gone. Lara felt a bit of sadness about never seeing the friendly lady again. Grandpa looked her way and waved. Michael jumped up and down in the wagon, squealing and waving.

"Mama! Mama! Did you get some land?"

Lara's heart warmed, and she couldn't keep the grin from her face in spite of the fact that she'd failed to get a claim, was exhausted from the long ride, and her head ached. She reined Sunny to a stop, slid down, then ran to her son, snatching him up in a big hug. "I missed you so much."

"Me, too. I was good, Mama. I'm taking care of Grandpa."

Lara's gaze raked over the older man.

"I'm fine. The spell wasn't too bad'a one." Grandpa's gaze shifted past her, and she knew he was curious about why a man had accompanied her.

"I'm glad. So where's Jo?"

He nudged his head to the side and back. "She walked over to the creek to wash off."

Lara scanned the area he indicated but didn't see her sister. "Is it safe to allow her to wander off now?"

He shrugged. "There ain't been many folks around, so I reckon it's as safe now as it was when there was hunnerds of people. Who's your friend?"

Gabe dismounted, grabbed Sunny's reins, and walked toward them with the two horses. He nodded at Grandpa then held out his hand. "I'm Gabe Coulter."

Grandpa slid off the end of the wagon and shook Gabe's hand. "Daniel Jensen. I'm Lara's grandfather, but I reckon she's told you that already. How do you two know each other?"

Glancing at Lara, Gabe grinned. "Your granddaughter rescued my horse when I first arrived in Caldwell. The train and crowd had spooked him, and she walked through the group of men, straight up to Tempest and calmed him. I was quite impressed."

Grandpa lifted a brow and eyed the bandage on her head. "That girl always was good with horses."

She kissed Michael. "Could you run over near the creek and let Jo know I'm back?"

"Yes, Mama."

She set her son down and watched him race off. "Stay where you can see us."

He swatted his hand in the air but didn't slow.

Now she had to explain Gabe's presence. "Gabe came to my rescue the day I hurt my hand. He took me to the doctor and insisted I get it checked out. Then he graciously replaced the food that was lost when that boy ran into me. Gabe even rented a buggy and brought me home. We saw one another in town several other times"—she sucked in a breath—"and he helped me when I took a fall off Sunny." She ducked her head. "Because of that, I didn't get a claim, but Gabe did, and now he's my boss."

Grandpa blew out a loud breath as if he were the one who'd told her tale. He studied Gabe as if taking his measure then nodded. "Looks like I owe you a big debt of gratitude."

Gabe pursed his lips, shaking his head. "You don't owe me anything, sir. I was glad to assist Lara. And to be honest, I need help on my claim to make a go of it. I'm hoping you'll be willing to work for me, too, as you're able, of course."

Grandpa straightened. "I'll have you know I was a sergeant in the War Between the States."

Gabe looked as if he were stifling a smile. "I don't doubt it for a minute, sir."

Lara turned to him. "My grandfather is an amazing horse trainer. He used to raise them."

"Well, that's providential since I plan on raising horses, too. How many head do you figure I can support on a quarter section?"

Grandpa glanced down at the ground. Most of the grass that had been there the day they arrived was crushed and had turned yellow. "If the ground is anything like up near Caldwell, you might be able to raise forty to fifty head on one hundred and sixty acres, although that might be pushing things if you have a rough summer with little rain."

Rubbing his thumb and index finger on his chin, Gabe nodded.

"I don't think I'll own that many for several years, and by then, I hope to have bought out one of my neighbors and have a bigger spread."

"What kind of horses you plannin' on—"

A shrill scream broke the quiet afternoon, and Lara spun toward the river, searching for Michael.

Chapter 22

Go away! Leave!"

Lara recognized her sister's voice, and relief melted her tension as her gaze landed on her son's backside as he faced the river.

"But, Ma—"

"Michael! I'm not dressed. Go away!"

Lara snickered and glanced at the men. "I had better rescue my son."

"Sounds like Jo's the one who needs rescuin'." Grandpa chuckled.

"Lara, are you back? Come get your son. I'm not dressed."

"Michael, come here." She started for the creek.

The boy spun and trotted toward her, a frown marring his sweet face. "Aunt Jo yelled at me."

She squatted down. "I know, sweetie, and I'm sorry. You surprised her. She's not angry with you, so don't fret." She placed her hand on his cheek. "It's all my fault. I didn't realize she wasn't decent. Let's go back to camp and wait on her."

He took her hand. "I'm hungry."

"Me, too." Lara glanced at Gabe as she strode back to camp, wondering what he thought about her family. At least they'd been able to talk to Grandpa without Michael overhearing.

While Gabe and Grandpa tended the horses and Michael ran

around pretending to be one, she checked the food supplies. There wasn't much for her to work with. She could whip up a bunch of pancakes and some hot coffee, but that was about it. She longed for the stocks of food back at the claim site, but those didn't help her now. As she sifted through the mess Jo had made of their supplies, she thanked God for the job offer and that Gabe won a claim. She couldn't stand the thought of what would have happened to them without his generosity.

Footsteps pounded her way, and Lara looked up to see Jo storming toward her.

"Why did you send Michael for me if you knew I was bathing?"

"I didn't realize the extent of your bathing. Grandpa said you were washing off, so I didn't expect that you would be undressed."

"I've never been so mortified in all my life." She flounced her long hair, flicking water on Lara.

Suddenly, Jo looked past her, and her eyes widened. "Who is that?" Her face instantly paled. "Was he here when I shouted that I was indecent?"

Lara knew she was referring to Gabe and fought back a grin. Jo was so bold that she was rarely embarrassed, and for some reason, it hit her as humorous. "Um. . .possibly."

Her sister's eyes narrowed. "I've seen him before." She gasped. "Is he that dandy that was sniffing around your skirts in Caldwell?"

"Jo! What a crude thing to say." She glanced over her shoulder, relieved that Gabe was probably too far away to overhear her sister. Then she realized what Jo said. "When did you see Gabe?"

"One day when he was talking to you. He was dressed all in black like a fancy undertaker or something." Jo glanced up at Lara's head as she ran a brush through her hair. "What happened to your head? And how is it you know him well enough to call him by his given name?"

Lara shrugged. "He's helped me a couple of times, like the day my hand got injured. Then during the race, Sunny stumbled and fell down a hill, throwing me. I don't know if I'd be here now without Gabe's help."

Jo's gaze zipped over to where the men had staked the horses. "Is Sunny all right? He must be if you rode him back."

Lara didn't miss the fact that Jo was more concerned about the horse than her.

The hairbrush suddenly stopped. "Wait a minute. If you fell and were injured, I guess that means you didn't get land. What are we gonna do now?"

Lara had never been so glad to have an answer to that question. "Gabe has offered me a job. Grandpa, too, if he wants one. Gabe won a claim and needs help to make a go of it."

Jo put a hand on her hip. "How convenient. He just happened to be right there when you hurt your hand and then again when you fell off Sunny. Why, a girl might think he was stalking you."

"He's helping and trying to protect me, like a true gentleman. What harm is there in that?"

"Good question. Have you asked yourself why he's always around when you need help?"

Lara watched Gabe talking to Grandpa as they walked toward them. She could hear the buzz of their voices but not what they were saying. Could Gabe have some ulterior motive for helping her so often? She shook her head, unable to believe it. She didn't want to believe it. The man had stolen her heart with his kindness. Part of the reason she wanted to work for him was so she didn't have to say good-bye to him. She hoped that, given time, they might grow closer—that he might come to love her as she was afraid she loved him.

"It all seems mighty fishy to me. I'm just sayin'."

Lara hated the niggling of suspicion that wormed through her at Jo's comments. Maybe her sister was jealous because Gabe hadn't offered her a job, but then he hadn't even met her yet. As he approached, he eyed her sister then turned his gaze on Lara and smiled, chasing away all doubts of whether he cared for her. A man didn't look at a woman like that—and totally ignore her beautiful sister—if he didn't.

⁓

Two days after meeting Lara's family, Gabe walked off the area for the house he planned to build. The view from the small hill would allow him to see a good part of his land from the second story. Lara knew about the house, but she had no idea of the size—or the fact that he hoped she'd share it with him as his wife once it was completed. Last time he was in town, he'd wired a carpenter he knew in Kansas City and made arrangements for the man to come to Oklahoma to build his house. In another week, Jerrold Parnell and his crew would arrive and the construction would begin.

He'd already ordered the lumber and needed to go into town to see if it had arrived and make arrangements for it to be delivered. Though he had some furniture, they would need much more. He had nothing for the kitchen or the spare bedrooms. Maybe Lara would ride with him and help pick out some furnishings from the catalogs at Mark Hillborne's store. What the man didn't have in stock, he seemed happy to order.

The whack of Luke's axe reminded him that he needed to get down the hill and resume his work of helping with the fence posts. He had just wanted to make sure the level place on the hill where he planned to build was big enough for the house he envisioned.

Gabe's stomach rumbled at the same time the dinner bell clanged.

Luke took another swing with the axe then covered his eyes and looked up the hill. "Was that the dinner clanger?"

"Yep! I'm coming down." He jogged down the grassy part of the incline then slowed his pace where it turned into the loose rocks that Sunny had lost his footing on.

Luke walked toward him, leading Tempest and Golden Boy, then tossed him the reins to Gabe's horse. "Hurry up. I'm starved. That woman of yours sure can cook."

Gabe mounted, remembering the near tasteless pancakes Lara had cooked the day they met up with her family. She was a wonderful cook when she had a good stock of supplies. And the game he and Luke had shot helped, too. He could hardly wait until the large garden they started planting yesterday began yielding fresh produce. The thought of eating newly picked corn on the cob and green beans made his mouth water.

As they rode toward the dugout, where they stored the food and Lara's family lived, he thought of how she'd outsmarted him by finding and claiming it first, but he really didn't mind. He preferred that she and her family not have to sleep outdoors. It allowed him to worry less about her safety, knowing no wild animals could bother them once the door was closed. It was still possible a snake or small critter might burrow its way through the dirt, but that probably happened when they'd lived in a soddy, too.

As Gabe rode closer to Lara's camp, his pulse picked up its pace. He longed to see her—to be close to her—whenever they were parted, as they were most days. It was the nature of working the land. Each person had their own tasks to do, and things worked well when each did their job. He scowled at the thought of Lara's sister. She ought to help more, but Lara didn't want to push her, because Jo didn't like being forced. She was just plain spoiled and lazy, if you asked him. Lara was too sweet and preferred to shoulder the burden of the chores rather than argue with her stubborn sister. Maybe he should talk to Daniel about it. The older man had done well since arriving here. Gabe had trouble keeping him from trying to do too much. Too bad Jo didn't take after him or her sister. From what little he heard, she sounded more like her brother who'd left the family when they had needed him most.

Michael ran toward them, waving. "Can I have a ride, Mr. Gabe?"

He reined Tempest to a halt, reached down, and tugged the boy up so he could sit in front of him. Michael grasped the saddle horn with both hands. When he leaned back against Gabe's chest, the boy's wispy hair tickled Gabe's chin.

Lara smiled and waved as they drew near. She untied her apron and draped it over a low-hanging limb of a nearby tree, brushed the loose hair from her face, and walked toward him. Her cheeks reminded him of the red rosebush his ma had when he was young. His heart warmed with love for this woman.

He dismounted and set Michael on the ground. The boy ran past her, yelling that he was starved.

Luke walked around the front of Golden Boy and took Tempest's reins. His lips tilted in an ornery smile, and his eyes twinkled. "You'd better hurry up and marry that gal before someone steals her from you."

Gabe narrowed his gaze at Luke, hoping his friend wasn't refer- ring to himself. Luke laughed out loud. "Not me, you dolt. Her sister's more to my likin'." He walked away, chuckling.

"I hope you're hungry. Grandpa and Jo caught some bass, and I fried it. Got a pot of rice, too."

He smiled, longing to take her in his arms and greet her like he dreamed of, but there were too many eyes watching. "That sounds delicious."

He held out his arm, and she looped her hand around it. "Do you suppose we could take a walk later?"

She glanced up at him. "I don't see why not. Just let me get Michael in bed first. "What did you want to talk about?"

"I plan to ride into Guthrie tomorrow, and I'll need a list of supplies you want me to pick up. Also, I want to talk about the house furnishings."

"Oh."

He hated the disappointment in her voice. What had she hoped to hear? The possibilities made his knees weak. He tugged her closer. "And maybe I'd just like to have you to myself for a while."

When she glanced up, he winked, once again bringing red to her cheeks.

And if things went as planned, he would steal a kiss or two.

Lara pushed the pins into her hair, hoping it looked all right for her walk with Gabe. She had hoped he had a more romantic topic he wanted to chat about than food supplies, although talking about his house would be something different. Her insides quivered as she thought about finally being alone with him. Whenever they were together, someone else was always nearby.

Lantern light flickered on the dirt walls, barely illuminating the area enough to see. Jo watched from her spot on the edge of the bed, arms crossed. "I don't know why you're primping for that man. I thought you were smart."

"What does that mean?"

"Nobody gives a person free land, just for working for them, unless they want something. Just be careful. And don't say I didn't warn you."

Lara blew out a frustrated breath. "You're too young to be so jaded. Gabe has done nothing to cause me to mistrust him. Grandpa even likes him."

"Well, I don't." Jo stuck her chin in the air. "But that won't stop me from going into town with him tomorrow."

"What?" Lara crossed the tiny room. "Why do you need to go to Guthrie?"

"I'm going to find myself a job. I've told you before that I don't intend to work land. I wasn't cut out to be a farmer's wife, and I don't intend to become one."

"Jo—"

Her sister held up her hand. "Don't bother trying to dissuade me, because I'm either going with Gabe or going alone."

Lara swallowed, trying to think of something that would sway her hardheaded sister. "You'd leave all of us? We're your family."

"All you want to be is my boss." Jo rose. "I am not your slave, and I don't intend to work for you anymore."

Lara's heart ached at the hatred in her sister's voice. "I never meant to be bossy, but there is work that has to be done, and I need your help."

Jo shook her head. "You'll do fine without me."

How would Jo find a job when she despised working so much? She couldn't bear the thought of her sister alone in an unfamiliar town. "But you're only sixteen. What will you do?"

"I'm not sure, but I won't live in a dirt house again." Jo yanked her spare dress off the peg and folded it. "I'll do whatever I have to."

"Don't say that. There are awful men out there who prey on beautiful young women. You have no idea of the horrible life some women endure just to get by. Why would you want that when you have a family who loves you so much?"

Jo shook her head. "You'll never understand, so don't bother trying. My mind is made up."

Lara's throat tightened as she fought the tears burning her eyes. She glanced at Michael on the far side of the bed, glad their discussion hadn't awakened him. "Have you talked to Grandpa about it?" Finally, she noticed a chink in her sister's armor.

"No. I can't. You'll have to tell him."

Lara gasped. "You'd leave and not tell him good-bye? It will break his heart."

Jo shrugged. "I can't do it."

A soft knock sounded on the door, and Lara answered. Grandpa glanced at her then Jo with a worried expression marring his normally happy features. "Gabe has come calling."

Lara nodded. She knew it would do no good to talk to Jo when she was in one of her moods, so she walked out but then paused and looked at her grandfather. "I think you and Jo need to have a talk."

"Lara!"

Ignoring her sister's angry cry, she strode to Gabe, her time with him ruined. Had Jo purposely picked that moment to tell her she was leaving, knowing how it would upset her?

Gabe held up a lantern with one hand and reached out with the other, taking her hand. "What's wrong?"

She shook her head. "Get me away from here. Please."

Gabe tugged on her hand, and she numbly followed as he walked toward the creek. Using the lantern to see their way, they jumped across at a particularly narrow spot and then meandered through the trees. Finally Gabe stopped, hung the lantern on a notch on a tree, and turned toward her. "Care to tell me what's upset you so badly?"

Her lower lip quivered. A tear ran down her cheek. "I've tried so hard to be a mother to Jo. She was so young when our parents died, and she has always been angry that I've tried to mother her and teach her proper skills. She resents that I ask her to help with the chores and things that need doing."

Gabe ran his hands up and down her arms, resting them lightly on her shoulders. "She is a bit headstrong, from what I've seen of her, but I doubt she really resents you."

"You're wrong—she truly does. I've always known it and tried to make allowances by not pushing her to work too hard. I had hoped as she grew older—" A sob broke loose, and Lara buried her face in her hands, unable to stop her tears.

"*Shh*. . ." Gabe tugged her closer, enveloping her in his arms.

She wrapped her arms around him, desperately needing his comfort. Next to raising her son, the most important task God had given her was to raise her sister to be a godly woman and to one day be a helpmate to her husband, but she'd failed miserably.

Gabe gently pressed her head against his chest as he placed soft kisses on her temple, driving away all thoughts of her sister. She sniffed, knowing she should step away, but she wasn't ready to. She was so tired of being strong for everyone else that she wanted to cherish this moment with Gabe, even if it meant nothing to him. No, that wasn't true. She wanted his hugs—his kisses. She wanted him to take care of her like he had been. She loved him.

Leaning back, she swiped her eyes with a handkerchief that she'd tugged from her sleeve and then wiped her nose. There was nothing less romantic than a runny nose. She smiled.

"That's better." Gabe brushed at the dampness on her cheeks with his thumbs as his gaze roved her face. "Lara, surely you know how I care for you. This isn't how I planned to declare my feelings, but I've fallen desperately in love with you."

Her heart quickened, and she brushed her hand down his cheek. "Me, too, Gabe. I don't know how it happened, but I've fallen for you, too."

His eyes glistened as her words lit a fire in them, and then he leaned down, claiming her lips and heart like he'd staked a claim on her land. But none of that mattered anymore. She looped her arms around his neck and pulled him closer, her lips crushed against his. Her rapid heartbeat kept a perfect tempo with his as he left little doubt to the truth of his confession of love. Having been a married woman, she knew the danger she was walking into. After a few minutes of wonderful ecstasy in Gabe's arms, she reluctantly drew back, allowing her rapid breaths to meld with his.

He pressed his forehead against hers. "Marry me, Lara. Share this land with me, and let's build a home and a family together."

She gasped at the unexpected proposal, and Gabe instantly sobered.

"I—I. . ."

She pressed her fingers to his lips. "Don't say anything. I was just surprised because we haven't known one another very long."

He nodded and seemed to relax.

"What I said was true. I care deeply for you, too, but I think we need a bit more time to get to know one another before we consider marriage."

The disappointment was obvious on his handsome face. He took hold of her hand. "Lara, I've never been married. Never really expected to find a woman I thought was as good as my mother, but I have. And I'm not letting you go. I realize you've recently lost your husband—" He looked away, and a muscle in his jaw twitched. He cleared his throat. "Take all the time you need to be sure I'm the right man for you."

"Thank you, Gabe. That's kind of you to not rush me. Your kindness is what first drew me to you."

He smiled. "I don't think anyone has ever said that to me before."

Lara took his arm and turned him back toward home. "I'm surprised."

He reclaimed the lantern and held it high, illuminating their path. Insects hovered around it as if needing the heat it shed. "I haven't always lived a life that I was proud of."

The comment jolted her for a moment, but then she assumed he was referring to his gambling days. "We all have regrets, Gabe."

She had plenty of them as she thought back over her years raising Jo and the many mistakes she'd made. She understood what he meant, but it still didn't stop her from wishing she could do things over.

Chapter 23

Shortly after lunchtime, Jo rode Sunny into Guthrie, with Gabe, Lara, and Michael following in the wagon behind her. Once again, Lara had intruded in her life. Why couldn't she just let her go rather than make the trip with her? It would have made things less painful for both of them.

Excitement pushed aside her frustration as she scanned the active town, far bigger than Caldwell. On both sides of the streets and for as far as she could see, tents had been erected and wooden buildings were in various stages of construction. Hammering echoed through the town. Surely, with so many new businesses going up, she ought to be able to find employment.

Her thoughts shifted to Mark Hillborne. Had the handsome man won his land and set up a store? She needed to find him, but it could take days with so many places to check. Since he came in on the train, it made sense to start first near the depot, wherever that might be. As if an omen, a loud train whistle blasted across the town. Jo looked for the smoke and found it on the lower end of Guthrie. Now, if only she could get rid of her escort.

But then she couldn't keep Sunny, as much as she'd like to. She huffed a laugh. Lara would probably have her arrested and strung up for horse stealing. No, that wasn't fair. Her sister might push her to work, but she never held a grudge.

A whistle drew her gaze, and a man in a plaid shirt and denim pants removed his sweat-stained hat and bowed. Other men along the street paused as she rode past, gazing, whistling, and shouting things that should have made her cheeks turn red. Jo secretly enjoyed the attention, but she kept her head pointed straight ahead, mostly for her sister's sake. She didn't want Lara to know how much she craved masculine attention. She would obviously have no trouble getting the respect she longed for. If only she could find a job and a decent place to live, then she could enjoy the stares of the town's men.

She had no idea where to look for Mark. Since Gabe was headed to a store in the depot area, she slowed Sunny and pulled into step with the horses pulling the buckboard. It was as good a place as any to start.

"Aunt Jo, can I ride with you?" Michael hopped up from where he sat behind the bench.

Her gaze shot to Lara, but her sister looked down into her lap. "I don't mind since we're in town."

Jo wasn't sure why Lara wouldn't let her son ride with her out in the countryside, but she kept quiet and pulled closer to the wagon. Gabe handed Lara the reins, stood, and lifted Michael up, handing him to Jo. She caught Gabe's stoic gaze as she settled her nephew in front of her. He was angry with her for upsetting Lara. Ah well. There was no helping that. Lara would keep her around her whole life, slaving away, if she could. Jo lifted her chin. It was past time she was on her own.

A shiver of concern crept up her spine, and she hugged Michael. What if she was doing the wrong thing, venturing out on her own? Grandpa had been more than a little stunned when Lara forced her into telling him her plans last night. He had argued with her, finally leaving in a huff. She'd read the pain in his eyes and knew he thought he'd failed her, just like Lara did, but they didn't understand. They never had. Losing the parents she loved so much had done something to her. Killed a part of her, deep inside, just like it had Jack. She didn't understand it herself—or maybe it was just the way she'd been made. She wasn't sweet and helpful like Lara. Even Michael took more delight in helping than she ever had. The only way for her to find her true self was to get away from her smothering family members.

She would miss them, especially Michael. Leaning over, she placed a kiss on her nephew's curly haired head. The boy gave unconditional love, something she so badly craved.

Gabe pulled the wagon to a halt, and Jo realized they'd ridden almost all the way through town, turning onto several other streets while she'd been lost in her thoughts. When she looked over at the store he stopped in front of, her heart lurched. Hillborne's General Store. How providential was that?

Excitement zipped through her as Gabe hopped off the wagon, helped Lara down, then turned to reach for Michael.

"Do you know Mark Hillborne?" she asked.

His brows lifted as he pulled Michael from the saddle. "You know him?"

She nodded. "We met in Caldwell."

"That must be where I've seen him before. After I left his store that first time, I thought I'd seen him somewhere. I think maybe we stayed at the same hotel in Caldwell, although we never actually met then." Gabe set the boy down then offered her a hand.

She shook her head and dismounted. "You all go on in. I want to walk around for a bit."

"But—" Lara started to say something then ducked her head and turned away.

Jo saw the hurt in her eyes and tried to ignore it. She didn't particularly want her sister to overhear her conversation with Mark, if he was there. Nor did she necessarily want Lara knowing where she was working and living. After letting Sunny get a drink from the trough, she tied him to a new hitching post and looked around.

All manner of shops had been established in the town that had been open prairie only a week ago. It was a bit boggling to the mind, and it excited her to think she might be part of something historical—the beginning of a town.

She really didn't want to look around, but she hadn't wanted to enter with her family. The man to the right of Mark's store had set up a cobbler business. He glanced up from his work and stared at her. "Can I he'p ye, miss?"

Jo shook her head and took off between Mark's huge tent and the cobbler's small one. At the back entrance, she peered inside, hoping to get a glimpse of Mark. Some other man—smaller and far less handsome—was helping Gabe as Lara and Michael looked around. Disappointment washed over her. Had Mark maybe gone out of town to purchase supplies? Or had he set up the store and hired a man to run it then returned to St. Louis? She hadn't realized how much she'd counted on seeing him again until that moment.

Someone behind her cleared his throat, and she spun, her heart racing.

"Can I help—Jo?" Mark's eyes blazed with recognition, and he stepped forward, taking hold of her hands. "I can't tell you how much I've hoped to see you again."

"Me, too." She peeked behind her and saw Gabe moving toward the rear of the tent. "Do you have time to take a walk? There's something I'd like to talk to you about."

He offered his arm. "I have all day for you, my dear."

She glowed, delighted with his attention and willingness to leave work to spend time with her.

"So, I'm guessing your family must have gotten a claim, otherwise you wouldn't still be in these parts."

"Not exactly. But that's not what I'm here for."

He escorted her across several blocks to the quieter outskirts of Guthrie then turned to face her. "So, tell me what you've come to discuss."

Jo sucked in a breath, her pulse racing. *Please say yes.* "I need a job, and I'm hoping I can work for you."

Gabe stared across the campfire at Lara, wishing he could say something to ease her pain at leaving her sister in Guthrie. Their late dinner back home had been a solemn affair with Michael exhausted from the long trip and Daniel and Lara silent and hurting after Jo had gone missing. Luke had prepared supper knowing they'd be late returning, but then he'd wolfed down his food and disappeared into the night.

Daniel scraped his half-eaten meal into the slop pot and set the tin plate on top of Luke's. "Guess I'll turn in, though I don't suspect I'll sleep much."

Lara rose and gave him a hug. "I'll be in soon."

He nodded and trudged toward the dugout.

Lara sighed. "I hope this doesn't bring on another bout of malaria."

Gabe rose and tugged Lara to her feet. "I'm sorry about Jo. I wish I knew something to say that would help you."

She shook her head. "I lost my parents—my brother—and now m–my sister." She choked back a sob as tears welled in her eyes. "Just hold me, please."

"Gladly." He stepped forward and wrapped her in the shelter

of his arms. Disappointments and hurts were a part of life, but the one that had rocked Lara's world today was equal to the rift made when the Grand Canyon, which he'd once read about, had cracked open. He could see her worrying herself sick over her sister when he wanted her to be happy.

He held her, rocking gently and enjoying their closeness. He'd never felt anything toward the few women he'd been attracted to in the past compared to what he did for Lara. He'd never been in love before, and now he wished he hadn't wasted so much of his life in a saloon. He also understood why his ma had wanted him to marry a godly woman, as he believed Lara was. There was a sweetness to them—a wholesomeness a man didn't find in a saloon girl.

"Gabe."

"Uh-huh?"

"I'll marry you."

Joy surged through him, but just like a soaring bird suddenly shot, his delight plummeted. He set her back so he could see her face in the flicker of firelight. "As happy as it makes me feel to hear that wonderful news, sweetheart, I don't want you deciding to marry me when you're so upset. It's too important."

"But I do."

"Good. I'll remain very hopeful, but I think you need to wait until your feelings aren't so raw to make that decision. All right?"

She nodded. "When did you become so wise?"

"I'd like to say I always have been, but it's not true. I suppose I've wised up since being around you. You make me want to be a better man than I have been in the past."

"That's a kind thing to say." She yawned and quickly covered her mouth. "I suppose I should go inside, but I doubt I will sleep."

He kissed her forehead then tugged her close again and gently claimed her lips. She melded against him, so small, compliant, and responsive. He traveled across her face, placing kisses on her temple, eyes, and the end of her nose, and then he found her lips again, where he deepened his kiss. She moaned and pressed against him, sending warning thoughts as his body responded. She was vulnerable tonight, and he didn't dare take advantage of her—he didn't want to. He hated saying good night.

But he had to.

"Lara, I'd better go."

"I know, but I don't want you to."

"Believe me, I'd rather stay here, too, but we'll both be sorry if I do."

"You're right, of course." She reached up and laid her palm against his chin. "Thanks for holding me. I really needed the comfort."

He kissed her palm, wrapped her arm around his, and walked her to the door. "Sleep tight, sweetheart."

"I'll try." Her lips tilted in a halfhearted smile. "Maybe if I do, I'll dream of you."

He chuckled. "I know exactly who I'll be dreaming about. Good night."

He stayed until she went inside and closed the creaky door. Tomorrow, he'd find something with which to grease it. After checking the fire to make sure it was dying, he gathered up the lantern and walked back to his tent, thinking on the day's events. There was a part of him that would like to paddle Joline Jensen for her insensitivity toward the people who loved her. The stubborn, independent girl was in for some hard knocks, he was afraid. He clenched his fist as he thought how hard they all had searched for her, but to no avail. Lara hated leaving, but Jo had made her wishes clear.

There was nothing left for him to do except clean up the mess she'd left behind.

After breakfast the day after Jo left, Daniel fell into step with Gabe as they walked up the hill to where he and Luke had been building a corral for the horses. "I want to thank you for all you've done for my family." He shook his head. "I don't know where we'd be right now if not for your generosity."

Gabe smiled, warmed by the man's expression of gratitude. "I'm happy to do it, sir."

Daniel walked beside him for a while, scratching his unshaven jaw. "I can see that you are, but I have to admit, there's a part of me that wonders why you want to help us. It's not natural for a stranger to take on another man's family."

"Even if Tom is dead?"

"So, Lara told you his name?"

Gabe suddenly realized his mistake, but it was too late. He wouldn't lie to Lara's grandfather. "No, sir. But I knew Tom a little back in Kansas City."

"That's quite a coincidence, ain't it?"

"I don't know as I'd call it that."

Daniel took hold of his sleeve, stopping him. He narrowed his eyes. "What *would* you call it?"

Gabe sighed and stared off in the distance. "Recompense. Restitution. Atonement."

"Sorry, but I don't follow you."

The time to come clean had finally arrived. He'd thought to tell Lara first, but maybe it was better that her grandfather knew so that he could comfort her without her having to explain. He had no doubt she would be angry with him. He could only hope she wouldn't go back on her desire to marry him.

He blew out a loud sigh and looked at the older man. "There's no easy way to say it. Tom came to my table one night, cocky and drinking, thinking he could double his month's pay. I saw him ripe for the pickin' and proceeded to do just that. I won all of his money, and later, when I walked home, Tom jumped me in an alley."

Daniel hissed.

"I'm sorry to say I killed him. It was self-defense, but the result is the same—I killed Lara's husband."

Daniel lifted his hat and forked his fingers through his thin hair. "Holy moly, Gabe. Have you told Lara?"

He shook his head. "I haven't found the nerve to, but I will soon."

"See that you do. I can't stand the thought of her being hurt again. The timing is lousy."

"I know."

"Gambling is a horrible thing. It robs from families and makes men into sniveling fools. I saw how Tom's witless choices hurt Lara and Michael, and I won't stand by and let another man hurt her again."

Gabe blinked, surprised by the man's vehemence. "I love Lara, sir. I have no desire to hurt her."

"I doubt Tom did in the beginning, either, but he did it all the same."

"I'm not Tom. Lara is a precious treasure to me, and the last thing I want to do is hurt her."

"I'm glad to hear it, but unless you give up gambling completely, you will hurt her—deeply."

"I have given it up. Whether Lara agrees to marry me and help me set up a home here or not, I'll not return to gambling. I've seen how it hurts families, and it makes me sick to think how many innocents suffered because I won the money that should have gone to them. It shames me, sir. That's one of the reasons I've tried so hard to help Lara."

"You can work your whole life helping people, Gabe, but that won't remove the shame from your heart or make amends. Only Christ can erase the guilt you carry and wash you clean again."

"You talk like my ma used to."

"She must have been a wise woman."

"She was." A rabbit hopping up the hill drew Gabe's gaze. It froze then spun and hurried away. Luke's hammering echoed across the peaceful hills. If only he could find peace.

"Gabe, you need to seek God. No amount of buying food or things or giving Lara land and a home will take away the pain you're feeling over killing Tom. I don't see as you had a choice, according to what you've told me, but I can tell it bothers you. Confess your deed and tell Him about the wrong things you've done and how you want to do better. Then ask Christ to forgive you. That's the only way to be whole again. This thing will eat at you, and no matter how much you love Lara, if you don't get rid of it, it will become like a rotten spot in a potato and ruin everything nearby. You understand?"

"Yes, but I don't know how to approach God. I haven't prayed since I was a boy, and even then, God wasn't listening. Why would He now?"

Daniel laid his hand on Gabe's shoulder. "He heard your prayers, son. He just didn't answer them the way you'd hoped. And there's no special way to talk to God. Just find a quiet place and tell Him what's in your heart like you talk to Lara."

Gabe knew it was time to quit running. He could never be the man Lara needed unless he faced God and admitted what he'd done.

"You go on. I'm supposed to take Michael fishing, and then I'll come and help you and Luke with the fence posts." Without waiting for an answer, Daniel plodded up the hill.

Gabe turned for the creek and soon found a shady boulder to sit on. He plopped himself down and stared at the water, glistening like diamonds in spots where the sun slipped through the overhang of trees. The peaceful lapping of water on the banks helped ease his tension. Where did he start? He knew he needed to forgive Elliott, but he didn't know how. He had to find a way though, because if he didn't, the awful memories and emotional pain would forever have a stranglehold on him. He was afraid they would choke the life out of him if he didn't find a way to break free of their grip. *Help me, God.*

He rested his elbows on his knees and his chin on his hands. "I don't know where to start, God. I've made a lot of bad choices in my life, ones I wish I hadn't, especially shooting Tom Talbot. Daniel says You can forgive me, and I hope that's true. I'm sincerely sorry for all I've done, and if I could do things over, I would. Forgive me, Lord. Please. I reckon I've always believed in You, but I was just too angry to pay You much attention. I aim to change that now and hope You'll make me a new man. Wash the ugly blackness from my life. And show me how to forgive Elliott. Please."

⌒

Gabe walked toward the dugout, feeling cleaner—fresher—than he could ever remember. He had a new hope for his life—a hope that he could change and maybe accomplish something important. And Lara was key to his future.

He had to talk to her, tell her about his meeting with God, and he had to tell her about his part in Tom's death. He wished he didn't have to, but the truth of the matter was that without Tom Talbot entering his life, he'd have never met the woman he'd fallen in love with.

Apprehension threatened to steal away his newfound joy. Would Lara hate him for what he did? Or would she see that he was only defending himself?

He blew out a loud breath. He would know soon enough because there she was, sitting under a tree near the dugout, mending something.

Gabe slowed his steps as he neared her, enjoying the serene scene. Other than his ma, he'd never known a woman who worked so hard. Lara's hands rarely stopped. Even when they'd driven to Guthrie, she'd been knitting with yarn he had purchased at Mark Hillborne's store. Shaking his head, he wondered how she managed that on the bumpy trails. He longed to see her in a new dress, but she seemed bent on making sure everyone else had something new first. Maybe he should just buy a dress at Hillborne's for her. He grinned. Next time he was in town that was what he'd do.

Putting his feet into motion, he quickly closed the space between them. Two of her goats bleated from their pen on the far side of the camp, and she looked up, offering him a meager smile. Her feelings were still raw over her sister's leaving, so maybe this wasn't the best day to talk to her.

But he was sure he'd felt God prompting him to do so. And he liked to think he was done arguing with his Maker.

"I didn't expect you'd be back so soon," she said.

He squatted in front of her, resting on his toes. "Could you spare a minute or two? I need to talk to you about a couple of things."

She laid her mending in the basket beside the chair she'd dragged out of the dugout. "I suppose so. Grandpa and Michael are fishing, so I can't start lunch until they return with the fish—if they catch some."

Gabe stood and helped her to her feet. Seeing her so melancholy made his heart ache.

"So, what did you want to talk about?"

He stared off in the distance, thinking of how to tell her.

"What's wrong, Gabe?"

"I had a talk with your grandpa—or rather he had a talk with me—about getting things right with God." He pulled off his hat and held it, rolling the brim. "He was right about most everything, and I knew it. The time was right that I made my peace with God."

Lara's eyes brightened for the first time in days. She reached out and laid her hand on his forearm. "Oh, Gabe. I'm so happy for you."

"Thank you. It does feel good to be at peace." He gazed into her lovely eyes, so afraid the next words he uttered would drive her away from him. He wanted to hold her and never let go, but they couldn't have a life together with Tom's death standing in between them. "I've been to church enough in the past to know that God expects us to make amends when we've done something wrong. And I need to do that."

Lara frowned. "I can't think of anything you need to apologize for. You've been nothing but kind to me."

He crushed his hat brim, so dreading to say the words, but he had to. "Lara, I need to tell you a story."

She nodded, looking curious.

"One night when I was gambling, a cocky cowboy sauntered over to my table. It was Tom."

She blinked. "My Tom?"

The goats bleated and fidgeted in their pen, probably sensing Lara's distress.

He nodded. "He seemed so sure that he was going to double his money, and I'm ashamed to say that I was more than glad to dissolve him of that notion. It was a challenge to me—and I was successful. And I've regretted it almost ever since."

Lara squeezed his arm. "You had no way of knowing about us and how badly we needed Tom's wages. Losing that money was his fault, not yours."

"Hear me out, Lara. I'm not done yet."

She lowered her arm. "Go on then."

"Later on, when I was walking back to the hotel where I lived, I cut through an alley to avoid a group of rowdy cowboys. Tom was there. He drew his gun and demanded I return his money. I wasn't of a mind to oblige him, and when someone hollered his name, distracting him, I drew my gun and fired at the same time he did." He swallowed the lump in his throat. "Lara, it was self-defense, but I'm the man who killed your husband."

"No. . .I don't believe it." Her face turned white, and she stood there blinking. She lifted her chin. "Wait. How did you happen to come to Caldwell?"

"It wasn't by happenstance. I came there to find you and give you the money I'd won from Tom."

She gasped. "Mr. Jones. He works for you?"

Gabe nodded, wishing Lara's dumb goats would shut up. The moment was stressful enough without their caterwauling.

Lara looked aghast. "You've been helping me just to ease your guilty conscience?"

He put his crumpled hat back on his head. "Maybe at first, but it wasn't long before I started caring for you. No matter what you faced, you did it with grace and determination, and I fell in love with you and wanted to protect you from more hurt."

She crossed her arms and stepped away, blinking back tears.

"And yet you've pierced me with the greatest wound of all. I was merely a project to you—a way to soothe your guilt."

"Lara, please. That was true in the beginning. I thought if I helped you and Michael, it would ease the guilt I bore after. . .you know."

"Only Jesus can wash your heart clean and free you from the guilt you wrestle with."

He nodded, remembering his ma had told him something similar more than once. "I just want you to know that even though my motive in helping you may have been wrong at first, it quickly changed. I helped because I wanted to ease your burden. Because I fell in love and hoped to make your life easier."

She held a hand at her throat. "Go back to work, Gabe."

"Lara. . ." He stepped toward her, and his heart nearly broke in half when she retreated.

"I can't be with you right now. Just leave. Please."

He ducked his head, feeling the sting of tears. This is what he was so afraid of. She hated him now. "All right, I'll go for now, but I want you to know that I meant it when I said I love you."

The goats' racket continued, giving him one good reason to leave.

She shook her head and turned her back to him. Gabe started to walk away, but something in the shadow of the trees caught his attention. A man—with a gun aimed at them—stepped out.

"Well, now. Ain't this just a scene out of one of them dime novels. I ain't been so entertained in years."

Chapter 24

Lara's heart pounded like the hooves of a runaway horse. Who was this man? What did he want?

Gabe slid closer to her. "There's plenty of food in the dugout. Help yourself, if that's what you're after, mister."

She stepped to the side to be closer to Gabe. She might be upset with him, but she still felt safer beside him. Thank God he hadn't already left. She eyed the rough-looking stranger. The bottom had dropped out of her world with Gabe's declaration, and now this. Uncontrollable shaking overtook her. *God, help us!*

The man cackled. "I will help myself to that food, soon as you folks skedaddle. That's my dugout, and this is my land. My brother's buried here, and ain't nobody else gonna live on it."

The goats were finally settling down, although Bad Billy stared at the stranger as if knowing the man didn't belong. Lara glanced around. She hadn't seen a grave, but that hardly mattered. She glanced at Gabe, and he waved his hand, indicating for her to get behind him. She eased closer when the man looked over at the goat pen.

Gabe slipped in front of her. "Look, mister, we don't want any trouble. I won this land and registered the claim legally, so there's no way you can expect to live here without the law stepping in. Why not just take all the food you can carry and move on?"

"Silas Stone may have been born in the morning, but it weren't yesterday morn." He pointed his gun at Gabe. "Send that purdy gal over here."

Gabe stiffened. "That's not happening."

"Now!" Silas stepped toward Gabe, waving the gun.

Bad Billy rammed the goat pen, obviously upset at the man's yelling. Lara couldn't let Gabe get shot. She moved to slide past him, but he grabbed her arm.

"Stay behind me."

"I won't let him shoot you if I can stop it."

"Ain't that sweet? Another lovers' quarrel. Get over here, lady, afore I plug your man."

Lara stepped around Gabe, but he grabbed her arm again and shoved her back, glaring at her. Suddenly a shot rang out, and Gabe jerked. He moaned and grabbed his arm. The goats bleated a frantic chorus, and Bad Billy butted the pen post again, causing it to lean.

"Next time, I'll shoot 'im in the gut. Ain't no gettin' over that."

Gabe straightened. "Run, Lara," he whispered over his shoulder.

She shook her head. "I am not leaving you."

He clutched his arm, blood oozing through his fingers. "There's no way this will end well. I shouldn't have left my gun at camp." He captured her gaze. "I love you, Lara."

And she knew then that she desperately loved him, too, no matter what he'd done in his past. "I love you, too. I don't care what happened before."

He smiled, though his beautiful eyes were filled with pain.

"Hey, lady. You comin' over here, or do I have to kill your lover boy?"

God help us! Please!

"Mama!" Michael suddenly ran out of the trees on the far side of the goat pen.

Lara sucked in a sharp breath. "Run, Michael. Run!"

Silas Stone pivoted and moved toward her son. Lara's heart nearly pounded out of her chest as Michael halted, looking confused.

"Hey there, little fellow. Nice to meet you."

Lara was sickened by the man's syrupy tone. "Run!"

Gabe started toward Silas, but the man snatched up Michael and turned the gun on them again. Gabe stopped, keeping one hand over his wound. Blood oozed from it, staining his shirt.

"I warned ya. I ain't leavin'." Michael squirmed, and Silas turned the gun toward him. "Hold still, boy. I wouldn't wanna hav'ta shoot ya."

Lara's mind raced. What could they do? She wouldn't leave her son. No matter what. *Where are You, God?*

"You two head on out. If I don't see no hide nor hair of you, I'll set the boy free in a few days."

"He's too young to be on his own." Gabe took a step toward Silas. "Give him to me, and we'll leave. Peacefully."

Silas looked to be contemplating Gabe's request. He hiked Michael up higher, holding him against his chest.

Suddenly Bad Billy cried out an eerie bleat that almost sounded human. Silas looked over his shoulder toward the pen. Billy reared up and then butted the fence again. The post cracked and fell over. Silas stepped back at the same time the goat retreated. Lara watched in horror as the goat leaped over the mangled fence and headed straight for Silas Stone. The man fired wildly, missing the goat. Billy ran straight for him.

Lara screamed. "Michael!"

"Mama!"

Silas suddenly spun, tucked Michael against his chest, and huddled over the boy as the goat ducked his head and rammed Silas in the back. He screamed in pain as he stumbled to his knees, dropping his rifle and curling his body around Michael. The goat reared up then rammed the man again.

"Billy! No!" Lara yelled. Gabe started toward the trio, but she grabbed his sleeve, stopping him. "Don't! Billy's likely to attack you, too."

Grandpa ran through the trees, his gaze wildly taking in the scene. He lifted his rifle, aiming it toward Silas.

"Grandpa, shoot Billy. Hurry!" Lara clung to Gabe's arm, afraid her son might get shot—might get harmed by the crazed goat.

Michael wailed as Silas roared in pain each time the goat rammed him, but the man courageously protected her child.

"Take the shot," Gabe cried.

Lara could see Grandpa's rifle shaking, even from across the wide yard. He took aim, but at that moment, the goat backed up and halted. Billy snorted, staring at the man on the ground, then trotted back to his pen as if to check on his nannies. Grandpa looked at her, lowered his rifle, and shrugged.

Lara ran toward her son, but Gabe caught up and jerked her to a stop. "Lara, let me look first."

She nodded, tears burning her eyes at the still forms on the ground, her heart ripping in two. *Don't take my son, Lord. Please.*

As Gabe approached the bodies, Grandpa kept his rifle trained on Billy. Gabe eyed the grazing goat then squatted on his heals. He rolled Silas Stone backward, and the man uttered no sound. Lara held her breath, watching her son. Suddenly, he unfolded his body, sat up, and leaped into Gabe's arms so fast that Gabe fell over backward, groaning and then chuckling.

Though weak with relief to see Michael was safe, Lara pushed her feet into motion. Michael climbed off Gabe, hopped up, and ran to her. She bent down and scooped him into her arms. "Oh, baby."

He hugged her for a short moment then pushed back. "I'm not a baby."

Lara laughed out loud. "No, you're a very brave boy, and I'm so thankful you're not hurt."

Michael dipped his brows, looking serious. "I was scared, but I didn't cry."

She hugged him again. "You're a very brave boy."

"Mr. Gabe is hurt."

Lara glanced at Gabe, who laid faceup on the ground. Grandpa had tied up Billy, so she set Michael down. "Could you please fetch my medicine basket from the dugout?"

He nodded and trotted off. Still shaking, Lara hurried toward the man she loved, praying his wound wasn't too severe. She couldn't lose him now.

Lara sat down beside Gabe, resting her hand on his chest. She blew out a relieved sigh at the strong, steady beat of his heart. "Are you all right?"

"Yes, but I decided to rest while I was down here since it looked as if the storm was over."

"I need to have a look at your wound."

He pushed up to a sit, grimacing. "I need to check on Mr. Stone."

"But you're hurt."

"I insist." He grinned at her, sending butterflies dancing in her belly in spite of all that had happened, then his expression sobered. "There's a chance he still could be dangerous."

Lara shook her head. "I think his dangerous days are past."

Gabe rose and walked over to the injured man. He kicked Mr.

Stone's gun away then knelt down and rolled the man onto his back. The right side of his face was covered in blood. "I suspect his back is broken, and it looks like his temple smashed against a sharp rock." He glanced up at her and shook his head. "He's gone."

Lara hugged her arms to her chest, thinking about the close call they had. "It may be awful to say, but I'm glad we won't have to worry about him returning."

Gabe clutched his wounded arm. "Thank God the man protected Michael. Maybe it's true that there's some good in everyone."

"You're right, and I'm extremely grateful for that, but he did put my son in danger in the first place."

The dugout door bounced against the side of the hill, and Michael trotted out with her basket.

Grandpa wrapped an arm around her shoulders then placed a kiss on her forehead. "I'm sure thankful everyone is all right. God was with us today."

"Yes, He was." Lara returned his hug. "Will you keep Michael busy while I tend Gabe and we do something with. . .Mr. Stone?"

He nodded. "C'mon, Shorty. We've got some fish to clean."

Michael held out the basket to her and glanced at Silas's body. "Is he a bad man?"

Lara passed the basket to Gabe then pulled her son against her. "Yes, but you don't have to be concerned. He can't bother us now."

"He's dead?"

"Yes." She kissed the top of his head. "Go help Grandpa while I doctor Gabe."

Michael leaned back, his brow puckered. "Is he gonna die, too?"

Lara's heart jolted at the thought. She smoothed Michael's chaotic curls and smiled. "No, sweetie. I don't think he's hurt that bad. You go on now, and don't worry."

Looking relieved, Michael ran to Grandpa and took his hand, and they disappeared through the trees.

"I do feel like I'm dying," Gabe muttered.

"Don't joke about such a thing."

Fast hoofbeats sounded behind her, and Lara spun, hoping Silas Stone didn't have a partner. Relief weakened her knees. Luke had come to help. She helped Gabe up and tugged him toward a chair she'd pulled outside earlier. "Sit down, and hold my medicine basket in your lap."

"Yes, ma'am."

She knelt beside him, dug out her scissors, and cut his sleeve off, even though she hated ruining the nice shirt. Gabe started telling Luke what happened. When she dabbed at the wound, Gabe jerked and hissed.

"Easy, there," he said.

"Don't be a baby, boss." Luke grinned. "It looks like it's only a flesh wound."

"Well, it's my flesh wound, and it hurts like—" He glanced at Lara and pursed his lips. Then he turned back to Luke. "Would you get that body out of here before Michael comes back? I don't want him seeing it again."

Luke nodded, picked up Mr. Stone, and tossed him over Golden Boy's back.

Lara focused on Gabe's injury. "It is only a deep flesh wound, thank the Lord." She cleansed the gash in his skin then applied some salve and a tight bandage. "There. That should do it." When she rose, Gabe did, too, albeit a bit shaky.

"Lara. . ." He grabbed her hand. "I hope you can find it in your heart to forgive me. I only wanted to help you and Michael in the beginning, to make things easier for you, but then you went and stole my heart, and I couldn't stand not being in your presence." He wobbled, and she tightened her grip on him.

"Sit, Gabe, before you fall."

He did as ordered, leaning his head in his hands. "I'm sorry for ever complaining about those smelly goats."

Lara smiled and gazed through the trees at the sky above. Today could have ended so differently. She could have lost the man she dearly loved. She could have become the victim of a horrible man. She owed God her gratitude.

And there was no denying that in spite of everything, she loved Gabe. The circumstances that brought them together were unique. She was sorry Tom died the way he did, but he died like he lived. Gabe might have thought he was helping her to ease his guilt, but she believed God sent him as an answer to her prayers.

After several moments of prayer, she stepped close to the chair, ran her fingers through Gabe's hair, and pressed his head against her stomach. He held completely still, barely even breathing. "Gabe, look at me. I need to say something."

He took a deep breath and leaned back.

"I want you to know that I forgive you for shooting Tom. I realize it wasn't your fault. Tom never should have called you out like he did."

He closed his eyes and breathed in deeply then looked up at her. "Thank you. You can't know how much that means to me."

"You asked me to marry you. Today, it's my turn. Will you marry me, Gabriel Coulter?"

The dull glaze in his eyes instantly changed to a bright gleam. He pushed up then cupped her cheek. "I most certainly will. There's nothing I'd like better."

She stepped even closer, careful of his arm, and leaned against him. He crushed her to his side, placing kisses on her head. When she looked up, she knew all her prayers had finally been answered. Not the way she'd ever dreamed though. God sent her a gambler who'd won her heart, and she looked forward to spending the rest of her days with him.

Jo handed the customer her change and smiled. "Thank you, Mrs. Cleary. Please come again."

"Oh, I will, deary. Thank you for your assistance."

With Mrs. Cleary gone, Jo relaxed, glad the store was empty for the first time in an hour. She skirted around the corner and straightened the bolts of cloth she and Mrs. Cleary had looked through. Wouldn't Lara be surprised to learn that she'd helped women pick out dress fabric and ribbon and lace to match?

Pride soared through her. She knew that if she found a job, she could live on her own. Today marked a full week of working in Mark's store, and it had been wonderful. Yes, it was work, but it was fun work. She especially enjoyed opening the crates and unpacking the new items. That was her favorite task so far.

She positioned two cans on a shelf to make a perfect line like Mark had showed her, and then she paused at the ready-made dresses. Mark had given her three of them as a celebration reward for leaving her family and starting life on her own. Plus he said she needed to look the part if she was going to work in his store, and wearing the dresses allowed her to tell shoppers how comfortable they were.

Footsteps sounded behind her, and she jumped and spun around. Richard, the other store clerk, wasn't due back from lunch for another half hour. Mark stood beside her, grinning. He glanced at the front of the tent then swept her into his arms, enjoying a long, slow kiss. Her heart pounded, and her breath fled as he deepened his embrace.

Reason returned, and she pushed against his chest. "Mark," she gasped, "what if someone walked in? Are you purposely trying to ruin my reputation?"

He shrugged, and his lips tilted in a cocky grin. "You are sleeping in my tent."

She sucked in a loud breath and slapped his arm. "But you're not there. You are staying in one of the hotel tents, and I sincerely hope you freely let others know that."

He rubbed the back of his neck, looking a bit like a cat who'd stolen his owner's meat right off his dinner plate. "I've been thinking about that. I miss my own bed. How about you and me sharing it?"

Jo batted her eyes, stunned at his suggestive comment. "I don't know what to say to such a horrid question."

He strode to the front of the tent, flipped the flap down, and stalked back to her. "Don't play coy, Jo. You know how attracted I am to you. Having you work here, sashaying down the aisles, smelling pretty, and casting me teasing looks is driving me crazy. I care for you. I want you."

Jo backed up, totally taken off guard. She'd never expected Mark to be so forward. "If you want me in your bed, you'll have to marry me."

He blinked several times, frowning, then he nodded. "If that's what it takes, let's do it."

Jo squealed and leaped into his arms. "I don't believ—"

Mark's lips crushed against hers, hard—probing. His hands roved up her spine and down low—too low. She wiggled and finally managed to get him to release her.

She bit back a smile at his puffy lips and the smoldering stare of his gaze. "When would you like to get married, Mr. Hillborne? I really think we need to discuss that important event."

"Today. Now."

Jo's heart paddled like a drowning woman. "Today? How? I need a dress. I have to prepare."

Mark waved his hand around the store. "Pick out whichever one you want, and then choose a ring. I'll go find a preacher."

She stood there in stunned shock as he ducked out of the tent, leaving the flap down. Joy replaced her surprise at his uncharacteristic behavior, but she was secretly delighted that he'd noticed her as she had him. And just think. . . "I'm getting married."

She raced to the dresses. She already knew the one she wanted—the off-white satin—and lifted it down from the bar. Then she hurried to the case of rings that sat on the shelf behind the counter. The ruby ring with a quartet of diamonds shone up at her. Every night, she'd carried the case to Mark's tent for safekeeping and had tried on each ring, more than once. The ruby one was her favorite, and it fit the best.

She spun around, happier than she'd ever been. Too bad Alma Lou wasn't here to celebrate with her. And to think, she was getting married before her friend.

Richard moseyed in, picking at his teeth with a toothpick. He stopped short and stared at her. "What's going on? Are you pretending to be a bride again?"

Jo beamed him a smile. "No pretending today. Mark and I are getting married."

Richard's eyes bulged. "Well, now, I shouldn't be surprised. I've seen the way he looks at you. Congratulations."

"Thank you. I suppose you can open the store since you're back. I need to get dressed."

She rushed away, enjoying the swish of the gown in her arms and the feel of the warm silver of the ring on her index finger. Wouldn't Lara be surprised to find out she was married?

Chapter 25

Excitement bubbled through Lara as Gabe drove the wagon through the streets of Guthrie. He had ridden to town yesterday and made an appointment with a minister to marry them. She peered at him, admiring his handsome, manly profile. His skin had quickly darkened as he worked in the sun each day, and his body had slimmed from the first time she'd met him. Her soon-to-be husband was a fine-looking man. But even better, he was now a godly man.

"You're staring." Gabe slid a glance her way and winked.

Heat warmed her cheeks, and she looked away, studying the town. Had only a week passed since they'd left Jo here? Where was she? Had she found work? Was she safe? The questions haunted her daily, but all she could do was pray for her sister.

Her only regret was that none of her family would be at her wedding. Grandpa was on the tail end of a bout of swamp fever and not up to the long trip to town. Gabe told her Luke had suggested they might like to spend their wedding night in town alone, so he offered to keep Michael and check on Grandpa.

"I want to stop at Hillborne's so you can pick out a ring."

"I don't need a ring, Gabe. We need so many other things that it seems frivolous to purchase a ring."

Gabe pulled the wagon to a stop in front of Mark Hillborne's store. "It doesn't to me." He grinned. "Consider it a brand."

She jerked around to face him. "A what?"

He picked up her hand and rubbed his thumb up and down her ring finger. "A brand of sorts. I want every man who sees you to know you're taken. That you're mine."

"Oh." Inside, she glowed with love for this man. "In that case, I will accept your ring."

"Good." He squeezed her hand. "Because I was going to get one anyway." He hopped down and hurried around to help her down. "I'm curious to see who Mark married. When I stopped by yesterday, his clerk said he'd up and gotten married, all of a sudden."

"That sounds odd, but then maybe it wasn't quite as sudden as the man thought. Surely Mr. Hillborne doesn't talk about his private life with his help."

"That may be true." He offered his arm. "But I don't care to talk about Mark's new wife. I want one of my own, so c'mon."

Blushing again, Lara took his arm and allowed him to lead her into the store. Her gaze shot to the nearest rack of thread and sewing notions. Gabe wanted her to pick out some fabric or several ready-made dresses, especially one to get married in. But she'd never had a store-bought dress before. That, too, seemed frivolous, but since she didn't have fabric or time to make the dress she had agreed. She searched for the dresses then moved toward them while Gabe strode to the back to talk to the man at the counter.

"I hear congratulations are in order." Gabe reached out his hand, and Mark shook it.

Lara glanced at the handsome store owner then sorted through the dozen dresses. She passed a brown calico with small yellow flowers and a dark blue one with stripes, and her hand halted on a beautiful pale green gown. It was far too fancy for everyday use, but she could save it for a Sunday dress once they found a church to attend. She held out the princess-style skirt, admiring the lovely color and the deep gathers in the back that added fullness. The matching waist-length jacket even had leg-o'-mutton sleeves.

"That's pretty. It almost matches your eyes." Gabe smiled, appreciation in his gaze.

Lara held it up. "I think it will fit, but I'd rather not spend the money for it without trying it on." She glanced around. "Do you suppose there is someplace where I can?"

"Let me ask Mark." He spun around. "Is there somewhere my bride-to-be can try on this gown?"

"I don't have a dressing room yet, but you're welcome to use my tent. I'm sure my wife won't mind. She's due to come back in here soon anyway."

"See," Gabe said as he took the dress from her. He turned back to Mark. "Just point the way, if you will."

Mark lifted a flap at the back of his tent, and they walked outside. He pointed to a smaller tent only twenty feet away. "Right over there."

Lara looked at Mr. Hillborne. "Um. . .maybe you should prepare your wife. We can't exactly knock on the door."

He glanced back at the store. "If you two will keep an eye on my stock, I'll let her know."

"Happy to." Gabe moved back inside the store a few feet and faced the front, even though they were the only customers.

Mr. Hillborne ducked into his tent and returned shortly with a woman in tow, wearing a lovely blue dress. Lara heard a gasp and lifted her gaze to the woman's face. "Jo!" She rushed forward but halted halfway when her sister didn't approach her. Jo looked less than thrilled to see her. "I've been worried sick."

"There was no need. I found a job within a few minutes of arriving in town, and as you can see, I am married now." She cozied up to Mark, whose face held a curious look.

"You two know each other?" he asked.

Jo's lips pinched, but when she gazed up at Mark, her expression turned all lovey-dovey. Lara's stomach ached. Had Jo married a man she'd only known a few days?

"Lara is my sister," Jo admitted to Mark as she turned back to Lara. "Go on in and try on the dress. It's time for me to get back to work." Jo marched past her with no further comment.

Lara's heart nearly broke in half.

Gabe narrowed his gaze as Jo passed by then hurried to Lara's side. "Are you all right?"

"No, but that doesn't matter."

Mark walked up to her. "I apologize, Miss Jensen. I knew Jo had a sister, but I had no idea that you lived nearby. She doesn't like to talk about her family."

"The name is Mrs. Talbot—for another hour, anyway." She smiled at Gabe. "It's all right, Mr. Hillborne. You couldn't have known."

"Well, please, go on in and try on the dress. We'll wait out here."

Lara no longer cared about the dress, but this was Gabe's wedding day, too, and she wouldn't let her sister's bad attitude ruin it. "Thank you." She turned to Gabe. "Why don't you pick out a ring and surprise me."

"Are you sure?"

She nodded.

Mr. Hillborne stepped forward. "If you'll allow me to look at your ring finger, I can show Gabe all the ones in your size."

Numbly, she held out her hand. He barely touched her finger then nodded. Lara stepped inside her sister's domain, not the least bit surprised to find it in disarray. The beautiful four-poster bed wasn't even made, and clothes littered it. Mark had obviously been generous, as two new dresses hung in an open wardrobe, and another lay across a chair. Lara hurried to dress then crossed to the full-length mirror in the corner. She gasped at the sight of herself in a new gown. It was the first store-bought dress she'd ever owned, and it was lovely. She patted several curls that had sprung free on the ride to town. At least she would look pretty for Gabe on their wedding day.

She rolled up her old dress and hurried out of the tent. She couldn't yet think of her sister as a married woman, even though she was. As she reached the store opening, she paused. What she'd like to do was march straight to the wagon and wait for Gabe there, but that would be wrong. And she wanted her sister at *her* wedding, even if she hadn't been invited to Jo's. *Help me, Lord.*

Lara stepped into the store, and Gabe's appreciative gaze shot to her. He let out a slow whistle that made her cheeks burn. She hurried toward him and leaned close. "Please behave," she whispered.

Gabe winked and turned to Mark. "We'll take the dress and the other things."

"Good. Come to the end of the counter, and I'll tally them up while the ladies talk."

Jo busied herself arranging perfume bottles. She picked up a duster and bustled across the store to the canned goods and started wiping them off.

Lara followed. "Jo, can we please talk?"

"What is there to say?" Jo sidestepped to the next set of shelves. "You're getting married, even though Tom is barely cold in his grave.

I'm married and quite happy, as you can see."

"I can't see that, but I hope it's true." She stepped closer and lowered her voice. "I can't believe you married a man you've only known a few days."

Jo barked a loud laugh and spun around. "I met him back in Caldwell. I've known him every bit as long as you've known Gabe. Besides, you have no say in the matter as I see it."

Lara sighed. "Please, Jo. I don't want to fight with you."

"Then what *do* you want?"

She looked at her sister, still a child in so many ways but all grown up in others. "I'd like for you to stand up with me at my wedding today."

The color washed from Jo's face for a moment before she seemed to regain her composure. "Thank you for asking, but I need to work. Mark has an appointment soon, and this is Richard's day off. We'd have to close the store and leave it unguarded, and I'm sure you understand why we can't do that."

What she understood was clear. Jo didn't want to attend her wedding or have anything to do with her. At least she could make a gracious exit and ease both of their pain. "I understand. It was good to see you and to know that you're doing well. I wish you and Mark the best." She spun around and hurried to the front entrance. "Gabe, I'll be waiting in the wagon."

Lara rushed out, determined not to cry. This was her wedding day, after all, and she wouldn't have Gabe marrying a red-faced woman with wet eyelashes. She carefully climbed onto the wagon, making sure to not snag her new dress. She wished Grandpa could have come to her wedding, but then she was glad he didn't have to see Jo acting as cold as she was. It would have hurt him terribly.

She stared at the new town. Several plots already had buildings on them made from fresh lumber. One man was painting the facade of his barbershop in red and white stripes.

Something thumped in the rear of the wagon, and then it creaked as Gabe climbed aboard. He touched her shoulder, and she turned toward him. "Are you all right, sweetheart? I know that was quite a shock for you. It was for me, too. Mark never said anything that would have led me to think he'd married your sister."

"I can't deny that Jo hurt me, but it certainly isn't the first time."

"Would you prefer to postpone the wedding for a few weeks?"

Her heart overflowing, she gazed into the concerned eyes of the man she loved so much and cupped her hand around his cheek, heedless to the spectacle they made. "No, Gabriel. I want to marry you right now. I love you, and I want you to be able to comfort me when I'm hurting. Maybe that's selfish, but I need you."

His wide grin cheered away the sadness. "Then let's get married, darlin'." He placed a quick kiss on the end of her nose then collected the reins and released the brake. "Hi'yah, horses. We have a wedding to get to."

As Gabe gazed into Lara's lovely eyes, he repeated his vows, promising to love, honor, and cherish her. He slid the ring he'd picked out—a beautiful emerald—onto her finger, excited to become a husband and father all at once. How had he been so incredibly lucky to have found such a compassionate, selfless woman to marry? His mother would have loved her as much as he did.

But even more, he'd made things right with God and had a new purpose in life. He'd learned that no matter what he did or how much he sacrificed, he couldn't atone for killing Tom Talbot. Only Christ could take the pain away and make him a new man. Lara's love and forgiveness had helped, too.

"Mr. Coulter," the minister said, "you may kiss your bride."

Gabe grinned, then he cupped his hands around Lara's sparkling face and melded his lips to hers. This kiss would be short. Quick.

But tonight, he would offer her all the comfort and love she needed.

And tomorrow was his birthday, and he and his new wife could celebrate again.

About the Author

Bestselling author Vickie McDonough grew up wanting to marry a rancher, but instead she married a computer geek who is scared of horses. She now lives out her dreams in her fictional stories about ranchers, cowboys, lawmen, and others living in the West during the 1800s. Vickie is the award-winning author of over thirty published books and novellas. Her books include the fun and feisty Texas Boardinghouse Brides series, and *End of the Trail*, which was the OWFI 2013 Best Fiction Novel winner. *Whispers on the Prairie* was a Romantic Times Recommended Inspirational Book for July 2013.

Vickie is a wife of thirty-nine years, the mother of four grown sons, and she has one daughter-in-law. She is also grandma to one precocious little girl. When she's not writing, Vickie enjoys reading, antiquing, watching movies, making stained-glass projects, and traveling. To learn more about Vickie's books or to sign up for her newsletter, visit her website: www.vickiemcdonough.com.

Other Books by Vickie McDonough

TEXAS BOARDINGHOUSE BRIDES
The Anonymous Bride
Second Chance Brides
Finally a Bride

Also Available from Shiloh Run Press

Gabriel's Atonement

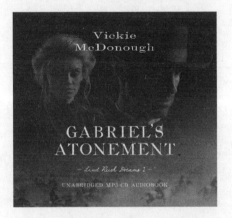

Unabridged Audiobook

Coming Fall 2015

Joline's Redemption

Land Rush Dreams
Book #2